Reviews for Tides of Change

Tides of Change is more than the love story of all time; it's a magnificent and thrilling adventure. For the followers of Atlantis and the Edgar Cayce Readings you will love the intrigue and possibilities this story brings to mind. Ms. MacIver is a master at creating the visions of Poseidon's world under the sea with all of its splendid colors, sounds and imagery. You'll find yourself staying up late reading this book, turning page after page until you've finished and then you'll miss the characters that have become a part of your life, you'll even worry about their safety. The book weaves the intimate stories of the residents of Atlantis with perfection. You'll laugh out loud, you'll cry and you'll applaud the heroin and cheer her on. I would love to see this play out on the big screen. I can envision a fantastic movie along the lines of Avatar.

—Kay Schlichting, Horseshoe Bay, Texas

Perhaps the concept of a paradise is a philosophical construct, but in Tides of Change, it is brought to life in all its potential romantic glory. It is warm, wise, funny, exciting and thought provoking. Its characters live and feel with all of their senses and so, too, will the reader.

—Cynthia Lidman, Chandler, Arizona

Susan MacIver's Tides of Change is extremely well done. The minute I started reading it, it was if I were in Atlantis myself. Her natural and easy writing abilities come through with her great level of detail and colorful descriptions of the people, places and things she presents. The storyline is new and fresh and I am looking forward to what is coming next! I was hooked from the moment I started reading!!

—Mark Platt, Santa Fe, New Mexico

Alien surroundings with believable people and just enough explanation to not get in the reader's way. Women who are both strong and have a bit of the romantic-plot frailty... You have written an excellent book...I enjoyed this hugely...Good job! I would recommend this book to all my friends.
— Idony Lisle, Style Editor

Tides of Change is a mystical, captivating story with romance, suspense and hope for an uncertain future. Once I started reading I found it difficult to walk away from and look forward to the stories continuation.
— Nancy Peebles, Avid Fiction Reader, Bothell, WA

In "Tides of Change," the first of three books in the Atlantis Chronicles, Susan MacIver takes you on a whimsical and fantastic journey to the bottom of the ocean and to matters of the heart. If you like fantasy, romance, intrigue and just a good story this is a book for you! Ms MacIver keeps us wanting more as she paints a wonderful picture with creative and descriptive wordsmithing. You are immersed in intrigue and relationships from the moment you are drawn into Atlantis and back topside. If you want a good read that you can't put down and leaves you wanting more "Tides of Change" is the book for you!
— Jim Pflueger, Avid Fiction Reader, San Tan Valley, AZ

Wonderful story, beautifully written. And the cliffhanger ending – I sure hope she's already working on a sequel (or series)!
— Rosina Wilson, Line Editor

TIDES *of* CHANGE

BOOK ONE OF THE ATLANTIS CHRONICLES

With love & joy –
Susan

SUSAN MACIVER

Cover Design by Monica Haynes; thethatchery.com
Interior Graphic Design by Colleen Sheehan;
wdrbookdesign.com

Susan MacIver
Visit my website at www.susanmaciver.com

Printed in the United States of America
First Printing: 2003
Published by Sojourn Publishing, LLC

ISBN: 978-1-62747-408-5
Ebook ISBN: 978-1-62747-556-3
Library of Congress Control Number: 2003111535

DEDICATION

To
My Beautiful Duke,
the husband of my heart and the love of my life.

ACKNOWLEDGMENTS

No one ever writes a book entirely by themselves. Anyone who has ever touched our lives comes into play in some way, no matter how small the influence. However, there are always and forever the people in our lives that we love the most. These loved ones bring to bear the largest influence that not only shape who we become, they in essence, help create the writing.

My son, Eric MacIver, whose touching poem, Clarity of a Moment, flowed so eloquently from Ni-Cio's thoughts has enriched my world beyond measure. What a joy you are! I am so proud of the man you have become. Wise beyond your years, your humor and your love have kept me going through times that seemed impossible. You are "the child of my heart," and there will never be enough words to describe how much I love you.

My version of Atlantis came into being when, sharing wine one night with my sister, Cynthia Lidman, she looked up and said, "The story should be about Atlantis!" Cindy, you are and always have been, my earth angel.

Tom Bird, you have disproved that old adage, "If it sounds too good to be true, it probably is." With a depth of kindness that seems boundless, you continue to help so many of us unleash the Divine Author Within. Thank you. And my heartfelt gratitude to your incomparable team; Sabrina Fritts, Executive Director; Mary Stevenson, Executive Assistant, and John Hodgkinson, Project Coordinator.

And once again, I circle back to my incredible husband, Duke...thank you for giving me such a safe and loving place to fall. Without you, there is no me.

With all my heart,
Susan
10/24/16

PRONUNCIATION

Aris – AIR/iss
Cleito – klee/ATE/o
Daria Caiden – DAR/ee/uh KY/den
Ennael – uh/NEEL
Eumelus – Yoo/mue/les
Kai-Dan – KY/dan
Kalli-Kan – KAL/ee/dan
Kyla – Ky/la
Marik – MAIR/ik
Na-Kai eva Evenor – na/KY ee/va ev/uh/nor
Ni-Cio evaw Azaes – NEE/shee/o ee/va UH/zays
Oia – EE/ya
Oomi – OO/me
Peltor – PEL/tor
Poseidon – PO/sy/den
Rogert – RO/jer
Travlor – TRAV/lor
Ylno – IL/no

The CANONS

I

As children of Poseidon you are granted the paradise that is Atlantis
In the purity of your actions will it remain thus

II

The healing power descends through my lineage
Live that you flourish
Attend not and you will surely weaken

III

No matter the form
All life is held sacred

IV

Whether in the heavens or the earth
We are bound by the same essence that creates life
Hurt another and you ultimately hurt yourself

V

Behold the miracle that is You
Cherish this offering

VI

The sacrament of love is inviolate
Written in the heavens before your time
Heart, mind and soul will bring you into awareness of your life mate
Act not until they speak as one

VII

Love is manifested within the smallest detail
Living thus will your life be enriched

VIII

Let your essence be filled with the joy of life
And spread that joy to those you touch

Far from earth's mad whirling,
deep beneath tranquil sapphire blue.
I descend, lured on by the whale's
siren song
Drifting over dark, silent chasms
of uncharted depths
Visiting chamberless cathedrals
of sun-banded coral,
and touching heavenless stars,
I feel a part of an awesome promise —
Life never-ending,
And something like coming home.

Cynthia Lidman

CHAPTER
1

Na-Kai eva Evenor entered her darkened chambers. Bent beneath the weight of her despair, she moistened her lips and tried to swallow, but her throat constricted so that she could hardly breathe. She lifted her arm seeking support and felt the cold of time-smoothed granite. Sagging against the wall, she tried to summon the voice command that would regulate the lighting, but her voice caught and nothing came.

A moment passed, she issued a telepathic thought-form and her quarters appeared bathed in subdued colors of gold and green. The lights continued to brighten until she could see her silhouette carved against the granite walls.

Beneath the soft fall of her warming robes, her body felt old. The abject horror of a truth she had never thought to face assaulted her once again. "If a new Healer is not found to take my place, my people will begin the inexorable slide toward extinction."

Her head pounded. She lifted her hands to massage her temples and noticed that the normal pearlescent glow of her skin had faded to resemble dry parchment. She was alone in this. There was nowhere left to turn, and no one else with whom to share this terrible knowledge. Her arms fell to her sides and she bowed her head. "There is no one else. Not one of them exhibits the least sign of the healing power. Within me was our continuance; without me is our end. Our underwater sanctuary has become our tomb."

Her hands shook. Her strength was gone. She gathered her robes and stumbled to the couch. She grasped the armrest, but her knees gave way and she slumped to the cushions. The plush seating adjusted, enfolding her form, but she found no comfort. Her thoughts spun. There had to be some way out of the morass, but all that she could envision was the hungry maw of a black void as it opened wide to devour her people.

She had no idea how to save them. Tears trickled over her cheeks and sobs crested in waves. She pulled her robes tighter, seeking warmth, and she sank further into the cushions.

How much time had passed before her shudders finally calmed, she didn't know. All was quiet. The only sound she heard was the ceaseless beat of her own heart. That steady rhythm brought her focus inward, and in the infinitesimal pause between each release, an idea glimmered on the periphery of her consciousness. Na-Kai examined that thought with horrified desperation. She tried to close her mind to such an act. To do this thing would be to go against everything she believed and had known to be true. However, the harder she argued against the idea, the more it dominated her. She lifted her gaze, swiped at her tears and pushed herself up.

She shivered with fear. Glancing at the door, she half expected someone to barge in to put a stop to her madness. She shook her head. Suddenly, flooded with energy, she began to pace. Her thoughts gathered speed, still she tried to banish the idea. Anything, any other idea than this would be acceptable. But the thought burrowed deeper and would not be denied.

Long ago, Poseidon had forbidden Healers to use their thought-forms for anything other than healing. Delving frantically through her memories, she tried to find a time when anyone had breached this command and it was as she

2

suspected. The law had never been broken. She didn't even know the consequences of transgression. Now, however, she was out of time and she was out of options. There was no other choice. She stopped and released her robes. Her spine stiffened like iron. Standing in open defiance of that ancient law, Na-Kai eva Evenor, Most Sovereign Healer of Atlantis, lifted her face toward the shrouded heavens. She raised her arms as though to challenge Poseidon himself. "I will not suffer this. It cannot be borne! I will do what I must. Whether you condone or condemn my actions, I do not care. I will enact the last and only rite that might somehow save your children! I will seek a Healer outside of the confines of our home!"

Na-Kai closed her eyes and forced her concentration inward. With the speed of thought, every atom within her consciousness coalesced, creating a powerful telekinetic form of incredible energy. Screaming with the effort, Na-Kai released it outward.

At a terrifying speed, the web of energy rocketed up and out of Atlantis. Through the very layers of rock and water that had become her home, it found its place in space and time and shimmered to a stop on the Greek island of Santorini. She knew that eons or minutes were as one, but for her people, time was of the essence. "We shall see what I have wrought."

Feeling as though her soul had been wrenched apart, she was unable to summon the strength to lift her robes. She reeled toward the couch. Dimly aware of the cushions that softened her fall, she plummeted toward oblivion.

CHAPTER

2

"*T*he woman's only been gone for one day." Slumped in his seat, elbows planted on the edge of his vast desk and both fists held against closed eyes, Evan Gaddes knew it was a bad sign to start mumbling out loud. So, rather than wait for a reply, he leaned back in his chair and ran his hands briskly, back and forth, through his sandy blonde hair.

The stiff tickle that brushed against his palms ignited his need for movement, and in a single motion he slammed his hands on the desk and rose to his full six-foot-three inches. His chair sailed backwards in a violent spin, and the noise of its four wheels rat-a-tat-tatting across the rug guard quieted when the chair clamored to an ungainly stop atop the thick pile carpeting.

Evan sideswiped a corner of his desk and paced. He felt the stretch in the backs of his legs and let his frustration carry him the lengthy span of the room. At the other end of his office, he paused long enough to run his gaze over the stunning Boston vista that opened below his top floor aerie. He turned around and thrust his suit jacket backwards. He shoved both hands into the pockets of his pants, hunched his shoulders, lowered his head and trekked back.

He passed the only painting he had purchased specifically for the space and halted. Evan glared at the Van Gogh in a silent demand for inspiration, but the artwork offered nothing, so he dismissed it from his attention.

His pace increased along with his anxiety, and the sumptuous trappings of his office faded from sight. He replayed their last night together.

Daria Caiden had pleaded with him to let the newness of their relationship settle, but he had refused to listen. He didn't think he was in love with her, but she had brought such color into his black-and-white, ordered existence that he had been captivated from their first meeting. He felt that if he could get her to forget reason, forget caution and forget that they had only known each other for three months and just, by God, marry him, he could at least keep her safe. He was wary of the schemes that Travlor kept hatching. Why the man needed to be rid of Daria, Evan had no clue. Travlor had not seen fit to fill him in as to the why of it.

What Evan had failed to realize was that Daria had fended for herself for thirty-two years, and she had developed a self-reliance that bordered on stubbornness. When she had informed him that she was "going away for a while to think," he thought that his adamant resistance to her departure would make her change her mind, so he had never even bothered to ask where she was going. But now, plagued with worry, he had only himself to blame, because he had absolutely no idea where she had gone. "How is it that everything I've achieved, and the plans I've laid, pale in comparison to you?"

Disgusted, he shook his head to clear the memories and stopped at his desk. He grabbed his cell phone from an inside jacket pocket and depressed the unlock button. The crystal display lit up, and once again, he felt his blood pressure start to redline.

He thrust the cell back into his pocket, loosened his tie, flailed open the top button of his shirt and yanked one end of the tie from beneath his collar. He heaved it across the desk and watched the beautiful slice of cloth glide gracefully through the air and fall to the floor in an expensive, colorful heap.

He leaned over the desk and punched the button on his speakerphone. He tried to sound composed, but the military bark that wound itself around his words assaulted his secretary's ears just as it did his own. "Has she called yet?"

He anticipated the impatient hesitation before he caught the hurried intake of breath and the sigh that preceded the answer to his question. It wasn't hard to envision the involuntary shake of his secretary's gray head as she struggled to temper her reply. "No, Dr. Gaddes, she still hasn't called. The moment she does, I promise to put her through. I'm sure everything is fine."

Evan grabbed the receiver and banged it back into the cradle. He gripped the edges of his desk as though he could wring a confession of Daria's whereabouts from the inanimate beast. The weight of his bleak life started to press down around him. "Enough, I'm through!"

He scrambled to reach the door and startled his secretary when he burst through to the outer offices. "The only call I want is Daria's. When that happens, put her through to my cell immediately."

Not listening for a reply, Evan waded through the tangle of the rest of his offices and staff. Several employees approached him but he brusquely waved them away. He decided he'd rather not waste the minutes it would take to summon the elevator and he certainly didn't want to get trapped by anybody in an inane conversation. Pushing his athletic abilities into maximum drive, he pounded through a fire exit and raced down thirty-three flights of concrete stairs.

Barely out of breath, Evan reached the parking garage and fumbled for his car keys. He remembered watching Daria hide the spare entry key to her apartment. He stood still, and a flood of certainty pulsed through his veins. Somewhere, inside that apartment, was the clue he needed to find her.

Climbing the stairs to Daria's alcove, Evan was determined to find something that would indicate her destination. Once assured of her safety, he would be able to consider his next step.

The key was exactly where he thought it would be, but as he opened the front door, a feeling of unease settled over him. It was the first time he had ever been in Daria's home when she was not there. To Evan, her absence felt like an unfinished song.

He reached for a nearby lamp and switched on the light. The room was bathed in a soft glow. Although Evan considered the space small, the decor spoke of the artistic nature of its missing occupant. Watercolors by local artists hung on several walls, and her bookshelves bulged with everything from the latest paperbacks to the works of literary heavyweights. Her furniture was overstuffed, rich with texture and shaded in moss greens, deep scarlets, dark blues and golds. Tables of subtle earth tones held different varieties of flowering plants, and jewel-toned candles completed a picture of warmth, relaxation and serenity.

Evan didn't quite know where to start; a cursory glance told him nothing was out of place. Daria wasn't compulsive about neatness, but she had always kept her surroundings clean and tidy. He remembered an inadvertent remark he had made. "Everything has a place, and every place has a thing." Daria had just laughed, thrown a pillow at him and initiated a wrestling match. The lovemaking that followed had been wondrous, at least for him.

He shook his head at the remembrance and the sudden pain it caused and jerked his thoughts to another tack. Evan crossed the living area and entered the study. He hoped to find something that would reveal her plans.

The room, too, was free of clutter. The antique desk she had been so excited to refinish was in order. No note pads by the phone with hastily scratched flight numbers, no crumpled papers in the trash, nothing. Even the light on the answering machine mocked him with its red, unblinking stare. Patience strung tighter than piano wire, Evan flexed his hands, momentarily overcome with the desire to destroy that mute machine. He turned to search the kitchen before he started tearing the place apart.

The kitchen yielded more of the same until he had no choice but to make his way to the bedroom, a room he had wanted to avoid. Too many memories of their nights together assaulted him as he entered.

Daria had designed a sanctuary that evoked her love of the tropics. She had draped netting in long, loose waves over and around a woven frame and she had piled the bed with pillows of every size and color imaginable. A ceiling fan stirred a gentle breeze, and plants of exotic beauty completed a scene of sensual delight. Evan could still smell the scent of her perfume and thought he would be unable to continue when he spotted an unusual book on her nightstand.

It was a World Atlas. He had not seen it before, and suspected that she had kept it in the bookcase by the living room window, until now. He crossed the floor, and time shifted into slow motion. He inched the book from the side table and felt the strength leak from his body. Filled with a terrible lethargy, Evan lowered himself onto the bed. A marker hung from the pages, and by imperceptible degrees, his fingers crept over the cover. Foreboding such as he had never known flooded through him as the book fell open to the page she had marked.

Evan bent in half and covered his face with his hands. A groan escaped his lips. He intoned the one word that made his stomach clench.

"Santorini."

CHAPTER
3

*E*van hurtled out of Daria's front door. He grabbed his cell and punched the number for his office. The phone rang and he raced to his car. As soon as his secretary picked up her end, he barked out his orders. "Book me the first flight available to Athens, Greece. Then book the fastest route to an island by the name of Santorini. I don't care if you have to charter something, just get me to that island as fast as humanly possible."

He yanked the car door open, and as he slid into the leather seat, revved the engine while he finished talking. "Cancel my appointments until you've heard from me. I'm on my way home, then I'm headed to the airport. Call me when you have the flight information. Oh, and call every hotel on that island and find out where Daria is staying!"

He tossed the phone onto the passenger side, threw the car into reverse and backed out. He ground the gears into first, and smoke filled the air as the tires spun, looking for purchase. When they finally bit asphalt, Evan laid down a perfect set of tracks. His car screeched out of the parking lot.

The flight was interminable. He had never felt so confined. As the engines droned over the Atlantic, Evan forced himself to some semblance of calm. He tried to grasp the implications of what had transpired.

Of all the places, how had Daria chosen Santorini? When she said she wanted time away, it had never entered his mind that she would leave Massachusetts, much less the United States. Evan banged his fist on the armrest. Time away was a weekend, not a jaunt halfway around the world!

He was afraid to imagine just how Travlor would react to this news. He had not contacted the man. Evan would know more once he reached Santorini. If he reached Daria in time, Travlor would never need to know.

He closed his eyes and leaned back into the seat. The drone of the engines finally lulled him into a fitful sleep.

When Evan cleared Greek Customs he was approached by a dark youth.

"Dr. Gaddes, yes? Please, this way." The boy gestured toward a shiny black limousine.

Evan sprinted toward the vehicle and threw his luggage into the open trunk. He slammed the lid down and had the passenger door open before the chauffeur had moved from behind the wheel. Evan ducked into the spacious interior and banged the door shut. "Do you know where to go?"

The driver nodded and started the car. Driven to an area of the airport where his charter waited, Evan climbed in, brushed past the assembled crew and buckled himself into his seat. The small jet was in the air within minutes, but to Evan the flight was another anxious consumption of time that kept slipping away. He drummed his fingers on the armrest, willing the plane to go faster.

CHAPTER
4

*C*radled in an early-morning cocoon, Daria Caiden sat and reveled in the feel of the soft down pillows against her back. With the covers strewn about the bed and her legs freed, she felt the first traces of a gentle breeze as it slipped through the open doors of her veranda. She watched the sheer curtains flare in a sinuous dance, then closed her eyes. She inhaled the aroma of the strong Greek coffee and blew across the top of her cup. She took a tentative sip. Replacing the cup to saucer with a soft chime, she smiled and nestled deeper into the pillows.

The salt-scented air teased her with hints of honeyed jasmine and ripe olive trees, and her tired mind relaxed in the profound comfort with which she was surrounded. The compulsion (and where had that come from?) that had driven her to this tiny island no longer held her in its grasp and she reflected on the reasons that had impelled her to this particular place at this particular time. Sipping her coffee, she let the memories come.

Evan Gaddes had invaded her life three months ago. He had pursued her with single-minded devotion, and though she had been somewhat flattered, she had tried to keep her distance. When she finally accepted his offer of dinner, she found that she quite liked him. Her heart ached when she learned that like her, he had spent a solitary and parentless childhood. His mother had died during his birth. His father had not cared enough to ever seek him out, and the man had never been found.

Evan had been entrusted to an old, ineffectual aunt and uncle who had been unequipped to cope with a child whose brilliance surpassed their own simple understanding. They had never understood the hunger that drove him. And though they loved him in their way, he never let them get close. Daria doubted that he had ever contacted them after he left their home. She shook her head, "What a lonely existence." She gazed out at the lovely scene from her hotel veranda and continued her review.

Evan received a doctorate in genetics with an emphasis in gerontology in his early twenties, and by thirty-five, he had amassed enormous wealth. He owned several patents on some of his most important discoveries, and the company he had built employed some of the best minds in the world. Evan had told her that it was just a matter of time before he and his team unlocked the genetic code linked to aging.

He had been justifiably proud of his accomplishments, but Daria knew that because of his dedication to clinical research, Evan had experienced emotions with her that he had never shared with anyone.

On a night with too much wine, Evan had uttered a statement that still haunted her. "I think every boy wants his father's approval at some time in his life."

She had tried to question him further, but Evan had changed the subject and refused any more discussion. Though he never talked about his father, Daria suspected he harbored a deep-seated need to know his sire.

Daria cared deeply for Evan, however, she wasn't "in love" and neither, she suspected, was he. She knew that even though they enjoyed each other's company, their innermost hearts still remained locked tight, barriers erect. So, his proposal during a tender, romantic moment had shaken her foundations.

Daria didn't think that being "in like" was enough reason to get married. So, she had turned him down. Soon their time together had turned into a tug of war, and the emotional turmoil and fights mushroomed. Bombarded by Evan's arguments as to why they should marry, Daria had been just as adamant that they should leave well enough alone. Pressured for a commitment she was unwilling to give, she had become desperate to end the fighting.

One Evanless night, she had wracked her brain for an escape and had ripped an old Atlas from her bookshelves. As she turned to reach a table, the book had flown out of her hands as though she had thrown it. Landing on the wooden floor, page side up, the book's hard thud resonated in her body. She bent to retrieve it and her eyes involuntarily shifted. Riveted by the sight of one small island in the middle of the Aegean Sea, Daria shuddered when she read the name. Santorini.

Seized by a sudden impulse, she booked the first flight out of the States and prayed that Evan would understand.

He didn't. "You're leaving? For what reason? If you need space, Christ, I'll give you space. You don't have to leave to get away from me!"

The ricochet of the slammed door accentuated his anger and his hurt, but Daria hadn't gone after him. He had never asked where she was going. How could she have explained the incomprehensible compulsion that drove her toward Santorini?

Daria sighed with relief, release and gratitude for the blessed peace, and she savored the last swallow of coffee. She placed the cup and saucer on the bedside table and a vague feeling of need swept over her. She frowned, slipped from the sun-warmed covers and donned a simple shift. The compulsion that had driven her to this small island in the middle of nowhere suddenly surged through her again.

Helpless against the driving force that exerted such a raw obsession over her, Daria hurried outside. Her body ached with a desperate need to be by the ocean. Her bare feet sank into soft, warm earth and she almost moaned with pleasure. Her steps quickened while her gaze played with the riotous summer beauty of Santorini.

The butter-soft yellow of early light washed the island in the golden daydream of an impressionist painting. Sounds of a nearby brook created delicate harmonies with the mourning doves as they sang the sun higher into a cloudless, azure sky. But even as Daria wished to stop and enjoy the scenery, her stride lengthened. It seemed that the more ground she covered, the more her pace increased.

She crested a small rise and caught her first glimpse of the Aegean Sea. It sparkled with such an intense sapphire blue that she had to shield her eyes. Mesmerized, heart pounding, she broke into a run. As she skimmed over the dark earth a stiff sea breeze pushed against her skin. She thought that if she lifted her feet a little faster, a little higher, she would take flight, and as she soared, her hair would leave a wake of golden contrails.

Daria neared the sun-bleached cliffs and a panorama opened before her that was primeval in its wild beauty. In her headlong rush to the cliff's edge, Daria suddenly stopped as though she had crashed into a glass wall.

Immobilized, barely able to breathe, a halo of light flickered over her body. She was blinded by the rainbow colors. As if in a dream, her dazed mind watched her hands reach to her shift and remove the clothing. Trance-like, she picked her way to the rocky cliffs. Standing on the brink of the precipice, and against her will, she raised her arms to the sea almost as if in praise.

All thought was silenced. Only movement remained. She stared in horrified fascination as her legs stepped to the very edge of the earth. Her toes gripped rock, and she tried with every fiber of her being to turn her body from the chasm. The attempt was futile. She felt caught in the relentless grasp of something otherworldly, as flames of electric light darted over her skin and her vision narrowed to a pinpoint. Fear was cast aside. Thought was suspended. And she took one last breath.

Protected from the immense height by the web of energy that imprisoned her, Daria was forced from the jagged cliffs. Diving headlong toward the Aegean, she squeezed her eyes shut as she plummeted into the restless sea. The ripples that bespoke her passage faded, and she was enfolded in space and flight and womb-like silence. Arms of sapphire water wrapped around her naked body with more intimacy than any lover, and down she swam. Pulled by currents of will and water, Daria descended until she could no longer see her hands. Her ears ached from the pressure and her lungs burned for air that was not there. Her body became sluggish and her strength evaporated until she could no longer continue.

Suspended in midnight quiet, she felt her hair settle, like seaweed, around her face and neck. Unable to move, Daria drifted. Darkness poured into her mind, and she waited to die.

$\mathcal{C}$HAPTER
5

Evan deplaned on Santorini, paid cash for a rental car and
with directions from the agent, careened out of the airport
parking lot and punched the accelerator.

He flew by lazy towns and recklessly passed slower vehicles
that moved with less purpose, all the while repeating his mantra.
"Daria will be fine, I have to keep her safe. Daria will be fine, I
have to keep her safe." His heart pounded in time with the words.
He blocked out any other thought. His sole concern lay in finding
Daria. His only hope was that he accomplish that mission.

In the tiny town of Oia, he took a wrong turn and roared a
curse. He wound through the twisted residential area with as
much speed as the turns would allow.

At last, Evan sighted the hotel that Daria had chosen. The
retreat seemed to flout the gods as it dared to cling to the side of
a plunging three-hundred-foot cliff. Sunlight glinted off
whitewashed stucco cabanas while scarlet bougainvillea crept
skyward with haphazard abandon. Far below, the brilliant blue
Aegean undulated with restless passion, and colors collided in
riotous counterpoint.

The car skidded to a stop and Evan admonished himself to
stay calm. Nevertheless, he tumbled out of the car and hurried
to the reception desk. Exhausted with the effort of the last
twenty-four hours, he pounded the reception bell as though his
life depended upon the very sound.

A young assistant peeked out of a hotel office and cleared his throat. He was bold enough to stride forth, but before he could get a word out, Evan voiced his demand. "The room number for Daria Caiden."

The young man replied in the time-honored tradition. "Sir, we are not allowed to give out that information. However, I would be glad to ring her for you and the young lady can tell you herself."

Evan gave a curt nod and sighed with relief. He crossed his arms and leaned against the counter. Daria's room was rung. An old wall clock marked the passage of time with ominous ticks of the second hand.

The youth re-cradled the handset and grimaced. "There is no answer, sir; apparently she has stepped out. She could be at breakfast or possibly she has taken a walk. We have a very nice path that…"

Evan felt his neck tighten with the first stirrings of a supersized headache. He rifled through his pockets and flashed a fifty-dollar bill. "Show me where she went."

Tired and strung out from his recent ordeal, Evan hit the path running at a fierce speed. He knew she would be there. He reached the crown of a hill and scanned rapidly for any sign of Daria. The strong Greek sun blinded him and his eyes watered. He blinked to clear his vision and as he did, he caught a sudden flash of light. Screaming Daria's name, he cut from the path.

Evan fought his way to the cliffs. He brushed past olive trees and leapt over dense underbrush. At last, he crashed into the open. He glimpsed Daria as she stood transfixed, arms raised to the sky, golden hair flying around her. He opened his mouth to yell, but another blinding flash pierced the sunlight and he watched as she simply disappeared!

CHAPTER
6

Ni-Cio evaw Azaes loved his job. The freedom he felt from racing through the world's oceans to collect water and air samples thrilled him. It brought him closer to the topsiders, and Poseidon knew that for him, the topsiders were a constant source of mystery and curiosity. The many hues and colors of their lives and cultures teased the edges of his imagination and called him like a siren song. He longed to explore their world. "Canon Law, Edicts!" he spat, "I have never understood why the mixing of Atlanteans and topsiders was forbidden. It makes no sense."

He tightened his hands on the console. He never attempted to dock topside, but that didn't mean he wasn't tempted. A rampant thought brought a moment of brutal honesty: *"If not for this job, and for Aris and his antics, I would lead a very dull life indeed…"*

Even Aris couldn't understand why his friend hadn't picked a life mate. Ni-Cio didn't want to explain. His best friend would never understand. Ni-Cio's mouth twisted as though he had tasted some sour seaweed. *"Atlantis is too much of the same…"*

He remembered his mother telling him, "Oh, my son, if wishes were only fishes you would be wealthy indeed."

She had tried to involve him with his schooling to help take his mind off his wanderlust, but studying about the topsiders only inflamed his thirst for adventure. He learned the hard way to keep his rebellious thoughts to himself. And so, when their

Council Leader, Marik, had asked if he would like to take over the job of collecting samples, he had jumped at the chance like a barracuda. He was grateful that Marik had given him that opportunity.

Lost in thought and engaged in reaching his assigned test site, the first sense of trouble seemed to Ni-Cio only a slight current shift. He frowned and shrugged his shoulders in an attempt to banish the feeling.

It was imperative that he retrieve the samples. Once presented at Council, they would provide irrefutable proof that the future of his home, his family and the lives of every Atlantean were threatened. The risk of discovery increased with each leap of Terran technology. And so, Ni-Cio ignored the first unsettling hints that nipped at the edges of his psyche.

As the speed of his biosphere's ascent increased, the vibrations of distress insinuated themselves deeper into his awareness until he could no longer concentrate on his race to the surface. He slowed his craft and searched for the source of the disturbance.

His thoughts circled through the surrounding blue, and he was captured at once by a feeling that rippled through his body almost like an electrical shock. Someone's life force was ebbing.

Ni-Cio tried to continue his task, but the vibrations grew more insistent. Against his better judgment he attempted contact before he diverted his attention back to the mission. *"Forgive me, I cannot stop...your life is precious, but I am not to interfere with your actions..."*

As his thought-form sailed through the sapphire water to find its recipient, Ni-Cio urged his biosphere into a moderate ascent.

A pall cast itself around his heart as he felt the motions of distress slow. He was aware that the last bit of oxygen had been reached. With the sudden release of that last breath, he stopped.

24

The light from his biosphere cut through the dark and flashed across a motionless form. A topside woman! Her skin sparked like a falling star and Ni-Cio would sooner have willed his own heart to stop beating than leave the woman to her fate.

Before her next inhalation, he positioned the biosphere next to her and the hatch dematerialized. He reached to gather her in. The hatch closed and seawater flowed outside in an eye blink. Ni-Cio willed the bioskin from around his head and breathed deeply into the woman's mouth. Her full lips parted to accept his gift, and for a moment, Ni-Cio felt lightheaded.

He pulled her inert form into a more comfortable position and the biosphere adjusted to its new rider. Questions swirled in aquamarine eyes before the woman lost consciousness. But in that instant, Ni-Cio sensed an elusive thrill of recognition. He felt he knew her. His hands slid down the graceful slope of her back and encircled the curve of her waist. Ni-Cio drew her closer until he could feel the drowsy beat of her heart against his own racing pulse.

"What have I done?" Ni-Cio looked wildly about, fearing that someone from Atlantis had seen his wanton disregard of the Edicts. His stomach clenched and he felt sick. The spike of his heartbeat spoke of his own rising panic. *"Leave her! I cannot bring her to Atlantis!"*

He didn't know what to do. Blindly willing the hatch to open again, he started to thrust her from the craft but his body acted of its own accord. The hatch shut yet again and the surge of water was once again expelled from the 'sphere. Bringing her closer, he peered into her face and tried to hear her thoughts. The woman remained unconscious, however, and he heard nothing. The icy water, caught like crystal teardrops in her feathery lashes, riveted his attention and he watched in fascination as salt tears trickled down her porcelain cheeks. He couldn't catch his breath, and he coughed as his heart quivered with an uneven beat. Her otherworldliness ignited his restless soul with an unquenchable fire. *"I will give my life to protect you."*

His decision made, it still took a tremendous effort of will to bring his craft around. He lifted his gaze and concentrated on the downward trek home.

CHAPTER 7

Ni-Cio knew that the action he took to save the woman would send shockwaves through Atlantis. What wasn't certain was how vast the repercussions would be. He had to be prepared for anything.

Holding the woman as gently as he could, Ni-Cio watched their descent. Colors outside changed and deepened. Orange flowed to red; green became blue and dark blue merged into an indigo night. The luminous headlights from his biosphere cut the unrelenting darkness into streaming bands of shadows, and Ni-Cio flew his craft around jagged mountains and over fathomless canyons. Finally, at the base of a sheer rock wall dotted with the soft glow of phosphorescent green, he brought his craft to a stop.

An almost invisible shadow briefly distorted the canyon walls, then swam into sight. Ni-Cio smiled. The torpedo-shaped, nearly transparent body lurked at the portal entrance and emitted rainbows of light while clicking a triple row of razor-sharp teeth. At the sound of its fretful swishing and clicking, a sound audible only to him, Ni-Cio knew they were home. He sent a gentle thought-whisper to his old friend. *"Peace, Gallendar, be still…"*

The menacing appearance of the ageless behemoth camouflaged a docile nature, however, he did not give ground to Ni-Cio at the entrance portal. *"My friend, do you know what it is that you do?"*

"I could not help myself, Gallendar…if you could, you would have done the same…"

"I would not be you for the world…you will need all your strength to endure the consequences of your action…I leave you to your fate…"

Ni-Cio watched as the fish lazily flicked its great tail and swam away. Admittance into Atlantis opened before him and his still unconscious guest.

He steered the biosphere into an underwater tunnel and navigated the winding cavern. Without the shimmering illumination of the green phosphorescence, and even with the lights of his underwater craft, the darkness of the portal was complete, so dense, that it seemed to have its own presence, its own layers of black. Ni-Cio traversed the portal and aimed the craft toward a light that unfolded like a rose.

As the light became more distinct, colors flared on either side of the tunnel, becoming brighter until the Atlantean surfaced into an arched chamber that was swathed in a soft coppery glow. Pinpoints of light glinted off granite walls, walls carved into fantastic shapes: unicorns, miniature elephants, heroes and mermaids.

Ni-Cio held the topsider as gently as possible and stepped from the biosphere onto the pool deck. His bioskin, which had provided protection and air, changed form, trailing away like a cloud. From a rack full of warming robes, Ni-Cio grabbed two to drape around himself and the woman. As he did, his thoughts called to his friend and Healer. *"Na-Kai…come, please…"*

A gentle rebuke soughed through his mind. *"Ni-Cio, not you…a stranger?"*

"She is unconscious…"

"Wait…I am coming…"

A sudden sharp slap burned across Ni-Cio's shoulders, causing him to jump. Holding the woman, he twisted around to see the piercing, black eyes and hawk-like face of his childhood friend.

Aris's smile pulled into a deep scowl of dismay. The sudden change of his friend's affable behavior punctuated the severity of Ni-Cio's transgression. Aris grasped the stranger's chin and tilted it to the light, then just as suddenly, let her go as if his hand had been burned just by touching her. "This topsider is way beyond her depth! By the gods, Ni-Cio, what were you thinking?"

Grabbing Ni-Cio's arm, Aris tried to drag him back to the biosphere. "Come on! We can get her out of here before anyone finds out!"

Ni-Cio wouldn't budge. "Aris, I need you to stand with me in this. Na-Kai is coming for her, and in my heart..."

Aris barged in, "Your heart? What an argument! That should just about convince the Council to let her stay. Have you finally lost your mind?"

Ni-Cio's heart sank. He was well aware of the repercussions his actions would dictate if he couldn't even convince his best friend that his decision had been warranted. Before he could defend himself, however, the sound of a deep bass voice reverberated through the hall, making both men jump.

"Who's lost their mind?" Marik strode into view.

The sheer size of Marik commanded attention and Ni-Cio felt dwarfed not only by the responsibilities of leadership that Marik seemed to wear so easily, he felt diminished by comparison. Ni-Cio's arms tightened around the woman and he straightened to his full six-foot height.

As he watched Marik's purposeful approach, Ni-Cio could tell how much he enjoyed his position as Council Leader. Marik had always led Atlantis with a firm sense of adherence to Canon Law. While he shared an abundance of love with all Atlanteans, it was no secret that he loved the children most of all. It was

Marik's dedication to his post, and the love he held in his heart, that Ni-Cio fervently hoped would work in his favor now. However, the disdainful sweep of Marik's water-blue eyes as he took in the unconscious form did not bode well.

Ni-Cio jostled his bundle into a more comfortable position as he watched Marik's eyes narrow to slits, and his heart sank along with his carefully nurtured hope.

"What have you done?" Sickly green striations curled over Marik's strong features, showing the fear that roiled inside him. "You are well aware of the Edict guarding against associations with topsiders. Put her out, now." As if the episode were concluded, Marik turned to go.

"Marik, I cannot. She is hurt!" Ni-Cio felt like he was drowning.

The Council Leader halted and when he turned around, Ni-Cio saw the glint of steel in his eyes that reflected his innate terror and repugnance of the foreign female. "You should never have brought her here. What possessed you to even touch one such as this, much less bring her into our midst? You know it is expressly forbidden. Must I order another to do that which you are unwilling to do?"

Ni-Cio had known his actions would meet with intense opposition, but he had counted on the reverence for life within the soul of every Atlantean to strengthen his position. He never thought his single act of compassion would be turned into a cold-blooded act of murder. "No, I cannot do this." He clung to the topsider, thinking Marik would yank her from his arms. His ability to reason vanished, and he knew a deep and abiding anger had taken over when he felt his eyes turn from vivid violet to a heat-filled purple. He swung on his friend. "Aris, speak to my defense! We can take this to a vote in Council. It is my right!"

Aris's skin rippled from orange to bronze, and Ni-Cio was stunned. Incapable of movement, he had to acknowledge the dire predicament into which he had brought the topsider with Aris's reply. "My friend, I would give my life for you, but do not ask my help with this, not this. You must do as Marik says and put her out. There is no other alternative."

Ni-Cio turned away from Aris and Marik, and with the backs of his fingertips, stroked the face of the unconscious woman. He heard the muted tread of Marik's feet as the Leader came closer. "I know your heart, Ni-Cio, but there is no Council decision to be made. The Canons teach us to revere life, yet the Edicts are what have kept us safe and hidden. We will not change what has worked for thousands of years. Go now and be done."

Ni-Cio's blood pounded and he spun to face his adversary. "I will not do this. I will leave Atlantis before I commit this unspeakable outrage!"

Aris and Marik released their fear and frustration at the same time.

"Ni-Cio, it is for the good of Atlantis that I tell you to do this!"

"It is law."

"We cannot interfere…"

Tempers flared and voices escalated until a regal whisper cut through the tumult like a knife. "Let me see her."

As one, they turned, extreme ranges of emotion reflected on their faces. Na-Kai had come. Marik and Aris parted to let her view the woman Ni-Cio gripped like a life preserver.

Na-Kai studied the unconscious topsider, then took her from Ni-Cio and settled her onto a nearby couch. The Healer laid her hand across the young woman's forehead. "You are safe. Awaken."

31

At Na-Kai's command, the young woman's eyes opened. Ni-Cio let out an anxious sigh and only then realized he had been holding his breath. He could tell that the topsider was unaware of the men grouped around her, and instead focused her gaze on the wise and beautiful woman who observed her. The topsider's voice trembled. "Who are you?"

Na-Kai neither moved nor spoke. With the Healer's hand still resting upon the woman's forehead, Ni-Cio could see her hesitation. His heart skipped a beat as Na-Kai's thoughts tumbled into his mind. *"You do not even realize the extent of this treasure you have brought us..."* The Healer passed her hand over the woman's eyes, and the topsider fell into a deep, untroubled sleep. Na-Kai eyed the men. "I would have her rest before she is questioned."

The maelstrom erupted. Na-Kai rose from the couch, and with the absolute authority of her years, silenced everyone with a gesture. "We will meet in Council. Regardless of what you may think, Marik, there are reasons to keep her with us. I will say no more until we are convened. I suggest you summon everyone with utmost urgency. I will be in my chambers until you are ready."

"Ni-Cio, see that this woman is placed under Kyla's care until I am ready for her."

They watched as the Healer turned with a grace that belied her years, and swept from the chamber. Ni-Cio turned to stare at the other men, and then at the sleeping topsider.

CHAPTER
8

Once Ni-Cio saw that Kyla had sequestered the topsider in Na-Kai's chambers, he retraced his steps. He walked back through the empty halls to rejoin his friend while his thoughts boiled over one another like sharks at a feeding frenzy. *"The Terran woman is in grave peril because of my rash decision. If the reactions of Marik and Aris are any indication, then it is a foregone conclusion that the vote at Council will not be any different. By the god of my fathers, if anything happens to her I will never forgive myself!"* He bowed his head and his heart began an erratic syncopation. Icy beads of moisture created a string of sweat at his hairline.

He angled down an adjacent tunnel and lengthened his strides. His breath seemed to wedge in his throat. He had heard the term "blind panic" in relation to topsiders, but for the first time in his life, he comprehended the idea.

He located Aris, but when he saw a look of obstinacy crisscross his friend's features with dark blue, Ni-Cio decided that diplomacy could wait. He grabbed Aris's arm and forced him into an empty side chamber.

They squared off. Aris's skin rippled red and gold streaks of flame. Ni-Cio knew the colors to be a perfect mirror of his own inflamed emotions, so he tried to still his jumping heart. But as he opened with his first persuasive salvo, it seemed that his heart had decided to leap from his chest and into his throat. He swallowed hard and tried to clear a path so that his words could slip by. "You must help me sway the vote."

A quick shake of his head and Aris crossed his arms. He set himself obdurately on both feet. "You heard Marik. You should never have brought her here. Her very presence endangers us all."

"Think about it, Aris, we are taught to revere the life-essence almost before we take our first breath. Surely, the third Canon prevails over the dictates of our man-made Edicts. It is unconscionable to suggest any other alternative."

When Aris didn't respond, Ni-Cio felt a slight twinge of hope. "How long have we been friends? I would not ask you to do that which I was unprepared to return in kind. Please Aris, with your help we can sway enough of the assembly so that the consequences of my actions need not reach such a terrible conclusion."

Robes flying, Aris pushed past Ni-Cio and turned around. Drawing several deep breaths, he struggled for composure and ran his hands through his long, dark hair. "I do not understand why you are unable to take her back to the unfortunate place you acquired her. At least then you would not have to put her out at depth."

In a gesture that made him feel like the supplicant he was, Ni-Cio turned his hands palm side up before lifting his shoulders in a helpless shrug. "She was trying to kill herself. I, intervened."

Aris's face and arms burned an incandescent scarlet, and it looked to Ni-Cio as if he was about to receive some painful physical damage. He girded himself for the rampage. "By all the gods, Ni-Cio, I do not believe this! How am I to help you? You have sealed her fate by your own actions. You know as well as I do, unless we are directly involved, it is forbidden for us to interfere in the actions of topsiders. Our safety and anonymity depends upon our adherence to that Edict. Surely you cannot have forgotten how the Council voted with respect to Travlor?"

Aris turned and headed for the door as if the discussion had been concluded, but Ni-Cio quickly blocked his exit. "Aris, you must listen. It was as if I was compelled. I cannot explain any better than to tell you that I was drawn to that exact place at that exact moment in order to save her. She is here for a purpose. I know this with every fiber of my being. On that, I would stake my life."

Ni-Cio thought maybe he had opened a small fissure when his friend stopped to scrutinize him in minute detail. "Ni-Cio, I know you are not given to rash statements any more than you are given to rash actions. Whether ordained by the gods or not, I have always been the one to make trouble and from my earliest remembrance, you were always the one who stood up for some of my more unfortunate schemes. It was you who placated and made peace."

Ni-Cio watched with dreadful hope as his friend's high coloring subsided to its normal bronze glow. The quiet earnestness of Aris's usually boisterous voice pierced Ni-Cio's soul to the core. The strong arm of his childhood friend dropped over his shoulders. "It would seem that loyalty outweighs Edicts. I pray you have not staked your life for a topsider. Reasons aside, it seems to me that you have done just that, my friend. I hope that we can find others who will appreciate your nebulous reasoning."

Ni-Cio felt the warmth and the support of Aris's body and he let himself be guided to the exit. They paused long enough to let the door de-materialize when Ni-Cio felt the sudden grip of Aris's hand on his neck. He knew that his friend had reached a decision.

"So be it. Let us converge upon the Council and do what we can to persuade the others."

CHAPTER
9

*K*yla sat next to the bed and scrutinized the topsider in minute detail. Her curiosity of their visitor ran wild, almost as wild as her innate fear of Terrans. She calmed herself by studying the beautiful woman who slept like the dead.

With hair the color of sunlight, she seemed to Kyla, to shimmer in the soft light of her quarters. When Ni-Cio had brought her in and laid her sleeping form on the bed, Kyla could tell that the woman was small by Atlantean standards. She surmised that the topsider reached just five-feet-six inches. Almost a head shorter than herself. Also, her skin tone was so much lighter than that of the Atlanteans. After Ni-Cio had left, Kyla had summoned enough courage to hold her arm next to the topsider's. The difference was amazing.

Kyla remembered studying the vast collection of information available on their processors, and to her watchful eye, the woman's form resembled that of a lithe, graceful dancer. Kyla wished that she herself looked as exotic and as beautiful.

The young woman stirred and Kyla yanked her arm away, fear slithering through her like an eel. She sat very erect in her chair and hardly dared breathe.

Daria had no idea how long she had been asleep, but as she felt her mind wind back toward reality, she replayed various parts of an unusually vivid dream. She remembered unrelenting darkness coupled with a sense of suffocation, a sudden intake of breath that made her feel like crying, and finally, a soft breeze with a voice like a goddess that calmed her worst fears.

With the gradual return of consciousness, her dream memories faded and she enjoyed a lazy stretch. She luxuriated in the touch of silken sheets that flowed over her body like quicksilver. Upon opening her eyes, Daria fully expected to be greeted by the vivid colors of her hotel room.

She screamed and scrambled to all fours while she grappled with the sheets. She yanked the fabric to her body, and skittered across the bed until her back was plastered against the wall. Her breath came in quick gasps, and she felt the sledgehammer beat of her heart as she clutched the sheets against her chest.

Her surroundings were unrecognizable. There were no windows, so there was no sunlight. The room was hidden in shadows, but she knew the walls should have been made of white stucco. Instead, her back pressed against solid rock. She should have been clothed, but all her frantic thoughts were cast aside as she stared into the ageless gaze of a green sea turtle. The reptile was so close that she could see the scaled lines of its face, like antiquated brickwork.

In heightened anticipation, Daria watched the gentle giant blink its thick, emerald lids. With elegant disregard, the creature turned and heaved itself back into a tiled pool. He swam away in regal splendor. Daria wrenched her gaze from the disappearing turtle to the form of a young woman seated next to her bed. The rise of panic in her voice joined with a symphonic crescendo of hyperventilation. "Who are you? Where am I? I thought I was drowning."

Daria struggled to maintain a grasp on her sanity. She felt as if she had slipped down Alice's rabbit hole. About to give voice to the endless scream that threatened to erupt, she paused when she recognized the same crazed look mirrored on the face of the other woman. In a diamond flash of clarity, Daria knew that the person seated before her was also riddled with fear.

From beneath the sleeves of her robes, the female raised hands that trembled in a gesture of conciliation, contrition or pleading. Her voice shook. "Please, my name is Kyla. I was told to watch over you, but now that you are awake, I am to escort you to Na-Kai's chambers."

Daria detected just a trace of an accent, but she was unable to place the woman's nationality. She exhibited a hint of Mediterranean influence. Swathed in the blue green shimmer of floor length robes, the outline of her slender form was visible, yet her hands were covered again and Daria guessed that the woman held them clasped tightly underneath the flowing sleeves.

Her long, black hair was swept up in soft curls, and it gleamed even in the subdued light. It was held in place in a style that was reminiscent of ancient Greece.

The woman stared back at her, and Daria was unnerved by an eye color that could only be described as topaz. They inspected each other carefully, but as they did, a swath of violet color rose in snakelike tendrils, and ribbons of color swirled across Kyla's full lips. Tracing a line over high cheekbones, the color continued to curl upward to vanish beneath her raven hair. Daria gaped.

Kyla glanced down and stared at her hands. "I am sorry. I am unable to keep my emotions hidden."

Daria clamped her mouth closed and swallowed hard. "I don't understand. Who are you? How is your skin changing colors?"

The other woman waited a heartbeat, then lifted her eyes to look at Daria again. "Come. Our Most Sovereign Healer is waiting, and there are many questions only she can answer for

39

you and for us. I will give you clothing, then we must go." Kyla stood, and after a slight pause, offered her hand.

Daria reasoned that for the moment she had no other recourse, so she crept to the edge of the bed and with a firm grip on the sheets, stood on unsteady legs. Ignoring Kyla's outstretched hand, she jerked her chin in a quick motion to signal that she would follow. The young woman shrugged and turned to lead her to the changing area.

After Daria had been fitted with a warming robe, Kyla escorted her through a complex series of tunnels until they came to a walled garden. They stopped before what looked to Daria like a solid wall, but she watched a portion of the stone dissolve like liquid.

Icy fingers of fear raced up Daria's spine. Kyla gestured for her to enter, but she was too afraid. Kyla placed her hand at the small of her back and gently ushered Daria through the door. After a tentative step, Daria spun around to see if Kyla had followed, but the door had re-materialized. She was sealed inside.

Blood pounded in her ears, and her body shook. Daria clasped her hands and stood motionless for a few heartbeats, then decided she might as well get on with it. She grabbed the long robe, turned back into the room and gasped.

The chamber was unlike anything she had ever seen. It felt as if she had come home. There were no hard angles, yet there were nooks and crannies and private places. Granite walls were softened by refracted light that glimmered in soft blues, greens, purples and golds. A domed ceiling of colorful mosaic tile was held in place by columns that had been carved with exquisite detail. Plush seating in muted sea colors made her want to sit down with a good book. Daria knew that the area in which she stood was no larger than the apartment she had left, but the intimate surroundings created an illusion of boundlessness.

She blinked her eyes. Her breathing returned to normal and Daria felt, rather than heard, an ageless voice whisper to her heart.

"Come, sit here, child…"

An older woman beckoned her, but her attention was drawn to a wall of gently falling water. The crystal liquid wound over the dark slate in lazy ribbons before slipping into the deep blue waters of a quiet pool. The ethereal sounds of a water sonata lifted to entwine with air so pure that when she inhaled, it stung her nose.

Caught in a sensual play of light and sound, Daria pulled her robe up and crossed the floor. As if in a dream, she sank into cushions fluffy as clouds. When the cushions moved underneath her and molded to her form, Daria was surprised that she felt no shock. She looked at the woman seated next to her.

Na-Kai reached for her hands and enfolded her in a touch that spoke to her soul of joy, love, laughter and timelessness. Na-Kai's voice washed over her, as soothing as the music that emanated from the waterwall. "You are a visitor to us. The first and only we have received in the thousands of years we have lived within this world. Until you have reached a decision as to your fate, we will give you safe harbor; therefore, I must share with you the knowledge you require in order to make your choice."

Daria frowned. She pulled her hands away and stood. She walked a few anxious paces and stopped. Wrapping her arms around herself, she snorted at the inadvertent gesture of self-protection and dropped her arms to her sides. She shook her head, shrugged her shoulders and turned to face her captor. "Well, let's start with the most practical questions. Who are you, and where am I?"

She noted the woman's hesitation. She seemed to Daria to be uncomfortable, because she cleared her throat more than once before she spoke.

"I am Na-Kai eva, meaning daughter of, Evenor. I am a Healer to my people. I am four hundred and seven years of age. You are in Atlantis."

A futile hope that she had misheard raced through Daria's heart. Even with everything she had seen, she couldn't believe what Na-Kai had just said. "Is this your idea of a joke? Who brought me here and how do I get out?"

Daria swung around and tried to find the exit, knowing even as she did that she would be unable to locate the door.

Na-Kai stood to face the frightened woman. "I would not joke about something so serious. Ni-Cio brought you to me. And though I know how badly you wish it were not so, now is not an auspicious time for your departure. Now please, tell me your name."

Na-Kai's voice soothed Daria's feelings of alarm and helped calm her a bit. Daria studied Na-Kai. The woman looked forbiddingly beautiful. No trace of her incredible age was in evidence, for she moved with the easy grace of a much younger woman. She glided across the room, and as she did, her long hair shimmered, sparking lights of pure silver. Every movement brought a play of luminous iridescence that emanated from her very being. With eyes the color of mother-of-pearl, she appeared almost translucent, and Daria found it difficult to look straight at her.

The sheer otherworldly quality of the woman chased away the last vestiges of Daria's bravery. She was utterly at the mercy of this woman. Her voice trembled and she balled her hands into fists to keep from crying. "Nici, who? I'm Daria Caiden and I'm done." Daria backed away from Na-Kai's cautious approach.

The Healer stopped her advance and tried to calm the young woman's fears. "Please, try not to be afraid. I mean you no harm." Na-Kai gestured to the couch. "Come and sit with me."

Daria didn't understand why, but she knew that the woman who stood before her was incapable of lying. However, Na-Kai's veiled warning introduced a new element to her fear, and she didn't want to continue. She wanted to be back in Boston, and wished with all her heart that she had never come to Greece. Na-Kai offered her hand. From somewhere deep inside, Daria drew upon a hidden reserve of courage and let the Atlantean lead her back to the cushions.

Seated again, she looked at Na-Kai. The ghost of a smile flitted across the older woman's lips and Daria realized that Na-Kai was afraid, too. Whatever they faced, she steeled herself to get through it so that she could get back to her life. "All right, why me, why now?"

"Daria, we are in need of brevity, and there is a much faster way for you to learn what you need to know. It is something we call a thought-form; it is our version of telepathy."

A barrage of questions tumbled from Daria's lips, but Na-Kai held up her hand. "Peace. Be still and hear me. We are a very old race. Evolving as we have through the ages, we have inherited certain gifts that ensure our survival. Our most sustaining and unique ability enables us to open our minds to each other. We are adept at reading thoughts. I would ask you to let me touch your mind, but know this, in order to do so, I must have your complete agreement. Should you have even the least reservation, I will be unable to continue."

Daria reached for Na-Kai's hands. When she looked down at the luminescent fingers interlaced with hers, it was difficult to determine where her hands ended and Na-Kai's began. She forced her attention back to the Healer. "Do you mean to tell me that anyone in Atlantis can read my thoughts anytime they feel like it?"

"No, I assure you, without another's complete assent we cannot enter. Your thoughts are blocked, until and unless you grant entrance.

"I would read your thoughts and in turn, have you know mine. Only then can you truly grasp the extent of what we are asking you to face. There is much for you to learn and our time together is short. I will let nothing happen to you until you have made your decision. Beyond that, I must await your answer."

Stung by sparkling currents of fear and curiosity, Daria shuddered. Lost in a swirl of emotions, she rose from the couch and walked to the waterwall. She gazed into the muted flow of water, entranced by the intricate patterns that formed, dissolved and re-formed. She watched as silvery streams of water coalesced into the misty figures of her mother and father. She tried to touch the reflection, but it vanished as the shock of cold water trickled over her fingers. She blinked away the prickles of tears that threatened, but her resolve had settled. She turned to face Na-Kai. "I will open my mind to you. Show me what I need to know."

She had no idea what kind of choice she was supposed to make, but of one thing she was certain, her life would never be the same again.

CHAPTER 10

N a-Kai bit back a smile watching Daria's purposeful stride. The determined expression on the face of the lovely topsider only served to accentuate her bravery. She waited while Daria stiffly lowered herself to a seated position.

The young woman sat erect with her gaze trained forward. She clasped and unclasped her hands and held her knees together as though they had been bound. Na-Kai was ready to begin when Daria jumped up and started plumping the pillows. She stepped back to survey the result, then pivoted and sat down again. Daria was still for a brief moment, then she began shifting her body in an effort to find the most comfortable position.

A peal of laughter escaped Na-Kai's lips. "Daria, it won't hurt. You may relax. You will only feel traces of touch. Why, I would liken it to the softest of breezes. You will barely know I am there."

Daria nodded and sank back onto the pillows. Her arms slid from her lap to rest at her sides. Na-Kai waited until Daria was still, then she scooted forward. She leaned over the topsider and peered into her guileless aquamarine eyes. Na-Kai lost herself in the depths of shifting ocean colors. Her thoughts sighed into Daria's mind with a touch as soft as the breath of a newborn and Na-Kai began to unlock the doors that would bring her to the answer she sought.

She wound through Daria's present thoughts: kindness, gentleness, trust, and confusion, the last to be expected. She probed farther and reached into the past. Wisps of loving relationships mingled with generosity and humor, compassion beyond her years and always, kindness that was freely given. Watching Daria's life unfold, Na-Kai witnessed the brutal car accident that stole the lives of her parents when she was only five. There had been no other relatives, so Daria had been ushered into a foster care system that had little regard for her needs, or her grief. Shuttled from home to home, she met families from all walks of life. Not one of them cared to give her a permanent place in their homes, or their hearts. She learned to protect her own heart and erected the barriers that helped her hide. The loneliness in Daria's soul touched Na-Kai in a way that the Healer never expected. She wanted to enfold her in her arms and comfort her, but as she wound through other scenes of Daria's life, she saw a resolute girl turn into a beautiful, caring woman. Fending for herself, she had taken any job she could find in order to save money and prepare for college.

Working her way through school, Daria made friends easily enough, but Na-Kai could see that she never opened the most secret chambers of her heart, or her thoughts, to anyone. Na-Kai wanted to cry. Swallowing past the lump that had risen in her throat, she blinked hard and continued to watch Daria's life unfold.

Her first real job had come right after graduation. An antiques dealer had snatched her up and had mentored her until she was capable of running the business. Daria traveled the world over, and Na-Kai could see how quickly the young woman adapted to other countries and other cultures. The degree of empathy Daria exhibited toward others was remarkable. Her ability to adapt so quickly would help her adjust to life in Atlantis. Na-Kai knew she would make a sublime Healer.

As lonely as Daria had been most of her life, Na-Kai saw that she had still managed to fill her life with love. Always the first to take care of a sick friend or shelter a stray animal, the young topsider never lacked for companionship.

Even so, it was not enough. Na-Kai had yet to reach the core component that would let her know that her search had not been in vain. On she probed. Tracing the bloodlines back before Daria, before her mother and before her mother's mother, Na-Kai watched generations fly by as she traveled backward, following always the maternal line.

Na-Kai descended beyond recorded time. The lines were becoming less tangled, more distinct and still she descended. Darkness flowed inward and a moment of doubt sparked. An almost palpable fear trickled into her awareness, and Na-Kai decreased her speed. She could not see it. It was not there. She had risked everything. She had broken a supreme law, and now it seemed that her sacrifice had been for nothing. The intensity of emotion that threatened to overtake her caused an instant's hesitation.

It was at that precise moment of exquisite apprehension that Na-Kai beheld a brief flicker. Light that was not light flared and disappeared.

Her heart leapt! With unerring precision, she pursued the path that had momentarily lit her way and then, she was there. It was as she had hoped. The key! She had reached the core component that was her irrefutable proof. She was vindicated. Her actions had been justified. With that blessed reassurance, Na-Kai gently disengaged her thoughts.

She knew that it would seem to Daria that there had been no passage of time at all. So Na-Kai wasn't surprised to see her startled look when she pulled away. Beleaguered by her own conflicting emotions, Na-Kai rose from the couch. She tried to still her mind, but her thoughts roiled. She stepped toward the waterwall. Daria's worried questions followed, but they hardly registered in her consciousness.

"Na-Kai, is everything all right? Were you able to read my thoughts?"

With her back toward the topsider, Na-Kai roused herself. "All is well, child. It is as I had hoped. Give me a moment, for I am quite overwhelmed."

Na-Kai let her fingers trail through the crystal water. She had so much to accomplish, and time kept slipping down its infinite track. Could she raise this young woman to the level that was needed before her own time was over? Would Daria even consent to the path that would be presented to her? Doubts flowed over her like the water that flowed over her fingertips. For Na-Kai, there were no other options. Fate had decided for both of them. It was time for Daria to be told. The choice would then be her own.

She gathered her robes and turned. In solemn silence, Na-Kai rejoined the young woman. "You are everything I hoped for, and yet, so much more. She reached to caress Daria's hair, and sighed as she felt the soft gold strands beneath her touch. "How is it that all our hopes are to be found in so small a package? You have no idea how special you are and what we, I, will be asking of you. Believe me when I tell you, were it not so, I would never burden one so young with the weight of this terrible responsibility."

Na-Kai felt the recoil as Daria jerked her head away. "What are you saying? I came to Santorini to have some time away from my boyfriend. The last thing I remember, I was standing on the edge of a cliff. I'm supposed to believe I'm in Atlantis, and suddenly you're calling me 'your hope'? I've had enough.

I don't want to hear anymore. I'm tired and I want to go home, now!"

Na-Kai placed her hand on top of Daria's wrist. "Please, I promise it will not be much longer. You must understand the reasons you have been brought to Atlantis. Once you know my thoughts, your questions will be answered and your moment of choice will be at hand. No matter your decision, know that I will be with you and I will let nothing happen to you."

Na-Kai paused and gave Daria time to consider the implications of her words. She knew the young woman was confused, yet she no longer tried to sway her. From this moment, the decision would rest on Daria's shoulders.

Daria's brows furrowed, and her face exhibited such a look of worry that Na-Kai wanted to take her in her arms and hold her as if she were her own child. Finally, with the utmost resignation, she blurted her last question. "How do I do this thought-touch?"

Again, Na-Kai granted the merest smile to lift the corners of her mouth. It was the only outward acknowledgement she offered to show Daria how proud she was. "You need do nothing. I will bring my thoughts to you. Relax and let them flow, try not to close yourself off. Many of the memories will be extremely unpleasant, but just remember it all happened a very long time ago."

Daria leaned back into the feathery cushions. She looked at Na-Kai but simply nodded her acquiescence.

CHAPTER

11

*D*aria's vision clouded and then was obscured. It was as though an opaque crystal wall had settled before her eyes. There was not a breath of movement, and there was no sound. The stillness and silence expanded, and as she waited, a feeling of unease began to creep into her consciousness. She started to object, but the first traces of color stirred at the periphery of her sight and she heard Na-Kai's soft whisper enter her mind.

"I will be showing scenes from life as it was before the sinking...but I must explain a bit about myself...Daria, I was very young when I became Most Sovereign Healer, younger than you, and I was terrified of the responsibility that I was to inherit...I was given a night in which to come to a decision to accept or reject the title...

"I grappled between my desire to help others and my fear of the tremendous duties that would fall to me should I accept...in the midst of my despair and as dawn approached, I was visited by Kai-Dan, the greatest Healer Atlantis has ever known..." Na-Kai held tighter to Daria's hand. *"Kai-Dan told me that while I was a good Healer, and that my abilities would be sufficient for the needs of my people, it was my inner strength that would be needed...I truly believe that Kai-Dan compelled you to the cliffs of Santorini so that you could be brought here...she foresaw our time of need..."*

Hearing Na-Kai's story, Daria was astounded. She loosened her grip and sat up. "What are you talking about? And how could Kai-Dan have any ability to bring me here?"

"The thought-form I created to find you," Na-Kai hesitated, then rushed on, "it is forbidden because it utilizes something similar to telekinesis. I have trespassed an ancient law laid down by Poseidon since the beginning of time. As for Kai-Dan, she had powers beyond any of us. I know in my heart that she has watched through time for this very moment to occur. When it did, she stepped in to help us find each other."

Signaling for Daria to lie back, Na-Kai continued her story, her thoughts winding gently through the young woman's mind.

"I do not know the consequences of my actions, nor do I care...it is enough to know that I have done what was needed, and that Kai-Dan was right...no other could or would make the choice I did...it was the only way to give my people a chance...

"Please understand, being a Healer has been the most important aspect of my life...I have not found a life mate within our walls, and I have chosen not to have a child...I have dedicated my life to others until my destiny brought me to this terrible choice that now involves you..."

Na-Kai took a deep breath and looked at Daria. *"She is so young and so naïve. I could just let her go, no one would be the wiser. I ask too much."* It was a thought, however, that she did not share and did not act upon.

Hopelessly shrugging her shoulders, Na-Kai gave up the last struggle. She sank down next to Daria. *"If you have no more questions, I will show you our history..."*

Daria, eyes still closed, squeezed Na-Kai's hand. "I'm ready."

Like clouds lifting after a fog, Daria saw colors start to form within the whiteness of her vision. The clouds stretched and thinned, and she caught glimpses of a far distant landscape. As the view came into sharper focus and the scene drew closer she was able to determine objects and people. The place she saw was one of unimaginable beauty. She sensed a harmony that existed between nature and people that had not been found before or since. It was Atlantis at the height of its majesty.

Fountains cascaded into pools of sparkling blue. Architecture blended into the surroundings so that it was difficult to tell the buildings from the landscape. Archways formed walking bridges over rivers that flowed into an azure sea. Colors and textures were rich and vivid. Trees and plants abounded, and the air was scented with their essence. Above all, the people were happy and busy. She was surprised to see so much bustle. Ships were in harbor, trade was brisk and spirits were high. A general sense of well-being permeated everything.

The scene abruptly switched to a clamorous gathering, and Daria could see that people were standing, sitting or clustered in tight groups. Serenity forgotten, everyone argued. Her focus changed and narrowed to one woman.

Dressed in robes of glistening white, the woman generated a feeling of calm amidst the turmoil. She appeared neither young nor old. With hair as white as her robes, her age was hard to determine. She was the Most Sovereign Healer of Atlantis, Kai-Dan eva Evenor. She sat quietly in the melee, but after a time, she shook her head and slipped away.

Again, a scene change. Kai-Dan talked to a group of people who appeared anxious to listen to her. When they dispersed, it was clear they were more than just upset. Daria sensed an urgency that bordered on panic. Daria shifted her legs and sank deeper into the cushions.

The next vision brought with it a tremendous feeling of doom. People worked furiously to construct tunnels inside the heart of a huge granite mountain. Provisions were stored in the tunnels even before they were completed. Outside the edge of her vision, she knew there were people who watched and derided the small band of Atlanteans as they continued their excavations.

Daria was afraid to see what would come next. She closed her eyes tighter, but the visions came anyway.

The view shifted yet again, and the assault on Daria's senses escalated. She had never witnessed such destruction. The immensity of the monstrous cataclysm shook her to her very soul. Everywhere people were either dead or dying, fires were rampant and flooding ravaged the land. Another shift and she was quite removed from the scene, and her view was once again from a great height.

With a suddenness that took her breath away, an explosion of immeasurable proportions occurred. A wall of fire engulfed the entire land, and in the blink of an eye, Atlantis sank beneath a raging sea.

Daria threw her hands over her eyes and wrenched herself from Na-Kai's thought-touch. She sat up. "How can you stand it? I can't watch anymore! Please, don't make me do this."

Na-Kai pried Daria's hands from her eyes and stroked her face. Daria's lips quivered, but when she tried to lower her gaze, Na-Kai crooked a finger underneath her chin so that Daria was forced to look at her. Na-Kai offered the only explanation she had. "Forgive me Daria, I know this is new to you. But I could see no easy way to prepare you. You have not lived with these memories as have we. It was long ago, and as you know, when enough time passes, even the most hurtful memories tend to soften. We owe our lives to Kai-Dan. She sacrificed herself to give us a remote chance of surviving the cataclysm."

"But, how do you know this? Can this even be possible? You weren't alive then. Where do these memories come from?" Daria could not seem to focus her scattered thoughts, so Na-Kai continued to stroke her face and hair. At last, Daria felt her mind begin to relax and she waited for Na-Kai to address her questions.

The Healer ran a hand over her own eyes, then settled back into the cushions. "The ability to read thoughts is an acquired trait that each of us masters over time. As we grow, our aptitude increases. As we gain strength, a time comes when our history awakens within our consciousness. For this to occur, we must be able to exhibit total control of both thoughts and emotions. By keeping our emotions at bay, we can view our history without reliving it."

Daria scowled. "So, why do you need me? What possible reason could you have for bringing me to Atlantis?"

"We have not yet reached the conclusion. There is much more for you to see. But once my thoughts have been shared, you will understand. Please, our time grows short."

Daria wasn't ready to continue, and she voiced the question to another puzzle that had bothered her. "In these visions, the original Atlanteans had normal skin tones. But your skin is not the same. Yours is almost translucent, and Kyla's changes colors. How did that happen?"

Na-Kai rose and faced Daria. "Evolution has a wondrous way of adapting. With the second generation inhabiting this sunken colony, variations of skin tone and coloring began to appear in the children. Successive generations came and went, and the coloring grew more vivid and more iridescent. We were granted a miraculous gift. Not only does our coloration serve as an indication of health, there is another facet of this most singular and unique gift. As children of Poseidon, we once again live and swim in his vast underwater realm. Swimming through the deep just as the fish we emulate do, we are undetectable by any but each other. Our coloring also serves as a most glorious form of camouflage."

Na-Kai lifted her arms and felt for the clasp at her neck. She unhooked the robe and pulled the sides apart. It slipped down her arms and pooled around her feet in a blue-green shimmer.

Daria blinked hard. Na-Kai wore a form-fitting suit that covered her entire body. Only her head, neck, hands and feet were exposed. The Healer pivoted and as she turned, lights flashed over her body like lightning. The material was semi-transparent, yet her more intimate areas remained concealed by glowing white dots that swirled over and around the material. "I am wearing a bioskin. As our history unfolds, you will see how this unique garment came into being. The bioskin generates energy to sustain us as we swim, and this pliable material can withstand the crushing weight of the ocean when we swim at depth. No Atlantean is ever without a 'skin for an extended period of time."

"Then why don't I need one of those, bioskins?"

Na-Kai bent to retrieve her robes, and after she had slipped back into the warm folds, she once again joined Daria. "Our technology is more advanced than Terros. We have a system of air flow that maintains negative pressure. We can go without bioskins in our home, but they keep us warmer than if we just wore the robes.

"I know you are overwhelmed, and if we had the luxury of time, I would introduce you to our ways in a much slower manner. However, I must have you prepared before the Council convenes. It will not take much longer."

*M*arik wound through the Council Hall. He was well aware that his stature as Council Leader would be more than enough to cause people to listen. "Remember the time Na-Kai urged me to stand with her against the others of the Council? She and I voted against Canon Law and the Edicts, and we have lived with the result of that strategy. I vowed that I would never let that happen again. We must not let her sway us now!"

He slipped these observations into casual conversations and made suspicion seem wise. Tremors of doubt raced through even the most objective citizens. "Our laws have protected us through the centuries. Should we cease to apply them now? Na-Kai is trying to reinterpret what our ancestors instituted long ago. She is bending the laws to fit her needs. Until now, our civilization's debates have never been questioned. We cannot condone Na-Kai rewriting our past."

Marik continued to introduce his will throughout the Council Hall. Some members were persuaded to change their minds. They decided to challenge their Most Sovereign Healer's impeccable authority, and Marik did what he could to buoy their arguments. "It is unimaginable that Ni-Cio has brought a topsider into our midst. However, it is inconceivable that Na-Kai has immediately placed the intruder under her protection."

Even so, Marik knew there were quite a few Atlanteans who felt that their Healer must have had a significant purpose to allow such an extreme breach of Canon Law and a primary Edict. So, he continued to apply subtle pressure between opposing mindsets. Tempers flared and discussions became heated.

Marik looked up from his current conversation in time to see Ni-Cio and Aris walk into a very unsettled group of their peers. By his count, he had already garnered quite a few votes and he hadn't noticed too much opposition.

He saw Ni-Cio exchange a nervous glance with Aris, and though Ni-Cio kept his voice low, Marik could just make out the strategy he was sharing with his friend.

"Find Rogert and his group. I will appeal to Mer-An and her assembly. If we can persuade them to stand with us, our task will be less daunting. They must be made to see that the third Canon Law should be upheld, because it takes precedence over the historically younger Edict."

Marik shook his head and left them to their task while he continued to garner more support. By the time he and the Council were ready to convene, uncertainty surged aggressively through the crowd. Opinions changed as quickly as an ocean breeze. He watched Ni-Cio and Aris cut a diligent path through the scattered groups, and even though he could tell that they were able to convince a solid number of Atlanteans to relax their adherence to Canon Law, he knew the majority still stood ready to condemn the topsider. He found confidence in that.

He had talked to too many council members who felt that Ni-Co had violated the Edict of Non-Intervention without regard to consequences, and by doing so, had introduced a severe threat to their social fiber. That Na-Kai upheld Ni-Cio's actions did nothing to sway their opinion.

The hall fell silent as a bell sounded ten sonorous chimes. Thus the High Council of Ten were summoned to their place upon the dais.

Marik knew that it was an imposing group of five men and five women who assumed their positions. In order to reach such elevated status, a person had to be a direct descendant of Poseidon.

He watched everyone settle. Their lineage was apparent, and Marik knew that each of them could trace their heritage through Atlas, or Eumelus his twin brother, or one of their brothers from the other four sets of twin boys that resulted when Cleito, an all-too-human woman, was taken to wife by a god.

When Marik took the center chair, the restless throng of two hundred quieted in silent anticipation. As Council Leader, he would open the conference, and those who were not physically in attendance would be conjoined by virtue of thought-touch so that they would miss nothing.

Any stir of movement ceased throughout Atlantis. Marik rose from his chair, cleared his throat and began to speak. His voice reverberated through the hall and sounded loud even to him. "Na-Kai has yet to make her appearance. She will join us presently, and the topsider will accompany her. In the interim, she has asked that I proceed.

"Within our immediate history, we have never convened a Council meeting on anything that posed such a threat to the structure of our lives. Therefore, I will dispense with the usual preamble. We know why we are here. Let us begin. As the rules of conduct have been established long ago, compliance to their defined order is still expected."

Marik eyed the raised podium that stood in the center of the circular assembly. Opinions were presented in a counterclockwise rotation; beginning with whichever group arrived first. He eyed the two hundred representatives, separated into ten groups of twenty.

The emissary for each cluster was one of the members of the High Council, and though Marik was the emissary for Rogert's group, they had been among the last to arrive.

He was relieved that Ni-Cio's group had not convened first, because he didn't want him swaying any more people than he already had. However, since anyone was permitted to address the Council, he wanted to prevent any intention Ni-Cio might have of taking the podium at the outset.

The general rule maintained that one person from each unit would be chosen to speak on behalf of the group. Marik had decided upon the first speaker, for he knew her well. Mer-An was not a particularly adept speaker, and although he didn't think he had tried to sabotage the outcome, by the gods he would do what he could to keep peace and eject the threat from his home.

He saw Ni-Cio at the back of the crowd, leaning against one of the columns. Grim determination spread through Marik. He raised his arm and signaled Mer-An to the podium. Marik took his seat, but his heart quaked, as he knew that the opinions set forth in this convocation had the potential of tearing asunder the life of every person in Atlantis.

CHAPTER
13

Ni-Cio's heart hammered against his chest as though excavating its way out. Blood raced through his veins at such velocity that he felt his skin turn dark gold.

He ran a hand around the neck of his bioskin to loosen its hold, and it struck him that he had never given the intimate, life-sustaining garment a second thought. Now, his movements felt constrained as though a large python were tightening its grip around his chest.

Ni-Cio found it impossible to stand still. He wanted to steal the topsider away and take her to a place of safety. He felt so jumpy that he grasped the pillar next to him. With the strength and stability of the column steadying him, he felt a measure of control return. But his fear ratcheted again as Mer-An brushed by him.

She wound through the throng and approached the podium. Whispers skittered after her like grains of sand striking rock. She hesitated before the steps and pulled a deep breath into her lungs, then proceeded up the stairs to the dais.

Ni-Cio saw her knuckles whiten when she gripped the edges of the stand for support. Her dark, sea-green gaze flowed out over her friends and family like the sudden wash of a shoreline tide. The silence was profound. It was as though everyone held their breath collectively. Ni-Cio's pulse bumped against his eardrums. And he realized that he, too, was holding his breath.

He was worried about Mer-An's opening statement. He knew her well and he trusted her as a friend, and although she was what the topsiders referred to as a "tomboy," Ni-Cio knew she had never liked speaking at Council. So, he couldn't be sure what she would say or if she would buckle beneath the weight of popular opinion.

She began and her voice was timid, halting. "I do not think I can speak for our group. We are too divided on this issue for any one person to assume that responsibility."

Variegated colors of uncertainty flickered over her soft features and her long fingers played over the smoothed edges of the podium. Ni-Cio was reminded of the rapid movements of an accomplished musician. He knew she was stalling in order to gather her thoughts. She looked down and her raven-colored hair fell forward, veiling her face in long, dark waves. Mer-An was silent for so long that Ni-Cio was afraid she wouldn't go on. He wanted to help, but just as he thought he should go to her, she raised her head and the rich tones of her voice sailed through the Hall with true strength.

"The Canons have been law from the very moment Poseidon delivered them to Atlas. Cleaving to those laws enabled Atlantis to flourish into the mighty power it once was. When we were thrown into the fires of hell, the Canons gave us the strength to survive the ravages of that dark time. To this day, those very Canons continue to uphold the society that we have become."

Her tone shifted in intensity, her eyes blazed and her fingers danced to a silent crescendo. "Without the Canons, we would have ceased to exist long ago. I realize that we, as a people, felt it necessary to enact other laws as our society changed and grew. However, this does not mean the original Canons should be ignored because of our inherent fear of topsiders!"

Dissent had been loosed. Voices erupted from every corner of the Hall so that Mer-An could no longer be heard. Ni-Cio was afraid that Marik would have to step in and take control, but Mer-An's patience was at an end. She raised her arms and slammed both fists onto the rostrum. The noise reverberated through the room like the crack of breaking granite, and the crowd was immediately subdued.

"Hear me! Where is it written that the Edicts cannot be challenged? Have we become so closed-minded and frightened that we can no longer reason?

"Na-Kai has been our Most Sovereign Healer for three hundred and seventy-seven years! Does this mean nothing? She nurtures us with her wise counsel. She heals us when we sicken. How many lives has she saved through no efforts of your own? And yet you would not even wait to hear the motive that dictates her actions? If nothing else, give Na-Kai the benefit of the doubt. Do not make your decision until we know why she harbors the topsider. We owe her that much!"

Ni-Cio pushed away from the pillar to survey the throng, and though Mer-An's arguments had been well said, he couldn't tell how many people had been affected enough for the "aye" vote needed to save the topsider. He rubbed the back of his neck to try and release the tension.

Mer-An turned and left the podium. Marik rose from his place on the dais and addressed the assembly. "Would any other speak from Mer-An's group?"

Ni-Cio let his breath leak out through clenched teeth and edged closer to see if anyone would come forward. Before the Council Leader could continue, the frantic sounds of sudden movement behind him created a disturbance that would not be denied.

Ennael, Atlantis's normally reticent composer, forced his way through the packed hall in order to gain access to the podium. The man barged up the stairs and grabbed both sides of the lectern. His voice reflected the strident tempo of his fear, and Ni-Cio knew without a doubt that his fright would infect others. He prepared to intervene.

"How can you let Mer-An sway you so easily? Of course Na-Kai has tended us. She is the embodiment of that revered title, Most Sovereign Healer. It is not by choice that she ministers to us. It is an obligation that befalls anyone who holds that designation. And what binds a person to perform those duties? The Canons! The laws are specific to our society and our needs. The Third Canon states, 'No matter the form, all life is held sacred.' Is it not true that all Healers hold life sacred anyway?"

Marik started to interrupt, but Ennael refused to acknowledge his upraised hand. The composer's words flooded the room with the force of a gathering storm. "When Poseidon handed the original eight laws to Atlas, the third law was superseded by the first law which states, 'As children of Poseidon, you are granted the paradise that is Atlantis. In the purity of your actions will it remain thus.' Poseidon knew then that the bloodlines had to be protected. Is there anyone who is ignorant of the consequences of transgressing that law?"

No one, not even Ni-Cio moved a muscle, and no one needed to be reminded.

"Over time, we have had to create other, more precise laws. The Edict of Non-Intervention strictly forbids participation in the actions of Terrans. The topsider was trying to kill herself. She was going to die!"

Ni-Cio flinched.

Ennael raised his arm and pointed a shaking finger straight at him. "Ni-Cio brought this person among us, and it was Na-Kai's foremost responsibility to uphold that Edict. Even though we hold life sacred, we must protect ourselves first! Ni-Cio is the one who intervened. Ni-Cio is the one who prevented the topsider's death, and it is Ni-Cio who must put her out at depth and let this travesty be done!"

Before the reverberations from Ennael's impassioned outcry could die down, the grisly words Ni-Cio had fervently hoped to avoid circled from every side.

"At depth!"

"At depth!"

He vaulted from the granite pillar and thrust his way through the shouting, gesticulating mob of Atlanteans and flew up the stairs to the podium. The shift of opinion had swung to support Ennael. If Ni-Cio couldn't do something, Daria would have no chance, and it wouldn't matter if Poseidon himself returned to defend the actions taken by himself and Na-Kai.

Ni-Cio stepped around Ennael as the other man left the podium. Ni-Cio raised his hands for quiet, but no one paid any heed. The tumult had become so loud, even the explosion of his shouted words couldn't stem the tide.

The noise was deafening, and Ni-Cio's horror mounted as he watched the fires of hate, fanned by Ennael, burst into a conflagration. He continued to shout and wave his arms in a furious bid for order, but no one paid him any attention. So, Ni-Cio was the only one to behold Na-Kai's arrival when she and the topsider penetrated the archway into the Council Hall.

$\mathcal{D}$aria knew she had to face the High Council, but the angry noise that assaulted her entire being made her legs shake so much that she didn't think they would support her. She followed Na-Kai through the archway and placed each foot with determined care and concentrated precision. With one false step, she felt she would be in a heap on the floor. She could imagine the outraged mob falling upon her like a pack of slavering wolves.

Her gaze bounced around the assembly like a crazed ping-pong ball until it chanced upon the man standing on the podium.

He waved his muscular arms in a wild arc, and hair that had been secured flew about his face in ragged, raven-colored strands. He moved with the explosive power of a swimmer/warrior and it seemed to Daria that he was responsible for the bedlam that had been loosed.

She could not, however, look away. For some odd reason, she felt drawn to him. Why? She had no idea, but the thought scared her almost more than the angry, shouting Atlanteans did.

The man turned to spur the crowd further, and froze. His purple eyes locked onto hers. Blazing with an emotion so intense, his stare seared her soul.

"How can he hate me that much without even knowing me?" She shifted uneasily and tried to place her guardian between herself and that man. Feeling violated by his stare, her heart pounded in her chest and her breath caught in her throat. The Atlantean lowered his arms, looking more dangerous than anyone she had ever seen. Her insides turned to ice and her heart stammered to a stop. *"If he could, he would attack me right now."* Confused and frightened beyond anything she had ever imagined, Daria grabbed Na-Kai's hand. She wanted with every atom in her body to turn and run the other way.

The man, however, chose that moment to relinquish his position. He left the stand and melted into the crowd. Daria willed her feet to move. She and Na-Kai continued the interminable walk to the dais.

Inching forward through the swell of bodies, Na-Kai hesitated and turned back to Daria. She felt the comfort of the Healer's strong embrace circle her waist. Na-Kai brought her lips next to Daria's ear. "We will get through this. I certainly thought more of them would be willing to give me audience before condemning what they do not understand, but their fear runs deeper than their need for reasoning. Do not forget to breathe, and follow me up the stairs. All will be well."

Daria's lips quivered and her voice failed, so she just gave a curt nod and tried to inhale. Na-Kai resumed her lead and Daria followed. Halfway up the stairs, Daria's legs started to give way and she tripped on the hem of her robes, almost falling to the ground. She grabbed the handrail and fumbled her robes out of the way. The noise level dropped to an expectant hush. All eyes turned to watch as they presented themselves before the High Council.

Na-Kai faced Marik and bowed. For a few moments, no one stirred. Then, the Council Leader placed both hands on the arms of his chair and rose. The two most prominent members of the

Atlantean hierarchy regarded each other with wary respect. "Na-Kai, you join us not a moment too soon. You probably already know that there is not much dissension in relation to the threat present among us."

Na-Kai inclined her head toward the Council Leader. "As I anticipated, Marik."

"We have not taken it to a vote, however, at this time, the High Council recognizes no need. The overwhelming feeling is apparent. The will of the majority must be upheld." Marik's ultimatum was met with a nervous murmur of approval, and from the back of the hall, the chant began.

"At depth! At depth!"

Before the room could once again erupt, Na-Kai held her arms up for quiet. The outcry waned, but Ennael propelled himself through the crowd and once again charged the podium. His skin was flushed an ugly purplish-brown color, almost like a bruise. It was evident that he was nearly sick with fear and rage. He raised his arm and pointed at Daria, making her cringe.

"You should never have been brought here! You have no idea how many laws have been shattered in order to give shelter to one such as yourself." His voice escalated, and he punctuated each statement with a slash of his hand. "We are not without justification in keeping our lives hidden from topsiders. We have seen how you treat each other, your environment, yourselves. We want nothing to do with you. You are a plague to us!"

Waves of antipathy and fear poured from Ennael so that Daria could no longer move. She wanted to yell a denial, but her fear rooted her to the stage. People began to stamp their feet in time to the chant, and she felt each percussive shock as it pounded up through the stage and into her body. Her belief in Na-Kai became her only basis in reality and Daria clung to that reality with every ounce of courage she possessed. With her head high, she focused on an empty point at the back of the hall and waited as the chants crescendoed.

"At depth! At depth!"

The roar gathered so much force that it felt to Daria as if she was in the midst of a hailstorm. Noise pummeled her from every direction, and her body shook so hard that her teeth clattered. The Atlanteans were out of control, and she knew that her life would see a violent end. Wild-eyed, she cast about for a way to flee the fury. Nothing was worth *this*, but Na-Kai's calm reassurance settled into her mind. *"Peace...be still...it is almost done..."*

Daria became removed from herself and watched the incensed mob gather for action. Angry hands surged forth to rend her from the dais. Before anyone could so much as touch the hem of her robe, however, Na-Kai eva Evenor, Most Sovereign Healer of Atlantis, descendant of Poseidon, god of the oceans, interceded.

With a sound that seemed to split the air, Na-Kai released a telekinetic thought-form never before seen on land or underwater, by any being, living or dead. The Atlanteans were hit with such tremendous force that everyone, even those outside the Council Hall, were instantly immobilized.

CHAPTER
15

*I*t was as though everyone but Na-Kai and Daria had been caught in suspended animation. Not one muscle twitched. Not one sound was uttered. Throughout the sunken province, the turbulent movements of an entire society had come to an immediate halt. The silence that surged through Atlantis was almost more frightening than the prior unrestrained disorder.

Na-Kai took Daria's hand and guided her from behind her protective intervention. Tremors raced through Daria's rigid body. She stared at the paralyzed assembly but tried to keep her face impassive. She didn't let her gaze wander either left or right. She was terrified to move, for fear of starting another riot. She squeezed a question past unmoving lips, and Na-Kai leaned closer in order to hear. "What did you do, Na-Kai? Are they dead?"

Na-Kai snorted and released Daria's hand. "Hardly. In what should have been an orderly exchange of opinions, I find this mob behavior untenable. Therefore, I loosed a telekinetic thought-form that has captured their undivided attention. Once I have been heard, I will release them. Even so, I cannot hold them indefinitely. Let us proceed."

The Healer faced the members of the High Council. "I speak to you now while my thoughts transfer to those outside the Council Hall. You bear witness to a type of thought-form we have been forbidden to use from a time before I can remember.

The only people among us who have been aware this power exists have been the Healers. Although the knowledge of this ability was passed down through the ages, its use was forbidden because of the lethal potential for misuse."

Na-Kai faced the mute assembly. "None have dared exercise this potent energy, nor has its power been needed until our time. I have employed this force twice. Once today to control the unrestrained riot you would have let yourselves become. And again..." Na-Kai hesitated.

She wavered in her stance, and Daria saw that she had been assailed by a weakness. Her eyes looked as though she could fall asleep. Daria thought Na-Kai would be unable to continue. She moved next to the Healer, and held her up with her own strength. "Na-Kai, are you all right?"

Na-Kai sent a quick thought to Daria. *"The thought-form used up much of my energy...I am heartened by your love and strength...do not worry child, all is well..."*

Na-Kai pulled Daria closer and took a steadying breath. Her words and thoughts reached every soul in Atlantis. "The only other time I have availed myself of this explosive force was in a desperate attempt to save your lives.

"I stand before you with Daria Caiden, a direct descendant of Kai-Dan eva Evenor. She is the only person I have found who exhibits signs of the healing power. I offer the only person to follow after me as your Most Sovereign Healer. Look upon your savior!"

Na-Kai suddenly released her hold on everyone. Expecting another outburst, Daria was shocked that no one moved and not one word was spoken. Curious looks darted over some of the upraised faces, but most of the people just stared.

At last, Marik roused himself. "Na-Kai, how did it come about that a topsider must be our only choice? I am at a loss.

How is she related to Kai-Dan? And if she is, how did you find her?"

The wisp of a smile passed over Na-Kai's face. She disentangled herself from Daria and approached the edge of the dais. Daria saw that she was still a bit unsteady on her feet, and that she summoned the energy that remained so that her voice would reach the back of the Hall.

"Prior to the downfall of Atlantis, many Healers lived throughout our history. Each displayed different levels of the healing ability, yet one would always rise to become the Most Sovereign Healer. Her power was the greatest of them all. Kai-Dan was the last and most revered Healer Atlantis ever knew before we were consigned to these icy depths. It was Kai-Dan who foretold the awful fate that would befall our people.

"However, there is one part of the story that has been purposely hidden from memory. Until this moment it was a closely guarded secret, passed down from Healer to Healer." Na-Kai stopped. She drew several deep breaths and cleared her throat. "Kai-Dan had a twin."

Shouted questions exploded around the room. As Na-Kai no longer had the strength to withstand the multitude, she bowed her head. Marik intervened. "Silence! I would have Na-Kai finish!" He gestured to the Healer: "Please, continue."

Na-Kai's eyelids drooped, but she lifted her head to finish. "Kalli-Dan was a Healer every bit as great as her sister. As the end drew near, both women felt that the chances were infinitesimal that anyone would survive the sinking. Regardless of the lengths to which the small band prepared, there was only so much that could be done. And though the sisters had given their people an outside chance to survive the catastrophe, they had no idea if the tunnels would hold."

Na-Kai shifted position and looked out over the assembly. "The Healers embarked upon another, even more desperate plan. Because Kai-Dan was the Most Sovereign Healer, she was surrounded with a thought-form generated by every Healer throughout the land. Smuggled out of Atlantis, she was sent into the world in an effort to ensure that some small remnant of Atlantis would endure beyond the end. Their last hope was that somehow her line would survive and continue through the ages. Kalli-Dan stayed behind to either live or die within this mountain refuge that has become our home."

Na-Kai stopped, and motioned for Marik to bring her a chair. The Council Leader hurried to comply. While she waited, a timid question from the back of the hall floated to the stage.

"Why was it necessary to hide the identity of Kalli-Dan?"

Marik returned, and the chair made a metallic scrape as he positioned it behind Na-Kai. Without a backward glance, the Healer sank onto the seat and leaned back. She rested her elbows on the arms and dangled her hands over the edges. Daria and Marik flanked her, and Daria placed a protective hand on top of her shoulder.

"It is difficult to say, except that times were horrific enough without the added loss of morale that would have occurred had the band of one thousand not had the strength and guidance of their Most Sovereign Healer. The ruse was most probably motivated by fear. Fear that the one thousand would not follow Kalli-Dan into the prepared shelter. If they balked, then all would truly have been lost."

The leap had been made. The Atlanteans understood that Daria was a miracle, the embodiment of the vestiges of a great line that had surfaced at their time of need. A tear slid down Na-Kai's cheek, and Daria hugged her. Dark heads bowed in a loving tribute for the sacrifice with which Daria honored them.

A murky figure, unseen by anyone but Daria, drew the shadows closer and slipped from the Council Hall.

CHAPTER 16

L ost in the multitude that swarmed the dais, Ni-Cio forged
his way through the press of bodies. Spurred by feelings he
could no longer deny, he elbowed friends aside who were trying
to congratulate him in an attempt to reach Daria.

Hemmed in by the crush of people that thronged the stage,
Ni-Cio felt the blood rise and he could only imagine the colors
swirling over his face. He muttered, "By the gods, I will scare
her to death."

He eased his progress and tried to calm his mind, but Aris
accosted him with his laughter. "Ni-Cio, you look ready to burst
into flames! Slow down, my friend."

"Aris, I must talk to her." Ni-Cio shoved through a few more
bodies before Aris grabbed his arm.

"Surely, you would not approach her now? Why, every last
one of us is trying to make amends for behavior that can hardly
be justified."

"Aris, unhand me now."

Ni-Cio saw the quick shrug after Aris dropped his arm,
but he chose to ignore the evident "I told you so" look
planted on his friend's features. He turned and bulled his
way toward the dais.

He saw Marik take Na-Kai's elbow, and escort her and Daria
down the stairs. Ni-Cio locked on the topsider. Dressed in a
long robe that glistened with purple and scarlet hues, Ni-Cio

admired the unconscious grace with which the topsider carried herself. The women descended the steps, and a shy smile lit Daria's face as she acknowledged the heartfelt wishes sent her way. She bent to shake someone's hand and caught sight of Ni-Cio. Alarm leapt into her eyes. He balked, knowing that his over-colored face was screwed into a terrible grimace. He couldn't help it. But her startled reaction to his approach told him that he had already scared her more than he thought he would.

She grabbed Na-Kai's arm, and Ni-Cio didn't need to read her thoughts to know what she said. "I need to leave. Now." She pulled Na-Kai toward the closest exit.

Ni-Cio's way was again blocked when everyone realized that their new Healer was leaving. People scrambled to offer their goodbyes. Ni-Cio was buffeted by the crowd so much that he almost lost sight of the retreating figures. Before the women left the Council Hall, however, Daria glanced back at him. The look on her face made him feel as though he was a curse, one to be avoided by any means possible.

He knew his coloring was somewhat alarming, but he was perplexed as to why he would engender such a reaction. Nevertheless, he threaded his way through the packed Hall. Reaching the passageway that Na-Kai and Daria had taken, he lengthened his stride.

Before the women neared the end of the tunnel, Ni-Cio had closed the distance. A tremor ran deep within his body, and he knew that Daria was aware of his presence. He wanted to break into a run and sweep her into his arms, but he reminded himself to keep his composure.

Na-Kai stopped their headlong rush in order to let Ni-Cio catch up, but the topsider refused to turn around. Her back looked as though made of stone. Ni-Cio was not very surprised when wisps of a thought-form teased the edges of his mind.

"Go a...way, go...away..."

He cleared his throat, and when his voice finally came, it sounded like a growl even to him, so he couldn't imagine how it sounded to Daria. "Hold, I would have a word."

Before Na-Kai could respond, Daria pivoted and pointed a finger in Ni-Cio's face. "Leave me alone! I have nothing to say to you. Na-Kai, please."

She grabbed the older woman's hand and almost broke into a run. Na-Kai, a look of surprise on her face, was dragged along in her wake.

Startled by the topsider's vehemence, Ni-Cio sent a thought-form trailing after Na-Kai. *"What did I do?"*

Na-Kai's response did nothing to solve the mystery. *"Later, Ni-Cio...we are both overtired..."*

The two figures receded from sight and Ni-Cio shook his head. He couldn't fathom what he had done to deserve such wrath. Aris had always said that the ways of women were at best a mystery, but by the gods, he had never believed him until now.

Ni-Cio reluctantly retraced his steps back toward the Council chamber. He slowed when a vague feeling of menace pricked the outer parameters of his awareness. Ni-Cio hesitated and scowled at this unusual perception of danger. Turning in a gradual circle, his thoughts scanned the area.

Other than that first disquieting impression, he could discern nothing. He ran a hand through his hair. "Surely my mind has not started playing tricks." He raised his eyebrows, scratched his head, then gave up and ambled to the end of the tunnel to find his friend.

The sounds of Ni-Cio's footsteps echoed off quiet tunnel walls, and eyelids that had been closed, inched open. With reptilian patience, Travlor examined the retreating form until it was out of sight. He inhaled and stepped away from the shadows and the granite walls that had served as the backdrop for his camouflage. He willed his heartbeat, which had been suspended to almost nothing, to regain its normal rhythm. He felt his own leprous gray coloring slither down the length of his body, as the colors that had given him the same appearance as the surrounding rocks leached away. Travlor was no longer concealed.

He needed no warming robes to cover his form-fitting bioskin, for the chill of Atlantis never sank into his bones. The bleakness that encased his heart was colder than any tomb, and he never again expected to feel the least measure of warmth.

Travlor surveyed the passageway, for he knew well the path the topsider had taken. He had spent countless hours pacing that avenue in the solitary, never-ending vigil he maintained over Na-Kai. The Healer would shelter that abhorrent woman in her chambers, so nothing could be done at this moment, but time, which had never before merited a thought, now became his mortal enemy. *"The topsider is here! Where you have failed, I will not!"*

Travlor released the thought-form. It scorched its way toward the surface to burn a track into the frantic mind of his only descendant. He watched with indifference as his son fell to his knees on rocky cliffs. Razor-sharp edges cut his hands, and the whitened rock became stained with vivid slashes of scarlet. He could feel the numbness that invaded his son's consciousness, and the ghost of a smile played over his lips. Evan's scream echoed through his mind.

"Travlor! Nooooo!"

CHAPTER
17

*D*aria woke with a start. The feel of her mother's embrace lingered in the confines of her dream-cluttered mind. She had whispered, something, that the release of sleep chased away like traces of fog on a sunny day.

She closed her eyes in an effort to encourage the dream to return. However, a tone sounded and the door dematerialized. Kyla entered, laden with a huge tray of food. "Good morning. You have been asleep for more than twelve hours. We thought you would be quite hungry, so Na-Kai had me prepare this tray for you."

A delicious aroma followed the woman into the room and wafted around Daria in a tantalizing dance. Her mouth watered.

Kyla set the tray on a table and laid out their feast. "I am the head chef of our kitchens, and I have brought you something special today. I think you will like it."

Daria threw the plush covers aside and scooted out of the comfort of her warm bedding. "Oh, it smells wonderful and you're right, I'm famished. I feel like I haven't eaten in a week."

She covered her new bioskin with a warming robe and hurried to the waterwall. She rinsed her face and hands, grabbed a towel and joined Kyla as she finished drying her hands. She tossed the towel aside and pulled out a chair. Intoxicated by the aromas, she reached for a freshly baked muffin. "Surely this can't all be for me. Please sit down and join me; there is enough for an army."

A timid smile lit Kyla's face. She accepted the offer and seated herself opposite Daria. She took a plate from Daria's outstretched hand and helped herself to the food. For a time, the companionable silence was only broken by the soft clink of silverware. However, as Daria began to feel her ravenous hunger subside, she wiped her mouth with her napkin, placed it beside her plate and pushed her chair from the table. She looked at the Atlantean and before she could stop herself, she released a flood of questions that soon had Kyla relaxed and laughing. They shared an intense curiosity about each other's life, and as the morning passed, Daria felt the beginnings of a lasting friendship.

At last, Kyla excused herself and started to clear the remains. "I so enjoyed our time together, but Na-Kai is on her way. It is almost time for your lessons to begin."

Daria laid a hand on the young woman's wrist. "One more question before you go."

The Atlantean set the stack of dishes down and waited.

"Kyla, you have to understand, I have, had a life topside. Na-Kai insists that our time is critical, but the lifespan of everyone here stretches over hundreds of years. She has told me that I should be able to acquire the healing skills within a few months; and yet, she refuses to let me leave. Why?"

Kyla lowered herself back into the chair. She refolded one of the soft linen napkins, and after she had smoothed the edges, she looked up. "No one in Atlantis lives beyond the age of four hundred and eight. Na-Kai is well beyond her four hundred and seventh year. The time is drawing near for her transcendence."

Daria shook her head and raised her eyebrows in an unspoken question.

Kyla pursed her lips and thought for a moment. "The closest example I can think of is to compare it to the Terran form of dying, although transcendence is quite unlike death."

She cleared her throat and scooted her chair closer to the table. "As we near the age of transcendence, the physical aspect of our bodies begins to metamorphose into pure spirit matter. I don't quite know how to explain it to you other than to say, we start to become transparent. At the vernal equinox of our four hundred and eighth year, the physical gives way to the spirit and in the course of one glorious moment, we are transcended. Even topsiders are given awareness of this incredible event when the sun meets the ocean at sunset and a brief emerald flash can be seen. That flash, more powerful than all the other flashes witnessed by topsiders, signifies that someone in Atlantis has left the physical existence behind and entered the realm of the spirits."

Daria groaned. She placed her elbows on the table and lowered her head into her hands. "Oh my God. This is surreal. I don't think I can learn any more without my head exploding."

Kyla reached across the table and took one of her hands. Daria sighed and looked up. The Atlantean could see the astounding loneliness that clouded the topsider's eyes, and she felt like weeping. She wanted to comfort her friend and tell her that everything would be all right, but she kept her thoughts to herself.

Daria struggled to understand. "I just thought Na-Kai's coloring was different. When I look at her, it's like looking into the reflection of the sun on a calm sea. She shimmers, and it's hard to look straight at her; she's already almost transparent."

Daria stared down at the hand that held hers and marveled at the difference in their skin tones. She didn't know she could feel so close to people who were so different from herself, but she still felt lost in the labyrinth of their world. "Could this transcendence happen accidentally?"

Kyla shook her head and gently released Daria's hand. "No, my friend; an elaborate ceremony is held, with every member of Atlantis in attendance. I will tell you this, should another Healer not be named and active in our community, the chances are great that none of us would reach the age of this singular event. Our Most Sovereign Healer is a battery, so to speak. She recharges us, and enables us to continue into transcendence."

"Oh, Kyla, to lose Na-Kai is unthinkable. I can't be what she is to you. You ask too much."

Kyla stood up and rounded the table. She knelt beside Daria and placed a hand on her thigh. "I know you are afraid, and I know how alone you feel, but you are also very brave. Come, let us sit in comfort. There is more I want to share."

Daria could see the empathy in her friend's eyes, so she followed the woman to the sitting area. She pulled her robes around her and settled into a chair. Kyla sat opposite her. "Daria, we will be sad when Na-Kai transcends, but when one person transcends, then another can be born. It is a form of controlled reincarnation, and it is a wondrous time. However, for transcendence to occur, not only must we reach the required age, we must also be filled with the joy of life."

Daria laughed at the memory of some rather irate Atlanteans. Kyla nodded her head as though she had read her mind.

"That idea may be difficult to accept after everything you have been through. But even though we experience the normal fluctuations of feelings, from the outright fear you saw at Council to the grief of the loss of a loved one, we still retain the joy of life. And it is this joy that is crucial. Without it, the miracle of transcendence cannot be fulfilled. Therefore, we try not to create hurt or bring strife, for we are all tied to each other.

Simply put, you are me and I am you. Why would we want to harm ourselves?"

Daria fell back into the cushions. She closed her eyes as she considered the implications. She felt tired and bewildered, and her tongue stumbled over her next questions. "What happens if you reach the age of transcendence and aren't filled with joy? Do you die a normal death?"

"Unless kept in health by a Healer, yes. But there is one other substantial benefit we derive from transcending. It is the gift of energy. At the moment of transcendence, a tremendous force is released. The energy that is freed becomes the fuel that sustains our world. It has been thus from the very hour Poseidon created Atlantis, and it will remain that way as long as the healing line continues. It is a miraculous experience, one for which we are eternally grateful. And, my cherished friend, were it not for you, we would *not* continue."

Daria's shoulders sagged, and she frowned. She crossed her arms and slouched low in her chair. She was overwhelmed, and she was more frightened by the idea of becoming their Healer than she had been about being ejected at depth. "I will never be able to do that. I can't be your Healer! I, I just can't do it!"

She stood up and walked away from Kyla. She massaged her neck muscles, and focused on one desperate idea. She faced her friend. "Couldn't Na-Kai choose not to transcend? If she didn't transcend, you would still have your Healer, and then you wouldn't need me."

Kyla flashed a small, understanding smile and shook her head. "Once you have immersed your soul in the joy of life, the feeling does not dissipate easily. But even so, day by day, Na-Kai would lose her strength, and with it her powers, until she could no longer sustain us."

Daria paced the room. "I cannot possibly become what Na-Kai is to all of you. No wonder she keeps telling me how critical the time element is. There isn't enough time! If I lived to be four hundred and eight and started this minute, I wouldn't be able to learn what was needed."

She twirled to confront Kyla, ready to launch a parade of excuses, but the Atlantean stood, holding up her hands. "You will be ready, Daria. You may be riddled with uncertainties, but Na-Kai knows, as do I, that you are the one. You will be our Most Sovereign Healer, and the abilities that will awaken inside you will equal those of Na-Kai."

Daria desperately wanted to believe Kyla's words. She already felt more at home here than she ever had topside. But she was daunted by the responsibility they had placed upon her.

Kyla closed the distance and embraced Daria. "If you cannot trust yourself, trust Na-Kai. She will light your way, and she will help you uncover the amazing gifts lying dormant within you. Of that, I have no doubt."

As though to emphasize Kyla's statement, the regal Healer appeared in the doorway. "Good morning. Are you ready to begin your first lesson?"

CHAPTER
18

*I*t looked to Aris as though Ni-Cio had once again wrapped himself within the golden haze of his ongoing daydream. He watched, bemused, as his friend lazed against one of the biospheres and absentmindedly tapped the side of his long leg with the tool that he had requested five minutes ago. His composure almost gone, Aris lunged for the tool just as Ni-Cio swung his hand up and used the implement for a backscratcher.

A slow smile lit the planes of his handsome face and Aris grimaced when Ni-Cio's voice once again took flight. "She is beauty personified, Aris. I have never seen one such as her. Why, she takes my breath away! I tell you, I would give my very heart should she have need. I..."

Not that he had ever had much, but Aris's small reservoir of patience suddenly dried up and he interrupted what promised to become an hour-long soliloquy. "I have heard enough! You have done nothing all morning but talk incessantly about that woman. You are causing me to lose my mind. I say either quit the oration and pay attention or go in search of her and be done with it!"

Aris held onto the side of the dismantled biosphere with one hand while he snapped the fingers of his free hand and jutted his chin in the direction of the withheld tool.

Ni-Cio looked abashed. He placed the instrument in Aris's outstretched hand. Aris turned to his work again, but the touch of his friend's hand on his shoulder brought him up short and he felt Ni-Cio crouch behind him. He gave up any thought of fixing the biosphere, let out a disgusted sigh, turned around and settled himself.

Ni-Cio's confusion was evident. Streaks of gold outlined the sharp angles of his cheeks, and his violet eyes deepened to purple as he struggled with his thoughts. "I would go to her even now. It is just that I am not sure what I should do. She seemed none too glad to see me when I would have talked to her after the Council meeting. Na-Kai has her in lessons that require her utmost concentration, and I am at a loss."

Aris almost laughed at the dilemma Ni-Cio presented, except for the fact that he had never seen his friend like this. He had witnessed the wild flirtations many a maid employed in the hope of gaining the attentions of his handsome friend. But Ni-Cio had always remained immune to matters of the heart. He never seemed to notice some of the most beautiful women Atlantis had to offer. Aris would have given just about anything to have them look at him in the same manner. Nevertheless, he was beginning to feel sorry for him.

Aris shrugged his shoulders, wiped his hands on a cloth and stood in order to address his addled companion.

"My friend, think of all she has been through. That poor soul was on vacation when suddenly, she is trapped in Na-Kai's three-dimensional thought-form, shot off a cliff, saved by her hero, told she is our only hope, then very nearly besieged by highly inflamed Atlanteans who would have been overjoyed to eject her at depth! Now, I ask you, how would you react to some unknown person trying to proclaim anything, much less speak of love, after all that? I would not only have stuck my finger in your face, I would have punched you in the nose."

Aris gripped Ni-Cio's arm and urged him to stand. "Give her a little time to get her bearings. Then profess your love to the rafters. I am sure she will be unable to resist. Meanwhile, I am weary of this work. Let us take a swim. We need to retrieve the pollution samples anyway."

Aris threw the towel to the floor and prodded his buddy toward the exit portal. Ni-Cio grumbled something unintelligible, but offered no other argument.

They passed through an arched doorway that brought them to one of the many exits that lent access to the open ocean. Before they entered the airlock chamber, they hung their robes on nearby hooks.

Stepping inside the airlock, their bioskins responded to their thought-commands and began to shimmer as though they had come to life. The white dots began to glow, and material that was already molded flawlessly around their bodies, moved to cover their exposed feet, hands and heads to create an airtight seal.

The doors materialized and the chamber filled with seawater. No longer able to use their voices, Aris sent a thought-form. *"Come, we'll check the harvest, get some exercise, and then retrieve the forgotten samples...by the time we get back, you will feel like a new man..."*

Aris slipped under the rising water, inhaled, and jetted out the open portal. He could feel Ni-Cio close behind. They flew through the liquid blue at lightning speeds and Aris felt his muscles lose their strain. He was certain that Ni-Cio was just as glad for the respite.

Surrounded by the startling beauty of their underwater world, Aris was filled with wonder, and he marveled at the life that he and the others had been granted. *"We are blessed, Ni-Cio..."*

His thought was answered with a feeling of awe as he felt rather than saw Ni-Cio's grin of agreement.

Na-Kai and Daria enjoyed only one small break in order to share the special lunch that Kyla insisted they eat, but once they had refreshed themselves, their studies immediately resumed. By the time Na-Kai indicated that the first lesson was at an end, Daria no longer had the strength to stand. She fell onto Na-Kai's feathery sofa, closed her eyes and massaged her throbbing temples. "I think my brain has seized. Even if you used a sledgehammer, I wouldn't be able to fit another thing in there."

A subdued tonal harmony emanated from the waterwall and Daria felt her neck muscles loosen a bit. Na-Kai walked across the room to join her. "You have surpassed even my expectations, and have given me reason to feel a tremendous amount of relief. I understand well the monumental effort that is required to assimilate the necessary teaching."

Daria winced and tried a few, slow deep breaths. "Well, I'm glad one of us feels that way, because it surely isn't me."

"Here, let me help." Na-Kai placed her hands on either side of Daria's head and found the temples. She began a slow massage and hummed a tone that synchronized with the note rising from the waterwall.

Daria felt as if every molecule in her body had been infused with a warm, gentle light. With each breath, her headache became less noticeable and her body felt weightless, like a feather that floated on still waters. Daria drifted in the comfort of the healing touch until she couldn't remember when Na-Kai had removed her hands.

Stirring at last, Daria eased herself into a more upright position. She looked at her mentor. "I feel incredible. Thank you."

Daria took the Healer's hand in hers and gazed into eyes the color of mother-of-pearl. "I appreciate your faith in my abilities, and although I hope your faith isn't misplaced, I promise to do my best to honor you and your people."

Na-Kai's eyes opened wide, and her beatific smile brought a hint of rose to color her cheeks. "Why, I would never have thought otherwise, my dear one. But you must know, we are 'your people' now."

Daria blinked hard and her voice shook. Tears pricked the corners of her eyes. "I hadn't thought about it that way. After my parents died, I was moved through so many different foster homes that I never felt I belonged anywhere.

"The funny thing is that the first time I met you, even though I was so scared, I felt like I had come home."

Na-Kai took Daria in her arms and held her close, and Daria felt her warm breath on her hair, a whispered caress. "You are now, and always shall be, part of our family."

Daria was suffused with such an infinite joy that she thought her heart would burst. She understood what Kyla had been trying to tell her because she could breathe it, she could touch it, and her soul reveled in it. As she pulled herself from Na-Kai's embrace, her being was filled with the unending music of love. She wiped the tears from her eyes and laughed with the sheer wonder of it. "So this is how it feels?"

Na-Kai smiled. "Now and forever."

A tone sounded and the door dematerialized. Kyla entered and Daria laughed her delight. "I don't know if I'll ever get used to that."

Kyla held out her hand for Daria. "Come. It is time for you to get to know your home."

*C*HAPTER
19

*K*yla led Daria on an adventure of exploration through the entangled passageways of Atlantis. Daria was entranced by the artistry reflected in the construction of their underground home. The interiors, while built with purpose, reflected an intimate attention to detail, and the eloquence of design mirrored the joy of living that was the heart and soul of the small community.

Daria marveled to see the play of light and shadows soften the granite walls so that they appeared to be draped in textures of rich, creamy velvet. Delicate lighting, attuned to their approach, brightened to illuminate their path and dimmed with their passage.

When she noticed that the slow adagio of light brought a breath of movement to the beautiful carvings and works of art on display, she stood entranced until Kyla turned her attention elsewhere.

Daria inhaled the heady aroma of exotic plants and watched with delight as they swirled in intricate dances with graceful streams. Kyla pointed out hidden byways where lazy waterfalls filled quiet ponds, and plush seating invited moments of relaxation and contemplation.

Wherever they went, a whispered cantata flowed around them, almost but not quite out of consciousness. It tantalized Daria with its haunting refrain. "What is it that I'm hearing,

Kyla? I feel if I could just concentrate hard enough, I would recognize that music."

Kyla chuckled and stopped, taking Daria's hand. "Forgive me, I should have explained that to you at the start of our tour. What you almost hear is a specific composition. Because we have open access to each other's minds, we had to create a way to mask out stray thoughts. With this innovation, random musings no longer bother us. Now, in order to hear someone, we must elevate our thought patterns above the music. "To borrow your words, we blow up the sound."

Daria was confused, so she searched her mind for Kyla's meaning. A burst of laughter followed her sudden enlightenment. "Oh, I think you mean, pump up the volume."

Kyla nodded, "Exactly. I have studied many idioms of your topside language and I love to use them whenever I can." She pulled Daria down a short hallway. "Come, I will take you to see some of the biospheres and show you our mode of transportation."

Kyla led her through an arched doorway and into a domed room. The room, while not big, was magnificent. Fanciful patterns had been artfully woven into cobalt-blue tile work, and the golden dome had been painted with powerful images of the old god, Poseidon. A soft amber glow lit the chamber, and Daria ran her hands over the sublime carvings that stood in relief against the granite walls.

Kyla walked to the edge of a calm, dark pool and with a flourish, pointed at several devices perched next to the water. "These are biospheres."

Daria could make no connection in her mind to what she saw, so she made no immediate comment. Instead, she cocked her head and scrutinized the spherical, almost invisible devices. At last, she offered a tepid observation. "They're quite small."

Kyla arched her eyebrows. "Well, they probably do look small just sitting here, but what you might not realize is that one of these 'spheres can adjust itself to fit as many as ten riders."

"You're kidding." Daria hurried across the floor and bent down to inspect the inside of one of the biospheres when two hands appeared, one on either side of her foot. In an explosion of air, water and bubbles, the upper half of a person surfaced.

Daria yelped and scrambled to back out of the way, but her feet couldn't find purchase on the wet floor. When the man catapulted from the pool, she frantically tried to keep from falling. She grabbed the strong arms of the unsuspecting swimmer and the man stumbled trying to catch her. Kyla backed out of the way, and both Daria and the swimmer fell to the slippery deck. Through Herculean gyrations, Daria's fall was cushioned by the man, and in a tangle of arms, legs and considerable confusion, she landed on top of him with a hard thump. She fought the hair out of her eyes.

"Oh my goodness, are you all right? I'm so sorry, I, you surprised me." She disentangled herself from the prostrate form and pushed her way to a kneeling position.

Ni-Cio clambered onto his elbows and laughed softly when he recognized the topsider. "As they say, at last we meet."

Daria gasped. Goosebumps rippled over her body and heat rose in her face. The man was even more compelling than she remembered. He was beautiful. Against her will, a smile pulled at the corners of her mouth in response to his greeting. Her heart fluttered into a much faster beat, and butterflies started to dance in her stomach. She wanted to melt into him. The magnetic pull of him drew her closer, but her heart slammed closed when the image of him inciting the angry Atlanteans invaded her mind. She shook herself and spat out her next word like she was trying to eject a bug from her throat. "You!"

She heaved herself to her feet, and Ni-Cio scrambled to regain an upright position. He towered over her, but even in the midst of her inner turmoil, Daria could feel a quiet strength from him. A vision of his arms surrounding her startled her. She quickly erased the thought from her mind and brought her face to within inches of his. Just as she readied herself to let fly another tirade, the tableau was rudely interrupted by another dripping Atlantean. Aris made his way out of the pool. "There you are. I didn't realize you had already come in..."

His sentence trailed off and he clamped his mouth shut. Silence crashed around them. Kyla stepped forward to help pacify Daria, but the topsider brushed her aside and jabbed her finger into Ni-Cio's muscular chest. All the pent-up fear and emotion she felt at the council meeting spilled out of her. She poked him hard with each finger thrust. "*You're* the one. *You* were the leader."

Ni-Cio was forced backward toward the pool under the fury of each jab. Daria's volatile accusations hung suspended in the air between them. He moved to explain, but Daria twisted from his touch and flung her last words as she pushed him with all her might. "You bastard!"

Ni-Cio again lost his balance. Launched unceremoniously back into the pool from which he had surfaced, he splashed a hefty wall of water onto the deck, drenching everyone. Dark water closed over Ni-Cio, and Daria stomped back to Kyla. Kyla looked at the pool, and then back at Aris, and then at her maddened friend. Daria's sharp order rang in her ears. "Get me out of here."

Kyla didn't know what to do. Daria glanced apprehensively over her shoulder and watched Aris help his sputtering friend out of the pool. She strong-armed Kyla out of the chamber, but not before she heard Aris's wry comment and Ni-Cio's infuriated reply.

"You know, I don't think she likes you at all. What did you do to her?"

"By the gods, Aris, I haven't a clue. But I will be damned if I just sit here! That woman is going to answer some questions."

Kyla had never seen such unjustifiable anger. She had no idea what Ni-Cio had done. She let Daria drag her in tow and tried to grasp the implications of what she had just witnessed. She pulled on Daria's wrists to slow their headlong rush. "Daria, what is wrong? Why did you push Ni-Cio into the pool? I don't understand." She dug her heels into the tunnel floor. "Wait! We mustn't go this way."

Daria spun around. "So, that's his name? Ni-Cio!" The spite with which she imbued the name made it sound more like a curse and Kyla couldn't find her voice against such unbridled antagonism. "I won't soon forget that. And just so you know, if you want me to stay, you had better keep that man away from me."

Kyla couldn't begin to imagine why Daria was so upset with her brother, but she knew if she asked any more questions it would only serve to further inflame the topsider they were so hopelessly dependent upon. She reached toward Daria in an effort to placate their would-be Healer. "Come, we must go back the way we came, and I will take you to our music room. Ennael would be flattered to give you an impromptu concert."

Daria glared at Kyla, and then around, as though she was being stalked. "I don't think I'm in quite the frame of mind one would need to enjoy a concert. Another time, maybe...." She approached the adjacent hallway and made a quick motion with her hand. "Why can't we go down there?"

Kyla blanched and shuddered. "Travlor lives down there. You will meet him soon enough. Come." She guided her friend toward another passageway, but stopped and closed her eyes when she heard Daria's next question.

"Who is Travlor?"

Kyla tried to gather her wits in order to give a quick synopsis regarding the enigma that was Travlor, when a dark shadow fell across their path. Ni-Cio stood like an immovable mountain, blocking their exit. A rumbled command bridged the short distance. "Kyla, if you would, please excuse us. I *will* have a word with this incomprehensible topsider." His tone conveyed the implausibility of broaching any disagreement. No one moved, but Kyla knew her brother and she knew full well the meaning of discretion being the better part of valor.

Daria clutched Kyla's wrist. "Don't you dare leave."

Her friend extricated herself and backed away. "Daria, I think I had better go check on Na-Kai." Kyla felt her face flood with striations of embarrassment, however, that did not stop her. She turned and fled the scene of impending doom.

CHAPTER
20

*D*aria stood blocked by the only person in Atlantis she despised. His nearness shook her to her core and her breath seemed to have taken a holiday. She marveled that her body responded to him without her consent. Her senses tingled and again, her traitorous heart wanted her to reach for him. She shook her head to wipe out the wanton images that raced through her mind, making her blush. *"What is wrong with me?"*

She squared her shoulders. Rather than look like a coward, she decided the best defense was a good offense. She narrowed her eyes, took a deep breath and advanced toward the magnificent Atlantean. "I must not have made myself clear, so, I will say this as simply as I can. I do not care to exchange words with you. If you started at this moment and apologized until the world looked level, nothing you have to say will ever, and I repeat, ever, make me forget!"

Ni-Cio leaned into what little space was left between them, and Daria detected the pristine scent of salt and rain. She had to elevate her head another foot in order to look him in the eye. "Apologize? I owe no apology. I came to find out how truly daft you are."

Daria's eyes widened and her mouth opened. "Daft! *Daft?* I'll show you daft." She elbowed Ni-Cio aside. However, before she could disappear again, he grabbed her shoulders and spun her around.

Daria fell into the depths of his dark violet eyes. Her breath and her heart danced in quick time and her awareness contracted to nothing but the feel of his hands. Her skin quivered, and a slow burn ignited deep within her body.

Ni-Cio seemed equally lost, and she didn't resist when he drew her closer. One of his hands slid down her back and the other moved to trace the contours of her collarbone. Her eyes closed. Even through her bioskin, a line of flame erupted where his touch lingered. His fingers caressed the curve of her neck until his thumb and forefinger came to a gentle stop beneath her chin. She tilted her head and his mouth touched hers. She tasted sun and wind and something reminiscent of the ocean. Her insides turned to liquid fire. She moved into him, but at the first touch of his body against hers, Daria started as if he had slapped her.

Her eyelids flew open and she recoiled. She raised the back of her hand to her mouth and wished she could wipe his kiss from her memory as easily as she wiped away the feel of his lips. "What are you doing?"

Daria was lightheaded, and she felt betrayed by the huskiness of her voice. She took a few steps back, glanced away and cleared her throat. "Better yet, what am I doing?"

She looked at Ni-Cio. His handsome face was hidden in shadow. He took a step toward her and the light slid upward, unveiling the purple blaze in his eyes. Like a butterfly on display, Daria felt impaled. She could not move. He took another step and the space between them dissolved. The heat of him caused her resistance to crumble. She wielded her only weapon. "Stay away from me. You're…just leave me alone. Please!" Forcing her body to turn around, she bolted toward the nearest passageway and willed herself not to look back.

Her feet pounded the floor in time to the wild thrumming of her heart. Beads of sweat curled off her scalp and the salt sting trickled into her eyes. She blinked to clear her vision and skidded around a corner. Throwing herself into the nearest offshoot, she slowed her pace in order to peer over her shoulder. Ni-Cio had not followed. She should have been relieved. Instead, she shook her head because whether she wanted to acknowledge it or not, she was disappointed he wasn't there.

She stopped to catch her breath. Glancing around to get her bearings, she noticed that the light in the tunnel had dimmed and seemed to withdraw from her. She rubbed her eyes and slowed her inhalations. Darkness slid over her as though an inky cloak had been pulled down the length of her body. Any semblance of light had perished beneath writhing hues of gray and black, and she shivered.

With sudden clarity, Daria knew that she was in the tunnel that Kyla had insisted they avoid. Her heart dropped into her stomach. Swallowing hard, she decided to take her chances with Ni-Cio rather than ignore Kyla's warning. Kyla had been very clear that Travlor was to be avoided.

She began to back out of the tunnel when a suggestion of light flared at the other end. Daria stopped. The curious flicker beckoned and now, she couldn't remember any warnings Kyla had given. Drawn like a fish to a lure, she stared at the flickering light.

Daria had almost traversed the length of the tunnel when a wave of nausea assailed her. She gritted her teeth and tried to keep the bile from rising any further. She felt dizzy and gripped the blackened rock wall to keep from falling. "I can't believe I'm saying this, but I would be glad to see Ni-Cio right now."

Colors swam before her eyes, and the rock, which she thought was anchoring her, dissolved under her hand. An overpowering convulsion ravaged her insides and she felt herself begin to lose consciousness. The chill of the stone floor rose to meet her when a pair of strong arms roughly lifted her in an icy embrace. She tried to lift her head. "Ni-Cio?"

"Not quite."

She heard the icy reply before blackness slammed down on her first tremors of fear.

Jolted from an uneasy sleep by a particularly fetid stench, Daria almost gagged, but before she could protect her nose and mouth, the odor dissipated. The hard contours of the bed on which she had been placed dug into her body, offering not even a semblance of comfort. No coverings or pillows were in evidence on the unyielding pallet, and she shuddered with a chill that seeped into her bones. Her brain felt fuzzy and she had no idea where she was, or how she had gotten here, but she was more than ready to leave.

She shifted her legs and pushed herself to a sitting position. She rubbed her eyes and remembered feeling very ill. She rose gingerly to a standing position and was relieved to find that whatever ailment had afflicted her was gone. She looked around the room.

She was quite alone, but the chamber reflected well the mark of its owner. An existence that once could have been viewed as disciplined had yielded to a barren reality that fed a grim subsistence. The few shapes of furniture in the Spartan surroundings were dark counterpoints to a greenish light that glowed weakly from one corner. A spike of fear returned.

"I'm in Travlor's chambers." Daria squeezed her eyelids shut and sent a hurried thought-form. *"Na-Kai? Come…please…"*

She approached the doorway afraid that it would not dissolve, but as she moved closer the door dematerialized, providing entrance to an antechamber.

She entered a room suffocated by monochromatic shadows. Light or color had long since been snuffed out. She hesitated to let her vision adjust to the profound gloom. The vague outline of a figure, shrouded in darkness, disentangled itself from the unrelenting black. And a voice, cracked and scratchy from disuse, haltingly whispered an eerie greeting. "I am...quite dismayed...to say nothing...of being...mystified...by your presence."

She almost slapped her hands over her ears. The tone evoked the image of a dust-covered cellar door, hinges rusty and groaning and creaking in rigid protest at being painstakingly forced open after the sad neglect of many silent years.

A hiss of movement and Daria was looking into a face so devoid of hope, she thought she would cry. Again, the clawing, straining, nails-on-a-chalkboard effort of speech. "I am...Travlor ...you...are feeling better...I trust."

Daria backed away and nodded. Her voice would not come. Her throat was dry and her tongue stuck to the roof of her mouth. To stand before the life-defying gray husk was almost beyond bearing. Fear edged out feelings of pity and her stomach recoiled again. She winced from the pain and her mouth tasted sour. She saw a flicker of contempt touch his eyes. *"Travlor creates this pain!"* But the thought disappeared before she could examine it.

Daria knew she should leave, wanted to leave, but she could no more will her feet to move than she could will herself to sprout wings and fly. She couldn't understand her lack of control over her own body, and her fear soared. "Who are you?"

"Sit...over there...I will...bring you...a tonic."

Flinching from his raised hand as though it held contagion, she crossed the room and lowered herself onto a stone seat that jutted raggedly from the wall. Travlor stood a moment as if in deep contemplation, then without a word, turned and stole quietly into another room.

With his departure, Daria's pain eased. She tried to quash the imminent feelings of danger that made her heart pound, but her foot bounced up and down in staccato bursts, belying the calm she struggled to exude. *"I should have stayed with Ni-Cio, at least I'm not afraid of him. But wouldn't Na-Kai have warned me if I had anything to fear from Travlor?"*

No matter how she tried to calm herself, she became more agitated. Nevertheless, it did not occur to her to look for an exit.

Travlor came back into the room carrying an opaque, flat, brown flask. He proffered the container. "This will help...you are unused...to our food...drink two swallows...before you eat. Your pain...will ease. You...may drink some...now."

Her senses jangled with alarm. She did not want to take anything from this person. He scrutinized her as though he was a scientist inspecting a new virus. Daria watched her arm lift on its own accord and she took the flacon. The bottle seemed to command its own power. Her hand inched towards her mouth and her terror rose as the spout forced its way into her mouth. Her thoughts raced. *"Please, I don't want to do this! What is this stuff? How is it that he controls me?"*

Her mind shut down. Closing her eyes, she drank. The taste was not entirely unpleasant, a hint of earthiness laced with honey, but the sound of Travlor's whisper was one of bone clicking on bone. And when he spoke, her fears lessened and her questions lost their importance. "You...will be better...now."

In truth, she did begin to feel better. She found she was no longer afraid and was discomfited by the ring of fear that had threatened to take hold. Remnants of anxiety faded, just as the last trickle of warmth leaves a dying ember. "Thank you. I do feel better."

"As it should be. Keep the tonic…with you…no one need know." Travlor glided closer to her and before she could step away, he encircled her waist with a swatch of black material, tying it securely.

He then took the flask from her hand and inserted it into a pouch concealed within the makeshift belt. An involuntary shudder ran through her at his touch, and the revulsion that had receded started to rise again. She jumped. A note sounded, alerting Travlor that he had a visitor. The man gave the appropriate response and the exterior door disappeared.

Ni-Cio walked into the chamber. Brushing by Travlor, he immediately took Daria's arm. She accepted his touch with more relief than she would have thought possible. His low voice flowed over her like warm silk, and she gratefully let him usher her toward the door. "You are needed. Kyla has been looking for you."

In disdainful acknowledgment of the gray figure that had melted back into the shadows, Ni-Cio stopped, looked over his shoulder, glaring at Travlor. "No need for you to show us out. I just cannot figure how Daria got in."

Daria wondered at Ni-Cio's hostile reaction, but as before, her concern took flight. Ni-Cio turned his attention back to Daria. "Are you all right?"

Another vision of his strong arms wrapped protectively around her came to mind. Daria did nothing to shake the image. "Yes, I'm all right. Shouldn't I be?" Greatly comforted by Ni-Cio's presence, she hesitantly removed his hand from her arm and turned to Travlor. "Will we see each other again?" She waited for a reply, but not a sound issued from the darkened chamber. She was glad when Ni-Cio again took her arm and led her through the door and into the light.

CHAPTER

21

*T*he encounter with Travlor exhausted Daria, and she felt more than ready to vacate the shadowed existence that circumscribed his life. It was difficult to remember their meeting, but the irony of Ni-Cio being the one to deliver her from that bleak residence was not lost on her. She glanced at him out of the corner of her eye. He had yet to remove his hand from her arm, and oddly enough, she did nothing to encourage him. She had never experienced feelings like these for anyone, and she was bewildered by her reaction to him.

Ni-Cio trained his gaze ahead, but Daria saw that his soft bronze coloring had become infused with warm rose tones. Faint traces of salt, wind and rain drifted around her and she inhaled deeply. She was startled to realize that the exhilarating scent was as much a part of her escort as his vivid violet eyes. *"I'm losing control and that terrifies me."* Amazed by that thought, she stumbled. Ni-Cio lunged to steady her, and once again, they were face to face.

The warm rose of Ni-Cio's complexion deepened. Otherwise, he did not move, it was as if he had become cast in bronze. Daria felt equally transfixed. She gazed into the depths of his beautiful purple eyes and never wanted to leave. A wordless passion play took flight on the wings of silence that swirled around them until, at last, Ni-Cio shook himself. "I would advise you to leave Travlor quite alone. He has nothing you need."

Daria wanted to bathe in his voice. *"Oh, my God! What is happening to me?"*

Ni-Cio leaned toward her and brushed a stray lock of her hair back into place. The electricity from that simple touch sang all the way down to her toes. Daria tried to cover her distraction. "How did you even know where I was?"

His tone was so low and intimate that Daria thought her knees would buckle. "I heard you. You sent a thought-form to Na-Kai, but I was still nearby. I knew you had to be with Travlor, so I came as quickly as I could."

She didn't know what to say. The significance of his role during the Council meeting had suddenly lost some of its impact. Still, she had to know. "But you led them against me at the Council meeting. Why?"

Ni-Cio furrowed his dark brow and cocked his head, his full lips pulled into a puzzled frown. "What are you talking about?"

"When I walked into the hall, you were at the podium leading the chant to eject me at depth." At the remembrance, Daria winced and backed away.

Color drained from Ni-Cio's face. "No, Daria! I was trying to subdue the crowd. The meeting had gotten out of control and I was afraid that if nothing was done, you stood no chance."

He stepped toward her and lifted her chin so that she had no other option but to look into those magnificent eyes. "I was the one who brought you into Atlantis. I saved your life, and as I stand before you, I would never do anything to hurt you."

The truth of his statement made her heart contract, and her thoughts spiraled. A hazy memory bubbled to the surface, and she remembered Na-Kai telling her that someone had brought her to them. She released her breath, even though she hadn't known she was holding it. Her heart trembled and she felt the last of her barriers crumble. She gazed, awestruck, at Ni-Cio. "*I, I could love this man!*"

She knew he had misunderstood her silence when he lightly touched her elbow. "Come, I will see you to Na-Kai's chambers. She was beginning to worry, but I have let her know that all is well."

"*I'm not ready to leave yet.*" Daria couldn't believe how quickly she was falling under this strange man's spell. She stalled for more time. She placed a hand on Ni-Cio's upper wrist. The color of her skin seemed to stand in relief against the bronze of his muscled forearm. It took a moment to gather her thoughts. "But you said I should leave Travlor alone. Why? Is he sick?"

Ni-Cio took her hand in his and lightly stroked the lines in her palm. Daria could hardly concentrate as he spoke. "Travlor is not sick in body. The man has never done harm to anyone that I know of, but he is a cause of great unease. Come, I will share with you what I know of his tragic story."

He led Daria to one of the garden retreats. She walked through a lush tropical garden, the gentle sounds of raindrops tapping subdued melodies on precisely placed stones. Those drops sluiced into small pools that were coaxed into delicate cascades that came to rest in an emerald green pond flowering with lily pads. Sequestered next to the pond were two overstuffed chairs.

Ni-Cio settled her into the billowy cushions, and she waited while he lowered himself onto the adjacent chair. Mesmerized by the play of light sliding over the golden bronze of his skin, Daria lost her train of thought. Flustered at her lapse, she attempted to pick up their conversation. "Please continue. If I am to live here, I should know everything I possibly can about you."

His lips curved into a lazy smile and Daria immediately realized her faux pas.

"Everyone, uhh, I meant, Travlor." She laughed at herself with easy joy, and Ni-Cio's echoing chuckle joined in.

He reached for her hand and placed the whisper of a kiss in her palm. He looked up and pitched his voice so low that it was almost thought. His violet gaze caught and held hers. "We will know everything there is to know about each other very soon. That is a promise from my heart to yours."

Daria's heart nearly burst with joy at the sensuousness of the dance they had begun. She couldn't find her breath.

With her hand entwined in his, Ni-Cio sighed and leaned back into his chair. He rubbed his eyes with his free hand and frowned. "Travlor is very reclusive. The man we left has a sickness of spirit rather than body. Travlor has literally walked the earth for eons. He is so old no one can begin to guess his age. We know only that he was alive before the sinking of Atlantis; how much further his history goes beyond that is a mystery."

Daria dropped Ni-Cio's hand and sat straight up. "Are you telling me that Travlor never transcended? I thought that wasn't possible. How can he still be alive?"

Ni-Cio sat up to face Daria and shook his head. "He has never spoken of his past to anyone, and his thoughts are so jealously guarded, no one has been granted admittance. I think he did not transcend because the joy of life seeped from him long before that event could transpire. He seems terrified of death because he refuses to give his body to the earth. So, as each Healer has come and gone, Travlor has been kept in health and therefore kept alive."

Daria glimpsed the sad world that Travlor occupied. "No wonder his life seems so dismal."

Ni-Cio continued. "But there is more to his story. Please be comfortable and I will finish."

Daria once again eased into the pillows. She closed her eyes against the foreign surroundings and waited for Ni-Cio to resume his account. "Travlor used to be the go-between from our world to yours. Because he never inherited our unique coloration, he was able to blend easily into the different communities. At regular intervals, he would leave Atlantis to record the progress of Terran technology, habits and spiritual development. We relied on his observations to keep us apprised of any threat your world might have presented to us."

Ni-Cio paused, and Daria sensed he was nearing the crux of the saga. She opened her eyes. "What I am about to tell you may not seem serious, but let me assure you, Canon Law is followed with strict adherence. Until you, there has never been a hint of dissension from what is written."

Daria could hear the sadness in his voice.

"Travlor transgressed a Canon Law that keeps him bound to this day. It is forbidden for him to ever leave Atlantis. Never again will he look upon the sky of Terros, for it was his misfortune to fall in love with a Terran woman. Together they conceived a child."

"Oh, Ni-Cio, that's unbearable. Why can't he be released to go to them and live out a normal life?"

"Daria, no one would have stopped him, but when he was brought before the High Council, Travlor revealed that both mother and child had succumbed during the birth. Na-Kai and Marik fought for his release from his duties, but they were outvoted. The others felt he had breached Canon Law one too many times. To ensure that he never again mixed bloodlines, Na-Kai was made to imprison him with a thought-form, and she was forbidden to use her healing abilities to extend his life.

It is impossible for him to leave. He cannot even access the halls leading to the exit chambers. Travlor is here until his death."

Daria had never heard anything so sad. "But his life is so devoid of hope. I can't imagine living like that. Can nothing be done?"

"Make no mistake, Travlor wants nothing done. It is not as if we turned our backs on him. He burrows so far into his own misery that no one can reach him." The tenderness in Ni-Cio's voice was unmistakable. "Again, I would say to you, leave him quite alone. He has nothing you need."

The strangeness of everything finally closed in upon her, and Daria could only nod her understanding and her acceptance. She was such an alien to the ways of this underworld. Would she ever truly fit in?

Ni-Cio must have felt her anguish and her bewilderment, because his eyes filled with concern. He rose and offered his hand. "Come, let us depart. It grows late and it is over time for you to rest."

When she stood, Ni-Cio took her in his arms. She laid her head against his chest and he stroked her hair. His mellifluous voice washed over her in waves of comfort. "All will be well, love. You will see."

And she knew this to be true. In his arms, everything was made right. Arm in arm, they slowly made their way back to Na-Kai's chambers.

CHAPTER
22

*I*n a solitary room, Evan lay exhausted. After the terrifying scene of Daria's disappearance and all that it augured, he had stumbled, bleary-eyed, back to the hotel. Spent almost beyond his endurance, he had taken a room, rinsed the dried blood from the cuts on his hands, given them some cursory first-aid, and then fallen on the bed to sleep through a dreamless twenty-four hours.

He opened groggy eyes to a sunlit room, and his first conscious thought rammed through a sleep-dulled brain. "Travlor has her!" His second thought followed with maximum velocity. "Then she is dead."

Evan never wanted to move again. He watched the dust motes swirl in listless patterns until he squeezed his eyes shut against the intrusive morning light. When the final realization came, he gathered the sheets on either side and crushed them in his fists. "I should have just killed her myself."

Sorrow welled up and then clamped down on him like a vise. Barely able to breathe, he held himself immobile against the torrent of emotion that threatened to tear him apart. A lone tear began its solemn descent from the corner of his eye. And then, as though a dam had broken, tears streamed from his eyes and his body began to shake. A deep, grief-stricken sob wracked his body as he choked her name. "Daria! Oh my God, forgive me. I'm so sorry."

Wave after wave of sorrow broke over him and it seemed to Evan that his whole life had dissolved into nothing but sadness and loneliness, the miasma of a loveless existence. Thoughts and memories pummeled him until he felt as if relief would come only with his death. And as the cacophony of his mind flatlined, a frantic thought-form finally made itself heard in a repetitious command.

"She lives! Evan…hear me…she lives! Evan…hear me!"

An indistinct picture of a subterranean room far beneath the surface of an uncaring ocean shimmered, mirage-like, on the edges of Evan's psyche. He summoned his shell-shocked thoughts into focus.

"She lives! Evan…hear me…"

Like a vulture circling its prey, the same thought-form spiraled through Evan's mind until it had insinuated itself into the vortex of his consciousness. He forced himself to inhale, and air cascaded into his painfully constricted lungs. He flexed his rigored fingers and the crumpled sheets slipped from his death grip. He heard his own ragged exhalation as his mind sluggishly sought Travlor. *"She lives?"*

The impassioned answer came. *"Yes…"*

"Daria's alive?"

Travlor's sibilant reply struck him like a blow. *"Yesssss!"*

Comprehension chased away the fog, and Evan felt the first stirrings of hope. He raised his body to a sitting position and his muscles creaked with stiffness. *"You didn't kill her?"*

"No…"

Evan's mind reeled. He couldn't imagine why Travlor had spared her life, and he didn't want to take the time to ask. He only knew that Travlor needed Daria dead to secure his release from Atlantis.

To that end, when his father had approached him with the idea of removing a troublesome female, Evan had promised to help. His conscience hadn't been bothered. The woman was just one more obstacle to be removed in his quest for the power and control that Travlor had said was his birthright. He had planned to hire someone to take care of the problem, but for some reason his curiosity had gotten the better of him.

He had become obsessed with the need to meet the one person who merited so much attention from the fearful personage he had reluctantly come to acknowledge as his father.

Evan rose from the bed and stood on trembling legs. He shook his head to clear the cobwebs and coughed. "Oh, yes, I was going to take care of everything until I made the arrogant mistake of meeting you face to face."

He moved to the window and his words slipped through chapped, bitten lips on a sigh. "Thank God you're safe."

As he stared out the window, nothing but the grateful cessation of his misery registered upon his consciousness until he formed the next thought. It plummeted to reach its diabolical recipient. *"Now what?"*

Evan pictured a jaundiced light that flickered from the maleficent stare of snake-black eyes when a thought-form descended upon him like a shroud.

"You…will come…to Atlantis."

Evan was stunned. In the years that he and Travlor had been touching minds, never had that suggestion even been hinted. Once Na-Kai was out of the picture, Travlor was to join him on Santorini and they would put into motion their carefully conceived strategy. Now, because of his failure to kill Daria and his inability to isolate her, everything had changed.

An uncomfortable feeling had taken root, and the tendrils that sprouted were an irritant to the raw ache of his reborn heart. Simply put, he no longer trusted Travlor. Father or not, Evan was aware that he needed to use extreme care when dealing with this demonic entity. With a marked decline of enthusiasm, Evan sent his thought. *"How?"*

"A submersible...I will guide you..."

The compulsion that clamped down on Evan's mind told him all he needed to know regarding the desperation that drove Travlor's every action.

He turned from the window. As he rubbed his hands over his face, the growth of whiskers scraped against his wounds. He knew that if Daria was to remain safe, he had to follow Travlor's commands without hesitation. And if he could get into Atlantis, he had a small chance of getting her out. He moved toward the door with a stride that taxed his stiff muscles and doggedly replied, *"I will come..."*

CHAPTER
23

*P*reparations for the celebration were well into the fourth day, and the majestic room had been transformed. Kyla stood at the main entrance of the Great Hall of Poseidon and surveyed the work. The massive granite walls had been draped, floor to ceiling, with centuries-old tapestries that were arrayed like royalty. The resplendent weavings caught and held the light, so that the threads glowed as though lit from within. Her gaze leapt from one hanging to another as the history of Atlantis, from the ancient legends to life after the sinking, sparked to life.

Immense, hand wrought crystal chandeliers, shimmering with soft pastel colors, hung suspended from arched ceilings. Long buffet tables had been laid with the finest cloth spun from microfibers of gold and silver. Abundant arrangements of strange and beautiful flowers spilled out of large cobalt urns and filled the air with their exotic fragrance.

At the grand entrance, a pool of glistening water shifted and Kyla watched as silver rivulets ran in a lazy whirl. As if by magic, a gossamer water sculpture began to take shape. It sailed above the basin and drifted in lazy circles. The exquisite masterpiece lingered only to dissolve into sparkling drops of rain as another creation, equally wondrous, rose to take its place.

Aris and Mer-An entered the Hall through a side portal, followed by a stream of Kyla's friends. All of them carried a dizzying array of trays laden with gourmet delicacies. The smell of early morning ocean spray and sun-warmed breezes surrounded silver bowls that brimmed with fresh oysters, steamed mussels, baked clams and abalone. Steam rose from some of the platters, and the enticing scent of aromatic spices, cushioned by the yeasty smell of hot bread, wafted throughout the Hall.

Kyla helped with the food placement as a vegetable stew that had simmered for hours in a nutrient-rich sauce was brought out in huge cauldrons. The tantalizing odor created a mouthwatering response.

Aris snatched a loaf of fresh bread and began to slather it with a thick layer of creamy butter. "Kyla, if they do not come soon, holding me back from this banquet will be harder than holding back the tides."

Kyla laughed when Mer-An slapped Aris's wrist as though he was a wayward child. "You have no self-control, Aris. Leave this table untouched. Na-Kai and Daria will be here soon enough. Surely you will not starve before their arrival."

Aris's chagrined look and tortured sigh was enough to make both women laugh. He jammed a bite of bread into his mouth, turned, and as he stalked away they heard his muffled sigh, "Women!"

Mer-An rolled her eyes in an exaggerated display of patience, long and suffering, but couldn't disguise her grin. "I have loved that man since I was a little girl, but sometimes, he tests my patience." She looked at her friend. "Truly, Kyla, he is not joking. Everyone is famished. When are they coming?"

Before Kyla could reply, Marik lumbered in, burdened under the weight of quartz crystal dishes of every imaginable size and shape. Followed by his similarly encumbered crew, he motioned for the tables to be set in the final preparations.

The heady scent of muscari elixir completed the scene, as crystalline pitchers, filled to the brim, were placed at easy-to-reach intervals. The gold-and-ruby liquid flashed rainbows under the light.

"We are almost ready..." Kyla's thought found its way to Na-Kai and Mer-An, and she heard the Healer's quick response.

"Our lesson has ended...let me know when to proceed..."

One last time, Kyla cast a critical eye over the room to see that everything was ready. The Great Hall dazzled even her expectations.

Kyla had wanted this particular night to reflect her feelings of awe and humility. That Daria would become their new Healer was reason enough to celebrate. That she would willingly abandon her life topside was a sacrifice so unselfish, Kyla had been stunned. Had the situation been reversed, Kyla knew she would never have been able to leave her home, no matter the reason. She took a deep breath and summoned Na-Kai. *"Most Sovereign Healer, we await your arrival..."*

Kyla was beginning to feel the effects of the long nights and harried days. She was ready to sit, relax and enjoy the festivities.

"We are coming..."

Kyla shifted her gaze to a small group of seated musicians. At her signal, the first strains of an enchanting concerto flowed through the Hall. Written by Enneal, the beautiful composition was an attempt to atone for his angry display at Council. He had poured his soul into the creation, and the music was glorious.

Dressed in their finest raiment, Atlanteans gathered to await the arrival of the guest of honor. Their beautiful robes swayed in the soft pastel light, and an incredible array of colors permeated the Hall.

Kyla stepped toward the main portal and rejoiced to see the emotions of love, at-one-ness and peace in the soft blue, green and lavender hues that played over the smiling faces of her friends and family. As she positioned herself on the steps of the main entryway, she knew that everyone had given their utmost to create this memorable tribute.

She turned when she heard the muted sounds of footsteps, and watched Daria and Na-Kai as they took their place beside her. All attention focused on the diminutive figure of the topsider as everyone placed their hands against their hearts in prayer attitude. The symbolic gesture of reverence continued in unison as everyone turned their palms up and out signifying their heartfelt acceptance of Daria.

Kyla saw tears in Daria's eyes and felt her startled reaction. Kept busy with her lessons, Daria had been unaware of the banquet preparations. Na-Kai clasped one of Daria's hands and Kyla heard the encouragement Na-Kai sent. *"Send them a thought-form...let them know how you feel..."*

With a nervous inhalation, Daria closed both eyes and furrowed her brow as she attempted to send her first Atlantis wide thought-form. Kyla grinned to see the studied effort of their young Healer and broke into laughter as Daria's thoughts reached everyone simultaneously.

"I am...play...love you...I...worth...dust..."

Before a larger reaction could be heard from the others, Na-Kai fired out the interpretation. *"I believe what our esteemed Healer meant was...I am overwhelmed at this display of love you give to me...I will always strive to be worthy of this moment and your trust..."*

Smiles, laughter and thunderous applause erupted.

"Speech!"

"Speech!"

"No, we probably wouldn't understand her anyway!"

"Let's eat!"

"I'm starving!"

All in all, it was a joyous throng that converged upon the buffet. Kyla grabbed Daria's hand and pulled her toward the heavily laden tables. "I'm afraid when it comes to food, we lack a certain propriety. I think it would be similar to your come and have it attitude."

It only took Daria a moment, "I think you mean, come and get it."

Kyla joined her friend's laughter. "Exactly. So you understand why we must hurry." Kyla led Daria to the head of the banquet. "Do not be amazed by how quickly the food disappears. We are always hungry."

Kyla gestured for Daria to precede her. As people good-naturedly jostled her for a closer position in line, Kyla turned in time to see Daria surreptitiously thrust a container back into her pocket. A question came to her lips, but Daria had started to heap food onto her plate, so Kyla thought better of it and instead grabbed her own plate.

They found an empty table and sat down to enjoy the feast. Daria took a tentative bite of the stew and Kyla watched with interest. She was delighted to hear her friend's garbled response.

"Umm, hmmm."

Kyla nodded in mutual assent and began to eat with gusto. At last, Daria slowed enough to compliment Kyla's efforts. "This is, without a doubt, the best food I have eaten in my entire life."

Kyla paused and smiled at her friend. "I do not think you realize how much energy we expend living in our underwater home. The bioskins generate a great deal of warmth, but our metabolism is such that we burn a tremendous amount of energy as well. There is probably no time in recorded history that an Atlantean has ever turned down an offer of food."

Daria gestured between bites. "Where did you get all this food? I don't remember passing a supermarket on our tour."

Kyla's eyes widened and she tucked into her food. "I believe the unexpected appearance of Ni-Cio had something to do with cutting short the rest of our tour."

Daria nodded and gave an unladylike snort. Kyla took her glass of muscari elixir and lifted it to her lips. As she savored the heady brew, she changed the subject. "We use aquaponics to grow much of our food and we also harvest the gifts the ocean offers. At no time have we ever been unable to sustain ourselves."

"Oh, so you fish."

Kyla almost choked and she quickly wiped her mouth with the napkin. "Daria, however limited, we communicate telepathically with most of the fish in the sea. They are our friends. Why even the suggestion makes me lose my appetite." She pushed her plate away.

Daria leaned toward her and placed her hand on the top of Kyla's shoulder. "Kyla I'm sorry, I meant no offense. I'm still trying to acquaint myself to your way of life, but it looks like I've still got so much to learn."

"My friend, you are beyond wonderful. Please do not let me cause you discomfort. Sometimes, your direct line of questioning catches me by surprise."

Daria seemed to have lost her appetite as well and Kyla watched with concern as she pushed her food around the plate. So, she was surprised at Daria's next question. "I haven't seen Ni-Cio. Will he be coming?"

Kyla glanced around but after having witnessed Daria's reaction to Ni-Cio, she didn't even try a mind link. "Knowing my brother, he is somewhere enjoying four plates of food. Don't worry, I promise not to let him bother you."

Daria's mouth dropped open. "Your brother? Ni-Cio is your brother?"

Kyla was about to apologize for her lineage, when the Council Leader rose and raised his glass to toast their new Healer. Marik's rich bass tones rebounded through the Hall. "Daria, I traditionally raise the first toast. As I present this glass in your honor, I wish you long life, love beyond measure and children to keep you young. Welcome to Atlantis!"

Cries of "Hear, hear!" accompanied his toast and the muscari flowed freely as others chimed in with their good wishes.

Tradition dictated that the next formal toast should come from the Most Sovereign Healer. Na-Kai rose to address her new apprentice. With her movements, streams of light flickered around and through her. She was almost transparent. The revelry quieted until a solemn hush had descended over the hall. The aging Healer raised her glass. "Daria, you are our continuance. Because of you, our lives will be lifted. Though you have doubts about your abilities, know this, in time, the full measure of the woman you are to become will unfold as surely as a flower opens its petals to the sun. With your presence, Atlantis is well and truly blessed."

She lowered her arm and paused. Still seated, Daria moved with uncertainty. She glanced anxiously at Kyla, and Kyla squeezed her hand in reassurance. Daria looked back at her mentor.

Na-Kai's voice filled with tenderness as she once again raised her glass. "Daria, I would take you as the child of my heart. From this moment I would be as your mother. I will teach you. I will love you. I will protect you with my very life. All that I am and all that I have will pass unto you, if you would have it so."

Throughout the Hall, there was not a rustle of movement.

Kyla saw the doubt flash over Daria's features. She knew that Daria was conflicted and she watched as her inner struggle played itself out over her beautiful face. The young Healer slowly pushed her chair back and approached Na-Kai. She stood before her mentor, and her beautiful contralto filled the air. "Having been alone so much of my life, the idea of becoming part of a family again is almost more than I can bear. I don't remember my mother very well, but I do remember being surrounded by her love. From the moment I was brought into Atlantis, you have surrounded me with your love.

"Na-Kai, it would be my greatest joy to take you as the mother of my heart. I will love you as a daughter would, and I will protect you. All that I am and all that I may become will be given to my new family. I will protect them with my life."

As Daria and Na-Kai wrapped their arms around each other in a fierce embrace, exaltation rang through every heart in the Great Hall. Their family was whole once more.

CHAPTER
24

*W*hen the food had been consumed to the last crumb, the toasts had dwindled to the occasional sentimental pronouncement, and the dessert had been cleared, the celebration suddenly gained a new momentum. People jumped up and shoved tables and chairs out of the way as the musicians began a set of foot-tapping, finger-snapping tunes. The dancing was fun, frivolous and frenetic.

Daria laughed to see people grab their partners and with joyful abandon begin spinning about the floor. Entranced by the bright swirl of color and people, Daria tapped a rapid beat with her foot, but as she swayed to the music, a strange lethargy began to crawl down her spine and seep into her bones. She thought she needed to sit for a while so she walked toward a set of discarded tables. Before she could lower herself into a waiting chair, a pair of strong arms seized her waist and spun her onto the dance floor. Startled, she couldn't hide her delight, "You're here!"

Ni-Cio flashed such a brilliant smile that her knees almost buckled. He pulled her closer and his words teased. "I see you missed my company."

She tried to think of a witty response, but the sound of his voice chased away all conscious thought. He guided her onto the dance floor and Daria was amazed to find how effortlessly their bodies blended. They danced as though they had known each other forever. The music climbed to a final apex and Ni-Cio began a gravity-defying spin. Daria clung to him, afraid that the g-forces would wrench her from his grasp and send her rolling, like a bowling ball, into the other dancers.

She was about to beg her handsome partner to stop so that she could catch her breath when the tempo slowed, and the music merged into a poignant number that evoked memories of lost lovers reunited. The indescribable feel of his body as it molded to hers awakened a response in her that she had never thought possible. She wanted to melt into him until she became his breath. She closed her eyes and surrendered to the feel of him as he led her in the slow, sensual dance.

With the intimate fusion of their bodies, Daria was overcome with a longing so intense she wanted to cry. She lifted her gaze. Not quite sure what she wanted to say, she stammered. "I, I…"

Strong fingers caressed her lips with a touch soft as a feather, and Ni-Cio's whispered response was pitched for her only. "Hold, my love. Nothing must be said now. We are here. Let your senses succumb to this tenuous moment. There will be time enough for talk."

His warm breath caressed her neck and her heart thrummed. Ni-Cio raised his head and their gazes locked. The recognition of all that would open between them was as real as the dancers that swirled about the Hall.

Ni-Cio lowered his mouth to hers. Their kiss was long and deep, filled with passion and promise. At last, Ni-Cio trailed a line of kisses to her ear and she heard his breathless whisper, choked with ardor. "We must leave before I make a complete fool of myself. By the gods, I could take you here before all the descendants of Poseidon and not care a whit who was watching."

Daria's passionate reply echoed his desire, "Not before I would have you."

He took her hand and they wended their way through the remaining dancers. They crossed to one of the portals and Ni-Cio turned into the passageway that led to his chambers. As they walked, wrapped in each other's arms, Daria began to feel lightheaded. Thinking it was the overwhelming nearness of the man next to her, she shook her head. Assailed by a violent attack of vertigo, she stumbled and nearly fell, but Ni-Cio caught her. "My love, are you all right?"

Overwhelmed by a feeling that bordered on an ether-induced need for sleep, Daria mumbled a response. "So, tired. I, don't understand."

Each step felt as if she were slogging through waist-deep mud. Suddenly, what little strength she had disappeared. Her arms slipped from Ni-Cio's waist.

Ni-Cio crushed her to his chest and stroked her back. His words barely registered. "Do not trouble yourself. You have been through so much, it is a wonder you haven't fallen asleep for an entire month." He swung her into his arms and hurried to his chambers.

Ni-Cio laid her upon his bed but Daria didn't stir. He pulled thick, warm covers over her shoulders and smoothed her brow. "Sleep, my dearest love."

He wasn't quite sure what to do. He walked to the waterwall and rinsed his face and hands, then lifted a chair and carried it over to the bed. With a quiet thump he settled into the soft cushions and propped an elbow on one of the arms. Resting his chin on one fist, he studied the topsider. Wondering at the rapidity with which this sleep had overtaken her, his lips twisted in a wry grin. "If I did not know better, I would think my male pride just took a tremendous beating."

As certain of Daria's feelings as his own, his thoughts took a darker turn. *"Still, this behavior seems highly unusual. Perhaps it is just that events have finally caught up with you."* He frowned. *"Even so, should I attempt to read your thoughts?"*

He leaned forward. Before he could begin, Daria twitched and moaned, and Ni-Cio could see that however deep her slumber, it was not restful.

He slid from the chair and onto the bed. He lay beside her and took her carefully into his arms. He released a gentle thought-form. *"I am here...rest and refresh yourself, troubles will wait for the morrow...know that you are my heart and it will always be so..."*

Ni-Cio felt an immediate response as her muscles loosed some of their stiffness. He took a slow, deep breath and calmed his mind. Eventually, he allowed his eyes to close, and he followed Daria into the realm where dreams are made.

An agonizing, heart-wrenching scream brought Ni-Cio to full and abrupt consciousness. He fought the covers, trying to extricate himself from the tangle until his focus was yanked back to the woman next to him. Daria sat straight as a ramrod, staring sightlessly into the night as though all the forces of evil were coming to annihilate her very soul. Ni-Cio grabbed her and pulled her back to his chest. His heart hammered against his ribs and he felt a panic he had never known. He tried to keep his voice even, "Daria, you are having a bad dream."

Deep into the nightmare, her body shook with fear and even though he held her, she gathered herself to scream yet again. Ni-Cio grabbed her shoulders and pushed himself to his knees. He looked at her, but there was not a glimmer of acknowledgment. Her eyes were in a trancelike state. He shook her as hard as he dared and initiated an urgent thought-form, *"Daria, awaken!"*

A swift inhalation of breath, and Ni-Cio knew she had disentangled herself from the grip of her terrible dreamstate. Daria blinked rapidly, her breath came in ragged gasps and she twisted and turned, wildly looking for something that was not there. At last, she threw herself into Ni-Cio's arms as if terrified that he too would disappear into the blackness.

A sound similar to a gentle keening issued from deep within her soul, and he thought his heart would break. Ni-Cio held her like a child, rocking back and forth, until at last, she calmed. "It was terrible. They were here and I couldn't do anything."

"Shh, shh, there is no need to remember. It was just a bad dream. You are safe. We are together and you have nothing to fear."

The power of the nightmare finally began to release its hold. Daria's body started to relax. They laid back and drifted, for a time, in the comfort of each other's arms.

Finally, without breaking the stillness, Ni-Cio initiated a thought-command and the lighting changed. He sent the whisper of a thought to Daria. *"Look up..."*

Overhead, the panorama of a night sky unfurled across the ceiling and a galaxy of twinkling stars spilled into the room. They danced though the dark like fireflies and chased the murky shadows away. Daria and Ni-Cio watched in wonder as shimmers of light splashed across the bed and painted their world in moonglow and starshine.

A beautiful smile lit Daria's face and Ni-Cio gently released her from his embrace. He crooked an elbow and rested his head on his hand. He was awed by her. A smile lit her face. "Ni-Cio, it's glorious!"

Glimmers of light flashed over the sensuous curves of her body, and a swift desire ignited within him. With her arrayed in starlight, it seemed to Ni-Cio that all light emanated from Daria. Her golden hair cascaded in loose waves over her shoulders and reflected colors like a prism dancing in the sun. With every breath, her porcelain skin sparkled with its own translucence. To Ni-Cio, she was heartbreakingly beautiful.

Had he not felt the bed holding him firmly in place, he would have thought he had entered a dream of his own making. "One from which I do not want to wake."

He caressed the small of Daria's back with a touch soft as down, and she shifted her gaze to look upon him. He was unable to take another breath. The moment had come. He raised his hand to trace the silken line of her cheek with the backs of his fingertips. "I would know your thoughts and I would have you know mine."

Daria's eyes were filled with so much love he thought his heart would burst. She reached for his hand and entwined her fingers with his, and the cadence of her voice washed over him like a gentle prayer, "Please tell me that this isn't a dream. I don't think I could stand having my heart broken again."

Ni-Cio lowered her onto his chest, "I will never hurt you. I will love you and protect you with my very life. You have nothing to fear."

They faced each other and his gaze spiraled into the aquamarine depths of her eyes. She opened her mind to the first tremolos of his thought-touch. Like a whisper of mist, he wound his way through the garden of her mind until he had encircled her very essence. The deepest core of Daria was known to him and he felt himself open to her fully and with love.

Through the exaltation of their communion, they took each other to higher peaks, higher skies. They were mixed and made one with colors dreamed through their eyes. They flew and were led to the sun. As their thoughts were softened and warmed, they awakened in each other's arms.

CHAPTER
25

*L*eaving Santorini was easier than Evan expected. One call and arrangements had been made for a mid-sized jet to be at his disposal. He had not inquired about a submersible, because the less anyone knew, the better. He needed to obtain the vehicle as fast as possible, and being unfamiliar with the laws regarding such acquisitions, he was prepared to circumvent certain proprieties.

After some thought, he had concluded that the closest deep water port outside of Greece was in Italy. Within easy reach of Santorini, Naples was where he had decided to begin the hunt.

The jet was on the tarmac, fueled and ready for departure. Evan left his car in the hangar and hurried over the hot asphalt. He vaulted up the steps and heard the captain greet him as he entered the fuselage. "Dr. Gaddes, welcome aboard, sir."

"We leave at once." Evan wanted everyone on board to know that he was not there to chit chat.

The captain's manner stiffened. "Certainly, sir, I just need to know our destination."

"Italy. Naples."

"Very good, sir. We will be in the air as soon as I finish the flight check."

Evan gave a curt nod and turned to take his seat. He was approached by a pretty, dark-haired flight attendant. "Good morning, doctor. We are fully stocked. Is there anything you would like before take-off?"

Lost in thought, he regarded her for the interruption she represented. About to decline, he changed his mind, "Scotch on the rocks and make it a double."

Before she could attend to his drink, he stopped her. "Is there access to a computer?"

Anxious to comply with his request, she opened an overhead bin and handed a laptop to Evan. "Do you need help getting it started?"

"Just the drink."

She left without another word. Evan booted the machine and heard the captain's announcement. "Dr. Gaddes, our flight time to Naples will be approximately two hours forty-seven minutes. Skies are clear and we will be flying at an altitude of 31,000 feet. We have been cleared for departure, so if you will please fasten your seat belt, we can be underway."

Evan ignored the request and didn't look up as he was handed his drink. He absentmindedly took a sip while he scanned through the information on the Web. He knew what he wanted. So he quickly discounted the luxury submarines touted as the newest toy for the wealthy elite. He needed a workhorse with the capability of exceeding 10,000 feet.

The jet's vibrations deepened. The plane started to roll and Evan sifted through a catalog of choices. As the wheels left the runway, he narrowed his focus to a streamlined machine called the *Oceanus VI*. The two-man submersible had been built by a deep-ocean engineering company for an Italian television station. The unit was highly maneuverable and could exceed depths of more than 12,000 feet. He took another sip. "There you are. Now, who is your owner?"

Evan glanced out the porthole just once at a sky of merciless clarity. The uncompromising blue circled the silver jet like a globe. Left alone, he lowered his head back to the computer screen, tenaciously burrowing through the tangled byways of the Internet, hunting the owner of a certain *Oceanus VI*. He never looked out the window again.

With the search over and his business about to be concluded, Evan allowed himself a brief respite. He settled back into luxurious leather seats as the driver of the limousine skirted the narrow, winding streets of Naples. The port would soon come into view. He closed his eyes and ran over everything in his mind one last time.

He had found his submersible, but he knew that persuasion had a price. Calls completed, funds transferred, he was headed to the final meeting that would transfer ownership. The Italian owner had suggested that a week would not be enough to learn all the detailed mechanics of the undersea vehicle. But when Evan had snarled, "I don't have that much time," the man had offered no more advice.

Evan rubbed his tired eyes and relaxed into the silence. Still, he could not quiet his mind and his thoughts circled back to Daria. "I don't want you down there any longer than you have to be."

That thought brought back some wonderful memories.

Evan had stood in the living room tapping his foot. With his usual impatience, he had glanced at his watch as she came from her bedroom. One look at his expression and she had strolled across the room, taken hold of his arm and unfastened his watch.

With an attitude of studied nonchalance, she had thrown it onto a nearby table and, half-jokingly, admonished him. "Tonight there are no schedules, no necessary meetings and no clocks. I intend to have your full concentration. If not, I'll just go back into that bathroom, draw myself a hot bath and leave you to your commitments."

He remembered being so startled that he had laughed out loud. No one ever dared speak to him in that manner, and in retrospect, that was what he loved about her. She brought out a lighter side he hadn't even known he possessed.

He opened his eyes and sighed. "Ah, Daria, I would give everything I have just to be certain of your safety."

He looked out the window to see that they had turned into a very crowded and busy port. Without too much difficulty, his driver found the designated dock and as he pulled in, Evan saw a portly figure step gingerly from the side of the Oceanus onto the cement pier.

Evan exited the backseat before his chauffeur could open the door and he was met by the eccentric television executive. With true Italian gusto, the man bypassed Evan's outstretched hand and grabbed his shoulders. His hearty bear hug was followed with a kiss on both cheeks. "Dr. Gaddes, a pleasure to meet you!" Only the hint of an accent colored his speech. "I have been looking forward to meeting such a direct man as yourself. I never thought to sell my beauty, but you are a difficult man to say no to."

Evan endured the niceties and eventually signatures were applied to contracts and the deal was finalized. He had acquired the ownership of a very powerful personal submarine.

Curious, the older man eyed him. "An instructor will meet you tomorrow to begin your briefing. Treat her well, my friend, and she will take care of you. Take her for granted and she is not so forgiving."

Evan scowled. "I will remember that."

"I do not think you are looking for treasure, so what could it be that makes you hurry so?"

Evan shot him one of his "looks" and the Italian shrugged his shoulders philosophically and slapped him on the back. "Ah well, no problem. Good luck with whatever you intend. Arrivederci!" With a grand salute and one last look at the Oceanus, he was gone.

Evan stood on the deserted pier, feeling as though there was more he should be doing. However, a freighter had been lined up to take him and the Oceanus back to Santorini as soon as he gave the go-ahead. There was nothing left but to find a room in a nearby hotel and sleep like the dead.

CHAPTER
26

*O*utside the confines of their biosphere, Mer-An and Kyla swam through crystal seas. They wanted to gather fresh seaweed in order to prepare a special dish with which to surprise Daria. They glided toward the kelp beds when a familiar family of very playful bottle-nosed dolphins swam by and convinced them that a game of swim and seek would be a wonderful diversion before they began their harvest.

Mer-An and Kyla were excited to join Shaka, the father; Oomi, the gentle mother; and Tashi, a mischievous baby boy who had joined the world just a few months earlier, in their spontaneous celebration of fun.

Players disappeared in all directions as Shaka assumed the role of pursuer. Thought-forms of laughter and jibes echoed through the water and jarred Shaka to begin his pursuit in earnest. While he focused his swimming prowess on Kyla, Oomi made certain that her baby was safe with Mer-An and then soared out of sight. Mer-An and Tashi slipped through the deep when Mer-An was pummeled by an exultant thought-form.

"HIDE WITH MEEEEE!"

She choked back her laughter. *"Tashi, you need not yell...I can hear you..."* She slowed her speed and signaled the young dolphin. *"Lead the way..."*

Tashi struggled to pass her with all the strength in his little body. In a final burst of effort, he took the lead. He veered sharply to the left, but Mer-An stayed right behind him. She knew he was headed for a huge coral outcropping in a nearby reef. Everyone was well aware it was his favorite place to hide.

"No one ever finds me here, Mer-An…"

"I know, Tashi, this is the BEST place…"

They darted behind the reef and curved into a small cave that the young dolphin had happened upon in one of his previous games. Tashi beamed with delight as he snuggled close to Mer-An.

"We have to be quiet…"

Mer-An smiled at his irrepressible joy, however, Oomi had entrusted him to her safe-keeping. *"I know, sweetest, but tell me if you need to go up for air…"*

She could tell he tried to quiet his riotous mind. The youngest member of the dolphin family nodded his head, eyes wide and on guard for his dad. Unable to contain his excitement, Tashi thought-whispered. *"Where did my Mama go?"*

"She was heading for the kelp beds…shhhh…" Mer-An placed her finger over Tashi's nose to signal their need for absolute silence.

A shadow flickered overhead and the figure of Shaka slid by. Tashi wriggled with the sheer suspense of it all as an ethereal voice wound teasingly through their minds.

"Taaash, son, where are yoooouuuu?"

Mer-An could feel the baby's excitement climb. So far he hadn't been able to finish a game because he would become too agitated to hold still and he would burst forth in a tornado of bubbles and chortles. *"Daddeeee, you didn't see meee!"*

However, this time he waited and Shaka swam on.

Tashi peeked out of the deep twilight and saw that the coast was clear. Mer-An knew that he was filled with pride for his newfound ability to hold still longer than he ever had. She hugged his soft, streamlined body before he flicked himself into the open blue and let loose with every spin and flip in his fledgling repertoire.

Thrilled by his new tricks, she stopped to enjoy the pure exuberance that poured from the whirling baby. With his advance toward the surface, Mer-An knew that he was in need of air. With a huge smile on his beautiful face, Tashi swam backwards to show off. He drifted upwards and sang a very loud, off-key dolphin song. He sang with such abandon that neither of them heard the approaching vessel.

Mer-An felt the vibrations before she saw the boat. She screamed a warning to Tashi and pushed her formidable swimming powers to their utmost. As hard as she tried, everything shuddered into slow motion. She could see that the young dolphin and the sea craft were on a collision course. The propeller slashing its way through crystal waters turned deadly.

Inch by torturous inch, Mer-An charged through the currents in a supreme effort to reach Tashi before the relentless propeller ripped through his delicate life. Mer-An heard the others answer her scream but she knew they couldn't help. They were too far away.

Tashi slowed his ascent, but he needed air and so he kept rising toward the surface. He was confused by the sudden commotion, and she knew that he thought they had switched to a game of chase when he smiled and rolled over to put on a lightning display of speed.

Mer-An cried with the effort as she exploded upward. Flying to cover the baby, she used the last of her strength to push him out of harm's way. She was aware of all motion as it slammed into real time, but the last thing she remembered was the propeller as it slammed into her.

CHAPTER 27

*C*haos erupted along with Mer-An's blood. Kyla tore through the water in a furious effort to reach her friend. Mer-An floated unconscious, and the precious life force pumped from her in ever-darkening clouds.

Tashi thrashed about and tried to push her lifeless form to the surface. With each new gush of blood, his raw panic could be felt as his shrieks raked through their minds. *"Mer-An! Mer-An!"*

Kyla and the dolphins converged upon Tashi and Mer-An. Kyla's mind was in shambles and her body shook so hard that she could barely function. She had never witnessed such trauma, and she almost succumbed to the blind terror that hovered on the edge of her mind. But Shaka's calm reassurance steadied her and helped soothe the anguish of his son. *"Tash, son, peace, be still…Kyla and I will help Mer-An…"*

Oomi used her body to gentle her son to the surface. *"Tashi…you need air, come…you can help Mer-An by staying safe yourself…"*

Mother and son swam out of sight and Kyla willed her bioskin to cover the form of her inanimate friend. She prayed that her 'skin would temporarily staunch the awful flow of blood, but as she stared at the horrific wound, it seemed to mock her meager attempt to help. She was terrified. She looked up at Shaka. *"If I don't get her back…"*

Shaka's firm command cut through her despair. *"Enough! We can do this...no more thought..."*

Together, they pushed-pulled the inert body as gently as possible toward the biosphere. Kyla was aware that Tashi and his mother watched from above, and she felt his fear when his frightened voice reverberated through her.

"Mommie?"

The question hung. Shaka and Kyla worked desperately to get Mer-An into the biosphere. At last, Oomi's hopeful reply flowed through Kyla's mind.

"Sweetest, Kyla will take Mer-An to Na-Kai and she will help her..."

Although Kyla knew that Oomi's quiet assurance was an attempt to calm her baby's fears, she was afraid that even Na-Kai's abilities wouldn't be enough. She had never seen such a hurt, and an unsettling conflict arose to tear at her heart. Relief that Oomi's firstborn remained untouched was at war with a deepening dread that the woman who had saved his life would be no more.

"Na-Kai...Mer-An's hurt...I am frightened...she may no longer be with us!"

Kyla's grief ripped through everyone's thoughts. Immediately, Ni-Cio helped Na-Kai and Daria rise from their prepared lunch. He guided them through the halls while Na-Kai sent her steady response. *"Kyla, quiet yourself...I must hear Mer-An..."*

Na-Kai signaled Ni-Cio to halt. She closed her eyes, and Ni-Cio knew that she was probing Mer-An's body for damage. Her audible gasp galvanized him. He took Na-Kai's arm and hurried her toward the entrance chamber. The Healer spoke with an urgency that Ni-Cio had never heard before. "The heartbeat is there, but it is so slow as to be almost undetectable. Daria, follow my lead precisely, but remember, pitch your voice an octave lower than mine."

Even as they raced to the entry pool, Na-Kai began the healing. Ni-Cio heard the odd tones and the singsong quality of her voice echo around and ahead of them and he knew that for Mer-An, it would be as if she had physically received an anesthetic.

Ni-Cio helped Na-Kai and Daria into the pool area. Others stood ready, and as Na-Kai pointed out positions, they quickly gathered around. No one spoke, but the tension mounted as each second created a mirror of endlessness. Daria stood next to her mentor, and though she pitched her voice lower, she sang in tandem with Na-Kai so that she could exert her untried talents without interfering in the healing efforts. Their unearthly tones continued unabated as they awaited Kyla's arrival.

Suddenly, Ni-Cio heard Aris's anxious voice as his footsteps pounded toward the pool. Ni-Cio crossed the deck and grabbed his friend as he entered the chamber. He held his friend back from the water's edge, but Aris's wild, guilt-ridden thoughts roared through his mind. *"It is my fault! By the gods, it should have been me…"*

Aris struggled to break Ni-Cio's iron grasp but Ni-Cio wrestled him towards the portal with a stern warning, "Aris…hear me…you do not help like this…"

"Let me go…I have to see her!"

Ni-Cio pushed his friend out of the room and willed the portal door to materialize behind them. His whisper was fierce, "Aris, you cannot see Mer-An! Na-Kai and Daria need to stay focused so they can help her, your interference will only make it worse!"

All at once, Aris's energy left him along with his strength to stand. He sank to the floor and when he looked up, Ni-Cio could see his heart in his eyes. "I love her, Ni-Cio, and I have never told her."

Ni-Cio wanted to run from his friend's desolation. In all their years together, he had never seen him like this. Aris sucked in a ragged breath and lowered his gaze. "I always thought there was time, and I enjoyed ignoring her because it made her chase me even more."

Ni-Cio knew that Aris wanted more than anything to be loved, and he coughed to clear the lump that had formed in his throat. He knelt beside his friend as he continued his heartbroken confession.

"She wanted me to go with her today to get...I don't even remember. I teased her, telling her that I had man's work to do and that I did not have time for her fun and games. Gods, Ni-Cio, if I had just gone with her, this would not have happened." Aris bent forward as though he had been gut punched and great shudders ran through his body.

Ni-Cio didn't know what he could do to comfort him, so he just leaned over and wrapped his arms around him. He held him until he felt Aris's grief begin to subside.

Aris fell back against the wall and closed his eyes. Silent for the space of several heartbeats, when he spoke, his voice quivered with resignation. "I cannot feel her." He opened his eyes, stared at nothing and repeated, "I cannot feel her."

Aris's vibrant coloring faded to a dull gray. Ni-Cio rose to his knees and grabbed Aris's shoulders. He shook him hard enough to get his attention. "Aris! You do not need to feel her! If there was no hope, do you think Na-Kai would expend the effort to try to heal her?"

A glimmer of acknowledgment stirred within Aris. Ni-Cio shook him again. "Daria is there as well, and though she is but beginning to realize her talents, she can help reinforce our Healer. Do not give up on Mer-An!"

Aris's color slowly started to return and Ni-Cio relaxed his hold. He dropped down next to his friend and shook his head. "I tell you this, my oldest and dearest friend, if Mer-An has the tenacity to keep chasing after you, then she has more willpower in one finger than I have in my entire being. She will come through this. Now, whether she continues to pursue you, *that* is something else altogether."

He put his arm around Aris, trying to lighten the mood. "For the life of me, I can't see why she would even bother."

Aris didn't rise to the bait, but the ghost of a smile played over his frightened face. He gestured toward the closed room with his chin. "Go back in, Ni-Cio. She will need you. I will be right here. But you must promise me, if things get worse, you will let me come to her."

All lightness gone, Ni-Cio stared into Aris's sad eyes. "Things will not get worse."

When he saw that Aris needed more, Ni-Cio swallowed hard and nodded. "Should Mer-An falter, I will make certain that you have time with her."

CHAPTER
28

*T*heir wait neared its unavoidable conclusion, and Na-Kai clasped Daria's hand. The Most Sovereign Healer did not let her healing tones diminish by so much as a breath as she encouraged Daria. *"You do well, child...I know your fear...just follow my movements...everything you do will only serve to enhance what I must do..."*

Daria responded with a gentle squeeze of her palm but she continued, unabated, to vocalize the peculiar chordal structure that Na-Kai had taught her. The Healer was heartened. She knew that Daria was frightened, but saw that neither her voice nor her thoughts wavered or lost projection.

Ni-Cio re-entered the room and stood next to Na-Kai. She was grateful for his warmth, but she was glad when he moved next to Daria. She knew that his nearness helped strengthen her.

Everyone strained to see the lights of the biosphere. Suddenly, they heard Kyla.

"We are here..."

The lights of the craft broke through the tunnel and the pool glowed yellow-green as the vessel surged to the surface. Drilled in rescue procedures, everyone knew their job so that movements were certain, well timed, and performed without hesitation. As the canopy dematerialized, Ni-Cio and Rogert pulled the buoyant machine onto a docking station.

No one talked and not one thought was exchanged. Kyla stepped from the craft and stood to one side while the men

147

lifted Mer-An's body to a prepared pallet. Her bioskin slipped away and Na-Kai began the healing, with Mer-An unimpeded by any clothing.

The Healer bent forward and placed her hands over the gaping wound. Every motion and every sound that she performed was mimicked by Daria in perfect synchronization. As they worked, Na-Kai felt a change filter through the room. The severity of Mer-An's injuries were such that doubts began to assail everyone's faith in her extraordinary abilities. In their collective memory, there was no time when she had taken so long to heal someone.

One by one, their hopes plummeted to fear. They waited for some sign that their Healer could bring Mer-An back. Na-Kai tried to ignore the dread that pervaded the others, but she felt her own flicker of doubt. She clamped down on the negative feeling, refusing to let herself be led. She lowered her head and intensified her exertions. The laceration still would not close, and Mer-An's breathing slowed until it stopped altogether.

Ni-Cio turned to summon Aris, when Rogert grabbed his arm and whispered. "Look!"

Na-Kai watched, fascinated. Daria placed the palms of her hands over the tops of the Healer's, compelling Na-Kai to follow her lead. The young Healer brought both sets of hands up and closed them in a semblance of the prayer pose. Still anchoring Na-Kai's hands between hers, she pointed their fingers downward. To Na-Kai's surprise, it was if their combined energy had been injected with tremendous force and focus.

Daria elevated her tonality to match Na-Kai, chord for chord, structure for structure, note for note. Na-Kai watched, and by agonizing degrees, Mer-An's skin began to close. Membrane attached to membrane, blood vessel adhered to blood vessel and severed nerve endings sought their mates as bone knitted to bone.

The temperature in the room rose with the heat that poured off Na-Kai and Daria. A wisp of smoke drifted from Mer-An's body, and the smell of cauterized flesh spread through the air. Na-Kai and Daria continued their work and the deathly whiteness that pervaded Mer-An's form lessened.

Gradually, the wound closed and Mer-An's breath, though still quite slow, took on a deeper, more regular rhythm. Spirits lifted when a tinge of pink seeped into Mer-An's skin, signifying the return of blood flowing through her veins.

Na-Kai continued to administer the healing anesthetic, but was able to relax her thought-forms to a lesser intensity. She was exhausted, but when Daria's hands dropped from hers and the weight of her small body sagged against the pallet, Na-Kai could not keep the fear from her voice. "Ni-Cio, take her! The effort has taxed her beyond her limits!"

The Atlantean rushed to Daria's side and lowered her to the floor. Na-Kai looked down. "Mer-An is not yet safe, and I cannot remove my hands. Rogert, get Aris to help you. Take Mer-An to my quarters so that I can attend her. Ni-Cio, see to Daria. The very moment I can release Mer-An, I will come to your chambers. I fear for Daria's safety."

Everyone jumped to comply. Kyla moved to support Na-Kai and the men picked up Mer-An's pallet. Ni-Cio lifted Daria. Her head lolled limply against his chest and Na-Kai heard his fear-engraved thought. *"Na-Kai, will she be all right?"*

"I do not know…the energy transfer taxed her…she is weaker than she should be…take her to your chambers…I will be there as soon as I can safely leave Mer-An…"

Ni-Cio entered his chamber with Daria's lifeless form draped across his arms. He hurried across the room and placed her upon his bed. Her eyes were open, but nothing registered. Dark smudges were visible beneath her bottom lashes. She was deathly pale and cold to his touch, and her golden hair fell in slack ropes across the pillow. Ni-Cio gathered all the blankets he could find and piled them on her. Finally, he slid under the covers to lie beside her and supply additional warmth.

He made no attempt to speak nor did he send the smallest thought-form. He knew the less effort she expended, the quicker she would regain her energy. He prayed she would fall asleep, but even that seemed to require an effort she did not possess.

If he had not been so still, he would have missed the thought that sighed into his mind. *"...Mer-An..."*

Ni-Cio raised himself onto an elbow and peered into Daria's eyes. He wanted to believe that he saw a flicker of acknowledgment move through aquamarine depths. He tried to keep the fear from his voice. "Na-Kai is with her."

He didn't want to risk any more of her energy, yet he didn't want her to expend any more thought worrying about Mer-An. "Her breathing has returned to a more normal state and her color has improved. Because of you, she will live."

Ni-Cio watched Daria's eyelids flutter and close. He knew she suffered from extreme exhaustion, but he was frightened. She looked shrouded in death and her sleep did not feel natural. He tried to touch her mind, but the blackness he encountered felt more like oblivion.

CHAPTER
29

*K*yla sent an Atlantis wide thought-form to allay any fears regarding Mer-An's recovery, but she also needed to convey the extent to which Daria had been the factor in Mer-An's continuance. She had to be certain that should anyone harbor a single doubt as to Na-Kai's choice of successor, there would not be one soul who could disregard the miraculous healing that had transpired. She flashed a record of all that had taken place within the close confines of the entry pool, and took a deep breath when she reached her conclusion. *"Mer-An is not out of danger...even now, Na-Kai administers her healing energy...she will not leave until Mer-An can be left to another's supervision...however, Na-Kai is depleted and Daria is in total seclusion...do nothing to disturb our Healers...they must have time to regenerate themselves..."*

Kyla grimaced and muttered, "How much time is anyone's guess."

She sifted through her memories in a silent review of other times and other Healers. She observed the duration it took for Healers to gain in strength, stamina and conditioning. No matter their ability, everyone began under the tutelage and close supervision of the Most Sovereign Healer. The young Healers started with minute energy transfers, and once those transfers had been mastered, the difficulty increased until the limits of their abilities had been defined. Always the lesson was reinforced that they must hold enough energy in reserve so that they could reenergize themselves.

Once they recognized how much life force could be used without depleting themselves beyond the point of no return, the Most Sovereign Healer released them to work on their own. Kyla was certain that Daria had not known her limits.

She added the final touches to the special meal and hoisted the heavy tray onto her shoulder. She almost groaned under the weight. She hurried from the kitchens. The nourishment was critical for Na-Kai, and the longer the healing, the more food was needed to help replenish the energy.

Aris and Rogert stood outside the entrance to Na-Kai's chambers, and they nodded as Kyla entered. She crossed the room and placed the tray on the dining table. As Kyla began to unload the food and glanced up, she almost dropped the tray.

Na-Kai sat, hunched over Mer-An. Her hands covered the ugly slash, but Kyla had never seen their beautiful Healer in such a state. Her robes were in disarray and her elegant, unlined face showed unbelievable signs of having aged. Kyla took a moment to collect herself, then carried a plate of food to the bedside table and lowered herself onto a chair next to Na-Kai. The severely weakened woman raised her head to let Kyla begin feeding her.

Na-Kai's hands never faltered and her tonality never ceased, but she continued to open her mouth to take the food like a helpless baby bird. Kyla knew that Na-Kai could not continue her efforts through the night. The rejuvenation of sleep was just as important as the food, but Kyla kept those thoughts to herself.

Between spoonful's, Kyla checked Mer-An's progress. She could see small improvements. That it had taken so long to bring her to this point was testimony to how close she had come to leaving them. It was that thought that had plagued her throughout the afternoon. She whispered, "I think she almost died."

"She did die," Na-Kai's voice fractured the silence, but the thin, reedy voice that Kyla heard made her doubt its source.

She apologized, "Na-Kai, forgive me. I didn't mean to disrupt your concentration."

"Do not trouble yourself, child. I am through for a time. I can do no more." A bone-weary sigh slipped from her lips. Her head fell forward and her body swayed.

Kyla grasped her arms and tried to shift her to the bed. "You must sleep."

Na-Kai struggled against that suggestion and a trace of thought, inflexible in its exhaustion, entered Kyla's mind. *"Take me...to Daria..."*

Before Kyla could offer another objection, Aris and Rogert appeared. They walked in with the pallet they had used to transport Mer-An and placed it next to Na-Kai. Aris lifted her slack body and Kyla saw the shock on his face when he beheld the transformation of their beloved Healer. He placed a tender kiss upon a forehead once unblemished by lines, and Kyla heard the deference in his voice, "As you wish, but we will convey you to her."

Kyla knew that their Most Sovereign Healer had not heard Aris's words. She had fallen into a deep sleep the moment he had lifted her into his arms.

CHAPTER
30

*P*repared to cease at the slightest disturbance, Travlor censured his breath and exhaled in increments. He had camouflaged himself so that he was indistinguishable from the rock walls of the cavern and had closed his eyelids, prepared to wait.

The thought-form that bound him to Atlantis had lessened, and had he not been supine, thoughts suspended, he would never have felt the shift. And so, he had abandoned his quarters to stand sentinel before Ni-Cio's rooms. *"Like an unopposed virus, I come to feed upon the weakened host."* Appreciating the metaphor, he almost chuckled until he heard a worried exchange echo from the far end of the corridor. Travlor suspended all movement, all thought. The words he heard covered him like a balm.

"Aris, I have never seen our Healer like this. She requires sleep."

"I agree, Rogert, but her anxiety for Daria supersedes everything. Careful, we're nearly there." The men hustled past.

Travlor cracked his eyelids and smirked. His thoughts erupted. *"By all the monstrous gods ever invented, I knew it would happen! Na-Kai, your time draws to a close and the topsider abomination will die too! Atlantis, spawn of Poseidon, I am done with you. Evan! Where is he? I must contact Evan!"*

Travlor raged with hatred, but one thought stemmed his jubilant tirade. *"You are not out of here...yet."* His gaze slithered across space and he scrutinized Ni-Cio's door. One infinitesimal heartbeat and then another. *"I can wait…what is a few more days?"*

Na-Kai's eyes were closed as she was carried into Ni-Cio's chamber. She was aware that everyone thought she was asleep, but she was hoarding her remaining energy. She slowed her breath until her relaxation was complete.

Ni-Cio lifted her into his arms and held her against his chest. The rapid beat of his heart told her of his fear, but her sole focus centered on the daughter of her heart as he lowered her into the comfort of soft bedding. She inhaled the crystalline scent that surrounded Daria and she knew she was ready. *"She sleeps too deeply, Ni-Cio…place my arms around her…"*

Ni-Cio adopted the deference of her title, trying to intervene. "Most Sovereign Healer, I know that she sleeps far below a normal slumber and I would do anything to take this burden as my own. But, please, you must have a care for yourself."

Na-Kai did not expend the effort to respond. She suppressed the beat of her own heart so that her system decelerated almost to a suspended state.

Ni-Cio could do nothing but honor her request, so he gently turned Na-Kai onto her side. He placed her arms around Daria, and Na-Kai cradled her as though she were a newborn.

A tender healing tonality floated into the moist air. Na-Kai wrapped the last reserves of her energy around Daria. She infused the comatose topsider with strength and tenderness and affection. Daria was on the brink of death, but Na-Kai sent her own essence into the very marrow of Daria's body.

At last, Na-Kai felt a change. The young woman's sleep rose to a less threatening pattern. The Healer's thoughts wound through Daria, seeking some form of consciousness. However small the recognition, it would be enough. It had to be. *"Daria, child of my heart...I am here...hold to my voice and grow in your strength...all will be well..."*

Several silent heartbeats passed until a blessed murmur whispered through Na-Kai, soft as down. *"Mama?"*

"Yes, child, I am with you..."

"Where are we?"

"In a very safe place..."

Silence for a time. *"Why are we here?"*

"So that you will know I am with you...always and forever...in this place, time has no beginning and no end..."

"Will we come here often?"

"Whenever the need arises...I will be here..."

So endless, the peace. Na-Kai could feel the music of their souls bathing them in light and love and joy. A shared timelessness.

"Mama, I don't want to leave..."

Na-Kai's sigh touched Daria in a loving caress. *"You have to, child...I will give you everything you need, but then you must leave..."*

"You won't be coming with me..."

The least hesitation before she answered. *"No..."*

"What do I need that you would give me?"

"Knowledge..."

The quiet stretched between them.

"Mama, I love you..."

"I love you too, sweetest..."

157

It seemed that the blackness held him immobile. But for Travlor, the eons he had been forced to traverse the worlds had endowed him with patience beyond revenge. A motionless state was as comfortable as breathing. Thus concealed, he lost track of time. Whether hours passed or days, he could not tell. And yet he waited. It was almost at an end, and he could feel it with every fiber of his existence. So it was that in the blink of an eye, the thought-form that had surrounded his every movement for thirty-five years, vanished. With the flash of emerald green, Na-Kai was no more. He was finally free.

He rammed his body out of the shadows and flew down the hallway. *"Now...Evan, I need you, now!"*

CHAPTER
31

*E*van ended the call, pocketed his phone and walked out onto the veranda. Scarlet bougainvillea leaves, buffeted by the sea breeze, tumbled across the concrete with a gentle rasp. He relaxed against the balustrade and felt certain that he had contacted everyone who might have questioned Daria's whereabouts. He didn't want her absence to cause alarm, so he had invented a plausible explanation, their elopement, followed by an extended honeymoon.

The hotel manager had been eager to accept an exorbitant amount of money to cover her expenses, and to believe that Daria's hasty departure was due to a family emergency.

Because he had regained a measure of control, Evan experienced the first feeling of relief since the onset of this burgeoning debacle. His gaze wandered over the startling landscape. The luminous Greek sun had begun its stately descent into the ocean, and rays of cloud-softened light drenched the island in gold. He took a deep breath and massaged the back of his neck. "It's going to be all right. I *will* see you again."

The glow of lamplight began to dot the island against the coming night, and Evan almost convinced himself that everything would turn out. But his sense of calm detonated as Travlor's command blasted through his mind, "Now! Evan, I need you, now!"

Evan scrambled out of his room, jumped into his car and sped toward the waterfront where his *Oceanus VI* was docked. Within thirty frenetic minutes, he was belted into the pilot's seat and he had fired the startup sequence. He detached from the moorings and shoved off. As soon as he dogged the hatch, the interior cabin was illuminated in a soft green glow. Evan motored toward the mouth of the harbor as fast as maritime law allowed and booted the onboard computer to access his nautical maps.

Travlor had rendered a rather vague idea as to his destination, so Evan had charted a course based on assumption and guesswork. But his estranged father had assured him that once he was within close proximity, he could guide Evan straight into the heart of Atlantis. Evan held a secret hope that the closer he came to Atlantis and to his father, the more his telepathic ability would become enhanced. If he could locate Daria on his own, he wouldn't even have to deal with Travlor.

As the reef dropped away and plunged to exceptional depths, Evan's angle of attack steepened and his descent gathered speed, his gaze locked on the computer screen. Although the outside lights were on, the murky depths became impenetrable as darkness closed around him. His concentration intensified, but Evan dared not slow his descent because if Travlor was free, something monumental had occurred to bring that to pass. He couldn't waste time in the execution of a technically safe dive.

The small submersible plummeted. Beads of sweat gathered at the base of Evan's skull and he felt a slow, sticky trickle wind down the back of his neck. He gripped the steering mechanism so tightly that his hands ached. He took quick gulps of air. His heart felt like it would beat a way out of his chest, and an irritating itch settled itself on the bridge of his nose to challenge his focus.

He blinked his eyes and risked a quick swipe of his brow. Several deep breaths helped him to lower his heart rate and regain some composure. He riveted his attention and his faith to a set of maps that had never known of the existence of a sunken colony. A world that had only ever lived shrouded in legend, mystery and once-upon-a-time longing.

At the precise moment the emerald flash blazed through Atlantis, Daria awakened from the netherworld that bound her. With the infusion of Na-Kai's healing energy, she had been strong enough to help the Healer transcend, so that Na-Kai had not been subjected to the trauma of a physical death. And although everyone was aware that their cherished Healer had forfeited what remained of her life in order to bestow the gift of a new beginning upon them, every heart in Atlantis was filled with deep sorrow at her unexpected passing.

Daria was transported to Na-Kai's quarters, and Atlanteans lined the way in tribute to their new Healer. The indigo color of their sad faces reflected their heartfelt mourning, but as she reached to touch their outstretched hands, traces of gold glistened through their sorrow, and she knew that they honored her with their love.

By the time they entered Na-Kai's chambers, Daria was ready to sleep again. Although she had regained quite a bit of strength, a full recovery would still take a while, and she was relieved to be back in the comfort of soft sheets and downy pillows.

Ni-Cio fluffed the covers and tucked her in, and he worried over her until Kyla pushed him aside so that she could lower a heaping tray of food onto Daria's lap. Ni-Cio moved to a nearby chair and sat down.

Daria marveled at the sight of the only man she could ever love, then glanced at Kyla. "I'm stuffed. You forced me to eat so much food after I woke up that I can't take another bite." Daria pushed the tray away and leaned back into the mountainous pile of pillows.

Kyla crossed her arms, and Daria was surprised to hear her deferential tone. "You are still not well, and in order to speed your recovery, you must consume a variety of foods in varying combinations and portions. This nutrition also helps accentuate your healing powers. So, even though you are full, I must try to entice you to continue eating. In that way, I am assured that you have received the additional calories you need to offset your accelerated metabolism."

Daria shook her head and signaled Kyla to remove the tray. "I'm sorry, Kyla, I am just too tired right now. Maybe later."

Kyla lifted the heavy tray and Daria heard an element of teasing tinge her voice. "You are doing quite well, Most Sovereign Healer. Certainly you have gained enough strength so that tomorrow we will force you out of bed to run the halls of Atlantis."

A mischievous glint lit Kyla's eyes and Daria was grateful to have her friendship. The nourishment Kyla had provided had increased her wellbeing, but she was still exhausted. "Kyla, I doubt I'll feel much like a footrace, but if you keep calling me by anything other than my given name, you will be surprised how fast I can climb out of this bed and come after you. Besides, I don't feel like a Most Sovereign Healer."

A deep rumble came from Ni-Cio, "If you rise, you will have to pass me, my lady. And I warn you, I do not mind seeing that you stay in that bed."

Though his tone was light, he was in earnest. Ni-Cio uncrossed his long, muscular legs and leaned forward, all pretenses aside. "You are our Most Sovereign Healer no matter your feeling. In our history, no healing has ever taken place such as you performed. Do not make light of the importance you hold for us."

Daria felt the heat rise to her cheeks and she ducked her head. Kyla rested an edge of the tray on the bedside table. "My brother is right. The sooner you get used to hearing the title, the faster you will move beyond that title. Your powers are as yet untapped. And I agree with him, you are probably the greatest Healer that Atlantis has ever seen."

Daria drew the covers up. Dazed by their assessment, she hid her shock with a change of subject and mood. "Kyla, just don't make me eat any more for a while, or the eruption of Vesuvius will look tame in comparison to what I will do."

Kyla raised her eyebrows. She gathered the tray, but her look was stern, "Very well. I will let you rest, but I will be back later. And full or not, you will eat."

Kyla headed toward the door, "It is time to see about Mer-An anyway. Aris has probably driven her into a relapse by now."

Ni-Cio chuckled, "No doubt."

Kyla left and the door re-materialized. Daria sighed and closed her eyes. She couldn't remember ever feeling so drained. Ni-Cio rose to join her. He settled beside her and took her in his arms. Daria snuggled onto his broad chest and inhaled the pure scent of him. "It will be all right, my love. You will regain all of your strength and more. Just be patient."

Ni-Cio held her and stroked her hair, and Daria's mind drifted. She thought about Na-Kai and all she had learned under her love and guidance. She didn't want to think about their last conversation, but somewhere in that final exchange was the perception of a significant warning. Something tugged at the back of her mind, but she was too tired to exert the effort needed to remember.

She floated on the edge of sleep and her mind filled with random thoughts. It occurred to her that when she had consumed the meal Kyla had prepared, she had forgotten to take any of Travlor's potion.

She stirred and took Ni-Cio's hand. Aimless thoughts tried to coalesce...Travlor...the warning...something about the potion...a thought-form... nausea.... "Oh my God!"

Ni-Cio sat bolt upright. "Daria! What? What is it?"

She grasped his hands and tried to rise. She shook so much that she collapsed against his shoulder. Thoughts, like bolts of lightning, burst through Ni-Cio's mind. *"Travlor! Ni-Cio, he was trying to poison me...Na-Kai discovered the poison when she transferred her energy...her thought-form no longer binds him, and I don't have the strength!"*

Daria could tell that Ni-Cio wanted to ease her sense of alarm by the care with which he settled her back onto the pillows. He hesitated as he took his arms from around her. She was frightened by the suppressed reassurance in his voice, for she could see his fury rise. "Sleep. I will take care of Travlor."

Ni-Cio crossed the room, and before the door materialized behind him, Daria heard his frantic thoughts summon Aris. *"Gather some men and meet me at Travlor's!"*

CHAPTER
32

*I*nside one of the lesser used exit portals, Travlor paced back and forth like a caged jungle cat. He waited for his son to surface. With each about-face, his stride accelerated, but his steps became more skittish. Heightened anticipation churned through his insides and he could smell the anxiety that poured from him, like a stench. His thoughts thundered with concussive force, *"If I am caught, any chance of leaving this underwater mausoleum will be over! I will meet Death with measured finality!*

"Even now, Ni-Cio and Aris have entered the main corridor leading to my chambers! An amassed group follows! The seconds tick, tick, tick, out of my grasp! I cannot concentrate! Focus! I must focus!"

An endless rage threatened to vomit from him. He clung to the fibers of his slowly shredding mind with frightening tenacity, "The light! It is there! I am free!" His thoughts spewed into Evan, *"You are almost here...I see a brightening of the tunnel walls...hurry! You must hurry!"*

The *Oceanus* crawled toward the pool entrance like a soldier navigating a minefield. So great was Evan's concentration, he barely heard the violent thought-forms that hammered his mind. The tunnel allowed no leeway for error, and at this depth, if the *Oceanus* were to spring a leak, thousands of pounds of water pressure would crush him with the same nonchalant disregard that an insect is squashed underfoot.

The black water took on a lighter cast and he knew that the entrance was near. After what seemed like an eternity, the submersible cleared the tunnel. Evan started a slow ascent. He tried to regulate his breathing and failed miserably. However, as a scientist, he was amazed how quickly he began to hyperventilate. He forced himself to calm down.

The *Oceanus* broke the surface and seawater streamed, like tears, over the bowed windows. Evan caught distorted glimpses of a solitary figure at the edge of the pool and he realized that he was afraid to open the door. The unknown would be made known, and the events that Travlor had set into motion would play out with implacable certainty. Unable to move, Evan felt the craft drift under its own volition until it bumped against a tiled edge.

The submersible slanted crazily to starboard with the impact of Travlor's body. The man clung like a leech while one fist frantically pounded the hatch. Evan heard the scrape of his metallic voice even over the engine noise, "Open it!"

The *Oceanus* rocked with such violence that waves splashed onto the dock and splattered the walls with black. The urge to turn around and leave almost won out, but the need to help Daria steadied Evan's hands. He reached to unfasten the hatch.

Travlor lurched into the submarine, catching his robes on the instrument panel. He heaved himself into the seat, yanked at the cloth as though offended by the grasp of instrumentation and turned to face Evan.

Evan was speechless. He looked upon the man that had fathered him for the first time in his life. The resemblance, although uncanny, still exposed their differences. They scrutinized one another until Travlor broke the silence.

"I...see traces of...your mother."

Evan's mouth was dry as dust. He swallowed hard to ease the passage of words. "How would you even know?"

The moment shattered.

Travlor relinquished his stare, "We leave, now!" He signaled the portal entrance. "It will not be long before a sweep of Atlantis is initiated."

Travlor's voice grated on Evan's frayed nerves. He knew that he had lost control of the situation, but he didn't balk, "What about Daria? Where is she?"

Travlor shifted in his seat and nailed Evan with a narrow glare. He seemed to consider his response, "They hold her against her will. If you do not get us out of here now, there will be nothing we can do!"

A whirlwind of emotion charged through Evan, hindering his ability to reason. He didn't want to trust this man he grudgingly accepted as his father, yet he couldn't think of another alternative. Against his better judgment, he swung the craft around. He adjusted the controls and took a deep breath.

Evan glanced surreptitiously at his father. What he saw made his blood run cold. The *Oceanus VI* plunged back into the onyx maze.

CHAPTER
33

"*He is not in there…I feel no trace of him!*"
The group of fifteen men gathered around Ni-Cio to force their way into Travlor's abandoned chambers, and under the onslaught of their combined energies, the door dissolved. They crowded into the darkened chamber.

Ni-Cio scanned the premises, but nothing moved, and even the air suggested an unused staleness.

Aris walked farther into the room and sniffed, "Do you smell that?"

Ni-Cio pushed by him and entered the kitchen area. The men followed, and as the lights came up, shadows scurried, like rats, into the corners. On a large stone table isolated in the center of the room there was a jumble of cooking instruments. A cloying smell assaulted Ni-Cio's nostrils.

A thick glass bottle lay on its side as though it had been knocked over in haste. The liquid contents dripped from the narrow mouth and oozed over the table in an ever-widening stain. Ni-Cio dipped a forefinger into the concoction and brought the oily residue to his nose. His eyes watered and he jerked his head away, "By the gods, this is Sacred Datura! Aris, if this was in the potion he gave to Daria, he truly intended to kill her!"

He signaled his friends, "Rogert, take Ennael and go to Daria. Guard her with your lives. Half of you follow Aris, the rest of you come with me. Search every room and every turn in Atlantis. This madman must be stopped!"

Thought-forms flashed throughout the community. Ni-Cio and his men sprinted through the tunnels and people catapulted into the corridors to help search for a person who for ages had barely merited a passing thought.

Ni-Cio and Aris led their men toward a fork in a passageway. They each took a different corridor. Ni-Cio careened onto the left path with his men on his heels. His thoughts swirled through his companions, *"Aris, take your men and start at the north exits...we will take the southern routes...count the biospheres...we need to know if any are missing...if he has taken a 'sphere, we will be able to track him!"*

The sounds of their racing footsteps faded down the opposite tunnel.

Urgency mounted and the hunt intensified. Still, no trace of Travlor could be found. Thought-forms poured into Ni-Cio as area after area was searched to no avail.

"Council Hall secure..."

"Nothing in the Great Hall..."

"Nobody in the kitchens..."

Ni-Cio and his group inspected the southern exits and accounted for all of the biospheres. He knew that Aris's cadre mirrored their actions in the northern exits. It was as though Travlor had been swallowed by the sea. Ni-Cio was baffled, and his men gathered around him while he queried Rogert. *"Rogert, are Daria and Kyla all right?"*

"They are fine...do not trouble yourself..."

Ni-Cio thought for a moment, looked at his men and contacted their Council Leader, *"Marik, are you in Council?"*

"I am here, Ni-Cio..."

"Aris, are you through?"

"Done and nothing is missing, Ni-Cio...not even a towel..."

Ni-Cio made his decision, *"All right…everyone convene in the Council Hall…immediately!"*

He led his men through the corridors at a dead run. They raced into the Council Hall just as men and women spilled into the room from every portal. The Council of Ten was seated upon the dais and Marik stood at the edge of the stage, ready to take action.

People converged upon Ni-Cio and bombarded him with questions. Information, everyone needed more information. Marik held his arms up in a bid for silence. "Ni-Cio, I cede the floor. Speak so that we might better understand what has transpired."

Ni-Cio swiped the damp hair from his face and strode to the podium. He leapt up the stairs and gripped the sides of the rostrum as if he had his hands around Travlor's neck, "Travlor has escaped."

The Hall echoed with the ferocity of his statement. Questions erupted, but Ni-Cio shouted above the noise and people settled. "We cannot figure how he escaped. Every biosphere is present, and a thorough scan was made of all the exits, as well as of every chamber small enough to hold a seahorse. We can find no trace." Ni-Cio paused. "We found Sacred Datura in Travlor's quarters. He tried to poison Daria so that when Na-Kai transcended, he could leave Atlantis at will."

Pandemonium broke out. Ni-Cio knew that no one could understand the depths to which Travlor had fallen. The shock of such depravity in their midst could be seen in the sickly green and yellow colors that swirled over the features of his friends.

The commotion would have continued except that Aris made himself heard over the noise, "What do you want us to do, Ni-Cio?"

Ni-Cio looked at Marik, and once the Council Leader signaled for him to proceed, he shared his plan. "We must treat this man with utmost care and caution. He is extremely dangerous and he will to do anything in order to achieve the goals he has set forth. You can put it to vote, Marik, but I think it is imperative that we find him. I suggest a search outside of Atlantis. He must be apprehended and brought back."

Marik nodded and took a rapid survey. The vote was unanimous. The Council Leader turned his black gaze toward Ni-Cio. "Take whom you will, Ni-Cio. Find Travlor and bring him back. This time, he *will* face retribution!"

CHAPTER
34

A quick count, and Ni-Cio knew he had more than enough volunteers. "Aris, you take the swimmers. Break into pairs and head for the exits."

Everyone chose a partner while Ni-Cio pulled his friend aside, "Take only the fastest swimmers. The rest can use biospheres."

Aris nodded and motioned to the men and women who were to follow him. He walked toward one of the portals and stopped. "There are fifty exits, but remember, once out of Atlantis, it's a systematic search. Scan quickly but be thorough. We have no idea what he is up to or where he might have gone." Aris glanced at Ni-Cio, "Ready."

Ni-Cio stepped in front of the teams of swimmers, "Be on your guard. I cannot stress this enough. If you find Travlor, do not try to take him yourself. Summon others. He is desperate enough to try anything. His energy wanes, but he is still stronger than most of us. Not one of us has ever faced a threat such as this."

Varying shades of red showed the grim determination housed in every heart.

"Very well. Remember, have a care for yourselves and each other."

He gestured a heartfelt goodbye and watched Aris lead his cadre out of the west portal. Ni-Cio addressed his remaining group, "This is how we will break out, two to a biosphere, one biosphere for each exit. I think Travlor is making his way topside. However, there are so many small islands that rest in our ocean, it is anyone's guess as to where he is headed."

He reached into the sash that surrounded his robe and pulled out a clear, wafer-thin marinus. He initiated the device with a quick thought. A three-dimensional map unfolded and soared into the air. Islands closest to Atlantis were highlighted in a yellow bioluminescent glow. People moved closer for a better look.

Ni-Cio enlarged the scene until everyone was encased in a nautical map of their underwater world. He structured the map to indicate orientation. The marinus twirled about and came to rest as it floated in midair. Views of the headings needed to reach the nearest islands were available in fly-by mode or in a stationary overlook.

Ni-Cio showed each team their exit and the island that was their destination. He held up his marinus, "Imprint your course."

A shuffling of robes was heard as Atlanteans extracted their devices. As fast as thought, their nav-systems were imprinted with the course and heading specific to each team. Ni-Cio looked over his group, "Our time grows short, so I only have this left to say. If you have not found Travlor by the time you have reached your assigned island, do not go topside. I cannot make myself clear enough on this point. Even if you see Travlor's body leaving the water as you are pulling up, do not attempt a topside excursion. Without knowledge of Terran ways, it would only lead to events I am not prepared to sanction. Look sharp and be wary. I want nothing more than to have Travlor back, but not at the expense of anyone here."

He sighed and again gave the gesture for a heartfelt goodbye.

Atlanteans raced to their biospheres. All hoped that a hasty conclusion could be reached with the apprehension of someone they no longer recognized as one of their own.

Ni-Cio, with his partner, Peltor, arrived at their appointed exit. Ni-Cio's thoughts found Daria, *"Love, are you all right?"*

A quiet return, *"I am well...look to yourself, Ni-Cio...I need you back..."*

Ni-Cio shrugged out of his robe. His bioskin sent shimmers of light cascading across the floor. He crossed to the pool and bent down next to a biosphere. *"Fear not, sweetest...I am back before you know I am gone..."* His muscles tensed and flexed as he and Peltor pushed the transport off the deck and into the dark water.

A return sighed through his mind, *"My heart already knows your absence..."*

Ni-Cio lowered himself into the biosphere and waited for his companion to settle behind him. He allowed himself one last reply before the mission engaged his full concentration, *"Until I am with you again, let your heart know this..."*

Daria's worries were forgotten when a thought-touch such as she had never known swirled into her heart. The radiance of Ni-Cio's love suffused her entire being until she felt she would burst with joy. She gasped and touched her heart, "I can feel him, Kyla. He is here with me."

A look of deep longing played across Kyla's lovely face. She sat on the bed next to Daria. "And it will always be thus between the two of you, Daria. That is the magic of love."

Daria reached for Kyla's hand. She recognized her friend's solitary yearning and she ached to ease her loneliness. "Kyla, I know your heart. Believe me when I say, it will happen for you too."

Kyla shrugged and she pulled her hand away. "You are right. Love comes in its own time and not a moment sooner."

She stood to leave, but Daria stayed her departure. "I probably shouldn't share this with you, but just as I know the color of your beautiful topaz eyes, I know that love approaches you. And it comes from a most unexpected source. Now, don't ask me who, what, where or when, because I'm a little fuzzy on those details myself." Daria laughed to cover her embarrassment and joked to soften the mood, "So, how do you like that for some down-home fortune telling?"

Kyla stood immobile for several moments, and with a look of wonder, she cocked her head and put her hands on her hips, "Is there no end to your talents?"

Daria lowered her gaze and plucked at an imaginary string on her bioskin, "I don't know what you're talking about."

Kyla plopped back onto the bed, "Daria, not every Healer is also able to foretell the future. After Kai-Dan, only two others illuminate my remembrance, and one of them had sporadic abilities at best."

Daria frowned and she sifted through her own memories. "I've no recollection of any premonitions before the age of five. But now that I think about it, after my parents died, well, I began to sense things. I just thought it was the loneliness. Maybe Atlantis has enhanced this ability."

Kyla shook her head and stood. She plumped some of Daria's pillows. "Maybe so. Nevertheless, it is time for you to rest. Rogert and Ennael are outside your door. Should you need anything, let them know, otherwise, I will be back in a few hours."

"Oh, no more food, please." Daria thumped her tummy, "I sound like a small watermelon." She yawned and rubbed her eyes. Nestling deeper under the covers, she turned onto her side to face the waterwall. "Kyla, have you ever seen anything in the waterwall?"

Kyla's answer was soft and low as she started out of the room. "No, my wondrous friend, and I doubt that I ever will."

The lights dimmed, and Daria felt herself carried to sleep on the waves of Ni-Cio's love.

CHAPTER
35

"Can you not make this pathetic excuse for transport proceed at a faster pace?"

Evan was disgusted. The corners of his mouth turned down in a deep scowl. The scrape of fingernails on a chalk board would be more preferable than the voice that issued from the person seated next to him. He sneered and baited his reply, "If you would like to take a swim, be my guest. I can't push this machine past her limits, or neither of us will see daylight."

Travlor spun around. Malevolence glared from his eyes and his words were infused with venom, "I am unable to swim anymore and a biosphere can be tracked. That was why I needed your assistance to get out of that wretched death cave. I grow older with each passing moment. The few abilities I had before Na-Kai entrapped me have deserted me as surely as your mother did."

A lump rose in Evan's throat. Years of loneliness bled through the old wound that Travlor had just laid bare. Evan tried to inflict just as much pain. "Maybe she would still be here had you not left her. I understand that you were nowhere around when I was born. She had no one else, Travlor. She was totally alone and in incredible pain when she died. I would be more inclined to believe *you* were the one who deserted *her!*"

The grip that clamped down on Evan's wrist was like steel. Evan yanked his arm but could not break the hold. He twisted to face the Atlantean and found himself looking into the merciless stare of shark-black eyes. "Enough! You know *nothing* of the circumstances. Son or not, if you ever dare speak of this again..." With one swift breath, Travlor released Evan's wrist. "Get us to Santorini, or your precious topsider will never see the light of day."

Evan was mortified to feel a tremor run through his hands when he re-gripped the steering mechanism. He struggled to regain his composure, so he took a deep, slow breath and stared off into the gloom. He trusted the computer to adjust their course heading.

The exodus from Atlantis was dazzling. Ni-Cio and Peltor watched swimmers burst from the exits like shooting stars. In their wake, streams of bioluminescence lit up the ocean deep like a shower of comets, and Ni-Cio knew that Aris's team would not leave one chasm, one crevice or one stone undisturbed. He looked over his shoulder at his companion. "Peltor, if Travlor could execute the poisoning of our Most Sovereign Healer, then he is capable of anything. The importance of finding this man is tantamount to surviving the sinking. If Travlor is left unchecked, I fear that this aberration could bring about our demise, swiftly and unmercifully."

Peltor squeezed Ni-Cio's shoulder, "We will find him. Aris's swimmers are scouring the area, and if Travlor is there, they will catch him as they cast their ever-widening net. Come, the others are leaving, let us depart as well."

Ni-Cio felt a small measure of encouragement, and as the occupants of the other biospheres deployed from their exits at velocities that mocked Terran laws of physics, Ni-Cio urged their craft toward their targeted island.

The search broadened, but it was clear to Ni-Cio that Travlor had gotten farther than anyone imagined. Still, he refused to admit that Travlor had somehow made good his flight.

Their biosphere raced through the deep and he and Peltor combined their energies to enable a wider sweep of the areas they covered. After passing through several miles of open ocean, Peltor broke the silence, "I feel nothing, Ni-Cio."

Ni-Cio did not deviate from the heading, but he was momentarily puzzled as to what they would do if Travlor were not found. He clenched his jaw and forced his awareness even farther, "We will find him. Do not let your thoughts falter. Hold suspect even the smallest movement that does not fit the regular oceanic patterns."

"But, Ni-Cio, we are closing on Santorini. The traffic will increase. How are we to determine if Travlor is among those vessels?"

"That question bothers me as well, Peltor. Travlor is adept at masking his presence, which is all the more reason that we find him before he comes into contact with others. I do not know how he could have come this far without the aid of a biosphere, and yet, none were missing."

People began reaching their assigned islands and their reports trickled into Ni-Cio's thoughts.

"Milos is in sight...nothing..."

"We have reached Crete...just regular marine travel, no sign of Travlor..."

"Talus and I thought we saw something, but it was just a local dive team...we are still heading to our destination..."

"Investigated an unusual vibrational pattern...just a personal submersible, still heading to Anafi..."

"Turning back...nothing at Karpathos..."

And on it went. No one had sighted the elusive target. Ni-Cio was well aware that the probability of finding Travlor plummeted with each negative report. It seemed that Travlor was nowhere to be found. Most of the teams had circled their destinations and were adjusting their headings for the return to Atlantis.

Unwilling to admit defeat, Ni-Cio decided to take one more look around Santorini. *"We will circle the island once more, and then we will meet everyone back home…"*

As he trained the biosphere to retrace their previous path, Ni-Cio kept focusing on viable alternatives that would explain how Travlor got out of Atlantis. He knew Peltor was beginning to feel badgered, but he was desperate. "Who had Anafi?"

"Ylno."

Ni-Cio sent a tentative thought-form. *"Ylno, you said you saw a submersible…how many people were in it?"*

The answer came immediately. *"We felt some vibrations that were outside our course heading and decided to investigate…one person was manning the craft…we saw nothing out of the ordinary, so we turned back to Anafi…"*

"How far off course did you go?"

"About 15 degrees northwest of our heading to Anafi…"

"Are you certain of only one man in the craft?"

"It was a very small vehicle and we made a quick sweep, but the inside was exposed because of the domed windows…there were seats enough to contain two riders, but only one was occupied…"

Peltor broke in. "What are you thinking, Ni-Cio?"

"I cannot stop wondering how Travlor was able to leave. It is almost as if he had help."

"Do you want to try to find this submersible?"

It was the opening he had waited for, "It cannot hurt, and we have found nothing here." He turned the craft, and the biosphere ventured once more into the open water.

182

Evan came to the uncomfortable realization that he and Travlor had veered off course. They had been so engrossed in scouring the ocean for pursuers that he had been oblivious to the navigational error. Evan would rather have jumped out of the submersible than give Travlor the news. He cleared his throat, "We missed Santorini."

Like the claws of an angry cat, Travlor's question raked the silence, "How can that be?"

"I'll have it corrected in a moment." Evan's hands flew over the instrument panel and he made the necessary changes. The *Oceanus* responded to the new coordinates and adjusted accordingly. "It won't be long before we reach port."

"I sincerely hope you are right. The longer you expose us to the open ocean, the more rapidly our chances of evading capture decrease."

They stared through the thick, bowed window into the murky blue. Hardly daring to breathe, Evan and Travlor waited in the gloom while their craft trudged toward Santorini.

$\mathscr{C}$HAPTER
36

$\mathcal{I}$nside the biosphere, Peltor and Ni-Cio suspended any unnecessary motion. They strained to feel the slightest mechanical vibration. The vast quantity of water they had moved through before with such ease now seemed an impenetrable wall. Their senses swept through crystal seas only to be met by an implacable silence.

Ni-Cio held the craft steady at one-quarter speed. Peltor had agreed that it was better to proceed with care and deliberation rather than risk missing the submersible through haste. At two hundred feet, the biosphere cruised in utter silence. If the submersible surfaced, they would be able to detect the vibrations through the surface chop. Any deeper, however, and the likelihood of missing the small submarine increased.

Ni-Cio knew that their chances of locating the vessel were slim, but he was compelled to try. He wanted to see the submersible with his own eyes. Something about it bothered him, and it had given rise to a nagging suspicion.

In a craft that traversed the oceans as silent as nightfall and as invisible as a breeze, heightened waves of awareness spanned out, and Ni-Cio and Peltor narrowed the search.

Evan was lulled into a trancelike state. Endless vistas of blue whispered past the domed windows. He had put Travlor out of his mind until the repellent sound of his voice slithered toward him like a snake.

"How much longer?"

Travlor's unnerving vocal dissonance replaced the steady mechanical hum of the engine and jolted him back to reality. The weighted question sank into his psyche as though a line had been cast and the hook waited to snag him without compunction. Evan studied the computer screen, wishing that willpower alone would already have them docked. Shocked at the vehemence with which he wished to be rid of his father, he knew that any answer short of "We're here," was not what Travlor wanted. So, he ignored the implied threat and ventured an educated guess, "We should reach the mouth of the harbor within the next eleven minutes."

Swirls of light mixed the sapphire water to turquoise, and an array of coral curled over the ocean floor. Acrobatic reef fish darted past their window in bright splashes of neon. Evan prayed for the floor to rise faster. He heard Travlor mutter under his breath, "Not good enough. No, not good enough."

His father turned to stare back into the deep. Travlor began to rub his hands together, vigorously, as though he was scrubbing for surgery. "I am extremely uncomfortable. We are no longer alone." He glared at Evan and demanded, "Faster. You must go faster!"

An irregular flutter skimmed the outer parameters of his awareness. Ni-Cio slowed the biosphere and waited. He sensed nothing out of the ordinary and although he thought to dismiss the perception, he coasted the biosphere to a stop. "Did you feel anything, Peltor?"

His companion was motionless for a few moments, "No."

Ni-Cio jerked his chin, "To the left, as far out as you can go."

The biosphere floated in neutral buoyancy and Ni-Cio and Peltor suspended their breath. They listened. Nothing. Seconds slipped by.

At last, Ni-Cio shrugged and glanced over his shoulder to address his companion when Peltor grabbed his shoulder and pointed. "There. Ni-Cio, I felt it!"

As one, they willed the craft to speed. The biosphere ripped through the great sea as easily as water passes through a sieve and the closer they came to the target, the stronger the vibrations became.

Excitement climbed. Ni-Cio tensed for the encounter, "It has to be the submersible."

"They have found us...no matter what you see or do not see, act as though nothing is amiss...you must convey that you are a man alone...if we are apprehended, you will never save Daria!"

Although Evan no longer trusted Travlor's motivation, he didn't question the fact that Travlor had detected the presence of the Atlanteans. He had always known that he and his father possessed unusual abilities. However, when he no longer sensed the man next to him, he couldn't hide his astonishment.

He swiped his palms down the legs of his pants, adjusted himself in his seat, and re-gripped the handles of the steering column. Worried that even a replied thought-form would alert their pursuers, Evan fixed his concentration upon their destination.

He began his approach into the harbor. A strange current buffeted the craft. Evan strained to catch a glimpse of the Atlanteans. When the alien vessel crossed his line of sight, he perceived a slight distortion in the water. As they passed, the *Oceanus* rocked, just slightly.

Fear rose like bile, and Evan was struck dumb by the mastery the Atlanteans wielded over their vast domain. It was obvious that their technological capabilities far outstripped anything available to him. It had been one thing to sail into Atlantis, oblivious of such odds. But witnessing the miracle of their science, Evan knew that he could never penetrate their midst again. He felt as though he had been punched in the stomach. He had missed the only chance he would ever have of helping Daria.

He fought to still his mind, but sweat poured off him. It wasn't possible to win against a race such as this. Evan was seized by a sudden impulse, he would throw open the door and surrender. His fingers inched toward the hatch. He grappled with his fear and forced himself to continue their ascent.

At last, the small craft entered the welcoming arms of the harbor, and as they breached the surface, moonlight flooded the *Oceanus*. Choppy waves splashed against the vehicle and Evan slowed his speed. He directed his craft to the waiting docks and did his utmost to block everything else from his mind.

"Something is not right." As Ni-Cio rounded the front of the submersible, persistence made him impatient.

Peltor let loose with an exaggerated sigh, "I have lost count of how many times we have circled, and I see nothing out of the ordinary."

Ni-Cio knew he was being stubborn, yet he could not help himself. "The man inside is afraid. His fear flows from him in waves. Why would that be?"

"I truly do not know. Maybe he had a mechanical malfunction and feared for his life."

Ni-Cio shook his head and his hair swished against his bioskin. "If that were true, he would have radioed a distress signal, which we would have heard. He has reached the surface and, it seems to me, his fear increases."

"Well, what would you do? He is about to dock."

"I would study him until his departure from the craft." Ni-Cio knew that Peltor had resigned himself to this last bit of surveillance, but he felt that his companion was about ready to give up. "It will not be much longer, Peltor. You have my word, we leave as soon as that topsider steps from the vehicle."

The biosphere hovered just below the surface, but as the submersible started to dock, Ni-Cio eased their craft into a position that allowed a better view. They waited, yet nothing happened. Peltor fidgeted. "Why does he just sit there?"

"I do not know."

"Ni-Cio, this becomes ridiculous. Obviously, the topsider's actions are incomprehensible to us. Why do we continue to watch him?"

Ni-Cio was just as baffled by the topsider's behavior. Nevertheless, he was not ready to leave. "He strikes a chord of recognition that I cannot quite grasp and because his comportment is so strange, I think we should see this through. Surely he cannot sit much longer."

Peltor's stomach rumbled. "Who knows what these topsiders are capable of? I am more than ready for a hot meal, but you are right. We do nothing until we are satisfied with the outcome of this watch. I just hope they will keep the food hot for our return."

Inside the cramped quarters of the *Oceanus*, Evan had suppressed the compulsion to throw himself on the mercy of the Atlanteans. However, his muscles had stiffened so that normal movement was impossible. With jerky, disjointed motions, he entered the shutdown sequence, but he had to repeat most of his actions because his fingers fumbled the wrong buttons or failed to turn the correct switch.

When he had finally turned off all the systems, he was surprised by the hard rasp of his ragged breaths. He wasn't certain what he was supposed to do. There had not been a hint of movement from Travlor. Because the Atlanteans watched and waited just below the *Oceanus*, he was reluctant to vacate the security of the craft. He reasoned that if he could outwait them, they might possibly lose interest and leave.

Without warning, Evan was overcome by such an intense feeling of claustrophobia that he could not suffer the vehicle a moment longer. He frantically undogged the hatch and almost ripped the door from its hinges. He gulped a huge lungful of fresh air and bolted from the *Oceanus*. He lurched over the floats, stumbled and fell to the dock on all fours. He skinned his hands and banged both knees. Evan groaned and lowered his head to the wooden planks. His body shook. No longer able contain his anger or his fear or his food, Evan retched until he had nothing left.

Ni-Cio and Peltor watched in amazement as the topsider fell to his side and lay motionless. Even from their vantage point, they could see the greenish pallor of his skin.

"Why, he is seasick, Ni-Cio. He endeavored to make land so that he could exit the vehicle before he became sick." Peltor chuckled and slapped Ni-Cio on the back.

Relieved, Ni-Cio joined in the joke. He smiled. "Now we can return home and share the story of how we trailed a hapless topsider through miles of open ocean so that we could witness this, this spectacle! The sheer lunacy with which our search has ended should be well received by an appreciative audience. I am weary, Peltor, let us leave."

Ni-Cio steered the biosphere through a long, sweeping turn. Before he headed out to sea, he looked back at his friend. "I do not suppose I can convince you to keep this to yourself?"

His companion never had the chance to reply.

"Peltor, look!" Ni-Cio brought the biosphere back around. The *Oceanus* had begun to pitch back and forth, even as Evan remained face down on the dock. "Peltor, there are no waves to cause such a violent motion."

His friend was silent.

Gripped by an invisible force, the topsider was wrenched to his feet and half carried, half dragged from the rickety pier. The biosphere shook as Ni-Cio disgorged his rage and frustration into one word, "Travlor!"

CHAPTER
37

Jagged black streaks stippled Ni-Cio's skin. He willed the biosphere to advance. Peltor knew the fury that blazed inside his friend, but when he discerned his intent he broke into the charged silence. "Ni-Cio, we cannot follow them. You were adamant when you gave the order not to go topside. It was wise to issue that mandate and we would do well to abide by it."

Ni-Cio's voice was hoarse with suppressed rage. He pointed at the *Oceanus,* and Peltor could see that his fingers trembled. "We almost had him, Peltor. By the gods, he was right there! Even now, we can take him!"

Peltor placed a hand on shoulders wound tighter than springs, and he tried to inject some measure of calm. "Ni-Cio, no. We must go back and inform the others. We know which island he is on. It is only right to inform the High Council and determine what course of action we must initiate, if any."

Ni-Cio gasped, and his voice was thick with wrath, "He nearly killed the woman I love more than life itself!"

Peltor dared not utter another word. Wisely he waited for Ni-Cio's anguish to subside. Ni-Cio swung his gaze back toward the empty docks, and the menace that filled his next words made Peltor quake. "It is not over between us, Travlor. I swear by all the gods, you will face retribution, and it will be in this lifetime!"

Ni-Cio slammed the biosphere forward and jetted from the harbor at tremendous speed. Peltor glanced over his shoulder and saw that the sudden displacement of water had caused a dark swell to lift from the becalmed sea. A rogue wave raced shoreward and flared to batter angrily against the vacant docks.

"I can walk." Evan yanked his body from Travlor's grasp. He felt disgusted by the physical contact and wiped his hands over his shirt. He heard his father sniff.

"It would not seem so."

Evan walked to the rental car. His lone shadow played over the pavement, but he noticed that Travlor gradually relaxed his camouflage. Color leached into his body like fluid poured into a glass.

Once Travlor became more visible, Evan saw no hint of the enormity of years that hung upon him. His equal in height, Travlor walked with purpose and vigor. His angular build, just this side of thin, suggested a hidden power that could explode at will. Evan considered his coloring just a hue below normal, however, it was not enough to attract undue attention. His shoulder-length hair reminded Evan of iron filings left too long in the dust, with illusions of black surreptitiously appearing among the gray. The man exuded such an air of superiority that Evan regarded him with careful awe. He struggled against the terrible spell that Travlor inspired and countered with a quick verbal jab. "I thought you didn't want to be found. Jumping out of the submersible and grabbing me isn't what I would call circumspect."

Travlor stopped. He turned to stare at Evan and his reply dripped with sarcasm. "I find that you irritate me. It is because of your lack of concentration that they were able to locate the submarine. Obviously, they suspected something, or they would not have bothered. I have been controlled by Atlantis for far too long to put up with any more waiting games." He took Evan's arm and urged him forward. "As the point is moot, let us find rest. We have much to accomplish in order to meet the goals I have laid forth."

They reached the car and Evan opened the passenger door. Travlor slid onto the seat. A sound assaulted Evan's ears that might have been a laugh, but sounded more like a screech, "Besides, they would never have come on land. They are ignorant of Terran ways and would stand out like sore thumbs."

Evan felt like a scared child. He slammed the car door to block the sound of Travlor's gloating and let his gaze wander over the moon-dappled landscape. He took his time. He needed a moment before he slid next to Travlor again. He sighed, "Daria, somehow I will find a way to help you."

He shook his head and let that thought create the impetus he needed. He rounded the car, opened the door and lowered himself onto the seat. He inserted the key, but before he started the engine, he turned and directed his attention to the stranger who was his father. He leaned forward and rested his arms on the steering wheel. "I realize you have your goals and you know that I'm willing to help. But you have to understand, if they are holding Daria against her will, it is imperative that we get her out as soon as possible."

He saw steel in the profile outlined from the glow of the interior lights and continued, "I don't want her down there any longer than necessary. God only knows what they will do to her."

"Do not trouble yourself about the topsider. She figures largely into my plans. I will not rest until her release." Travlor blinked like a sun sleepy reptile and with a weary sigh, sank back into the leather seat. He did not deign to look at Evan.

The words did nothing to assuage Evan's fears. But at this juncture, he knew that he had no choice. He had to follow Travlor down the path that was beginning to unwind. Like thunderheads cresting over a blackened horizon, the premonition of disaster he had suppressed until now began its slow, ominous build.

CHAPTER
38

Ni-Cio and Peltor burst into the subdued hall. The other teams had convened to await their arrival and had been fed. Everyone was tired and wanted to go to their families, but Ni-Cio and Peltor needed to refresh themselves and they did not turn down the food that was offered. Seated at a table, Ni-Cio could tell that the mood was somber almost to the point of defeat. The reddish hues on Peltor's face reflected his own agitation, but he listened as Marik stood to address the assembly.

"First, I congratulate all of you. The search was conducted very well."

Ni-Cio knew that the Council Leader was trying to buoy their disappointment. However, since Marik elicited no response from anyone, he continued, "I must remind you that nothing like this has ever occurred during your lifetime. Do not be so hard on yourselves, especially you, Ni-Cio. We had no reason to suspect that Travlor was capable of such actions. That you acted so quickly gave us the only chance we had of capturing him." Still no response. Marik shrugged his shoulders and lifted his hands, palms up. "We know where he is. That is extremely favorable."

Rogert, ever the pragmatist, rose. "What are we to do about it? We cannot go topside. We would never be able to blend, no matter the subterfuge."

Aris spoke up, "We cannot monitor him because he hides his thoughts."

Peltor looked up from his plate, "Only the gods know what he is up to."

Detesting his people's general feeling of helplessness, Marik tried to elevate the mood. "We may not need to know his intentions. That he has fled Atlantis would lead me to believe he is glad to be rid of us. It could be that we will never encounter him again."

Ni-Cio thrust his plate aside and stood, his chair clattering against the stone floor. He scanned the room. His anger found voice, "That is a naïve presumption! Does anyone truly feel that Travlor poses no more threat to us?"

He walked to the dais and turned to face the tired teams. "Because of his obsessive need to leave Atlantis, the man very nearly killed Daria. We lost Na-Kai too early and yes, Travlor hides his thoughts, but somehow, he has found an ally who was able to breach Atlantis and help him escape. If we do not concern ourselves with this matter, I feel there will be grave repercussions. It is a matter of such import that none of us should rest until we have apprehended this monster. And damn the consequences of going topside!"

Cries of assent clamored against the protests.

Ni-Cio waited for quiet. "I know that events seem as though they have spiraled out of control, and that the tranquility with which we have lived unravels. But it is the first time in living memory that we, as a people, have had anything to fear."

Marik flushed striations of blue. The truth of Ni-Cio's words could not be denied. "What do you propose?"

Before Ni-Cio could respond, Kyla entered the western portal, Daria by her side. She still looked quite fragile and she clung to Kyla's arm for support, but she carried herself with an imposing air. Her confidence in her position and her feeling of belonging was beginning to manifest itself.

Kyla walked slowly, allowing Daria to catch her breath. People parted to make way. Daria's gaze swept over the crowd. Finding Ni-Cio, she smiled. Ni-Co didn't know how it was possible, but she was even more radiant than he remembered. He watched with love and admiration as Daria made her way to the base of the dais.

She faced the gathering and her apprehension was evident. The clear tones of her voice, although weak, sailed through the assembly. "Ni-Cio is correct in his assessment of Travlor. However, even he doesn't know the peril that Travlor represents. As much as I don't want to acknowledge it, I have to say that you, we, can no longer live as if nothing can touch this blessed world. If we do that and bury our heads in the sand, then all our lives are endangered."

Fear flashed across people's faces but no one spoke. They waited for their Healer to continue.

"It is highly improbable that any of you could find Travlor and bring him back to Atlantis without topsiders becoming aware of your existence. You cannot hope to walk topside with impunity. The colors that camouflage you so well in Poseidon's domain would be your undoing on Terros, and Travlor will stay topside until such time as he feels compelled to return."

Daria looked at Ni-Cio as though seeking his strength. He sent her a loving thought, then nodded for her to continue. She inclined her head just slightly and looked out over the Atlanteans. "You have been surrounded by such peace that Travlor's nature is probably incomprehensible. But he is more dangerous than you can possibly imagine. He will return, and when he does, we must be ready."

Startled reactions writhed through the Hall with the speed of a cracked bullwhip.

"Ready? What does she mean?"

"What should we do? What can we possibly do?"

"We should at least try to bring him back!"

"How has Travlor come to this? Surely he would not harm us."

"I say we get him whether or not we are discovered!"

"What is the danger of leaving well enough alone?"

"How can she know with any degree of certainty that Travlor will be back?"

Above the increasing din of questions, conjecture and panic, Kyla raised her voice and shouted, "Know this! Our Most Sovereign Healer is gifted with foreknowledge!"

Silence blanketed the room and Daria shifted, somewhat embarrassed. "I wouldn't call it foreknowledge, exactly, it's just, well, sometimes I have these feelings and as far back as I can remember, these premonitions or feelings or whatever have always served me well. But I can understand if you don't believe me."

Ni-Cio could tell that Daria had reached the edge of her strength. He hurried to her side, wrapped his arm around her waist and held her. He signaled Peltor to retrieve a chair, which Daria gratefully accepted.

Ni-Cio spoke for everyone, "You misunderstand, my love. No one doubts your ability, but you keep mystifying us with your gifts. That you have come to us at our hour of need is more than apparent." He knelt by her side and enfolded her hands with a loving touch. He pitched his voice for her only, "The meeting will conclude very soon, do you grow overly tired? If so, I will take you back to your chambers."

She stroked the side of his cheek and traced the lines at the corners of his eyes. She looked at him with concern, "I'm well enough to finish. We must come to a resolution. It's imperative."

He studied her for a moment, then nodded abruptly and stood to face his friends, "Marik, put it to vote. Travlor is a threat that must be reckoned with."

Marik surveyed the assembly and came forward to announce his decision, "To a person, all feel that Travlor poses a significant and imminent danger. However, in the minds of a few, there is lingering doubt as to whether anything could or should be done. Because these are questions that must be resolved, we will meet again on the morrow."

Marik crossed the stage and bent to address Daria, proving his high regard for her abilities. "How soon should we anticipate Travlor's return?"

"No sooner than one month. No longer than three." Her reply created an audible gasp from all that had crowded around.

The Council Leader looked stunned, but he stood and made his announcement. "We are adjourned. Go, take your rest and more needed refreshment. Look to your families. Tomorrow, be prepared to come to resolution. It is of paramount importance that we reach a decision as to how we react to this menace."

CHAPTER
39

Daria resolutely rejected Ni-Cio's offer of transport. She knew she had to continue to gain strength, and the only way to do that was to put one foot in front of the other. However, she was still weak enough that she stood between Ni-Cio and Kyla, and let them escort her back to her chambers. They strolled leisurely, but in an added effort to conserve her fragile strength, no one offered conversation.

Everyone was glad for the respite that the coming night promised. Walking toward Daria's quarters, they saw tiny pinpoints of light beginning to shine from darkened cavern ceilings. Like stars in midnight skies, they twinkled, signaling the end of a traumatic day. Moonlight fell onto walkways and a whispered sonata drifted on the night air. Their softened footfalls lent a subdued syncopation to the enchanting melody, and Daria leaned her head against Ni-Cio's arm. A sleepy hush descended upon Atlantis.

As Ni-Cio and Daria drew closer to her chambers, the unfulfilled passion between them stirred. A sensual tango of unspoken love mingled with the music of the nighttime quiet. Their heightened feelings swirled between them like the luxurious scent of warmed perfume.

Kyla laid her hand on Ni-Cio's arm when the sound of footsteps echoed off the tunnel walls. They turned at Aris's approach. A look of worry was evident on his comely face. He was a study in seriousness, "Kyla, has Mer-An received her nourishment today?"

Before Kyla could respond, Mer-An's tender, mocking laugh sighed through everyone's mind.

"Kyla has seen to my needs very well...leave her to attend Daria...all I require is you, Aris..."

The Atlantean flushed a deep rose, and traces of dark purple ringed his eyes and colored his lips. Everyone's laughter mixed, witnessing Aris's rapid need to depart at war with his elegant manners. Ni-Cio ended his dilemma. He elbowed his friend in the ribs. "Unless you intend to dine with us, I would say your ministrations are requested elsewhere."

A luminous smile spread across Aris's face and lit his dark eyes. He hesitated for a fraction of a second, winked at his friends, did an about-face and departed in such haste it seemed that he had sprouted wings. The sounds of his joyful exuberance followed him until he disappeared from sight.

Their soft laughter continued as they entered the walled gardens leading to Daria's quarters. Kyla paused, "I believe I will decline your generous invitation for dinner tonight. I am tired from the stress of the day. Daria is progressing very well and it would be better for you to spend the time together. Besides, I feel like a squeaky wheel."

Daria laughed. Kyla's misplaced attempts at interpreting topsider slang were especially endearing, "I think you mean a third wheel."

"Exactly."

Ni-Cio started to protest, but Daria interrupted. She loosened her hold on Kyla's hand and hugged her friend. "Thank you, Kyla. Take heart, your time is near."

Their gazes met and held, and Daria let the willowy Atlantean behold the truth in her eyes. Without another word, Kyla smiled at her beloved brother, kissed Daria on the cheek and took her leave. They watched until her shadow merged into night.

Daria sighed and turned to enter her chambers. Ni-Cio followed. She walked to the waterwall, ran a finger through the crystal water, and then turned to face Ni-Cio. "It's hard to be alone while those around you find love." Her heart contracted when a look of disquiet crossed Ni-Cio's features. She took a step toward him, "Do not fret, my heart. I don't think she will be alone much longer."

Daria's worries were suddenly forgotten. Passion so intense blazed into Ni-Cio's violet eyes that it ignited a response deep within her soul. Her breath deserted her. In a single stride, they met in a fierce embrace. Hungrily received into each other, their kiss was long and searching and deep. Their bodies melded together and the fire that burned between them caused any more thoughts of Kyla, of dinner, of outside threats to disappear.

The only moment that existed was the breath they shared and the world they created with their love.

CHAPTER
40

*T*he morning sun blinked a lazy eye over the watery horizon. The first tentacles of light crawled across the sleeping island, sending night shadows in search of their own repose. Through the open windows of Evan's room, filmy streaks of yellow light snuck over twisted bed covers to rest tentatively upon his tired face. In sleep, the worries that permeated his waking moments had found little relief. Dream-haunted visions prickled disjointedly through his mind and turned his restful slumber into a determined effort to keep his eyes closed.

Travlor had risen and tended to his morning ablutions, the sounds of which could be heard through the thin walls of the adjoining room.

Evan stirred and gave up any pretense of sleep. He stretched and sat up. Massaging the aching muscles of his neck, he tried to loosen the knots that dammed the flow of blood to his brain. He knew that Travlor would be full of plans and counter-plans, and he felt ill prepared to handle his schemes.

A crisp knock on his door signaled that the day had started. Feeling sluggish, Evan rose to admit the person who had swept events into his life that were entirely out of his control. It was as though he was trapped in a flood with no lifeline, no hope and no chance of rescue. Never before had he felt so helpless. His temples throbbed. He reluctantly opened the door to the man who seemed to hold his fate in clawed, gray hands. He shuddered at the mechanical rasp of Travlor's speech. It seemed to pierce his eardrums.

"You are slow to rise. Wash the sleep from your face and let us break our fast. I am famished." A wicked light glinted from hooded black eyes and the ghost of a malevolent smile flitted across cruel lips.

Evan sighed and trailed to the bathroom in an attempt to erase the indications of despair that he knew marked his face. He took three aspirins from his travel kit, filled a glass with tepid water and washed them down in one swallow. He needed a clear head, and he could not afford to succumb to physical weakness.

He showered in a burst of speed, ran an electric razor haphazardly across blond whiskers, and shrugged into a pair of jeans and a comfortable T-shirt. He located his discarded loafers and slid sockless feet into the soft brown leather. Feeling somewhat refreshed, he decided that a good breakfast would help.

Reckoning with Travlor presented an onerous challenge, and if he wallowed in self-pity and uncertainty, then he would never be able to best the alien creature that had sired him. The blood of Poseidon surged through his own veins as well, and although he had never thought much about a bloodline that hearkened back to a god, Evan was determined to utilize the time with Travlor to his utmost advantage. The way out of this Travlor-inspired nightmare was to become familiar with the enemy. And his god-forsaken father had all the knowledge he required to help him get to Daria.

He opened the bathroom door and stepped into the room. He grabbed his keys and wallet, then brushed past Travlor, "Let's move."

Evan and his father walked into the morning sunshine. Evan basked in the soft glow of first light, almost feeling that anything was possible. For a brief moment, he let himself believe in happy endings.

Ni-Cio was first to awaken, and his heart soared with love for the woman asleep next to him. Last night would forever be engraved in his memory. The love they shared had its own singular clarity that lit corners of his soul he hadn't even known were there.

He relived the sensuous, all-consuming passion that had marked their physical consummation, and he yearned to give voice to his soul's song. In his life, he had never experienced the feelings that she evoked.

He carefully withdrew his arms from beneath the weight of her, feeling the silk of Daria's skin caress his hands. Ambient beams of light glistened over the lovely contours of her body and bathed her in morning-soft radiance. Ni-Cio was loath to take his eyes from her, but he slid noiselessly from the bed.

Collecting a small, frosted-glass tablet, he padded to a nearby sofa. Deep in thought, he burrowed into the cushions. With his thoughts, the words began to flow from his mind onto the paper-thin tablet.

He heard Daria drowsily move to find his embrace. Before she could fully awaken, he sent a whispered thought, *"I am here, my love…sleep, I will rejoin you shortly…"*

A smile lifted the corners of her lips and he knew that she had flowed back into her dreams. Ni-Cio worked until, satisfied, he yawned and stretched. Rising, he placed the pad on the bedside table and slipped between the covers. He took Daria in his arms and watched the tablet begin to glow. The words of his heart rose through the dew-scented air to become etched forever upon the waterwall.

CLARITY OF A MOMENT

Simple experiences form the heart of life.
Encapsulated doses of pure joy -
that lighten the soul and steal away the thoughts that haunt us,
even for a moment.

At some point unknown and unforeseen, during a mind's unrest,
arrives the solace of these singular times.
The moments pass, bearing only revered remembrances of happiness.

These moments arrive perfectly in harmony with the soul's thirst.
And after many years pass,
remain within.

Precious parts of life, which are most sweet
when arriving amidst turmoil.
An eye of a storm, their beauty is apparent only at their core
and when remembered from a great distance.

Time separates these moments
from their surroundings
to provide clarity.
Proof that they are worth their price.

We must live for these moments,
for their existence defines us.

My love,
You have defined my life. Ni-Cio

The warmth of Daria's body enveloped him. She opened her eyes and the sacrament of their love found expression once again in ecstasy.

*E*van could see that he and Travlor made an imperious pair as they walked into the empty compound. Followed closely by an elderly Greek man whom Travlor treated more like a simpering minion than a once proud property owner, they surveyed the area.

Vacant housing stood shoulder to shoulder in bleak military precision. Evan's analytical gaze followed the succession of ruler straight rows that stood in unoccupied formation. The empty courtyard, enclosed by the single-room accommodations, formed a determined rectangular alliance against the encroaching countryside.

The Greek showed Evan and Travlor the first cottage. The old door had to be shoved open. When they were inside, the owner flipped a wall switch. A thin trickle of light spilled from the shredded shade of a lone floor lamp and the gloom pulled away from the shallow pool of light.

"This suits our needs perfectly…"

Travlor's thought coincided with his ideas, *"Agreed…"*

They found each unit to be a carbon copy of its dilapidated neighbor. The kitchenettes, which may or may not have functioned, included two small sinks, an antiquated ice box and a stove hardly big enough to cook a chicken.

In the miniscule bathrooms, one toilet, one sink and one moldy shower stall argued for their share of the cramped space.

And crammed into a dusty corner of the main room, thin, cotton-ticked mattresses sagged through the frames of rusted iron bunks.

Travlor leveled a stare at the islander and the old man flinched. "How many acres did you tell me were contained within this property?"

The Greek accent was thick as it issued brokenly from a tongue unused to the harsh English language, "I believe to be...," he hesitated and counted in Greek. His toothless smile held great pride as he raised two fingers, "Two hundred."

"Why don't you speak his tongue?"

"Because I don't want to..." Travlor turned and walked out onto the slanted porch.

While Evan waited, he tried to ignore the imploring look visible on the old Greek's face. He knew how much the sale of his property meant. Travlor's voice scoured the air, breaking their uncomfortable silence, "You indicated there was ocean access."

A moment of doubt entered the old man's rheumy eyes as he stumbled through the interpretation. He gestured for Evan to follow, and he hobbled out the door to peer at Travlor. "Yes, yes, come, I take you."

He led them out of the compound and pointed to a path that wound through a decaying vineyard where years of neglect were in sad evidence. The wizened Greek indicated more through sign language than words that he would be unable to follow. He shoved a stubby, work-hardened forefinger in the direction they were to take. "Go and go and go, you see."

Evan nodded his understanding and he and Travlor began to scramble through the choked vegetation, the vague path all but disguised by the gnarled and withered limbs of long-dead grapevines. Veined branches, like old, brown fingers, plucked at their pant legs. And Evan was sorry to see that the only green in sight was the jealous green of overgrown weeds that had long ago sucked the life from each tender, struggling vine.

At length, they came upon a windswept cliff and navigated a careful descent along an uneven trail that clung to the steep hillside with stubborn Greek tenacity. Eventually, the powder-dry path spilled them, in a swirling cloud of dust, onto a deserted, rock encrusted beach.

They picked their way to the high water mark. As they looked out over the sparkling Aegean, a stout sea wind battered their shirts and pants and caused the material to snap as smartly as flying flags. The strident cries of seagulls sounded overhead, and they had to shield their eyes against the harsh noonday sun. Birds careened effortlessly through rising thermals. Blue green waves lifted and plummeted in a relentless battle against the frayed shoreline. As Travlor turned to Evan, his weather beaten voice rose above the pounding surf, "The swells indicate a sharp decline in the sea bottom! It's perfect!"

Evan had to shout back, "When do we begin?"

"Immediately Take care of the acquisition and do not be generous. Any amount you give that relic will be more than he would ever have made. Once you have procured ownership, we begin recruitment." Travlor briskly rubbed his hands together.

Evan felt his father's exhilaration begin to wax.

"We will accomplish our first goal, soon, very soon." Travlor stared out over the open sea and raised his arms, claw-like hands flung outward. "Once that is done, there will be no one to stop us!"

Evan was sick of his gloating.

"The world is mine!" Travlor folded the fingers of one bony hand into a tight fist. His laughter climbed the scales in a screech that challenged even the shriek of the gulls.

Evan's insides churned. Revolted by the unbridled ambition of a father he wished he had never met, he attempted a more

215

complex thought-form, *"Let's get back…as you say, we have much to do…"*

Travlor ceased reveling in the glow of his unearthly vision, and his thoughts seared Evan's mind, *"I see that your abilities grow…very good, I would even say amazing…I would not have thought you could achieve this level so quickly…"*

Evan could tell that Travlor blocked his next thought with a calculated glance from behind veiled lids.

As one, they turned to begin the climb to the summit. Leery of events that had made their interdependence a necessity, Evan knew that his father was not willing to lower the barriers that would allow him to forge even the smallest bond or initiate the tiniest shred of trust. He knew, without a doubt, that he would have to watch his back.

CHAPTER
42

*I*n the underwater conservatory, Aris and Mer-An could see that breakfast had become a silent and hurried affair. There was none of the usual bonhomie that typified the beginning of a new day. Beyond the invisible domed barrier that separated air and ocean, fish darted in shimmering bursts of color, while plants, subject to the mercurial mood of the changing currents, swirled in graceful whimsy. It seemed that even the sublime beauty of nature's canvas had failed to lighten the mood.

While they waited for Daria's tray, the only sounds that disrupted the worried hush were the occasional chimes of silver against crystal and the soft scrape of chairs when families rose to depart. Skin tones were subdued, the more muted hues indicative of the need for introspection. Individual thoughts seemed to imitate the shifting tides.

Everyone knew that the repercussions of their vote would initiate the most momentous event in their living history, implications that would remain locked in Atlantean hearts and minds forever.

Ni-Cio had declined the walk to the conservatory. He wanted to safeguard the precious reserves of energy that Daria was beginning to store. Instead, he had invited Aris and Mer-An to share breakfast inside the gardens of Daria's antechamber.

Aris shouldered the huge tray that Kyla offered, and he and Mer-An made their way from the conservatory. Entering Daria's gardens, it was clear that their breakfast, though far from raucous, would enjoy a lighter atmosphere.

Daria was already seated, so Aris settled the tray on a nearby table. Ni-Cio walked out and helped Mer-An move the contents to the dining table. By unspoken consent, any discussion of the coming Council meeting was avoided, and their laughter flowed in gentle eddies as they seated themselves and began to eat.

Once everyone had enjoyed a good portion of their food, Mer-An decided to share some of Aris's nursing antics. "One night, I remember waking and I was no longer in pain. It felt wonderful, but I was trying so hard to be quiet. My Aris had finally fallen into an exhausted sleep. And though I had not moved, he must have sensed something, because all of a sudden he sprang from his prone position as though a swarm of jellyfish had attached themselves to his well-appointed backside!"

Ni-Cio thumped his knee and everyone chuckled.

Mer-An continued, "He had gotten tangled in the sheets and fell off the bed headfirst. He hit with such a jolt, I thought all of Atlantis must have heard. He kept muttering, 'Are you all right? Are you all right?' And even though I tried to get his attention, I do not know how long he rolled around on the ground before he finally got his bearings."

Mer-An held her sides, joining in the laughter. "All I could see was this ceaseless flailing of arms and legs and his muffled voice rising with each roll as he kept mumbling, 'Are you all right?'"

Mer-An reached for Aris and took his hand in hers. The light of love shone from beautiful green eyes. "I doubt I would have recovered as quickly if you had not provided such caring, entertainment."

Even though it had been at his expense, Aris had enjoyed the story. His love for Mer-An sang through his heart, and he would have done anything to hear her laugh. He mustered a serious demeanor, but he could not hide his grin. "At your service, my lady, you have but to flutter those long lashes and I am prepared to flail anytime, anywhere."

Ni-Cio grinned at Aris. "I have had to submit to his ministrations as well. I can only reiterate what has been suggested before, 'It is truly a gift from the gods that Aris was not designated as our Most Sovereign Healer.'"

Ni-Cio's teasing laugh erupted and Aris could tell that he was ready to relate one particular episode that he didn't think needed to be shared. He decided to stem the onslaught of Aris bashing that he knew was imminent. "Yes, yes, and as you are well aware, I have never professed to a hidden genius where that particular talent is concerned."

"Thereby making the consensus unanimous!" Ni-Cio's good-natured ribbing continued until the laughter had subsided to the occasional chuckle.

Daria leaned forward and placed her elbows on either side of her plate. "It's wonderful to see the love you two have for each other. You have such a close and easy camaraderie. I hope it will always be this way."

Aris thought he saw a momentary shadow flit across Daria's face, however, before he could inquire, she changed the subject, "We should leave for the Council meeting. We should be there before the others arrive." She pushed her chair back from the table and stood.

They quickly cleared the table and placed their dishes inside a nearby cubicle. The items were whisked to the kitchens below where they would be cleaned.

Ni-Cio took Daria's arm and Aris placed his arm around Mer-An's small waist. They walked to the corridor leading to the Council Hall, and the good humor that had marked their meal vanished. The day's purpose was about to begin. Passing through the main portal of the Council Hall, Aris wondered if any of them had the vaguest idea of what would ensue from the coming vote.

CHAPTER
43

*T*en resonant chimes echoed through the hushed corridors of Atlantis. The solemnity of each strike mirrored the grave looks on the faces of each Council member. Marik took his usual position at the forefront of the dais, looking very much the part of an ancient, implacable god. His steel blue stare raked over the subdued gathering as he waited for the last note to fade.

All eyes were anchored upon the Council Leader when his thunderous voice crashed through the quiet and startled some members so much that they jumped. "I have had time to think about the plight that has been thrust upon us. That which we have feared has finally come to pass. Our precious anonymity has been placed in jeopardy, not by inquisitive topsiders, as once we anticipated, but by a treachery so heinous, it is hard to comprehend that it is endemic of Atlantis.

"The knowledge of Travlor's depravity has shaken the very foundations upon which we have based our lives. That this fact could paralyze us into inactivity is a distinct possibility. That the hour has come for each of us to take a stand for all that we hold sacred is a harsh reality. Retribution for such a traitor should not be denied, but I ask myself, at what cost? I stand before you even now with my heart torn asunder. The Canons state that all life is to be held sacred. What we have never addressed are the lengths to which we can and should protect *our* lives."

Marik paused to survey the ten council members. Ni-Cio knew that many of them were companions who, through the years, had shared Marik's friendship and laughter. The Council Leader shrugged his large shoulders and faced the crowd, "The issues are clear. The choices are not. Our Most Sovereign Healer has told us that Travlor will return, and that we must be ready. Some of you feel that we should damn the consequences, land topside, capture the traitor and bring him back to face punishment. Others are convinced that nothing should be done other than to leave Travlor to his own devices.

"These are harrowing choices, which I am sure many of you pondered throughout the night. However, I take this time to remind you that there are still questions that must be answered." The power of Marik's voice rose. Each question struck its intended target, "Do we risk exposing ourselves to topsiders? If we leave Travlor to his plans, what ill does his return bode for us? If he returns to attack, do we fight? If he wins, are we ready to submit to his domination? If he does not attack, do we do nothing and hope that he is done with us?

"It lies within each of you to determine the outcome of what must be done. But keep in mind, once the decision has been cast, it will be met with full compliance. Half-measures will be held in the same regard as the treasonous evil that has fled the sanctity of our home."

The Council Leader lifted his palms in a gesture of supplication, "I would that events had not unraveled as they have. We have been brought to this juncture at this appointed time with only our hearts to guide us. The only counsel I would offer is to be true to your feelings and know that all will be well."

Marik started to cede the floor, but hesitated. His brows knitted together and the creases that outlined his glittering eyes deepened. It was clear that he had made his decision, "The discussion will proceed. However, I exert my right as Council Leader to bypass the rules that govern the right of first speech. I choose to signify first speaker." He walked toward the High Council with quiet deliberation and extended a strong hand to their newest member.

"Your wisdom is more crucial to us than we could ever have expected. Your experience topside may open our thinking in ways we could never achieve on our own. I ask that you address the Council, not only as our Most Sovereign Healer, but also as a native Terran woman."

Daria accepted his outstretched hand and Marik guided her to the edge of the stage. The august leader bowed his head, then took his position with the others of the High Council.

The mantle of Most Sovereign Healer had settled itself in all its grandeur upon Daria's capable shoulders. The very light of her mother line radiated from dark aquamarine eyes, and her aspect was one of powerful majesty. The strength and clarity of her voice rang throughout the Hall.

"The Canons were created by Poseidon. He entrusted them to his oldest son, Atlas, who in turn gave them to the children of Atlantis. Only eight Canons were handed down, yet the wisdom of those commandments nurtured and guided your growth as a people. You have flourished through tremendous adversity, and that alone is a testament to your acceptance of those profound and eloquent ideals. The significance of eight Canons is a reflection of eternity. The ideals that Poseidon set forth are elemental in their simplicity, yet each one stands as an unshakable universal truth."

Daria took a moment. Ni-Cio felt her gaze fall upon him, and as he met her glance, their love seemed a tangible presence. Shimmering from one to the other, it filled the space that separated them and enclosed them as one.

A wistful smile lifted the corners of Daria's generous mouth. Her lips trembled and tears glistened at the corners of her eyes. Her voice shook with emotion as she continued, "My heart and soul are here. I would give my life to retain the peace and the joy under which you have thrived. Having lived topside, I want nothing more than to stay with you, but I feel strongly that we are faced with an almost insurmountable challenge. If we choose to ignore that challenge, it could bring about the complete collapse of Atlantis, and I cannot, I will not let that happen!"

"No!" Ni-Cio saw into her soul and was terrified. He knew her intention. He struggled to the stage, shoving startled members out of his way. "No, Daria, you cannot do this!" He leapt to the dais and grabbed her shoulders. He crushed her to his chest as though she was already gone.

She raised a hand to his cheek, and her caress calmed him enough so that he could hear her thoughts. *"I am the only one who can leave...I know Travlor's thoughts, even though he believes himself to be inscrutable...his aim is to destroy me..."*

Ni-Cio faced his friends and gestured wildly, "She would go topside to deal with Travlor herself rather than endanger Atlantis should this fiend decide to attack!"

Under a tsunami of objections, the arguments poured in.

"You cannot leave us!"

"You are our Healer!"

"Must Travlor be sought out? Perhaps he is done with us."

"I vote we stand and fight."

"We would protect you with our lives!"

Daria released Ni-Cio and lifted her arms. The noise abated and her voice rose with conviction, "Travlor will come. Make no mistake. His goals are immutable. He is willing to die for the cause that he has set forth, and should he fail, he is prepared to kill as many of us as possible!"

Ni-Cio glared at Marik.

"Let us put it to vote right now. You said yourself that there comes a time to stand and fight for that which we hold sacred." Ni-Cio faced the crowd, his voice harsh with disdain, "Would you let this woman sacrifice herself? Do we hold to the Canons only as a shield? Have we become such cowards that we are unable or unwilling to stand against an aggressor who tramples the very ideals we have sworn to uphold? Poseidon himself would sanctify a defense of our lives!"

Ennael approached the rostrum, and his plaintive tone grated on Ni-Cio's nerves. "Ni-Cio, no one wants Daria to give herself for us. Yet how do we fight? Battle tactics are as foreign to us as the topsiders themselves."

Disjointed cries of "Hear, hear!" could be heard, but one voice rose above the others.

Aris faced the fearful composer, "Ennael, we can learn. Studying historic strategies would enable us to develop our own."

Daria broke in with a new idea, "I could go topside without confronting Travlor and try to learn what he plans before it becomes necessary to defend ourselves. If we have that knowledge, then we know how to proceed."

Sounds of clapping and shouts of approval burst through the Hall.

"Enough!" Marik seized the floor, "A vote should not be required, as your feelings are clear almost to a person. However, since we have waived the rules that would normally govern this meeting, I stand on precedence with this issue."

At his signal, the members of the High Council gathered around him and the vote of every Atlantean was tallied. The silence was deafening. Everyone awaited the fateful decision.

Marik looked over the assembly and the bass timbre of the Council Leader's pronouncement exploded through the halls of

Atlantis, "A unanimous decision has been reached. For good or ill, we set ourselves to stand against the approaching storm!"

Throughout the Hall, cheers erupted. The decision coursed through Atlantis like lightning. Down and down, thought followed thought as the defiant jubilation gained momentum.

In his mind's eye, Ni-Cio could see the people who waited outside the bowels of Travlor's tainted nest. As they joined their thoughts with the others, their roar of defiance caused the grisly walls of Travlor's desolate chambers to vibrate. His domain slowly gave way, and a wall of granite rained down, obliterating the last vestiges of his evil.

The battle lines had been drawn.

CHAPTER
44

Exterminators Wanted

Containment of deep-sea scavengers
Situation critical
Environment toxic
Comprehensive knowledge of underwater combustibles
Provisions supplied
Contract in place
Payment in two disbursements; balloon upon completion
Forward resume; click here to email

*T*he covert ad generated more interest than Evan would
have believed possible. It had posted for the last week on
an innocuous website, and his email was flooded with resumes.
He and Travlor had scoured hundreds of unofficial biographies
that spanned the globe, and to narrow the field had been a
grueling, research intensive task.

He rubbed his aching eyes, yawned and blew out a huge
sigh. As he leaned back, the front legs of his chair lifted
precariously off the floor. He slowly rocked back and forth and
studied the man seated to his right. Travlor's features were

highlighted in the unnatural glow of the laptop computer. "How many more of these do you want to go through? I thought we only needed enough men for a small task force. The number of resumes we're throwing into the recruitment pile represents enough men for an army."

Travlor's attention wavered from the screen to him. At length, Travlor addressed the screen, "I need one hundred battle-tested mercenaries. They will be under my direct command and will lead the soldiers who await my signal."

Evan quit rocking and the chair fell forward with a thump.

"Avarice is such a noble trait. I admire anyone who can be bought without as much as the blink of a greedy eyelid." Travlor turned from the laptop and smirked.

Evan jerked his chair to face his father, "Just what the hell are you talking about?"

"I make reference to a certain drug lord who has come under my...auspices. He has graciously agreed to supply eight hundred men for the task at hand. Even with that number following us into Atlantis, we are not guaranteed success." Travlor returned his stare to the screen. Continuing to scroll through the emails, his fingers worked like the legs of a spider.

Evan couldn't believe what he had just heard. He rubbed his hands over his hair, then raised his arms above his head, "My God, Travlor! What do you think is going to happen? You told me these people have no weapons and have very little defense other than their own camouflage. All I want to do is bring Daria home safely and be done with this escapade."

Travlor thrust his chair backward and looked at Evan. Half his face was shrouded in darkness and the other half radiated the gleam of millions of photons. His countenance took on the look of a macabre mask, making Evan shudder involuntarily. "I am well aware that that is your primary expectation. However, I have motivations behind my actions that prevail against your limited view of the situation."

"Well, maybe it's time to enlighten me as to *your* view of the situation. I don't particularly enjoy flying blind, and your evasiveness could prove highly detrimental to *my* situation. And everything else aside, this is getting totally out of hand." Evan crowded Travlor's space.

A tug of will emerged and they stared at each other with ill-disguised contempt. Evan knew that his father did not have access to the slightest bit of human emotion, but he had to appreciate the obdurate look staring back at him. He wished that a tiny fissure, just wide enough to let an infinitesimal amount of compassion for the son he never knew, could slip into his father's consciousness. However, it was clear that Travlor did not want to accede to him in any manner. A slow blink of the lids and Travlor skirted the issue.

"Right now, we focus on the monumental chore of selecting the most useful men relevant to our mission. Once we have secured the men who will accompany us, and we have embarked upon a rigorous training regimen then we will talk."

Travlor resumed his painstaking search through the multitude of emails, concluding, "We still have much to do prior to transporting the recruits to the island. I suggest you engage yourself with securing the area, stocking the compound, and locating the equipment requisite to this operation. I will handle the locals. We don't need any curious visitors dropping by, and we certainly don't want speculations running rampant as to our business."

Evan sneered, "And just how do you propose to keep the execution of this campaign under wraps? As small as this island is, I would think our actions have already been the subject of much heated conjecture."

"The degree to which we can influence the human mind is about to expand your horizons. Have I not explained how easily these topsiders can be compelled? Their impressionability is as pathetic as it is useful to our purposes."

He shook his head and gave up. "Well, when you are prepared to exhibit this remarkable talent to augment the skills I have already acquired on my own, I will certainly relish the opportunity for enlightenment."

Loathe to be sharing space with such a repellent creature any longer, Evan pushed away from the table. He stretched to unkink his back, and when his fingers rammed into the corrugated tin ceiling, he decided he had had enough. He crossed the floor in two strides and opened the door. Crisp night air tumbled into the cramped space and Evan stepped out onto the sagging porch.

He didn't want to acknowledge the implications of what little information Travlor had deigned to tell him. Circumspection had to be the best route, so until he determined how far he was willing to follow his father, he would forge ahead with extreme caution.

He sighed and looked back at the apparition seated before the computer. It bothered him to think that Travlor looked darker than the surrounding shadows. "Tomorrow I'll go into town. I need to start making connections in order to get the provisions you seem to require for this mission."

Travlor made no move to look up or reply. The gaunt figure remained bent in fevered concentration as a litany of mercenary militarism scrolled before his soulless eyes. Evan shook his head and closed the door.

"*I*'m telling you, the best idea is my idea." Ni-Cio dropped the damp cloth he had used to wipe his hands. With a weary sigh, he looked up from the disassembled biosphere to continue the persistent discussion that Daria would not drop. He called upon his reservoir of great patience and explained yet again. "It is not safe. I do not want you alone on that island with Travlor." Ni-Cio unwound and rose to stand over Daria. He took her hand and led her from the pool area.

He, Aris, Rogert and three others had been assigned the difficult task of educating themselves in the gruesome art of war. With vast libraries housed in their data warehouses, they had studied different philosophies, from the great Chinese philosopher-general Sun Tzu, to the more current battles fought and won by the Americans in the well-executed Desert Storm operation.

"You do not seem to understand the danger that Travlor holds for you." They had learned much, but plans for their own defense had yet to be decided. A week had passed and Ni-Cio was worried. He could feel Travlor's black shadow gather force like a mounting wave.

He led Daria toward the kitchens, but she stopped and made Ni-Cio look at her. She released his hand, "You don't seem to understand the danger that Travlor holds for every one of us. Do you want him to descend upon us with no knowledge of the might he will bring to bear? Unless we can meet him on equal ground, we will have doomed Atlantis before the first skirmish."

Ni-Cio understood the logic of her argument, but before he could counter, Daria rushed on. "Ni-Cio, all I have to do is locate Travlor, which shouldn't be too hard, all things considered. Once I know his whereabouts, I just have to verify that he is readying himself for an assault. I won't have to come anywhere near him."

He could tell that she had readied her last bit of leverage.

"If it will make you feel better, I could take Kyla with me. Her coloring is not nearly as intense as some others' and with very little effort she should be able to blend in."

He realized that he had lost the battle. Still, he tried one last salvo, "Your energy has not yet returned to one hundred percent."

Excitement lit her beautiful face and he knew it was over. "Ni-Cio, I have reached ninety-five percent. That is more than sufficient for the task I have in mind. With Kyla's presence, I will have all the help I need."

Reluctant as he was to let this idea come to fruition, Ni-Cio could see the apparent sense her arguments made. Should Travlor not plan an attack on Atlantis, their worries could be halted immediately. However, should the suspected strike come, their position would be strengthened if they had some idea of the enemy's intentions.

Ni-Cio relented and Daria hugged him as tightly as she could. He kissed the top of her head. He feared for her safety with every molecule of his body. He heard her muffled voice.

"I promise, everything will work out. I wouldn't do this unless I knew I would be coming back."

Ni-Cio held up a finger, "I am not quite through. There is a condition."

Daria pulled away and looked up at him.

"I will accompany you and Kyla."

Her eyebrows shot up and she laughed, "Ni-Cio, I love you more than I can say, but I have to tell you, you cannot possibly blend."

He tried to smile and instead planted a kiss on her forehead. "Do not be so quick to point out the obvious. I will stay in the biosphere, and should you need my assistance, I will be near enough to reach you. And hang the consequences of being seen by topsiders."

"Then we should proceed immediately. The sooner we know what we are up against, the sooner we can initiate our course of action." A wide smile crossed her lips.

Ni-Cio halted her headlong rush and wrapped himself around her retreating form. He brushed her hair aside and as he ran his lips over the delicate skin on the back of her neck, he teased, "We proceed nowhere until I have visited the kitchens. I am overly ready for dinner after which I will be prepared for dessert. As you are to be the last course, I suggest we get a good night's sleep and begin our other activities on the morrow."

The length of their bodies touched at every possible juncture and the heat that flowed from Daria aroused his insatiable desire. Her husky reply ratcheted up the stakes, "Must I wait for you to dine? As you are a man of varied appetites, I may be able to think of something that will hold you over until dinner is served."

"Woman, I am your humble servant. Whither you lead, I faithfully follow." He nuzzled her earlobe and his hands wandered down the length of her arms.

Their breathing deepened until their need for food yielded to a passion that transcended every other care. Daria entwined her fingers with Ni-Cio's and pulled him down the passageway toward his quarters.

Assembled in the exit chamber, Kyla and Daria waited for Ni-Cio to ready the biosphere.

Prior to the miraculous breakthrough that had introduced the bioskins, Atlanteans had utilized many different garments in their continual quest for warmth. Through the efforts of some of the finest seamstresses in Atlantis, Daria had shown them how to remake a few of the older garments into newer fashions that could pass topside.

Over their bioskins, Kyla and Daria wore loose fitting clothes of pale earth tones. Their attire complimented the western styled fashion of long-sleeved shirts and pants. In place of the pliant pedisoles that adhered comfortably to the bottoms of their feet, they wore woven sandals that could pass for more normal footwear.

Their hair had been pulled into neat plaits and secured under scarves. Everything about their identity had been simplified in an effort to create unremarkable appearances that would enable them to move about unnoticed. To help hide Kyla's blush of Atlantean coloration, Daria had asked Aris to grind some volcanic talc into a very fine powder. The white powder had hidden the more vibrant tones, although if she was scrutinized, the difference would be patently obvious. Daria had said that most topsiders were fairly unobservant, so she was certain Kyla would be fine.

Even though Daria had reassured her that her disguise was more than satisfactory and that they would not be conversing with anybody, Kyla was still agitated. In the whole of her life, she had never anticipated moving among the people of Terros. She had never harbored the least desire to meet such strange, unpredictable, otherworldly creatures. Everything about them was so different that no matter the culture, they were an enigma. Other than Daria, who seemed to her more Atlantean than topsider, she simply preferred never to let the mystifying Terrans enter her thoughts.

Nervous as she was, she had to admit that her curiosity was aroused. When Daria had suggested her undercover idea, instead of dismissing it out of hand, Kyla decided to accompany their new Healer on this uncertain adventure. Her trust in Daria was so complete, she never entertained the slightest notion of denying her request. Still, she was extremely grateful that Ni-Cio would be close at hand. She never remembered her brother being afraid of anything and his presence helped calm her worst fears.

Ni-Cio finished his inspection and pushed the craft into the quiet pool. He smoothly lowered himself into a prone position at the helm and turned to offer his hand to Daria. His upper body was supported by thick padding that adjusted to his form and his legs rested at slight angles and fell to either side.

"It kind of reminds me of the rocket motorcycles topside."

"Come, love, it is very comfortable and the craft will conform to the contours of your body." Daria looked clumsy and unsure of herself, but trusting Ni-Cio, she clambered into the biosphere and settled behind him. She looked at her friend, "Oh, Kyla, a cloud couldn't be more comfortable."

Waves sloshed over the pool deck and licked at the brown sandals that covered Kyla's feet. It was her turn. Her heart started to beat triple time. She knew she could end the charade before it began, or she could step into the craft and ascend to an unfamiliar world from which she might never return. Her resolve crumbled. She hesitated.

"Kyla, it will be fine. I won't let anything happen to you. I promise from the bottom of my heart. Topsiders are not the monsters you envision. Besides, you might even enjoy this escapade."

Ni-Cio added his encouragement, "Kyla, you are the sister of my heart and Daria is the love of my life. I would not draw another breath if I thought any harm would come of this scheme."

Kyla squared her shoulders and made a last-minute adjustment to the foreign garments. She slid effortlessly into the waiting vehicle. Her eyes widened and she started to hyperventilate. She felt as though it would be her last taste of Atlantis. With one deep inhalation she nodded to her companions, "I believe the topside expression is, let's rock and roll?"

When Daria could not hide her surprise, Kyla knew that she had gotten it right.

Daria raised a fist to the sky and yelled, "Exactly!"

Their excited laughter became encapsulated as the canopy materialized and Ni-Cio willed the biosphere into a dive.

CHAPTER
46

Ni-Cio piloted the craft through the opening of a protected harbor. He kept the biosphere just under the surface until he glided to an effortless stop beside a crumbling concrete pier. In apprehensive silence, Kyla, Daria and Ni-Cio surveyed their chosen landing.

The dock stood as a decrepit testament of better times. Connected to a deserted boathouse and hidden from the surrounding warehouses, the unused condition of the wharf promised a small degree of privacy for the women to disembark. Harbor activity progressed at its normal morning pace, but by virtue of their location, their actions would remain concealed from roving eyes.

In one swift motion, Ni-Cio allowed the biosphere to tether to a nearby piling, and he disconnected his thoughts from the drive mechanism. His calm command flowed through the craft, "As soon as the canopy opens, I want Daria out followed by Kyla. I will submerge when you are on the dock."

He turned and Kyla could see the full force of his purple glare. Cobalt colors rippled over his features. Her brother was on edge, but he struggled to keep his feelings in check so that she could remain somewhat calm.

"At no time do we break contact. If I feel the slightest change in the thoughts of either of you, I will be out of this craft before you can take your next breath. Your safety is of paramount importance. Agreed?"

"Aye, aye, Captain!" Daria saluted crisply while Kyla tried to regulate her breathing.

Ni-Cio pinched the bridge of his nose and closed his eyes. With a great show of forbearance, he shook his head back and forth. His raven hair brush lightly against his square shoulders, "You try my patience, woman!"

Daria took Ni-Cio's hand and brought his fingers to her mouth to kiss the tips. Her solemn affirmation washed over Kyla like warm water. "Agreed, my love. We will not break contact."

Ni-Cio peered over Daria's head at Kyla. Her dread inhibited her capacity for speech. All she could do was nod her agreement. He opened the canopy.

Daria was first out of the craft and turned to help her friend. Kyla scrambled onto the pier, helpless, as her hands raked Daria's back. She struggled to remain upright but had to bury her face in Daria's shoulders. Frantic, she clung to Daria. Her breathing escalated to a wheeze.

From the moment she exited the biosphere, Kyla felt as though she had entered Dante's version of hell and she reeled. As the radiance of the unfiltered sunlight blinded her, tears streamed down her cheeks and her eyes felt as though they had been skewered and sewn shut.

From every direction, strange odors assailed her nostrils so that she gagged with each intake of breath. A cacophony of noises such as she had never imagined ground upon her hypersensitive hearing. She cringed from the pain. Her senses were so violated that she thought she would pass out. She prayed that she would. Anything would have been preferable to the indescribable, insufferable, excruciating experience with which she had been ambushed.

Her brother felt her panic, *"Kyla, are you all right? Daria, answer me! I am surfacing!"*

"Stay there…I have to get her inside the building…she needs time to adjust!" Daria covered Kyla's head with her arms and dragged her over uneven ground.

Kyla registered a loud crash and she stumbled over something. She heard a door slam and Daria pushed her inside a room that was dark and cool and most of all, quiet.

"Kyla?"

Kyla knew Daria was trying to talk, but she couldn't seem to make herself respond. Daria pulled her through the room and propped her against something solid. She didn't think she could stay on her feet and she felt her eyes start to roll back in her head as her knees gave way. Daria grabbed her waist and lowered her to the ground. *"Kyla, slow your breathing…I am here…focus on my voice…"*

Kyla's mind felt like shattered glass. It took every bit of strength to comprehend what Daria was trying to tell her. With her eyes clamped shut, she drew one shaky breath and then another.

A sustained atonal healing harmony flowed into her psyche, soothing her until the rigidity in her body began to subside. Daria's efforts were working well enough, but she was far from comforted. *"I cannot do this, Daria…by the gods, it is worse than I imagined…no wonder topsiders want to damage things…"*

Daria gently pried Kyla's hands from her aching ears. Kyla opened her eyes to mere slits and processed Daria's whisper as though it had been sent through an amplifier. "Don't move. I'll be right back."

Kyla recoiled from the sound, closed her eyes and nodded her understanding. She sat with her back pasted to the solid wall. Her hands were clapped over her ears, but she still heard Daria as she wound through the building.

Finally, Daria once again settled next to her. *"Kyla, I found some welding supplies…these are goggles…I will pull them over your head and down over your eyes…they will shield you from the sun…"*

Kyla took her hands from her ears and waited. Daria placed the sun shield over her head and with a gentle tug, stretched it across her eyes. Daria adjusted the fit, then Kyla heard her soft thought.

"Open your eyes…"

Kyla did as requested. She blinked to clear her vision and relaxed just a bit. The dark material mitigated any fears that she had been blinded forever. She smiled weakly and watched her friend tear open a small package.

"These are earplugs…they will help protect your ears…" Daria rolled the yellow material between her fingers and gingerly inserted one and then the other into Kyla's ears. She ventured a normal tone of voice. "Is that better?"

Kyla grimaced. "It helps. Thank you."

Kyla trembled as she tried to stand but Daria stopped her. "Let's wait just a moment. You need a little more time to get your bearings." Daria stroked her arm, "I'm so sorry. I never imagined what a shock the Terran world would be to your senses. Don't worry, we will get through this one way or another. And if it's too much for you, I'll go by myself."

One deep inhalation was followed by a very determined exhalation. Kyla didn't want to hold up their mission any longer, "I believe I am ready to try again."

Daria sent a quick healing probe. She must have been satisfied, as her next thought found its way to a very worried brother, *"We are ready to try again…don't even think about getting out of that biosphere…I will come to you…"*

Daria helped Kyla stand and led her toward the exit. She cracked the door and looked back, "Kyla, the goggles and the earplugs will help buffer you, but nothing has changed outside. It is your decision whether to stay or go."

Kyla prodded Daria with a gentle hand. "We go."

Daria nodded. "Just be prepared."

Pulling the door open, she walked into the Terran morning with Kyla in tow. They crossed to the docks but Daria stopped. "Can you stand it?"

Although still overwhelmed by the intensity of sight and sound and smell that was the makeup of topside life, the articles Kyla wore helped mute her senses. She knew it would be enough to let her process her surroundings without succumbing to them. "It is better." She swallowed hard. As she gazed at her surroundings, she still had to lift her hands to shield her eyes. And she winced, even though the noise was more muffled. However, Kyla got her first look at the topside world, "Daria, even the pictures I have seen do not compare. It is so beautiful!"

Daria smiled and held up the spare earplugs and goggles she had found. "I'll be back. These are for Ni-Cio."

Kyla knew that their visit topside had been parceled into precious sweeps of time, so she was not surprised to see how fast Daria hurried to the biosphere. She watched her friend kneel and throw the purloined objects into Ni-Cio's hands. *"Under no circumstances do you come out of that contraption unless you are wearing those...we won't be long..."*

Daria ran to Kyla and took her by the hand, "We have to hurry. This may be a small island, but it'll take a while to locate Travlor and believe me, we don't have the time to waste."

Kyla increased her stride and tried hard not to look like the gawking alien she knew she was.

CHAPTER
47

$\mathcal{T}$he picturesque village of Fira crowned the top of an impossibly steep and winding trail. Kyla and Daria forged their way up the narrow road, forced to keep their talk to a minimum in order to conserve energy. They placed one foot in front of the other and Daria kept her head down, avoiding eye contact with anyone. However, Kyla was seduced by the wild beauty of the volcanic island and she couldn't help staring about.

She tried hard for an air of studied nonchalance, but she felt ridiculous. Her gaze jumped from one sight to the next. She drank in the windswept terrain. The scenery of a land she never thought to see spread out before her with unadulterated abundance. It seemed to Kyla that the path they followed twirled over the cliffside with the same delirious abandon as tempest-tossed seaweed.

She glanced up, dazzled by the domed roofs that billowed over each other like earth bound clouds. The whitewashed buildings stood in stark contrast to the blazing blue of the Mediterranean sky and the volcanic black of the island soil. She was mesmerized. Even beneath the dark shield of her goggles, the white-hot gleam of stucco made her eyes water.

She stumbled over her feet because she couldn't keep her eyes on the ground. Their upward trek continued, but Kyla's pace lagged until she could no longer withstand the temptation.

Entranced, she came to a full stop. She spread her arms and lifted her face into the wind, wanting to embrace the entirety of Terros. Daria came to rest beside her and Kyla heard her quiet voice.

"I felt exactly the same way when I first awoke in your chambers, although a lot more frightened. It was overwhelming."

Unable to drag her eyes from the spectacle spread out before her, Kyla shook her head, "Even though we have books, and processors that resemble your computers, they do not do justice to the indescribable beauty of Terros. It is magnificent."

The moments passed in silence until their time limitation niggled at the back of Daria's mind. "I would give anything if we could spend more time. Forgive me, we must continue, but there will be a time when you will come back."

Kyla glanced at her friend, curious as to why she would make such a statement. However, she was afraid to waste any more of their time or of Daria's efforts. She bottled her questions and set a determined pace, and she and Daria soon reached the summit.

They entered a small store and Kyla waited while Daria tried to interpret directions to the town square. Their initial plan was to locate the marketplace, as it would be the focal point of village life. The second part of their plan leaned heavily upon the fervent hope that in the midst of the noisy back-and-forth of the local gossip, they might hear of any unusual occurrences.

Tired and winded from the hike, they were relieved to find that they were very near the square. They exited the store and stopped to rest in the shade of its veranda. Daria leaned back against the railing, but Kyla bent as far out as she could so that she could enjoy the view.

"The market is within a few blocks of us. How is your Greek?"

Kyla, intent upon watching the foot traffic, thought nothing of her reply, "Fluent."

"What?"

Kyla was surprised to hear the shock in Daria's voice. Then it dawned upon her that she had impressed Daria with her linguistic capability. She felt rather excited and self-important. Even so, she considered the fact that she spoke Greek a fairly mundane bit of trivia. She faced her friend, "Daria, consider our past. Where do you think this thriving Greek culture inherited their language?"

"But, you speak English so well!"

Kyla laughed at Daria's bewildered expression. "You are aware that our lifetimes are quite extended. Did you think that all we do is swim around underwater and congregate to eat?" She was greeted by a puzzled shrug. "Well, as much as I love to swim, and eat, if that was all I had to do, I would be bored in no time." Kyla smiled and raised her palms, "We study, Daria. We all have a love of learning and languages are just one facet we cultivate in our quest for knowledge."

"Once again, I am reminded of how little I know about my adopted family. How many languages do you speak?" Daria laughed, although it seemed a bit uneasy to Kyla.

"Hmmm, that is a good question. At the moment I am fluent in forty-three languages and fifteen dialects, and I am in the process of learning nine other tongues."

The topsider shook her head, sprang from the rail and dusted the backs of her pants. Kyla studiedly copied her movements.

"Well, you just made our job forty-three times easier. Let's head to the marketplace and you can speak some Greek!"

The day had acquired an incandescent shine and Kyla excitedly followed Daria toward the central square.

CHAPTER
48

*P*eople thronged the square. Tourists and locals basked in the late morning sun, enjoying the balmy day, as they strolled leisurely through the busy marketplace. Quaint shops and outdoor cafes lined the square and seemed to crowd one upon the other with the same festive disarray as children's building blocks. Gentle breezes flowed through kitchens and bakeries, and the mouthwatering aromas of the island's most magical culinary delights drifted through the air to entice hungry customers. In the background, the lively music of a local trio completed the charming island setting.

Daria and Kyla lingered in the deep shade of a covered terrace and observed the press of bodies that crowded the marketplace. Though Daria trusted that her appraisal of human nature was on target, she checked to be sure that Kyla's powder still concealed her distinctive coloration. She tried to distract the nervous woman from the bustling scene. "Kyla, don't worry, we'll just walk around the square to get our bearings. Keep your ears open, and if we're lucky, we'll hear something." Daria took a deep breath, "It's now or never."

Kyla nodded dumbly and grasped her hand so tightly that Daria was afraid she would lose circulation. She winked encouragement and guided her friend off the terrace and into the bright sunlight. When Kyla tripped and Daria heard her breathing start to escalate, she slid an arm around Kyla's quivering waist and gently steered her into the square.

Daria helped Kyla walk as casually as possible, and other than the occasional admiring glance from some of the men, no one seemed to notice anything untoward. That fact alone helped bolster their confidence.

Daria released her arm from around Kyla's waist. Content to follow in the footsteps of her friend's meanderings, she could tell that Kyla looked more relaxed. Daria knew that Kyla had never been exposed to so much variety. The beautifully displayed wares of local artisans stood next to stalls laden with island produce. Clothes in bright colors dangled from hangers while street vendors hawked their wares.

Kyla ran her fingers over everything in sight. "I cannot concentrate on the conversations for wanting to run my hands over everything I see." She stopped at a colorful display of silk scarves.

Daria whispered, "Don't feel bad, everything is new to me too. Since this is our first pass, let's just enjoy ourselves. All we're trying to do is get a sense of this place. If by some cosmic accident we hear anything, great. Otherwise, let's soak in the atmosphere. If we haven't learned anything by the second pass, that's when we'll start worrying."

In stunned bliss, they continued their tour and wound through the shops and byways of the boisterous marketplace. Daria took notice of the well frequented taverns, cafés, and coffee houses, and as the clock wound toward lunchtime, she decided that a visit to a local café would increase their chances of overhearing the information they sought.

After she considered their options, she stopped Kyla. "I was thinking that if we went into one of the cafés we might hear some interesting rumors. The only problem is that we have no money. We would need at least an hour inside the restaurant, which means we would need a table, and obtaining a table would require that we order something. If we just loiter aimlessly, I think we would arouse suspicion."

"I am not sure about the currency you require. I saw that some of the stalls were happy to barter their goods for other products." Kyla grabbed Daria's forearm and touched Daria's earlobes. "Maybe we could find someone who would be interested in purchasing your earrings."

Although they weren't costly, Daria had bought the diamond studs years ago as a present to herself, and she had forgotten that she still had them on. "Kyla, you're a genius. Follow me." Daria took off both earrings and they hurried across the square.

They chose a covered stall that was slightly removed from the other shops and stood adjacent to a vacant alley. By virtue of its location, the vendor was more or less isolated from the mainstream traffic.

The stall was swarmed by a family of island farmers and Kyla explained that they were trying to trade their wine for some of the clothing. Kyla and Daria watched a heated session of bartering as both parties attempted to gain the advantage.

Kyla listened and once an amenable exchange had been reached, she interpreted the results for Daria. The farmer's wives gathered the coveted garments, and as one unit, the family turned and shuffled away. It was obvious to Daria that they were quite satisfied with their acquisitions.

Kyla had taken the earrings from Daria. She stepped forward and she opened her palm. The Greek woman couldn't suppress a gleam of appreciation and Kyla initiated the bargaining.

Daria watched Kyla and the owner haggle in earnest, until a point was reached where both women stopped, obviously delighted with the outcome.

The vendor slipped the earrings into her side pocket and eyed Daria. She must have decided that Daria was harmless enough, so she began to count the money into Kyla's outstretched hand. Once she was finished, she waved goodbye and ambled over to another stall. Daria grinned to see the woman show off her latest purchase while Kyla's laughter rang with joy.

She shouted her victory, "Daria! Look, I did it! We have currency!"

"You were wonderful. I'm so proud of you!" Daria wrapped Kyla in a big hug. But their celebration was cut short when Daria felt a tentative touch on her shoulder. "Daria?"

She turned to see who could conceivably know her in this out-of-the-way marketplace on this one tiny island in the middle of an impossibly immense ocean. She gasped and uttered the only word that she could force through her constricted throat. "Evan!"

CHAPTER
49

*E*van heard the alarm in Daria's voice as she scrambled to conceal the person behind her. "What are you doing here?"

Speechless, he stared at the woman before him. His mind had stalled. Before he could summon a reaction, however, someone or something stepped from behind Daria, and ripping the goggles from her face, issued a startled cry.

"Travlor!"

Evan stared open mouthed as the chimera approached.

Daria tried to step in front of the creature, "*Travlor?* Kyla, he's not Travlor!"

The only thing Evan realized with any certainty was that the incredible vision was female. She looked ready for battle. Her face was colored with jagged streaks of cobalt blue and her eyes devoured him like flames of fire.

A gust of wind barreled through the alleyway and tore the scarf from her head. Evan stood in horrified fascination as dark hair uncoiled with the speed of a serpent and billowed into the air. The strands thrashed her neck and shoulders and looked as though they would strike him down.

"*She is Athena the warrior goddess! Fear and trembling, fear and trembling.*" Ridiculous, random thoughts fired through Evan's brain as he tried to spur his body into motion. But he could not think of a way to motivate his wonderstruck standoff. He registered that Daria had shoved the woman into the narrow alleyway. She had grabbed the woman's angry face and held it firmly.

The creature's stare bore into him with laser-like intensity, and she would not look away, even though Daria shouted for her attention. "That is *not* Travlor. Kyla, look at me. That's Evan. He's an old boyfriend!"

Evan willed his feet to move, and with jerky, unsure motions he approached the women.

Daria released one hand, holding it up. "Evan, don't come any closer. I'm trying to avoid an island-wide panic."

From his vantage point, Evan saw the woman struggling to get around Daria. Vehemence seethed from her and she looked ready for battle. Her topaz gaze darted back and forth as she looked at Daria and then back at him. At last, he saw a look of dawning comprehension settle over her features. She stopped her struggle, and her flushed coloring slowly receded. She shook her head and backed away from Daria. Glaring at Evan with wary eyes, she self-consciously smoothed her hair into submission and replaced her goggles.

Evan looked at Kyla with dumfounded awe. He was afraid that if he blinked, he would miss something. In his life, he had never seen such an eerily exquisite woman. With her defiant appearance, he had become spellbound, and his thoughts had fled so that he felt like the village idiot. He couldn't even remember why he had come to town in the first place. To cap it off, her blazing entrance had suspended any astonishment he had felt at finding Daria alive and well and unrestrained. Curiosity flickered between Evan and the woman.

Daria's voice broke his trance, "Well, I guess one mystery has been solved."

Kyla marched up to him. Her revulsion spoke volumes as her glance swept over him with undisguised disdain. She snarled, "He is the son."

Evan finally located his speech center. He ignored the implied insult and rounded on Daria, "What the hell is going on? What are you doing here? I thought you were being held against your will. And who is this?"

"I need an explanation from you as well," Daria stepped between Evan and Kyla. She looked around and indicated an enclosed café, "Let's find a better place to talk. This could take a while."

Evan scowled at both women and nodded, "It looks like a fairly quiet place and something tells me I'm going to need a drink."

Kyla's thought-form jangled through Daria's mind one octave below a shout, *"You said we would not be talking to anyone...I am not familiar with the procedures...and this person's presence does not bode well!"*

Daria attempted to soothe her rattled friend, *"Just follow my lead...everything will be all right..."*

"It had better be all right...because it looks to me like we are in one hell of a mess!" Evan's thoughts whipped through both women. He enjoyed their stunned looks, feeling as though he had initiated a small victory in this normal day that had been turned on its head. "When in Rome, right?" He grasped Daria's arm. He hesitated for a heartbeat before he took Kyla's arm and then he propelled both women toward the open doors of the café. "Let's move."

Inside, they settled into a corner booth and placed their orders. Once the required protocol was finished, it seemed that no one knew what to say or where to start. The silence grew heavy until Daria offered a tentative apology, "I'm sorry."

The dam broke, and Evan used his snarl like a slap, "Why Santorini? What could have possibly made you choose this one place? Was I so reprehensible?" He leaned back against the banquet and crossed his arms. "Obviously, you don't need my help. You seem to have made it out of Atlantis rather easily."

Daria lowered her gaze and shook her head. When she tentatively looked up again, he knew she could see the sorrow in his eyes. Silent, he waited for her explanation.

"I would not have hurt you for anything in the world. You have to believe me when I tell you that I did care for you! It's just that both of us were never going to open our hearts to each other. We were both too closed..." Her sentence trailed off and a funny look crossed her face. "Why do you keep insinuating that I was being held captive?"

Evan snorted and narrowed his eyes. He uncrossed his arms and leaned forward, palms on the table, "Travlor convinced me that you were in danger and that the Atlanteans..." he glanced at Kyla, "would not release you."

As Evan lowered his elbows and rubbed his temples, he couldn't stem the sarcasm that dripped from his voice like rain, "I am supposed to be helping him gather an army so that we can initiate your rescue."

Daria leaned over, placing a hand on his forearm, "It's time to stop beating around the bush. I need to tell you everything that has happened."

"So it would seem that Travlor has his own agenda and is not above using his only son to achieve his goals." Finishing the remains of their lunch, Daria reached the end of her narrative.

Evan took a stiff drink of his scotch. "My dear old dad, what a corrupt piece of flesh. I never trusted him, but once I helped him escape, I couldn't figure any other way to help you other than to follow him back into Atlantis. Ironic, isn't it? I was using him, too. Makes me a chip off the old block."

He swallowed the rest of his drink and set the glass down. He stared at the melted remnants of ice and swirled the cubes with one finger. "When you left, I knew you weren't in love with me. But I wanted you so badly. I thought that if I could get you to marry me, I would be able to keep you safe and eventually I could make you fall in love." He stopped, raised his head and gazed into Daria's aquamarine eyes, "You were the best thing that ever happened to me." He winced to see the compassion in her face.

"Evan, love has eluded you from the moment of your birth. I know how lonely you've been."

He pushed his glass aside, "You don't understand. Travlor and I had plans. The only reason you are alive is *because* I wanted to love you. I was supposed to have you killed." Remorse washed through him with such force, he thought he would have to leave. He waited for Daria to say something. When she remained quiet, he knew that she didn't know what to say.

As he was about to get up, Kyla reached across the empty space and took his hands in hers. The richness of her voice warmed his soul, "Know this, Evan, it makes no difference, your intent. The only thing that matters is that you did not follow through. A heart can change."

His breath stuck in his throat. Caught off guard by such a genuine display of affection, he tried to cover his embarrassment, "I guess anything is possible."

He suddenly felt shy and a crooked smile lifted one corner of his mouth as he looked at Kyla. He didn't want her to let go of him, and when she relinquished his hand, he felt as if he had lost something precious. He was baffled as to why he should feel that way. Feeling very awkward, he was almost glad when

Daria barged into the silence and flooded it with a dose of reality.

"With or without you, Travlor is determined to attack Atlantis. We have to know the extent of his firepower. Evan, it's imperative that we find a way to defend against his assault. If we don't, we could all perish."

Evan pushed his plate aside and leaned toward the women, "Listen, my car is close by. I can get you near enough to see the compound but with Travlor there, I won't risk taking you any closer. You need to know that he has finished selecting his leaders and some of them have already arrived to help set up camp."

A waiter approached the table and Evan waited impatiently as he cleared the dishes. As soon as the young man was out of earshot, he picked up his train of thought.

"After everything you've told me, and the things I've seen at the compound, it's clear that Travlor needs to be treated as an extreme threat. The man has a ferocious desire for power, but now I'm afraid that his need for vengeance has taken over everything."

Daria's voice was hushed, "We know how he feels about me, so at the risk of sounding melodramatic, what are his intentions other than wanting me dead? Has he told you his plans?"

Evan shrugged and shook his head. "No, he's been extremely close-mouthed, and no matter how hard I try, I can't read his thoughts. But I can tell you that he's recruited one hundred highly trained mercenaries. He's preparing them to lead a squad of over eight hundred soldiers and the list of equipment he has secured looks like he's preparing for Armageddon."

"Oh, my God!" Daria grabbed Kyla's hand. "It's worse than I thought. I don't know how we can defend against a force like that!" She looked down at the table and cast her gaze about as though seeking ideas. When she looked at Evan, her fear was palpable. "We have no weapons, Evan. These people have done nothing but live in peace for thousands of years."

She wrapped her arms around herself and rocked back and forth. At last, she stopped. "Is the compound private, and do you have ocean access?"

"Yes and yes. Travlor has surrounded the camp with a thought-form that keeps prying eyes from seeing anything other than a deserted vineyard. But he made sure that the property has ocean access."

"Where is this compound?"

"Near Perissa, not far."

Daria scooted out of the banquet and Kyla followed. "Take us there. Ni-Cio will meet us at your dock. This is more than I can decide by myself. We need his help."

The women waited outside as Evan took care of the check. He heard the thought-form she sent to Ni-Cio and he could tell that she tried to keep from infusing him with her panic.

"My love, the threat is very great...Evan is taking us to Travlor's compound...it is near Perissa, and there is hidden access from the ocean...he will give you the coordinates...meet us there..."

Walking out of the restaurant, Evan heard the reply.

"I am already on my way...look to yourself and Kyla...I will be there shortly..."

Evan hid his deepest concerns as he showed the women to his car, but his mind circled to the one conclusion he did not want to face. Travlor was hell-bent on a path of destruction and Atlantis was his prime target.

Accelerating toward the compound, Evan finally understood his role in the malignant play that his father directed with such cavalier disregard. His eyes never left the road, and though he kept his voice low, he knew that Kyla and Daria heard his urgent conviction, "Travlor has to be stopped, even if I have to be the one to do it."

CHAPTER
50

*O*bserving the military escalation in Travlor's compound, they sat in bleak silence. With an unhindered view, their only cover was the dry, wind-whipped grass that hissed and gyrated around them like thousands of angry snakes.

Ni-Cio surreptitiously followed the line of Evan's thoughts and found them, settled low to the earth. He knelt by Daria and nodded at Evan. Evan almost laughed at the astonishment on Ni-Cio's face. It was clear that the Atlanteans had no trouble noticing his resemblance to Travlor. Ni-Cio's stare was covered by his shaded goggles, but his laconic statement hit home, "No doubts as to who sired you."

Evan was riled, "For your sake, let's hope the likeness ends there."

Kyla placed her hand on Evan's forearm. "There is no reason for us to think otherwise. Were it not so, you would not be here."

Evan was startled by her support. But before he could comment, Daria shifted their attention back to the compound.

"I can't believe so many of them are already here. I've counted forty-five men."

Even as they watched, a line of cars turned into the compound in a haze of blood red dust. The drivers stopped just long enough to disgorge the brutal looking occupants, but it was clear that they didn't want to dally as they brought their vehicles around and exited the premises faster than they arrived.

Dark green duffels, glutted with belongings, were thrown to the ground in repetitious, dull thuds. It was evident in their swagger that the men were calculating each other's expertise. Disdain seemed to rise from them like summer heat waves. The cocksmanship of their interaction reflected an egotistical savagery that lurked just beneath the surface.

As though conjured from thin air, Travlor appeared among the men, dressed in battle fatigues. He walked through the steroid enhanced mercenaries with an air of command as he designated roommates, assigned sleeping quarters and made certain that his orders would be followed to the letter. The natural authority he exuded would have mandated obedience from anyone, but Evan knew that the compulsion he employed as he faced each man ensured an unwarranted, unscrupulous, inhuman fidelity.

"How long do you think it will be before Travlor launches his attack?" The candor with which Ni-Cio spoke made it clear that he trusted Evan's judgment.

Evan did not take his eyes off the movement below, "With men like those, it won't take much to get them ready. My best guess would be one month, depending on how quickly Travlor can accumulate the supplies."

"Then our time is more limited than I thought. Everything we do from this point is crucial." Ni-Cio took Daria's hand and Evan knew that he tried to reassure her. "We will be ready." He turned back to Evan, "What do you plan to do now?"

Even though he tried to hold it in, a derisive laugh managed to escape. "Well, since there's no need to rescue Daria, I doubt I'll be ascribing to the assault theory." He looked at the three people who flanked him and knew with unequivocal certainty where his path lay. "It would seem that the strategic position in which I find myself could offer quite an advantage to the people of Atlantis."

No one seemed surprised by his offer, but Kyla shook her head and her face looked sad, "I can only imagine how difficult this must be for you, given that he is still your father."

"He is an aberration. My only motivation for helping him was money. Until Daria came into my life, enhancing my fortune was the sole motivation for anything I ever did." Evan fell silent for a moment, lost in thought. He shrugged his shoulders, then looked at Kyla and confessed, "It's not something I'm proud of."

The unexpected need for Kyla's approval caught him off guard, and made him feel uncharacteristically self-conscious. Evan cleared his throat and looked away from the beguiling Atlantean. He indicated the direction from which Ni-Cio had come. "Let's move. There's nothing more we can learn by sitting here."

Everyone scrambled through the grass and followed Evan over the ridge and down the incline. The biosphere had been left well above the high water mark and rested in the miserly shade of a scraggly copse of trees.

Ni-Cio explained to Evan why the biosphere appeared invisible, "It has a pliable outer material that adapts to any element, and reflects the surrounding area, so that it is virtually invisible. The biosphere remains undiscovered unless someone accidentally stumbles over it."

Ni-Cio pulled the downsized craft toward the water. As he did so, Evan stepped around the group to get a better look. "I think it's lucky for us that Atlantis was never interested in world domination. If this is an indication of your technology, we would've been in serious trouble." He walked around the biosphere and inspected every line and curve of the magnificent craft. He bent to peer into the interior, trying to cover the wistfulness in his tone, "Another time, perhaps, I'll enjoy a ride." He straightened just in time to see a pensive look cross the Atlantean's face.

Ni-Cio sent his thoughts to Evan only, *"I know your feelings for Daria...that you are willing to accept her as a friend indicates a tremendous depth of character...for a man like you, it is not easy to put someone else's needs above your own...I am grateful that you have chosen to help...you would have made a formidable adversary..."*

Ni-Cio offered his hand to Evan, "I would be proud to give you that ride."

The men viewed each other in the heat of the afternoon sun. Evan had used Ni-Cio's exchange to discern the character of the Atlantean. With nothing hidden between them, a silent alliance had formed. "Take care of her." Evan knew his meaning had not been mistaken when Ni-Cio gave a slight nod of his head.

Evan looked at Daria, "You gave me more than I had a right to expect. I will give my life to protect your happiness."

Daria couldn't speak. She just threw her arms around Evan in a tight embrace. For a time they held each other. The steady rise and fall of the waves was the only sound to break the silence. When at last they parted, Evan faced Kyla, "I will do everything in my power to see that your home remains safe. But when the day comes that I claim a ride in that amazing machine, I would rather you be my pilot." He grinned.

Kyla touched his face in a feather caress, "I would be honored to be your pilot and I promise to keep my appearance a shade less extreme than that of the banshee you first encountered."

Evan smiled and mimicked her effort at levity, "I'm grateful my smoking remains aren't still warming the grounds of the marketplace. I think it's safe to say even Athena pales in comparison."

Beneath the white covering of talc, a deep hue of rose colored her cheeks and mouth. He laughed and the joy he felt was more than he ever remembered. "Just about everything pales in comparison. I will look forward to that ride."

He stepped back and outlined his idea, "I'm going to continue to follow Travlor's orders. At some point, I will do what I can to jeopardize his plans. Failing that, the moment I learn his strategy I'll relay his intentions, which should help direct your defense."

The biosphere increased in length to contain the three riders and Ni-Cio climbed in at the helm. Evan waded through the water to help the women. Before the hatch materialized, Ni-Cio spoke, "I know your heart. Do not blame yourself. The fault lies with your father. It is his twisted soul that has brought us to this. Your help is what is important now."

Evan narrowed his eyes against the blinding glare of water-reflected sunlight. He backed away from the biosphere, but he sent an adamant thought, *"If retribution for the sins of the father aren't visited upon the son...you have my solemn oath...I will not let you down..."*

Ni-Cio, Daria and Kyla simultaneously signed a heartfelt goodbye. There was nothing more to be said.

The topsider watched the canopy materialize to enclose the people who, in the space of one afternoon, had changed his life forever. With the fluid symmetry of a dolphin the craft arched across the water and in the blink of an eye, disappeared beneath a curl of sapphire waves. The surge raced forward to tug at Evan's legs as though begging him to come, too. He felt more alone than ever.

263

CHAPTER
51

*T*he swell of bodies packed the Council Hall and people jostled for room. Those who couldn't fit inside had inserted themselves as close as possible to the portal entrances. Every man, woman, and child of Atlantis was present and all eyes concentrated on Ni-Cio.

The last half hour had passed quickly as Daria, Kyla and Ni-Cio had taken turns reporting the results of their mission. But everyone still waited to hear what strategy they had devised. Ni-Cio reached the end of his account. "We will proceed as if we have only one month to prepare. I do not think Travlor will be able to produce the equipment he needs in that space of time. Nevertheless, we must be ready. If we are given longer, consider it a gift from the gods. Now I cede the floor to Our Most Sovereign Healer."

Daria was anxious, however, she kept her demeanor calm and tried to look confident. Everyone had been shaken enough and it would not serve the best interests of her new family if they discerned the extent of her fear. She took her place by Ni-Cio again, glad for his strength, and she felt relieved that her voice sounded unafraid, "The Council Hall is one of the largest chambers in Atlantis, and because of the safety of its location, it will become our hospital. I have asked Ylno to see to those preparations and she will designate the members of her team. The children who are too young to fight will be sheltered there."

A skittish murmur circulated the Hall and Daria waited for the noise to subside. "Kyla is in charge of staffing the kitchens. Although you are used to collecting and harvesting food only as needed, it is prudent to see that the pantries are well stocked."

From the back of the Hall came the worried questions that were on everyone's mind.

"What about weapons? How are we to defend against the kinds of devices you have described?"

Ni-Cio cleared his throat, "The importance of your questions weighs upon us all. Let us finish outlining the initial plans, then Daria will speak to that issue. She has had an idea with tremendous merit. One that I believe could mean the difference in our chances. Right now, I ask your patience. The basic plans that will aid in our survival have to be laid out first."

Ni-Cio waited for any response. No objections were raised, so he nodded and moved to the next stage of their strategy, "It is crucial that we supplement our fighting skills. The games that we have enjoyed as sport must be rechanneled into exercises of deadly intent. We must retrain our bodies and we must harden our minds."

Daria looked over the faces of Ni-Cio's friends and family. There were still a few who refused to accept the need for battle, while others hoped for some miraculous occurrence that would spare Atlantis from all-out war. But with his next statement, Daria knew that he would send a seismic shock. "To that end, I hereby invoke *The Cabala of Ares*. Barring our smallest children, and those over the age of three hundred and fifty, everyone is to become proficient in the technique of Last Strike."

Throughout the Hall, a collective gasp arose, followed by strangled cries. Marik jolted from his seat and hurried to Ni-Cio. "Ni-Cio, is that truly necessary? I understand that we can do nothing to deflect Travlor's assault, but I ask you, is the threat justified enough for such an action?"

Daria watched with sadness as their Council Leader came to understand a truth that even he hadn't wanted to believe. Marik raised his head and straightened his shoulders, power radiating from every line. He acknowledged Ni-Cio with a quick nod and approached the edge of the dais.

Not until he had everyone's full attention did he speak his heart. "My friends, we have abided in peace for so many generations that we no longer give thought to our freedom. Why, it is as much a part of us as the beat of our hearts. But I remind you, we have witnessed Terran societies dominated by the iron fist of tyranny and the results are catastrophic. Tyranny prospers always at the expense of the human spirit.

"Unless we sustain the values that have given reason and purpose to our existence, then I ask you, what is our purpose? There is no liberty when the right to choose is taken away. If we submit to Travlor because we are afraid to fight, do you think that he will be merciful? If so, you are letting nightmares chip away at your reason. Hear me when I tell you that if we let our fear of Travlor override our desire for freedom and our readiness to defend that freedom, then he has already won and we might as well *be* dead!

"We have come to a harrowing juncture in our lives, but let us not give in to a fear that would paralyze us. There is only one choice. Once again, we must fight for our right to exist!

"On this day and at this hour I say to you, do not fear Travlor. Instead, fear the loss of freedom that would kill our spirits! Remember, freedom has never been free, it has always come at a very precious price. But by the gods, I for one am ready to pay it!"

As one voice, a thunderous roar circulated as the people of Atlantis joined in accord.

"Freedom! Freedom! Freedom!"

A spectrum of blue and gold tones shone upon every face. Daria, struck by the purity of their intent, and humbled by the lack of hate that could have motivated their actions, beheld their magnificence. She knew that the reasons that led these people to make a stand would help them come together into an extraordinary fighting force.

Ni-Cio signaled for Aris to join him.

Aris rose from his chair and walked to the front of the dais. His affable demeanor was absent, and his expression was so severe that Daria almost did not recognize him. Aris took the floor, "We will split into squads. The leaders of each squad will see that a rigorous training schedule is employed. Once you have been assigned to your squad, you are not to leave that unit. The group of men and women to which you are assigned will become your family. You are to eat together, you are to sleep together, you are to train together. You will become each other's lifeblood!"

He glanced at Ni-Cio and stepped back. Ni-Cio nodded at Rogert. The robust Atlantean took his place beside Aris. Although usually reticent, as part of the group assigned to study battle strategies, Rogert had uncovered an innate talent as a tactician. "The groups will rotate. When you are not training for combat, you will be placed in lookout positions. Though we are fairly certain Travlor will not attack within the month, and we have Evan Gaddes to warn of movement in our direction, we will still engage our own surveillance system. Our people will be stationed outside Atlantis as well as inside. All exits are to be covered at all times."

Ni-Cio motioned the other five members of the study group to join them.

Mer-An took her place by Aris and addressed everyone, "Those of you not actively utilized as lookouts, or involved in combat training, will be drilled in fight and fall back procedures. Should the outcome not favor Atlantis, our last stand will be in the Great Hall of Poseidon. The portal openings must be fortified and food and water stored so direct access to the Council Hall has to be built. We cannot afford to waste the precious time we have."

A commotion started, but Marik spoke and everyone quieted, "At present we have enough guidelines in the structure of our defense. I think we would now like to hear from our Most Sovereign Healer. I am fascinated to discover what ideas she might have that would produce a weapon with which to fight this fiend."

Daria felt much less certain of her idea than when she had originally suggested it. She glanced at Ni-Cio, and he smiled his encouragement. "I don't know, but it occurred to me, I mean, I think it might be possible to use our thoughts as a weapon," she now had everyone's undivided attention.

"Na-Kai unleashed an incredible power when she generated the thought-form that brought me here. It was a tangible energy that I was unable to resist. She also used it on you in the first council meeting I ever attended." Nervous laughter twittered through the room and she smiled, "None of us need to be reminded of that, but if we could learn to reproduce that energy on a smaller scale, we might be able to wield our thoughts in a physical manner."

Ni-Cio quickly added to her idea, "It might even be possible to use our thoughts to form barriers or shields. If we can learn to do this, it would give us a measurable advantage."

Daria's inspiration spread like wildfire as people grasped the possibility of her idea. Marik's eyes gleamed, "How would this training begin?"

Daria considered his question. "In our last exchange, Na-Kai related the abilities needed to tap into this power. She specifically warned against its use until I had acquired the proper resistance to the drain of energy that would follow an event of this magnitude. I am not even close to the level required or I would not hesitate to utilize this energy in our defense. However, on an individual basis, we should be able to lower the power of this thought-form even as we attempt to replicate it on a smaller scale. This would enable us to acquire enough energy to serve as weapons or at the very least, shields."

Lost in a whirlwind of emotion, for a time, no one said a word. At last, Marik approached Daria and bowed. When he straightened again, a wide smile spread across his face. "Most Sovereign Healer, we are amazed and honored. You have introduced a concept that gives us cause to hope and it might well tip the scales in our favor!"

Cheers rocked the Council Hall and applause broke out, accompanied by shouts of gratitude. With a grin that spread almost ear to ear, Ni-Cio took Daria in his arms and gave her a rib-cracking hug. She was dizzy with the magnitude of her responsibility, and as she clung to the man who had become her strength, she prayed with all her heart that her idea would work.

It was with obvious relief that Marik faced the gathering. "Daria, you have given us reason to believe that we can succeed."

Shouts of joy drowned out the Council Leader's voice. Marik raised his arms and waited. Silence fell like drops of rain, as his next pronouncement boomed into the stillness like thunder, "People of Atlantis, we are united in a powerful will to resist!" His determined features broke into a triumphant grin. "We awaken with a resolute and fierce fighting spirit!" Marik's final words shook the air, "We have been given the ability to overcome! Let Travlor break upon the rock of Atlantis!"

Within the pandemonium Daria sensed a change. Galvanized by confidence, the people of Atlantis dared to believe that they could withstand the approaching cataclysm. A feeling that had been noticeably absent ignited in every heart, including hers. Daria recognized the feeling and that feeling was everything. It was hope.

CHAPTER

52

"*You must be more precise, and your pace must increase...*" The cryptic words scraped through his mind like a furrow being ploughed. Evan ignored the man standing next to him and leveled his concentration toward the target. Like a form of Chinese water torture, the scene crept toward an altered vision, drop by incessant drop.

The courtyard bustled with soldiers being grilled and drilled, but by excruciating degrees, the suggestion of a deserted, dilapidated winery began to appear. As though a scrim had been lowered, the ghostly outlines of people could be seen moving behind an overlay of the abandoned vineyard.

Evan sweated from the exertion. He squinted until his eyes were nearly closed and he ground his teeth together until his jaw ached. All of a sudden, the intensity of his focus left and the vineyard scene dissipated. The soldiers were once more the true reality. He was ready to give up. "It would be easier to get blood from a turnip."

"Do not cease!"

At the harsh command, Evan felt his father's presence slip into his mind. He redoubled his exertions and watched in awe as all live movement totally disappeared. The compound looked as desolate as it had on the day of its purchase. Evan felt his efforts ease and in one brilliant flash, he seized upon what Travlor had tried to tell him and was now demonstrating.

"You make it too hard."

The criticism stung, and with the impatient disengagement of his father's intervention, he felt as though Travlor was fed up.

He knew that Travlor had expected his vision to yield, yet somehow he was able to hold the falsely vacant image in place. He thought he detected a tinge of pride as Travlor acknowledged his accomplishment.

"Yesss, that's it. That's it!"

Evan blinked and allowed his dry eyes some momentary relief. He slowed his breathing and was relieved to feel his mind unwind, bit by stiff bit. He decided that this newfound ability was similar to exercising a muscle that first needed flexing. He released his concentration and the scene immediately shifted to the build-up of military activity. But in the blink of an eye, the reality of vacant housing stood, refuting any rumor of life within the old winery. The only movement came as a loose shutter banged mournfully against siding sagging with age.

Evan nearly lost control of the vision when the man who had not allowed an emotional interchange of physical touch in thirty-five endless years clapped him on his back, "You do well. You do very well!"

Shocked by the sudden touch of recognition, physical as well as emotional, Evan scrutinized his father. It would be farfetched to think he saw a glimmer of happiness, but he thought the negativity that pervaded his father's every waking moment had relaxed an infinitesimal amount. "I still feel that I am exerting more effort than is needed. How am I to sustain the façade and continue my other duties?"

Travlor's abrasive reply cut through the wind, "Never lose awareness of what you are doing, but let the thought become so automatic that you need not access it consciously."

Before Evan could ask what he meant, Travlor elaborated, "It is like your breath. You are aware that you breathe but it is not something you must consciously decide to do. Locate a secluded area in your mind and it is there that you store this tedious task, so that it no longer interferes with your normal routines." Travlor hesitated and stroked his chin. "I seem to remember a game that Terran children play. It has something to do with one child placing an object in plain sight while the others attempt to discover its location. That is the area you seek in which to store this repetitious thought-form where it is at once in sight yet it intrudes not into conscious action."

As he utilized Travlor's advice, Evan scanned the convoluted interior sections of his mind. He located a quiet offshoot that fit the description and willed the continual thought-form into position. When he was certain the chain would remain unbroken, he directed his attention to the wind driven clouds that scuttled past in haphazard formations. He whistled in atonal spurts until the suspense became too much. He sent an apprehensive glance toward the compound. The old winery, unwavering in its image, stared back.

Travlor nodded with obvious satisfaction and clasped his hands behind his back. He started the descent, and as Evan watched his father's figure recede, Travlor's thought touched him with more approval than he ever remembered, *"You will soon surpass my own abilities...it is just as well..."*

Shocked, Evan realized he had never considered that one day his abilities would outstrip Travlor's. He also recognized that he and Travlor had been standing in the precise spot that had provided cover for himself, Daria and the Atlanteans. It seemed ironic that the first civil exchange between them should take place on the exact site that Evan had inaugurated his betrayal. For some reason, that thought made him surprisingly uncomfortable.

273

CHAPTER
53

*T*he buildup of arms increased daily. It alarmed Evan to witness the amount of weaponry at their disposal and the skill with which Travlor's mercenaries wielded the armament.

He kept a close eye on the training drills that occurred at odd intervals of the day and night, but he learned nothing. The grueling exercises honed a deadly proficiency into a cohesive fighting unit. His repeated attempts to discuss the assault strategy were met with stony silence as Travlor zealously guarded any details of his master plan. His father did allude to a time in the near future when he would reveal the entire layout.

Nevertheless, Evan was religious about the pretense of his single-minded involvement. His ability to shield the compound no longer required even the least effort, it had become as much a part of his being as his arm or leg. Because of the visual deception he created, there was not one person on Santorini who suspected anything out of the ordinary even though Travlor's entire fighting force was present and accounted for.

Evan was judicious in his attempts to augment his evolving skills. He studied every scrap of tutelage that Travlor offered, and under his father's watchful eye, his ability to compel people excelled. Supplies arrived by the truckload, and as soon as the unloading was complete, the drivers who reported to Evan were sent away with no memory of having been in the vicinity.

Although Evan focused on gleaning the facts of the invasion, in the deeper recesses of his mind, an alternate plan had been conceived the day he had met Kyla. Before one topsider set foot on Atlantean soil, Evan had made the decision to kill Travlor.

Prior to acting on that idea, he had to uncover as much information as possible. Should his attempted patricide fail, the Atlanteans needed whatever data he could gather to have even a marginal chance of staving off the incredible army that flourished under Travlor's command.

Evan bided his time. A careful and consistent communication between himself and Ni-Cio occurred on a priority basis. Evan reported every development relevant to the Atlantean defense effort. Though he relayed only cold, hard facts, he knew that his anxiety was clear to Ni-Cio. Evan was unable to hide the degree to which he felt Travlor had the advantage. In one of their exchanges, Ni-Cio had tried to bolster his flagging spirits by sharing his hope for the realization of one of Daria's ideas. But Evan wasn't comforted. In his mind, Travlor's army was just about invincible.

As a testament to Travlor's meticulous plotting and his and Evan's vast financial reserves, preparations continued like clockwork. Three weeks into the regimen, a huge freighter hove into sight and moored off the coastal access to their encampment. Equipment necessary to the underwater phase of Travlor's operation was housed on or around the ship. And with the commencement of their ocean training, a flotilla of Zodiac boats was purchased in order to ferry the men to the freighter.

Travlor and Evan accompanied the soldiers on one of their first open water exercises. They boarded the large ship and Evan and Travlor made the rounds to view their newest acquisitions. Astounded to see two refitted transport submarines, an armada of *Oceanus VI* submersibles and two drilling subs complete with extensive underwater drilling equipment, Evan confronted his father. "I don't understand the necessity of this type of equipment. The people you have described have never exhibited any signs of aggression, and if you're to be believed, they don't even have weapons. If you're unable or unwilling to give me the salient details at this point, I can only surmise it's because of your distrust. That being the case, I don't see any reason to continue our association. I know where Atlantis is and I'm quite ready to take my chances in an attempt to get Daria out of there on my own." He jabbed a finger at the submarines, "This is ridiculous. It's what we topsiders call overkill, and to be honest, I'm tired of financing this madness!"

He turned to leave, and managed four determined steps, before the gruff command reached his ears, "Hold!"

Travlor shortened the distance, "You are quite right. It is time to disclose the general details. Follow me."

Evan had known that sooner or later Travlor would placate his need to know. He guessed that now was as good a time as any. Without waiting to see whether he complied or not, Travlor ducked through a nearby doorway and proceeded down a long, narrow passage. He stopped before a closed metal door and turned the handle. Travlor stepped over the bulkhead into a small room. Having followed him in, Evan was startled to see a superb lunch, artfully arranged on a table draped in white linen. Polished silver gleamed in the dim lighting and bubbles of icy champagne created a sheen of condensation on crystal flutes. Evan's guard moved to high alert, "I'm not sure what to make of this."

Travlor indicated a chair. As he seated himself, Evan could see that his father relished the sight of such a sumptuous meal. Travlor pointedly ignored the fact that Evan had not yet taken a chair. He slid a napkin to his lap and sampled the expensive beverage. Evan heard the noisy smack of his father's lips as he lifted the glass to the light.

He twisted the flute one way and then the other, "Ah, one of the true pleasures of topside living!"

Evan couldn't understand why the scarred sounds of Travlor's voice, a blatant juxtaposition to the beautiful crystal, didn't crack the glass.

He hesitated. When he had played his trump card and threatened to pull the plug on the financing, he had not been certain Travlor would accede. He truly had been ready to go to Atlantis to offer help in whatever capacity they needed. He had been prepared for anything but this.

"Try not to look quite so shocked. Terros offers many wonderful comforts. I felt it time to enjoy some of the smaller luxuries. You have more than earned this splendid lunch," Travlor hoisted his glass and drank.

Evan slid into the designated seat, but he was leery of the sudden turn in behavior and his mind burned with suspicion. He eyed the cold lobster as if it might spring from his plate and seek recompense for its demise. He doubted he could eat anything. His entire attention was focused on the person seated opposite him.

The hallucinogenic nature of the episode took on even more surrealistic proportions when the ghost of a smile flitted hauntingly across Travlor's narrow lips. "Eat. There will be time enough, once we are done, to discuss the overall plan of our operation."

Evan called upon every particle of his heightened awareness, but he could not detect a hidden agenda. For all intents and purposes it was what it appeared, a shared lunch between father and son. Something stirred in Evan's heart that he was desperate to avoid. He needed to despise the person on the other side of the table. Any slide toward compassion for his father had to be staunched at once. He surveyed the table, and as he could offer no significant reason for abstinence, he lifted his glass of champagne and tilted it toward Travlor, "Bon appetit, regardless of consequences."

Travlor offered a curt nod and the lunch proceeded in strained silence. It was evident to Evan that the meal was Travlor's attempt to recognize his efforts.

When he finished his coffee, Travlor lowered his cup with a daintiness that was somehow comically incongruent with the character that Evan had come to know. With a soft clink, the cup found its place on the saucer and signaled the end of the meal. Travlor pushed away from the table and extended his long legs. He crossed his ankles and looked at Evan. "You had some pressing concerns that I am now prepared to address."

Evan wiped his mouth and tossed the napkin aside. Leaving the table, he walked to a leather couch and settled himself on the arm. He leaned forward, hands on knees. "Daria's safe return is my primary focus. But my next problem is the amount of equipment we have purchased, followed by the number of men we have employed. If Atlantis is as defenseless as you have indicated, why this buildup?"

Travlor quirked an eyebrow, "I never said they had 'no weapons.' If memory serves, I merely stated they had never used any weapons. There is a difference."

Evan thought it a perfectly evasive lie, so he tapped his foot and waited.

Travlor uncrossed his ankles, pulled his legs back and sat up. "The topsider is surrounded by one thousand Atlanteans. Four hundred men, four hundred women and two hundred children of various ages. The children and two hundred older Atlanteans, can be discounted. Of the roughly four hundred men and women left, it will be they who will provide an impressive resistance. I can assure you there will be nothing easy about freeing the topsider."

Evan was astonished to see the lines in Travlor's face deepen.

"Make no mistake. Because of an excessive, terror-driven fear of discovery and the necessity of retaining the topsider's healing abilities, the men and women of Atlantis *will* fight to the death."

Evan took a deep breath and let the air out in a gentle exhalation as though digesting the new information. "All right, then, what is the plan? How are we to rescue Daria? And what weapons do we need to be aware of?"

Travlor pushed himself from the chair and went to a set of cabinetry secured against the opposite wall. He pulled out one of the drawers, and from his viewpoint, Evan saw several tight rolls of paper. Travlor grasped one of the rolls, closed the drawer and joined Evan on the couch. He unrolled a blueprint on the coffee table and used various books and ashtrays to hold the curled ends. Evan slid down the armrest to sit beside his father. The blueprint was a diagram of the inside of Atlantis.

Travlor went through a quick synopsis of the layout and oriented him to the design of the underground city. He spoke while he highlighted the exits. "As you can see, there are fifty exits. The Atlanteans will not fight in water. It is impossible to use their fighting skills while inside the biospheres. They will make their stand in Atlantis, probably in the Great Hall. Therefore, it is of no importance whether they know of our coming or not.

"However, to distract them from the force of our invasion, we will blow all but one exit in a timed maneuver, utilizing the personal submersibles. That action will sever any chance of escape. At the same time the men are sealing off forty-nine departure routes, one of the smaller subs will be deployed to drill an opening through the remaining exit for an all-out frontal assault."

Travlor threw the highlighter to the table. Evan watched it roll across the blueprint to teeter on the edge of the table.

"You have asked what weapons they have," Travlor pinned Evan with a look. "You need to understand the danger that awaits our invasion. For as long as I can remember, the people of Atlantis have trained in what would now be called *The Cabala of Ares.* Taught by the god of war himself, the children of Poseidon were instructed in this arcane and secret fighting art. Along with an entire series of moves designed to defend against an attacker, Ares introduced a technique that loosely translates as *Last Strike.* The application of *Last Strike* was always strictly monitored. It was to be used only as a last resort, and even then, only if the threat of death was imminent. Poseidon still questioned the wisdom of allowing anyone knowledge of this deadly skill."

Travlor picked up the highlighter. He rolled the stubby, yellow marker slowly back and forth between his fingers. "This method of combat is more ancient and far more deadly than the martial arts employed by topsiders. Mastery of this technique is requisite to reaching our fiftieth year. The execution of this particular maneuver makes a lethal weapon out of absolutely anything."

In one fluid motion Travlor turned and hurled the blunt marker. The force was such that Evan heard the whining objection of air molecules being viciously thrust aside. Wood splinters peppered the floor and the highlighter shuddered to a stop. The marker was imbedded inside the thick cabinet door by more than half its length.

Evan jumped up and spanned the room in two rapid strides. He examined the highlighter, even trying to pull it from its lodged position. The effort needed to extricate the marker was impressive. Evan spun around and held the highlighter as though it had assumed the properties of a highly venomous snake. He couldn't utter a sound.

Travlor took his cue, "Though they may not have actual projectile weaponry, you can now comprehend when I tell you that in their hands, everything becomes an instrument capable of inflicting a swift and certain death."

Dazed, Evan walked to the dining table and sank to a chair. He placed the highlighter in his shirt pocket and shook his head. "I would never have believed this if you had not shown me."

Dryly, Travlor concluded, "Hence the build-up."

CHAPTER
54

"*I* am writing this log as a testament to my people's fortitude. If we do not survive, by the grace of Poseidon, it is my fervent hope that this record will.

"The briefing ended with my signature affixed to the log. Our community is now separated into designated groups and there has been a whirlwind of preparations. With only one month in which to set the groundwork, increments of time have ceased to exist. Days melt into nights, back into days, until the incessant activity is now a controlled frenzy. We snatch sleep in broken fragments.

"Different groups of men and women make their way to the gymnasium. In hours of grueling exercises, their weary bodies have been pushed to the edge of endurance. The *Cabala of Ares* demands and has exacted the utmost precision in all their movements. Everyone has trained and retrained in this most lethal discipline. With the reemergence of the fatal *Last Strike*, I no longer see the peace-loving character of my people. They have diverged into a second nature, so deadly as to be unrecognizable.

"Those not involved in combat training have helped in other critical areas. The construction of the tunnel access leading from the Great Hall to the Council chambers was completed in a matter of only two weeks. From the surrounding seas, food supplies have been culled and brought in to be processed.

Enormous quantities of food and water are packed in the kitchens and the Great Hall. Fortifications proceed as every portal into the Great Hall has metamorphosed into a battlement from which a desperate last stand can be waged.

"Ylno reshaped the Council Hall into a viable hospital. Children too young to fight are engaged in making and rolling bandages. They make beds and secure the instruments necessary for simple surgeries. They have also been given a critical yet simple task from our Healer, creating shaded eye coverings and earplugs for every person in Atlantis.

"The older members of Ylno's team are tasked with inventing the more complicated medical equipment and they garner blood supplies. Even though Daria has the responsibility of healing the worst cases, we know that her talents will be stretched to their limits. Alternate plans for medical aid is integral to the survival rate of the wounded.

"Rogert has designated the lookout stations, and after the massive reorganization, teams are now dispatched to every interior pool access and every exterior exit. An ocean watch utilizing the biospheres is even now underway along with sweeps of the outer perimeters of Atlantis, which occur with growing frequency.

"The tremendous swing into battle readiness is exacting a toll on our overworked population. Nevertheless, swatches of time are set aside for the most crucial element of our defense. Every Atlantean to hold the designation of *Warrior of Ares* is standing by to learn how to turn their thoughts into weapons. With preparations well underway, I have sent the injunction for our Most Sovereign Healer to begin her instruction.

"May Poseidon's blessings be with us all." End

Attested to this day: Marik evaw Mneseus
Council Leader to the High Council of Ten
Atlantis

Seated as if in repose with her eyes closed, Daria had been joined by her first set of pupils. Ni-Cio, Aris, Mer-An, Rogert and the rest of their tactical study group awaited her tutelage. The members of the High Council were in attendance and Kyla and Ylno rounded out the gathering.

The new group had been instructed to relax in whatever position felt most comfortable. Some reclined, others sat cross-legged on piles of pillows, while a few leaned into the quiet corners of the darkened room.

One by one, Daria let her thoughts flow into their minds. She guided each of them as she located the fundamental position from which the physical reality of a thought-form could be generated. After she had shown the last person, she was prepared to continue. Her modulated tone circulated through hopeful minds, "Now that you know from which region you originate the thought-form, focus every particle of energy into that tiny space. Let it flow into your mind like water filling a capped jar."

She waited patiently, allowing them time to envision the energy transfer. Their concentration was palpable. The effort they expended would bring each of them to the brink of unconsciousness. She knew they were almost there.

She pitched her voice low, "Even though you feel that your container has reached maximum capacity, continue to force the energy into the limitation of space until there is no choice but to explode out of confinement. *That* is the power that becomes tangible."

She felt her words resonate in Ni-Cio's mind as he detonated a single train of thought into the dying echoes. The telekinetic evolution was instantaneous. His thoughts blasted outward in a tremendous release of energy and Kyla was knocked to the floor. She screamed as fiery trails of electricity singed her eyebrows and the acrid smell of burnt hair filled the room.

Daria watched the room erupt in a dangerous array of different external manifestations. A violent release exploded out of Aris and a hole six inches in diameter appeared in the wall next to him. At least Mer-An had encased herself in such a tight shield of energy that Ni-Cio's blow ricocheted off her and narrowly missed his sister.

The velocity with which random thought-forms whizzed through the air caused everyone to abandon decorum and adopt an attitude of duck and cover. With the exception of Kyla, everyone had succeeded in some aspect. However, it was patently obvious that the expenditure of energy had taken a tremendous toll.

Daria got up from her prone position and wound through the exhausted, inert bodies. "If I had known how quickly everyone would pick this up," Daria commented, "I would have been more careful in the seating arrangements. At this point, target practice might be an excellent idea." She helped Kyla to her feet, and checked to be certain she was unhurt.

Her friend apologized, "I am sorry, Daria, but I could not make anything happen. I do not understand."

Daria brushed some ceiling dust from Kyla's shoulders. "Kyla, not everyone will reach the same levels. And as you can see, this ability will not help much if after one transfer, people collapse."

She surveyed everyone for indications of internal damage and was reassured to find that the only repercussion was the intense energy drain. "We're going to maintain exclusive training with this form of defense. If you thought re-initiation into the *Last Strike* was difficult, I promise you, this process will make that look like a walk in the park."

Tired groans could be heard as her friends shuffled into more upright positions. Ni-Cio was the first to recover. However, he lowered his head to his hands with a gentle moan. "Daria is right. If this is the result of just one release, then it is not much help. Regardless, the time it will take to gain mastery of this latent energy works against us."

Aris couldn't even muster the strength to mutter, but everyone heard his whisper, "It will work. It has to."

Marik eased himself out of a corner and stumbled to a couch. As the cushions enfolded his body, he sighed. "I cannot begin to imagine the energy Na-Kai expended. It is a wonder she ever walked again."

Daria saw the slow nods of agreement as Kyla accosted her. "What did I do wrong? Why was I unable to make anything happen?"

Daria was baffled. "I don't know, Kyla, I'm as confounded as you. Perhaps if you could describe what you experienced?"

She furrowed her brow. "I could feel the gathering of energy, yet when I attempted to force it outward, it just seemed to collapse upon itself, if that makes any sense."

Daria shrugged. "Maybe too much energy flowed into the area and there wasn't enough strength to focus the thought outward." She had one idea, "We could try an experiment."

Ni-Cio lifted himself from his chair and stretched. "What are you thinking?"

"The only thought that comes to mind is a focus point. Something like, I don't know, a mirror?" She frowned, "Never mind, that even sounds crazy to me."

Aris gaped at Ni-Cio and his excitement propelled him from the pillows, "Crazy no, brilliant yes! Remember the ancient healers? Some of them used crystals to help focus their energy!"

Everyone but Daria seemed to understand what he was talking about.

Marik stood, and with renewed energy, clapped Aris soundly on the back. "By the gods, he is right!" He looked at Daria, "A crystal would not only help focus a healer's energy, in many cases, it magnified their efforts."

Mer-An sprang from her seat and vaulted toward the door. Her thoughts raced through the others, *"Do not go anywhere...I have crystals..."*

They didn't have long to wait. Mer-An reentered the room with a black case. Once she opened it, everyone could see that it had been crammed with different shapes and sizes of quartz crystals. She dumped all of them into a glistening heap on the floor and pointed at the pile. "Would one of these work?"

Everyone gathered around and waited as Daria poked through the selection. She sifted through the gleaming minerals and carefully studied the glacial clarity of some of the single pieces. Then, all at once, she began thrusting the crystals that had formed into beautiful families to one side and rifled quickly through the single minerals. As she moved to discard one of the clusters, the fingertips of her right hand inadvertently brushed against a small, insignificant looking piece of quartz. A faint sensation tingled through her palm as though someone had drawn a thread up and out of the pads of her fingers.

Her hand trembled. She grasped the milky crystal and raised the unassuming piece of quartz to her eyes. An impeccable sliver of ice-clear transparency shimmered back at her. Barely the width of a strand of hair, the thin line spanned the length of the crystal.

She handed the cloudy mineral to Kyla and whispered, "This one. Try this one."

Kyla looked at the small crystal, then looked a question at Daria. "Just as I showed you. Let your thoughts flow inward, only this time, direct the flow through that piece of quartz. When you are ready, release the energy back out through the crystal."

Kyla half-joked as she pointed the crystal at the door, "Maybe everyone ought to get behind me."

There was no argument. Everyone crowded behind Kyla and waited for her to begin. Daria watched Kyla's eyes close as she held the piece of quartz firmly in her hand. They did not have long to wait. A stupendous physical blaze leapt from the crystal and ignited the darkened room with jagged streams of light. An incredible shock wave of energy slammed into the door, and with one jarring crack, all that remained of the door was a wisp of black smoke and some charred cinders.

Kyla's eyes were huge, "That just might do it."

Daria could hardly catch her breath, "Oh, my God! Is everyone all right?"

All at once, she was surrounded. Ni-Cio swung her into his arms and danced around the room, throwing her into the air. The exultant cheers and accolades deafened her. The room came alive and everyone hugged and shouted and jumped with excitement. Daria couldn't keep the grin from her face and she laughed as Ni-Cio twirled her in a circle.

Suddenly, Mer-An's clear voice penetrated the exultant noise, "Daria, look!"

Ni-Cio slowed his mad celebration. All eyes turned to Mer-An. Gesturing wildly, she shouted, "Kyla did not collapse! Her energy is still with her!"

CHAPTER
55

Ni-Cio's thoughts transferred to Evan as he completed his recitation of the prevailing events, *"With enough crystals, we will have the ability to defend against Travlor's invasion and we will suffer none of the backlash of the intense energy drain..."*

Evan still maintained misgivings, *"I hope you can find the supply of crystals that you need...the army that Travlor has under his command grows in strength and cunning with each passing day..."* Ni-Cio's return surprised him.

"There is concern regarding your safety..."

Idly, Evan wondered who had expressed such worries. He stood alone on the rocky beach where his friends had left him. He bent to pick up one of the water smoothed stones. Hefting its weight, he reared back and launched. The rock sailed over the incoming waves. Skipping across the water, it barely made a splash upon entry. He considered his reply.

He had left the compound because of a desire for privacy. However, he had discovered a part of himself that had just wanted to keep walking. He envied the waves their freedom. Evan rubbed his neck, feeling the first twinges of a headache. *"I have yet to feel anything suspicious...preparations escalate and I am still kept apprised of the planning...there is no cause for alarm..."* He tried to keep the despondency out of his thoughts, but the choices he faced seemed as though they would conquer him.

"Evan...this is not your fight, and there would be no blame if you chose to explore another path..."

Evan suddenly felt very old, *"I have only one way open to me…the time has come and gone when other options could be taken…"*

He sighed and the gentle expulsion of breath was yanked from his mouth and carried away on the impudent laughter of sea wind. *"I will do what I can, but watch your exits…they are the key…Travlor will destroy all but the one…do what you must to prevent that from occurring…"*

"I will inform the High Council and the exit guards will be doubled…we do not have the ability to fight in the entrance tunnels, so we will have to let Travlor's men plant their devices…once they have retreated, we can move the explosives outside Atlantis…if we are granted the time…"

Evan knew the Atlantean was ready to break contact, *"Ni-Cio, if I had known Daria was safe, I would never have aided Travlor…"* His remorse weighed upon him like a thousand-year-old curse. He turned to make his way up the rocky path when he heard Ni-Cio's reply.

"Everyone follows their own destiny…had you not been the avenue of Travlor's freedom, he would have found other means…no matter the alternative, there was a high probability that Daria would not have survived…"

Because of the truth in Ni-Cio's calm reply, Evan found partial absolution from his deep sense of guilt, *"Thank you for that…"*

"You honor us with your help…as my sister indicated, yours is a difficult and complicated entanglement…look to your safety…Travlor is not above killing his own son should he become aware of just where your loyalties lie…"

Evan picked up one more stone and hurled it with all his might. It seemed to soar forever before it curved into the sea. He hoped one day it would find its way to Atlantis. *"Understood…I will keep you informed…"*

"And I will give Kyla your regards…"

Evan couldn't help himself. A small smile tugged at the corners of his mouth as he ended communications and started his ascent back to the compound.

CHAPTER
56

*D*aria had stolen a few rare moments of privacy and had come to her chambers for a much needed rest. On her bed, one arm thrown haphazardly over closed eyes, she tried to let the musical tones of the waterwall soothe her to sleep. But she couldn't concentrate. Her thoughts circled in a turbulent loop.

Her first students had progressed to the point where they could instruct others, and she knew that as each Atlantean learned to harness their telekinetic abilities, the teaching would spread exponentially. Within the next two days, all of Atlantis would receive the pivotal education. However, it was apparent that not everyone could obtain the same level of success. Abilities varied to an unbelievable degree.

It was truly a godsend when Ni-Cio and Aris discovered that those with lesser talents could combine efforts to produce the same caliber of energy as those with more explosive abilities. They also determined that there was a finite limit to the forces that could be combined. Those with a high degree of thought transference, when joined by an equal or greater ability, simply canceled each other out. The result was the obliteration of any power.

She was heartened to see the vast enhancement of such latent powers. But with each passing day, she wished she could do more to help with the defense. She was terrified that no matter how fast everyone developed their abilities, it wouldn't be enough to stand against Travlor.

The odds of finding the specific quartz crystals that contained the necessary glacial striation were against them. And even though the speed with which the Atlanteans mined was inspirational, so far they had only unearthed one hundred stones. More! They needed to do so much more!

Her endless inner dialog was interrupted when a chime sounded. She didn't feel like getting up. She removed her arm from her eyes and watched listlessly as the door dematerialized and Ni-Cio entered. He seemed to fill the room and her heart leapt. Again that sublime feeling of coming home.

His voice, low and tender, was filled with concern, "You have found no rest. Your thoughts run ceaselessly."

She propped herself on an elbow and held out her hand. She had dimmed the ambient light, yet as Ni-Cio walked toward her, his skin rippled a golden bronze that played over him like a lover's hands, her hands. The fluid symmetry of his movements thrilled her and reminded her of a tiger shark, beautiful, unpredictable and inordinately dangerous. Underneath his bioskin, lean muscles pulsed with magnificent power. His violet gaze held her captive.

She lost herself in the angular lines and planes of him as he walked to the bed. Sliding effortlessly under the silky sheets, he took her in his arms. An acute perception of the passage of time and the imminent possibility of the passing of life abruptly filled Daria's heart. She clung to Ni-Cio with all her strength, "*I cannot be without you...*"

His lips found hers and the exquisite tenderness of his lovemaking enveloped her in a fragile cocoon of comfort and security. His breath traced a warm line down her neck. "*You are my passion...my only love...worry not, for we will forever be alive through each other...*"

Before her entry into Atlantis, the misty dream of a transcending love had sustained her during her young life. Now, no matter what happened, she knew that the reality of the blazing love she shared with Ni-Cio would sustain her for the remainder of her life. She closed her eyes, thoughts finally quiet, and gave herself fully to the clarity of the moment.

*T*he tactical study group had left their assigned duties to meet at Marik's behest. Seated around a small table, they listened as Ni-Cio stood before them, "Evan Gaddes has given me the plans for the initial assault." He took a deep breath as everyone shifted in their seats, "It is not good."

Marik looked at Ni-Cio, "Nothing about war is ever good. Just tell us what you know."

Ni-Cio didn't waste any more time on a preamble, "A squad of men will be dispatched to plant C4 explosives in all but one of our tunnels. Travlor plans to seal the exits in a timed detonation. Once our attention has been diverted, the invasion will proceed through the only existing tunnel. His men will be equipped with automatic rifles, flash grenades and advanced body armor. Travlor has stipulated nothing less than total annihilation. No one in Atlantis is to be left alive."

Aris jumped to his feet. Variations of fire red twined with incandescent yellow, coloring his expressive face, "I will take responsibility for one of the tunnels. We will not be caught like rats in a trap!"

Rogert glowed a radiant bronze as he pushed from the table to stand next to Aris, "I will take a tunnel as well. The explosives will have to be moved."

Chairs were jostled aside and everyone stood. There was no hesitation as every member of the group volunteered for the hazardous duty.

Marik was filled with pride. He eyed the courageous men and women standing next to each other. Touched and humbled by their offer, it was still not one he could accept. He gestured for everyone to take their seats, "I am sorry, but your willingness to sacrifice yourselves is more than Atlantis can bear. The chance of surviving the relocation of explosives is almost nonexistent and even with the speed of the biospheres it is unlikely that anyone will return. It is because of that awful probability that I overrule your offers. Understand that your leadership in the coming days will be indispensable. One of the sad consequences of war still applies, others must be placed in harm's way to keep the leaders in a position to lead."

Mer-An interrupted with a concern they all shared, "How will you make the selection?"

Marik felt his strength diminish with the abhorrent task he had placed upon himself. He shuddered, "I will seek volunteers. Should the required number not come forward, a random drawing will finish the selection, though I do not foresee that becoming a necessity. I am certain that I will obtain more than enough offers. It is an odious task, one I never dreamed I would have to perform."

A deep sadness ran through him and with great effort he stood and adjourned the meeting. The burden of his responsibility made him feel old. He signaled Ni-Cio to accompany him and the younger man followed as everyone else departed to other tasks.

They walked through the empty hallway in silence and Marik appreciated the time Ni-Cio gave him to collect his thoughts. Every now and then, minute shudders of different excavations could be felt underfoot. It was a dismal reminder of the changes that had befallen Atlantis, and a bleak projection of changes yet to come.

They reached an alcove and Marik stopped to watch the sparkling fall of water as it tumbled into a dark pond. Lost in thought, he took a moment before he settled onto one of the benches. When Ni-Cio joined him, Marik unburdened himself, "I do not want to waste anyone in the tunnels, but the problem presents a fundamental need for redundancy. Ni-Cio, should someone fail, is it imperative that a backup be present?" He studied the man who would follow him as Council Leader, then continued, "The questions then follow; how many men represent enough redundancy? Two, three, four? Must we guard every tunnel? And more importantly, what are the ramifications if we let Travlor's men blow a chosen portion of our access routes without sacrificing our people?" Marik slumped over and rested his elbows on his knees. His body was tired.

Ni-Cio placed a hand on one of his shoulders, "I understand your hesitancy to send anyone into such a dire situation. But becoming part of a bomb detail does not necessarily equate to a sentence of death."

Marik's irritation surfaced and he jerked upright, "We have no knowledge of Terran explosives! How are we to know whether the devices that Travlor's men use can even be moved?"

Copying Marik's earlier posture, Ni-Cio rested his elbows on his knees, "You designated a tactical study group. Within that group, one of the teams has acquired a comprehensive knowledge of explosives. They will pass that information to every volunteer so that they will have an intimate understanding of Terran armament. The volunteers will be able to recognize whether the bombs can be moved or even dismantled."

Marik sighed and Ni-Cio hurried on. "In regard to your other questions, there is no mathematical certainty of the success of anything we undertake. However, I argue strongly against picking and choosing the tunnels we hope to guard. Every passage is a question mark. Some will stand; others will not. That is a foregone conclusion. It is impossible to discern the end result. Therefore, the point becomes moot. Every tunnel must be guarded. And since we cannot afford a higher sacrifice, redundancy is out of the question. Only one person can be spared to guard each exit."

"Your logic is faultless, which is why you are to follow me as Council Leader." He saw Ni-Cio start to object and he rushed on, "I know your heart, Ni-Cio. You have never wanted the position, but you are the only choice. The others have always looked to you for guidance."

"Let us not talk of this now. We have other worries," Ni-Cio started to rise, but Marik held him back.

"There is another decision we must make," Marik shifted uncomfortably. "Should neither of us come through this battle alive, who else can we designate?"

Ni-Cio's eyes went dark. It was a thought he had never considered. He felt cold all over. The thought of never seeing Daria again almost made him sick. He shrugged, "I cannot help you. This is not something I have even considered, but apparently, you have." He turned to his leader, "What are your thoughts?"

"I lean toward Rogert," Marik glanced at his protégé.

Ni-Cio nodded, "He is an excellent choice. Should things not go our way, he will be a steady hand to guide people through the aftermath."

Marik shook his head and hoisted his body from the stone bench. He felt as though he were moving through sludge. "In the coming days, I will depend even more strongly upon your counsel. I would ask that you make a list of qualifications unique to the tunnel detail. It is an odious task I ask of you. However, before too many Atlanteans step forward, it would be helpful to have a breakdown of requirements. Thus will the field of volunteers be narrowed."

"I will have the list within the hour."

Marik left Ni-Cio's company. He felt as though he was drowning in sadness. His thoughts flowed back to the seated figure,

"Your quick response is appreciated...our time runs out..."

CHAPTER
58

*H*e could feel the slow disintegration of his powers. As each second rounded into another hour, Travlor was keenly aware of the passage of time, for with it came the inescapable corrosion of age. It was an issue that, until now, had never been a consideration. With so much time stretched carelessly behind him, he was more determined than ever to wring the most from the time that remained.

The lightning growth of his son's abilities did not disturb him. It would still be a while before Evan realized his full potential, and as yet, he posed no substantial threat. Travlor knew that once Atlantis was taken, they would be well on their way toward his ultimate goal, a goal for which he had groomed Evan since earliest childhood.

As for his current ambitions, he could see that his army was nearing readiness. He chuckled as he watched a cadre of soldiers sweep through combat maneuvers. He was quite pleased with the caliber of men he had hired. Standing in the planked shade of Evan's dilapidated porch, he announced his decision, "The offensive launches in less than a week."

The drills he had developed were being executed to near perfection. Every soldier had proven that he could perform splendidly whether underwater in the submersibles or on land and his captains had honed their squad's timing to the split second. Travlor was ready to unveil his battle plans.

The boards creaked as he entered the squalid cabin. He crossed his arms over his chest and leaned against the wooden doorframe. Studying his son seated at his computer, Travlor elected to share his news, "It is time to summon a meeting of our captains."

Evan's fingers ceased their keyboard dance and he relaxed into his chair. He swung around and leaned a forearm against the table, "When do you want me to gather the men?"

"After mess tonight will be fine."

"So, you have a date?"

"I have," The pause lengthened as he savored his waiting game. Travlor received the impression that his son squirmed, yet he saw no actual movement. Evan sat quite still. He relented, "Less than a week. In three days, we go."

Evan didn't seem as enthusiastic as Travlor had thought he would be. "And you're certain it's necessary to kill every Atlantean?"

What little patience he possessed deserted him. Travlor slammed the door. He walked to the desk and stood over Evan. He enunciated each word with diamond-tipped precision, "Again, if you want your precious topsider, that is the only option."

Evan rose and stood toe to toe with his father.

Travlor looked into the hard glint of steel gray eyes and refused to blink. It was clear that neither of them wanted to give ground, but he knew that Evan was determined not to succumb. The tension mounted. It seemed to Travlor that their test of wills had become too evenly matched. He drew a long breath and relinquished his stance, "This could take all day." He glowered at his son, "You do not know the tenacity with which any survivors will pursue us. In order to bring their Most Sovereign Healer back to Atlantis, if even one person lives, we will be hunted to the ends of the earth. We will never have a moment's peace!"

Evan threw his arms in the air, "All right! The subject is closed. I will get Daria back any way I have to."

"Do not worry, the topsider's return is important to both of us," he tasted those words on his tongue and wanted to spit them out. God, he detested that woman!

Evan went to the door. With his hand on the knob he turned back to Travlor, "I will inform the men of the meeting. Will you dine in the mess tonight or will you take your meal in your cabin?"

"Why don't you join me in my cabin? We will dine apart from the men tonight."

Evan turned the knob and opened the door against the screech of warped wood. "I'll bring the wine," Evan slammed the door shut.

With his departure, the shriek of wood sounded to Travlor like a vehement protest.

"*Three days is all you have left!*"

Ni-Cio closed his eyes. It was upon them. "*We are not without defenses, Evan…the volunteers who have come forward to guard our tunnels have steeped themselves in knowledge of Terran explosives… they will be ready…we have successfully gathered two hundred quartz crystals so I can promise to meet their arms with weapons just as deadly…Travlor's men will be tested to the utmost…as will we…*"

Ni-Cio sat alone in the room where he had met with Marik and the other tactical leaders. He hunched over the table and waited for Evan to finish.

"*Travlor is unveiling the assault strategy tonight…the next two days will be used to drill the men in simulations of the invasion…if I learn anything more, I will contact you immediately…if you do not hear from me, proceed as though nothing has changed…*"

Ni-Cio knew that something wasn't right. "*Why would we lose contact?*" No answer. He reiterated. "*Evan…why would we lose contact?*"

The topsider's reply was more nonchalant than Ni-Cio would have liked. "*It's just a precaution…we can't foresee what the fates have ordained…*"

Ni-Cio's thoughts flew skyward, "*That is true, however, one is wise not to tempt the fates…*"

"*Well, there is a topside saying, 'God helps those who help themselves'…it's about time God aligned himself on our side…*"

Ni-Cio knew there was nothing he could do to prevent Evan from any action he planned against Travlor's men. He just hoped Evan knew what he was doing. He sat up when he realized there was a good chance that he and the topsider might not see each other again, "*Look to yourself, Evan…*"

Several heartbeats passed, "*Look to yourself, Ni-Cio…*"

CHAPTER
59

*E*van knew the mercenaries sensed a change. As battle hardened as they were, they had to know that the time was near when drills would cease and reality would decide who made it to the final payment and who didn't. Evan figured that since Travlor normally took his evening meal with the men, his absence, coupled with the meeting after dinner, would tell them all they needed to know. Evan's adrenaline was in overdrive.

Seated at a rickety table inside Travlor's cabin, he and his father awaited the meal that had been ordered earlier in the day.

Evan's anxiety ran rampant. His pulse raced and his nerves jangled. His breathing was shallow and he was terrified of what he was about do. The sordid room pressed down on him, feeding his claustrophobia. Evening shadows scrabbled toward him over the splinter-infested flooring. It was impossible to concentrate. Twice he had asked his father to repeat his words.

A knock sounded at the door, but to Evan, the noise invaded the room with the force of a jackhammer and he jolted in his chair. He checked to see if Travlor had noticed. The man gave no indication of having seen his startled jump, or if he was choosing to ignore it. Sweat gathered at the base of Evan's spine.

Travlor issued his command. "Come."

A bull moose of a man entered the room and drained what little space remained in the close quarters. He rolled a cart laden with food to the table, silently placing the dishes before Travlor and Evan. Once the transfer was finished, he turned to leave. As he moved back to the door, the curt order came.

"Hold!"

In one motion, the man turned and came to attention. Always suspicious, Travlor examined the soldier. He motioned him over and imperiously pointed at his food, "Taste."

Without so much as a flicker, the beefy man bent to retrieve a knife and fork. The table jiggled as he sliced a slender portion of meat. He chewed thoroughly and swallowed. Nothing happened, so Travlor inclined his head toward the rest of the meal. The soldier methodically tasted every bit of food on both plates.

Once the grisly ritual was complete, Travlor dismissed the man with a cursory wave of his hand. Evan watched the door close after the hulking figure. The harsh thump emphasized his sense of being sealed in.

Travlor began to consume his meal with hearty abandon. Evan tried to eat, but the first swallow of food hit his stomach with the force of a wrecking ball. He reached for his water but his hands shook so much he could hardly lift the cup. When Travlor spoke, he almost hurled the glass across the room.

"You seem uneasy tonight."

His father carved a fat section of blood-rare steak. Evan swiped at his brow and cleared his throat, "I'm fine."

Travlor paused. The speared filet dripped blood, "A certain amount of nervousness is expected prior to battle." He thrust the meat into his mouth and chewed with gusto, "It will pass."

Travlor bent to enjoy more of his meal. Evan thought he might pass out when all of a sudden he felt quite removed from his body. He observed himself push back from the table, "I purchased a good wine today. It will complement our meal."

Evan saw himself rummage through his backpack to bring out an opener and a bottle of imported red wine. He watched his body cross to the kitchenette and uncork the beverage. He sniffed the moistened end of the cork, but discerned nothing out of the ordinary. He grabbed two glasses and poured the ruby-red liquid, then shuffled back to the table and lifted his hand. He held his breath and presented one of the glasses to his father.

Travlor accepted and raised his glass. He swirled the wine around and around, then held the goblet under his nose. He inhaled and arched his eyebrows, "You did well."

Evan let the air out of his lungs and sat down.

Travlor lifted his glass in a toast, "To the desired result of our long planning."

Evan tilted his drink toward Travlor. He noted in microscopic detail the jagged lines of his father's hand. As though he was under the influence of a powerful hallucinogenic drug, time slowed and everything became magnified. The bystander in Evan saw the fine hairs splayed over the backs of Travlor's hands, the slight pulse of blue veins under gray skin, the drops of moisture that glistened on his father's lips, the sheen of the glass as he raised the drink to cruel lips.

Then came the preeminent moment, a moment that produced a rift in Evan's perception of time as it moved forward through space. It was a moment when the concept of time ceased to exist and in all the universe nothing moved. It was an offering, an aperture of time in which he could stay his father's hand and create a different path or...

Evan watched the cyanide-laced liquid splash into his father's mouth. Travlor swallowed. The seconds stretched into hours. The poison finally took effect. Travlor contracted into a violent seizure that wracked his entire body. He lurched up and fell forward. Under the impact of his weight, the small table gave way and smashed to the ground.

Evan bolted to one side. He grabbed hands that had been drawn into rigored knots and pulled his father from the broken meal. He dragged the contorted figure to the swaybacked bed and wrestled Travlor onto the musty blanket. He let go and stumbled backward. Tears leaked from his eyes as Evan waited for the poison to finish its work. His father wrenched from side to side in excruciating death throes.

At last the contortions subsided. Evan felt for a pulse. Nothing.

He labored to stand. There was no need to hurry. He gathered his backpack and stepped over the remains of dinner. At the door, he looked back at Travlor's distorted body. Evan had to remind himself that his singularly horrific act had indeed had some basis in reason. A low moan rose from deep inside and leaked through his closed lips. Evan left before the moan transmogrified into a wail.

CHAPTER
60

*B*linded by shock and tears and grief, Evan stumbled down the perilous cliffside trail. The night breeze wound about him in serpentine tendrils and dust drifted into the air to clog his nose. Finally, the rocky shoreline rose to meet him. He blundered onto the beach and lurched toward the Zodiacs.

Losing his footing, he tumbled onto one of the rounded rubber sides. He clutched the Zodiac like a life preserver and dragged the night air into his seared lungs. He couldn't seem to get a deep enough breath. Nausea coursed through him and his throat filled with a sour taste. He gave up. As he fell onto the gritty, sand covered stones, wave after wave of gut-wrenching heaves ravaged his body. Evan spewed the contents of his stomach until he thought his insides would surface.

Ribbons of saliva trailed like tentacles from his mouth. His body shook uncontrollably. He curled into a fetal position and wrapped his arms around his knees. The giddy face of a full moon peeped from behind wind tattered clouds and Evan closed his eyes so he wouldn't have to look at the vacuous smile. He had never known such anguish, and he was so absorbed in the throes of his suffering, that the sharp clap of rocks almost escaped his attention. However, in the dim recess of his misery, he realized that he was no longer alone. Harsh words ground into his ears.

"There he is! Grab him!"

Yanked to a standing position, Evan was roughly restrained between two musclebound soldiers. Even though he was exhausted and weak, Evan tried to compel the men to release him. He hadn't quite collected his thoughts when he heard a vindictive snarl.

"We came to tuck you in. It's beddy bye time." A Taser short-circuited him into oblivion.

The soldiers grappled the inert body with savage expertise and Evan was hoisted onto massive shoulders in a fireman's carry. O'Donnell took the lead. His weighted buddy brought up the rear.

"Hit it!"

At a fast trot, they made a brisk ascent up the winding cliff. When they reached the top, the lax burden was transferred to O'Donnell, and they double-timed it to the compound.

Their heavy footsteps pounded up the emaciated stairs and shattered the quiet as they shoved into the shell of Evan's cabin. O'Donnell pitched the motionless body face down onto wooden boards that groaned with the effort.

He and his partner worked well together. They were quick and they were silent. With brutal strength, O'Donnell twisted Evan's hands behind his back and bound his wrists with zip ties. He used one foot to hook the rung of a nearby chair and dragged it to his side. He jerked Evan into the seat. O'Donnell draped Evan's arms over the back of the chair while his partner tied each of Evan's ankles to the wooden legs.

Not one word had been exchanged since they had left the beach. They inspected their handiwork. Satisfied that they had executed their mission as expected, they stood. They quickly exited the cabin, unconcerned that they had left their boss's son slumped, unconscious, in a ramshackle room of atrophied remains.

He moaned. He tried to lift his head, but his body felt as if it had been set on fire. Shock waves of pain darted from his head, down his spine and into every concussed nerve ending. Evan twitched his arms and an electrical shock sizzled to his fingertips. He tried to ignore the pain and move his legs. His synapses screamed for him to stop. He ceased his struggles when he found that his hands were secured behind him and his ankles were strapped to the chair legs. He raised his head and blinked his eyes. God, even his eyes hurt. He was seated on a wooden chair inside his cabin. A sliver of moonlight oozed through the grime of one tiny window and lit the room in a tepid yellow glow. Evan shook his head and felt his brain knock against his skull.

He began to get his bearings and wondered how long he had been out. He remembered the mercenaries and the lightning shock of the Taser, but that was about it. The floorboards creaked.

"How *truly* careless of me not to have had my man sample your selection of wine."

Evan's head snapped up, and whether he wanted to or not, he bucked against his bonds. Travlor stepped from the shadows. Evan went still as Travlor glided closer. He felt like a rabbit that waited for the strike of the cobra.

"I suppose one is never too old to learn another lesson. For that unforgettable reminder, I have no one to thank but you."

Evan had no idea how his father could be alive. Dressed in crisp fatigues, he looked as though he had just come back from his tailor. Evan couldn't help it, his voice shook, "Hu, how?"

Travlor's mimic was pitch perfect, "Hu, how, what?"

Evan tried to reconcile himself to the phantom that stood before him. He stared at his father.

Travlor's top lip lifted but it wasn't a smile, "Ohhh, let me guess, you were trying to inquire as to the state of my health? Quite right. Naturally, the first question to enter your mind would be 'How is it possible that you are still here?'"

Evan blinked, feeling as though his lids were filled with ragged shards of glass. His heart ratcheted into fight-or-flight mode and it beat so hard he thought it would burst.

Travlor flowed across the floor and even the ancient floorboards remained silent beneath his tread. He grabbed a chair and settled himself in front of Evan. His manner seemed almost congenial as he leaned in, "You have much to learn regarding the power of the abilities we have inherited. In retrospect, I never expected you to develop yours so quickly, although your progress has been most entertaining. It is a shame to stifle such raw talent. I must even confess to a bit of fatherly pride."

Evan snorted, "You've never been a father."

Travlor looked nonplussed. He leaned back and lifted his palms, "A vocation to which I have never aspired."

"Why aren't you dead?" Evan wanted to smash that smug attitude.

His father stifled a yawn, "An unwelcome event that will occur in due time. But to address your question, one of the many perks of being sired by a god is an innate ability for poison control."

"You make no sense," Evan sighed, wondering if he really even cared. He yanked his arms and feet, but the bonds bit into his skin and he gave up.

Travlor cocked his head to one side and examined the fingernails on one hand, "The blood of Poseidon runs in our veins and the blood of a god is imbued with a very special chemical makeup."

Evan closed his eyes and shook his head. He pursed his lips and looked back at Travlor, "You're telling me that you are immune to poisons? Then what did I witness, an inspired act?"

The smile that flickered over Travlor's lips gave his face a debauched twist, "Do not misunderstand. I am not immune. What you witnessed was a true regression into an extreme amount of physical pain. As a matter of fact, you should derive some comfort from the knowledge that you came perilously close to achieving your goal. A larger ingestion of that particular selection of wine and I would not be before you."

Travlor's black, amoral stare locked on Evan, "To elucidate my point, I seem to recall a trite topside saying, 'Blood is thicker than water.' However, in our case, I would inject the word poison at the end of that phrase. Ignore the pun.

"Questions aside, son, I am poised to hear the explanation for your actions. I feel I am owed," Travlor fell silent and he crossed his arms.

Evan couldn't meet his stare. He glanced around the room and focused on the frayed lamp cord. He swallowed hard against the remnants of stomach acid and his fear, "I have found that killing doesn't come as easily to me as it does to you. There was a time when I thought it wouldn't bother me, and I was more than willing to follow your ambitions. I was living under the delusion that ruthlessness was the mark of a real man."

Evan stopped, but Travlor pressed, "And now?"

Evan raised his gaze and looked at his father. He shrugged, "Now? I've come to the realization that a real man protects life. It is the lesser man who seeks to destroy life."

Something that sounded like a chortle spat from Travlor's mouth. He stood and paced. The floorboards shrieked. "What an epiphany you must have had! I am curious, though. How did you rationalize killing me? I would be fascinated to learn how you reconciled that bit of attempted patricide with your newfound philosophical doctrine."

Travlor barged into Evan's space and brought his face to within inches of Evan's. Evan pulled back. Looking into his father's eyes, he felt like weeping, "There is no reconciliation. You were the unfortunate lesser of two evils. I can no longer condone the mass killing of innocent people."

Travlor bared his teeth and uttered a maniacal snarl. He whirled around, and with rabid strength, wrenched his chair overhead and hurled it at Evan.

Evan threw himself to one side, but not before the wooden missile grazed his head. The chair crashed into the wall behind him. Shattered pieces of wood bounced around Evan as he lay on his side, stunned from the blow.

Travlor sprinted to Evan's side and grabbed his shoulders. He yanked him upright as though he weighed no more than a rag doll. Slamming Evan back into place, Travlor lowered his contorted face to his son's, showering him with spittle, "You are my first and only prisoner! Enjoy the little time you have left!"

Travlor shoved Evan and stood to go. When he reached the door, he gripped the knob with superhuman strength. His hand almost glowed it turned so white. Battling to suppress his rage, Travlor did not look back, but when he had calmed himself enough to speak, Evan heard his sorrow, "I no longer acknowledge you as my son. Once the meeting has concluded, upon my orders, you will be executed."

The old door opened with barely a whimper and Travlor slipped from the room. He stepped across the porch and descended the stairs. Evan watched the solitary figure fade to black.

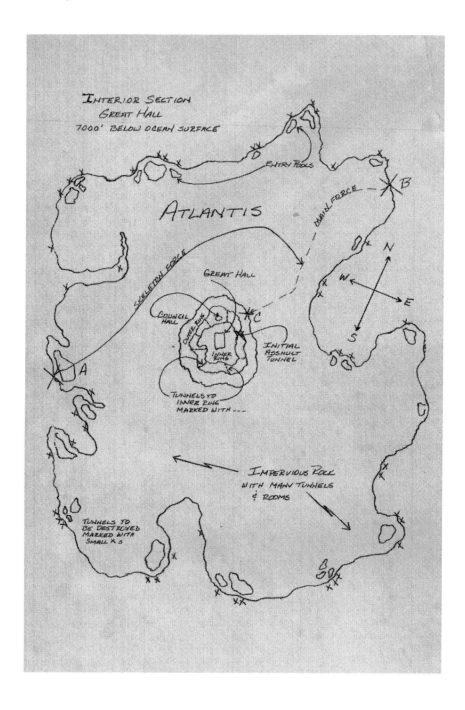

318

CHAPTER
61

*T*ravlor stood before a substantial wall map. His captains had gathered around while their men sat in the available chairs. He finished marking the forty-nine exits and turned into the room, "I realize the strategic disadvantage of eliminating so many tunnels. But again, I stress the necessity of containing the enemy. I want no one to escape."

His eyes traveled over the faces of his men and once again he reinforced his orders with an intense compulsion, "When these exits have been blown, the first submarine carrying a skeleton force will begin its enlargement of the remaining tunnel, here."

His forefinger traced the solid line of tunnel A, so that his soldiers would know where the advance would start. "This sub is important in that it will be used as a decoy. They will defend this position and will believe it to be our only port of entry."

He switched to another quadrant and indicated tunnel B on the diagram. His finger followed a different line, marked in dashes. It was this innocuous little line that had been absent on the blueprint he had shown to Evan. "It is here that the second driller will be deployed. The transport subs, ferrying the rest of the troops, will follow. Drilling will proceed quickly as there will be less ground to cover. Every submersible will follow the transports into Atlantis. By my calculations, the men will be in position by the time the first tunnel has been breached. Tunnel

A provides the semblance of a frontal assault while we gain the advantage by bringing the force of our army through this tunnel in our surprise rear assault. We meet at this juncture."

Travlor showed his men where the passages joined.

One of the men raised his arm, and Travlor nodded for him to proceed.

"The target doesn't have knowledge of this rear tunnel?"

Travlor placed his black pen on a nearby table, "As for anyone living in Atlantis, this tunnel does not exist and never has." He appreciated the sly approval of the mercenaries. Travlor arched a brow and smiled, "Well, with thirty-five years of captivity under my belt, I had to keep busy doing *something*."

Smatters of coarse laughter rippled through the room. When the noise settled, Travlor picked up again. "The entry access that leads to the eight tunnels ringing the Great Hall has been designated C."

His finger tapped the diagram at that tunnel, "It is tunnel C that will lead us to the initial assault tunnel, here."

He faced his men, "Gentlemen, take this tunnel and we open access to the inner ring."

He pointed to one of his captains, "Your men will spread through the inner ring placing a contingent of men at the openings of the other seven tunnels."

Travlor pointed at another man, "You will lead your men around the outer ring dispersing squads at the openings of the same seven tunnels."

He took his place in the group, "I remind you, take no prisoners. There are to be no survivors, save one. Make no mistake, this woman must be secured unharmed."

He circulated copies of Evan's only picture of Daria. Travlor could see the glitter of blood lust rise in ugly, parasitic eyes, but every man present made it clear they agreed to his terms.

"Fine. We go in two days."

A cheer sprang from the soldiers and they slapped each other on the back or traded high-fives. Travlor had made certain that they would peak when he was ready to move. The men were eager to flex their well-financed war muscles. He raised his voice over their rowdy exchange, "Sim-drills commence immediately."

One of his captains handed smaller versions of the topo map to each of the men.

Travlor waited until they were quiet again, "Remember to keep your explosives to the bare minimum! I do not want to risk bringing the mountain down upon our heads. Any questions?"

There were none, so Travlor dismissed all but one. The soldiers filed out of the room and the designee came to the front of the room. Travlor perched on the edge of the table. He examined the man and appreciated the level of fitness his captain had achieved, "You lead your men well."

"Thank you, sir. I have worked with most of them on other assignments."

"Good. Then you will know who is best suited for the job I have in mind."

The mercenary offered no response.

"The man shackled in my cabin is to be executed. He is extremely dangerous. I need someone capable of carrying out my orders, yet someone who will not be missed in the sim-drills."

"I would use O'Donnell again, sir."

"Fine. He has five minutes to meet me outside my son's cabin."

"Sir!"

The man exited the room to find O'Donnell while Travlor gathered up the rest of his papers. At length he left to meet the guard.

Travlor walked through the deserted grounds and glanced at the full moon. He ducked his head and hunched his shoulders. He felt the tidal pull deep within his body, and it made him want to howl like a madman. His thoughts started to spin. He refused to think about his only son in any terms other than the betrayer that he was, "No, not son! Deceiver, liar, traitor! Just like your mother!"

Travlor could go no farther. He bent over like an old man and a shudder rocked his body. His temples pounded. He rubbed his forehead to try to blot out his thoughts, "*I should be the one to kill you! Yet, I cannot pull the trigger.*"

The pressure in his head built until he looked skyward. He raised a shaking fist at the impervious yellow watcher, "I will give you something to howl about!"

Whether his threat was aimed at the moon, or whether he referred to Evan, even he could not say. He forced himself across the courtyard toward Evan's cabin.

O'Donnell waited on the porch and Travlor could see that he was fully armed. Travlor did not take the stairs, instead, he waited until the bulky mercenary stood before him, "I assume your captain has filled you in on the detail."

The man shifted, "Yes, sir!"

"Very well. Not until I am out of the compound and aboard that freighter are you to carry out your orders."

"Understood, sir!"

Travlor's thoughts boiled. He rubbed his temples until his skin felt bruised. He finally stopped and glimpsed up. He caught the sly look of depravity that winked over the face of his hired killer. Unable to control his thoughts any longer, Travlor turned and fled the compound.

CHAPTER
62

"*My endeavor has failed…there is nothing I can do…*" The disappointment Ni-Cio felt pierced his heart. He had held to a secret hope that somehow Evan would be able to thwart the invasion, "*Are you well?*"

"*Travlor has…detained me…but I am well enough…*"

Before Ni-Cio could offer aid he heard Evan.

"*Do not come after me…it's too dangerous and you are needed in Atlantis…*"

"*I cannot leave you there…*"

"*Ni-Cio, Travlor is capable of anything, including changing the day of the attack…if I am here, I still have a chance…stay where you are…once the men have left the compound, I'll find a way to get…*"

The thought was never completed.

"*Evan? Evan!*" Their contact had been severed. Ni-Cio bolted down the corridor, "*I have lost contact with Evan!*" His thoughts poured into his friends as they prepared for their final strategy meeting.

Aris answered for the group, "*He warned us that that might happen…*"

Ni-Cio rounded a corner and the door dematerialized. He barged into the meeting, "We have to help him!"

No one moved but Aris, "Ni-Cio, it was a chance he was willing to take. We cannot risk anyone in a rescue effort. Travlor's men outnumber us as it is."

Marik stood, "Sit, Ni-Cio. This is our last session. It is time to finalize the strategy and take our posts." He pulled out a chair and offered it to Ni-Cio. "We cannot help your friend, nor would he want us to."

Much as he wanted to argue, Ni-Cio knew their logic was sound. Everyone in Atlantis was needed; their time was at hand. With a heavy heart, Ni-Cio sat so that Marik could begin the summary.

The Council Leader pulled a marinus from the pocket of his robe and activated the three-dimensional diagram. An interior map of Atlantis materialized to hover over the table. The exits had been highlighted, and the routes glowed red neon. "Our forty-nine volunteers have done their homework. Once we have concluded the meeting, they will be dispatched in biospheres to their posts. I have asked Peltor to head the group, and he will report directly to me."

Ni-Cio refused to dwell on the implications of Marik's statement. He trained his attention on the map.

The Council Hall glowed yellow as Marik continued, "The Council Hall has been completely sealed off. The only access is through the new tunnel that connects to the Great Hall."

Colors bloomed over the diagram like sea anemones as the marinus responded to Marik's voice, "Ylno has a trained staff of twenty-five people to assist in the hospital. Kyla heads another twenty-five, who will help with the stored supplies and, if necessary, lend support to Ylno. Children under the age of twenty-five will be kept within the confines of the hospital area.

"Inside the Great Hall, the bulk of our forces will be stationed behind the interior barricades. They will be split into ten squads with a member of the High Council commanding each squad. A select command force will stand at each of the casement openings. They are ordered to fire at will should Travlor's soldiers break through any of the eight tunnels leading to the inner ring." Marik sat down and yielded the floor to Ni-Cio.

Standing, he reoriented the map, "This gives us a fighting force of around four hundred men and women. We will not waste manpower defending the route Travlor has selected as his point of entry, here." The tunnel appeared accentuated in black. "Even though the crystals supplement our arsenal, we cannot hope to overpower his men without the advantage of cover. Instead, we will employ the tactics of guerilla warfare."

Eight green spokes appeared as the tunnels that radiated from the corridor surrounding the Great Hall were highlighted. "There are eight corridors that grant access to the Great Hall of Poseidon and twenty people will be secreted throughout each of them. They will be stationed at the outermost end of each portal. Their mission is to slay as many of Travlor's men as possible before falling back to help defend the Great Hall. It will be in the Great Hall that we concentrate our defense, and it will be there that we stand or fall."

Ni-Cio indicated the tactical study group, "The six of us, along with Talus and his mate, Riina, will lead the guerilla squads. Marik and the High Council will command the forces in the Great Hall and Daria will be ready with Ylno in the Council Hall. Are there any questions or comments?"

Rogert jerked his chin at Ni-Cio, "Would you have us select our own teams or will you determine the squads?"

Ni-Cio shrugged, "What would make you more comfortable?"

The taciturn man frowned, "It makes no difference."

Ni-Cio looked for other comments, but no one wanted to offer any. "Very well. I would say choose your own teams, but be ready to take your positions within the next two hours."

Everyone nodded their understanding. Ni-Cio sat down and the map disappeared.

Marik stood back up and rested his hands on the table. He leaned into the group, "We will need to have the rest of the biospheres brought to the Council Chamber. I do not intend to let Travlor's men steal or destroy our only mode of transportation. Rogert, if you could see to that?"

"I will see to it as soon as the meeting is adjourned."

The Council Leader smiled, "Rogert, I would that I had just a jot of your unending supply of calm."

Laughter eased a bit of the tension.

"If there is nothing else, then I believe this meeting is adjourned." As chairs scraped, Marik raised his arm, "One last thing."

Everyone halted. Ni-Cio had never seen their leader look so sad as Marik signed a heartfelt goodbye, "Look to yourselves."

CHAPTER
63

"This entry will be the last that I am willing or able to make. Let it be known that I am humbled to lead such a courageous people. No matter our hope, I fear that the outcome will not favor us. Should I last this day, I can only pray that I lead my people well. Beyond that, I can see no further. It is now in the hands of the gods. So be it.

"In the depths of our home, there is nothing more to do. Now we wait. We wait in heightened anticipation for the first merciless, concussive blasts of the explosions. We wait to hear the sounds of drills ripping through the protective layers of our home. And we wait for the first unholy reports of gunfire. Vicious sounds that desecrate our sanctuary and signify Travlor's inexorable return. Sounds that are harbingers of death and destruction and ruin. For every one of us, down to the smallest child, has been taught that in war there are no victors. There are only survivors.

"In the unremitting, oppressive black of the underwater tunnels, Peltor and his forty-eight volunteers are poised in their lonely vigils. Isolated from the rest of us, their motionless biospheres hide their presence so that the rapacious intruders will never know that they are watched. Tied to their families through continual thought-touch, their selfless courage and heroic actions will be instantaneously perceived by their loved ones, whose appalling task it is to bear witness to the success or failure of their missions.

"Throughout the pathways of Atlantis, it is almost as though sight and sound have never existed. The blackness is so thick, I choke upon it. Every particle of light has been extinguished and with it every sound indicative of life. It seems a frightening simulation of the deathly hush that will descend upon Atlantis should Travlor's will be done.

"Our guerilla units are secluded in their own obsidian nightmare. They are stationed at various intervals in each of the eight corridors leading to the Great Hall of Poseidon. They have been selected as our first line of defense because the twenty members of each unit are the undisputed masters of the *Last Strike*. They carry in their packs simple everyday items that range from eating utensils to rocks to hair combs. The items are small, and by themselves innocuous, but in the hands of these elite men and women, every item will prove as deadly as the bullets they soon face.

"Each of these warriors has been entrusted with one precious quartz crystal. They harbor the minerals inside a special pouch within their bioskins. But I know that while they are alone and in the dark their hands check from time to time to be certain the pocket still contains their secret weapon.

"The Great Hall of Poseidon has been transformed into an impressive fortress. Barricaded inside, we still move about. The advantage of nominal illumination makes our wait more endurable. But I hardly recognize anyone behind the eye coverings we wear. And though we are filled with as much dread as the men and women outside the fortress walls, it is wonderful to see that life refuses to be put on hold. Our children still play games, older Atlanteans still share stories, and love still prevails.

"Enclosed but for one connecting tunnel, the refurbished Council Hall, now a hospital, stands undisturbed and patientless. However, everyone in Ylno's group lingers in fearful apprehension of the first bloody signature that heralds Travlor's deadly arrival. I cannot bring myself to dwell upon the horrors that must assail our Most Sovereign Healer, but I have never seen one such as her. Without her, we would surely be doomed.

"May Poseidon's blessings be with us all." End
Attested to this day: Marik evaw Mneseus
Council Leader to the High Council of Ten
Atlantis

Daria excused herself and walked from the hospital into the dimly lit tunnel. Her uncertain steps echoed off the rough-hewn, unadorned walls. It was with immense sadness that she ran her hands over the obvious marks of hurried construction. The mournful absence of beautiful detail was a stark testament of function dictating the form. The tunnel's cold, forbidding presence spoke to her of darker days yet to come.

As she walked, shadows pooled and descended to prowl the floor in inky black shapes. She started at the smallest sound. She wanted to talk to Ni-Cio. She wanted to feel his arms wrapped around her and hear him tell her that all would be well.

Though they were conjoined through thought-touch and she could pinpoint his position to the millimeter, she dared not risk communication. If he lost focus at the wrong time, it could mean his death. That was not something she could face.

Midway through the passage, Daria stopped and retreated into the anonymity of the darkling shadows. She leaned against the dank rock wall and shivered. She pulled her robes closer and wrapped her arms around her body. Daria was so frightened that she found it hard to concentrate. She felt smothered by fright.

So, she had stolen this time to assess her fear. She knew it was not self-motivated. She was not afraid of her own death. The indescribable fright that coursed through her was for her adopted family.

Intimate with the crushing feelings of loss and bereavement, she knew that before this horrific ordeal had reached its apocalyptic end, death would reap an overwhelming reward. She sank to the floor and covered her face with her hands.

Overcome with regret, she wished with all her heart that Ni-Cio had let her confront Travlor on her own. If he had, she felt sure that none of this would be taking place and everyone would be safe. She choked back a sob. As she opened the door to the feelings of hopelessness and despair that assailed her, an ethereal voice touched her mind and whispered to her beleaguered soul.

"Daria...child of my heart, have you not yet realized that the gift of life precludes anyone from being safe?"

Daria closed her eyes against the tears that coursed down her cheeks and she buried her face in her robe. She hugged her knees and her shoulders shook, *"Na-Kai!"*

"I am with you, my beloved...peace, be still..."

All at once, Daria felt the comfort of Na-Kai's healing presence. Her parched soul drank the joy of Na-Kai's love and she lifted her face and laughed out loud, *"You're here!"*

Na-Kai's tender reply caressed her, *"I am always with you..."*

Daria drifted in the love that Na-Kai bequeathed her and reveled in the nourishment of a mother's care. But after a time, thoughts of Travlor crowded her and Daria bowed her head, *"Na-Kai, I don't know what to do...I'm so afraid..."*

Na-Kai chided with a gentle laugh, *"Child, trust yourself...you will know what to do..."*

"But all this could have been avoided if I had just gone to Travlor..."

She heard Na-Kai's soft sigh, *"Daria...you do not know that...events have unfolded as they should..."*

Daria shifted to her knees as if she were a supplicant, *"So many lives will be lost..."*

"And yet, others will be spared...Daria, events will play out...but you must not despair or lose hope...in life and in love, there is always hope..."

Na-Kai began to sing, and as the music of the spheres washed over her and flowed through her, Daria's despair lessened. Her spirit became lighter, more at peace. She felt Na-Kai's presence start to recede, but the Healer's final words streamed into her heart and bathed her soul.

"It is time, child...remember, you are stronger than you know... always follow your heart, therein lies the joy...and thus, the love..."

Daria gathered her robes and stood. Travlor's army was at the door. The first dim sounds of detonated explosions reached her. She wiped her tears and lifted her face. She walked back toward the light of the infirmary and toward the shrouded future.

It had begun.

CHAPTER
64

A full day lost to a demented, bullet-headed sadist. The first Taser blast administered by the two goons who had found him had seared him into oblivion. But with each subsequent hit, Evan had experienced a lessening of the terrible effects, the result being that his periods of unconsciousness had begun to lessen. Nevertheless, with the last hit, he had lost more time than he intended.

Alone in his sorry excuse for a domicile, Evan was aware that a change had taken place within his body. It was as though with each shock of the Taser, another hidden door had unlocked. With the last hit, the doors had disintegrated and energy had streamed into his being, coalescing into the forefront of his consciousness. Not quite certain how to utilize this newfound energy, Evan was ready to put it to a test.

He heard the heavy clomp of his captor's boots as he marched up the wooden stairs. Evan let his head hang to one side and feigned a disoriented, groggy demeanor. His back was to the entrance, so he listened to the stubborn groan of the ancient door as it resisted the soldier's inward push. Evan marked O'Donnell's three unhurried steps, then heard the sudden zzz, zzt of the Taser springing to life.

A wicked laugh issued from his left and Evan felt the heat of the man followed by the reek of garlic-tainted air that surrounded him. Evan knew that the hired thug deliberated as to the most advantageous placement of the prongs. He tensed.

Through slitted lids, he watched the man's gleeful face come into view. He knew that the mercenary enjoyed his sadistic game. Saliva glistened at the corners of his rubbery lips and Evan was curious to see if it would drool down his chin. The disgusting excuse for a human started to rub himself. Evan closed his eyes. He couldn't watch anymore, but when the man lowered the Taser, Evan knew the minute he stopped.

Evan opened his eyes. The lascivious smirk that had painted the brute's ugly face was gone. The soldier grunted. He strained to bring the weapon into contact with his target. To Evan it was almost comical. It appeared as if the man's entire arm had been frozen in concrete while the rest of his body wriggled like a fish on the end of a hook. Evan smelled the stench of his fear.

The man finally realized that his struggles were useless. A beastly grunt gurgled up from his chest and he looked at Evan. Terror distorted the planes of his face as his eyes bulged and his mouth dropped open. Saliva trickled over his lips. The soldier watched fascinated as his hand, through no volition of its own, turned away from Evan. The jaws of the Taser inched toward his own body. The man emitted a high-pitched scream. He tried to throw the weapon away, but Evan had hit his stride. In a flash, the Taser bit into the soldier's beefy chest. His eyes rolled up into his head, and in a shower of small epileptic seizures, the man slumped to the floor. He lay in a loose pile at Evan's feet.

Evan was stunned. He glanced around, half expecting an army of mercenaries to burst through the door. Then he looked back at the man. He tried to understand how he had initiated the energy release. He bent forward and stared at the ties that bound his legs to the chair. He focused on the restraints and felt a quick surge of energy gather in his forehead, and then a small push forward, and it dissipated. Littered across the inert form of the soldier, pieces of plastic skittered to a stop.

With even less effort, Evan unfettered his wrists. He stood and rubbed the raw patches. He jabbed at the dispatched guard with his foot. The man didn't move.

Evan raised an eyebrow and stepped over his unconscious ex-captor, "I guess I have more ways to skin a cat now." He grabbed his backpack and made for the door.

At a dead run, he raced through the empty compound and located his truck. He yanked the door open, threw his backpack inside, jumped into the seat and fumbled for the visor. The key fell into his hand and he thrust it into the ignition. Evan ground the starter, pumped the accelerator and the engine sprang to life. He backed away from the kitchens and spun the truck around. Urging the vehicle through the front gates, he turned onto the main road in a spray of gravel that rained against the undercarriage. He sped toward the docks, tires sliding over the gravel paving as he fought the steering wheel. *"Ni-Cio! Ni-Cio! It's Evan!"*

Ni-Cio did not reply, but as Evan took the winding turns like a madman, he felt his mind open. He witnessed the carnage through Ni-Cio's eyes.

Hemmed in on both sides, Ni-Cio and the remains of his unit fought for their lives. Half of his squad lay dead, their lifeless bodies strewn about the tunnel floor. Ni-Cio and the ten survivors waged a savage war against the invaders and took more lives than they gave. Their shields held steady and blazes of lethal energy poured in continuous streams from their outstretched crystals. Men screamed and fell in both directions. The Atlanteans slashed their way through the rear attackers as they tried to reach the gates of the Great Hall.

Evan nearly ran off the road. He had to close his mind to the mayhem and he jammed the accelerator to the floor. His truck hurtled toward the wharves, but he feared that he would be too late.

He veered into the marina, and even before the vehicle skidded to a stop, he was out of the truck. He sprinted over the dock and threw himself at the submersible. He opened the hatch and clambered aboard.

His hands flew through the startup sequence, and with as much speed as he could muster, he piloted the *Oceanus* out of the harbor. Evan forced the vehicle into an immediate and dangerous dive. He had to make it to Atlantis before Ni-Cio's time ran out. If he pushed the little submersible past her limits and he didn't make it...he refused to think about that. He rocketed toward Atlantis, and his thoughts fired toward Ni-Cio with lightning speed, *"Hold any way you can! I'm on my way!"*

CHAPTER
65

*T*ravlor's enormous submarines were in position. The drilling had gone more easily than planned. The equipment had worked without a hitch, and at any moment, Travlor expected to breach the walls of Atlantis.

Travlor, along with the bulk of his men, were stationed inside the sub he had designated for the rear assault. As he watched his men work, he received a report that nineteen submersibles had been lost, "So, we destroyed only thirty tunnels."

He signaled one of his captains, and the man came to a smart salute. "Once we have secured the tunnels, and I have the woman, you are to make certain that the nineteen remaining tunnels are brought down. Is that clear?"

"Yes, sir!"

"Fine. Inform your men."

The man exited the bridge. Travlor turned and tapped his fingers on the command console as he counted the minutes before they would begin the land assault. It did not take long. The subs ripped through their targeted passageways in record time and submarine hatches were flung wide. His men clambered down steel ladders and dropped to the tunnel floors. Travlor entered the caverns of Atlantis with an army over eight hundred strong.

Through radio contact, Travlor followed the progress of his squads as they swarmed the tunnels. With the aid of lumalights, they soon secured the empty corridors and quarters of Atlantis, and Travlor and his minions converged upon the eight passages that led to the Great Hall. He halted to let his men regroup before they began the advance through the initial assault tunnel. He was proud of his units. They had trained hard, and they were ready.

"Men, this first tunnel will be the hardest, but we bring our might to bear. You have trained for this moment. It is time to unleash the fury of our war machine!"

Cheers rose with guttural savagery and rolled through the halls like thunder. Travlor raised his arms and roared, "We outnumber them, our firepower is superior and you are battle-hardened! Let them feel the heel of your boots as you grind them to dust!"

Travlor's hands closed to fists and he gave the signal, "Take that tunnel!"

One hundred men poured around Travlor and threw themselves into the portal opening. The sound of automatic gunfire was deafening. Travlor counted the seconds and was surprised. It was taking longer than he expected.

Through the haze of smoke, he saw one of his men stagger back out of the tunnel and he grabbed him by the neck, "Soldier, you are retreating! Get back in there, now!"

Sweat and breath poured from the man and his wild look rolled from Travlor back toward the tunnel, "We fight a demon!"

Travlor laughed and shoved the mercenary away. He insinuated a thought into the man's brain. The soldier did not hesitate. He hefted his rifle, ducked his head and sprinted back into the tunnel.

Talus's mate, Riina, led the twenty men and women inside the initial assault tunnel. Travlor's men gushed through the entrance, but the Atlanteans stood their ground and defended their passage. With desperate courage and deadly skill, the twenty engaged the might that bore down upon them, and for an honorable time, they held.

Nevertheless, their crystals began to shatter. One by one, Riina's companions fell until she stood alone, the last defender between Travlor's hordes and her people.

Riina's thought-forms blazed and she fought with concentrated ferocity, however, she could not fight forever. As she neared the end of her strength, she knew that she was losing control of her shield effect. She straightened up and lowered her trembling arms. Looking into the eyes of her killers, she signed a heartfelt goodbye. The men opened fire.

With the tunnel taken, Travlor waded indifferently through the bodies of the fallen and signaled the next contingent. Another bloodthirsty cadre poured through the tunnel. The muffled sounds of their boots pounded a steady rhythm as they navigated the death-riddled passage.

The soldiers reached the inner walkway that ringed the Great Hall and they began their second massed assault. Firing into the battlements at will, they provided cover for the units that followed, so that half of Travlor's hirelings blasted toward the inner entrances of the seven remaining passages.

The inner and outer rings were soon overrun with Travlor's men. The Atlantean guerrilla units were cut off from the Great Hall and effectively trapped inside their tunnels.

Travlor stayed in contact with his units, and as the separate battles raged in tunnels-turned-war-zones, Travlor led the rest of his men as they prepared to break through the fortress walls of the Great Hall. Under a fusillade of cover, Travlor's bomb detail surged forward and planted inward-firing explosives on two of the outer walls.

Thick, acrid smoke hung so that it was difficult to breathe. A curtain of gray haze made it impossible for the defenders in the battlements to pick out targets, so there was no return fire.

Bloodcurdling screams of pain mingled with the wretched cries of the dying in a horrifying symphony of death. But it was music to Travlor's ears and he reveled in the sounds. Every life that was extinguished brought him closer to victory.

Surrounded by an impregnable thought-form, Travlor stood and waited for the detonation. His men gathered behind him. With a sudden release of pressure, Travlor felt the concussive blast, and the entrance into the Great Hall gaped open before him. He and his men surged over the bloodied remains of the dead and dying. He led his army through the smoking rubble. With lightning speed, Travlor and his death squads infiltrated the Great Hall of Poseidon.

Marik rose with a cohesive fighting force against Travlor's inhuman killing machines and Travlor could see that they fought tenaciously to repel his lethal intruders. It was a chaotic clash as Terran hit men waded into the midst of Marik's fighting unit.

Travlor, wielding nothing more than his thoughts, searched through the scene of erupting anarchy. His mission was to locate the abhorrent topside woman, and surrounded by an elite guard of twenty-five of his most vicious combatants, he marched through the destruction with unruffled impunity.

Ni-Cio and his team fought for their lives as they faced an overwhelming number of invaders, *"To the rear...it is our only chance!"*

Their thought-shields deflected most of the bullets from the frontal attack, so he relentlessly urged his men back toward Travlor's rear offensive and the inner ring, *"Break their assault and we can make the Great Hall!"*

Ni-Cio knew that their only chance of survival lay in reaching the inner ring. If they could break through Travlor's rear assault, he could get his team within reach of the Great Hall. But every inch of ground they gained was paid for with precious human currency. They had not even reached the halfway point and Ni-Cio was down by half of his men.

"Ni-Cio! Ni-Cio! It's Evan!" Evan's cry broke through his concentration. Locked in mortal combat, he didn't reply. He just opened his mind so that the topsider could witness the devastation.

"Hold any way you can! I'm on my way!"

Ni-Cio surged forward as he and the remainder of his unit fought ferociously on.

Ni-Cio and nine of his men finally cleared their tunnel as the bone-jarring blasts of Travlor's explosives detonated. They were thrown to the ground by the force of the blast. Ni-Cio nervously surveyed the rock over their heads and he knew that the Great Hall had been compromised.

His command seared through the minds of the remaining units, *"The Great Hall has been breached! We are needed now!"*

He and his men picked themselves up. They were joined by Aris and twelve of his team, along with five of Talus's warriors. Heavy smoke flowed around them like a raging river, obscuring their vision. Ni-Cio felt as if he had been thrust into hell.

The stragglers gathered around him. Before he could issue his orders, the figure of Mer-An materialized out of a muddy cloud of gray smoke. She dragged two broken bodies while her last man brought up the rear. His thought-forms fired steadily back through the thick haze.

Ni-Cio and the others sprinted to help her as a thought blazed into their minds.

"I am almost with you, Ni-Cio!"

Before they could reach Mer-An, Rogert and eight of his men burst from their tunnel. Two of Rogert's team grabbed the men from Mer-An's hands, and as one, they turned to protect their retreat.

Of the one hundred and sixty Atlanteans chosen to defend the interior tunnels, the thirty-nine remaining men and women crowded around Ni-Cio to receive their final orders. He looked into their weary faces and knew that all of them were nearing the end of their endurance, "If we cannot repel the forces from the Great Hall, I am afraid that all is lost. Look to yourselves and do the best that you can."

He prepared to lead his courageous fighters into their last pitched battle when a passionate cry reverberated through the corridor, halting their forward rush.

"Ni-Cio! I am with you!"

Ni-Cio glanced over his shoulder and squinted. His team dropped into defensive postures. A lone figure emerged from the smoke and the gloom and he recognized the topsider. Ni-Cio almost laughed. A surge of energy entered his body and his heart beat with renewed hope, "You are slow to join us!"

Evan caught up to the group and breathlessly clasped Ni-Cio's outstretched hand. Ni-Cio could see the toll that Evan's journey had taken, but he also recognized a bond of brotherhood that would never be broken.

Evan eyed the group. He nodded and took a deep breath. He glanced at Ni-Cio and jerked his chin in the direction of the Great Hall, "Let's move!"

Shoulder to shoulder, Ni-Cio and Evan led the ragtag band of fighters into the shadows of the Great Hall. Ni-Cio knew it was a gallant charge, he just desperately hoped that it would be enough to turn the tide.

CHAPTER
66

*N*i-Cio and his warriors raged through the cavernous opening into the Great Hall. Those who still had crystals scorched a path through the backs of their unwary assailants. Together they exploded into the ranks of Travlor's entrenched army with arcing flashes of telekinetic energy.

From his position, Ni-Cio saw that Marik and his group were pinned behind a barricade. He cleared a swath and Marik seized the advantage. He leapt from cover to lead his group in a valiant counteroffensive. As he waded fearlessly into a barrage of hostile fire, his battle cry rang through Ni-Cio's heart, "For freedom! For Atlantis!"

His followers streamed from behind their barriers, and those without crystals launched anything they could grab with the efficacy and ferocity of guided missiles.

To Ni-Cio, it seemed that Marik wielded his crystal like a broadsword. His face was suffused with brilliant bands of blue and gold, the colors of honor and incorruptibility. The aging Council Leader fought with reckless abandon and leveled ten men before his shield flickered, and failed. A hail of bullets brought him to his knees. His last thought found Ni-Cio.

"Lead them well…" Marik's powerful form sank to the floor.

Ni-Cio went wild. He rallied Atlanteans from every direction and they redoubled their efforts.

Aris and Mer-An guarded each other's back and burned a fatal swath. Rogert led his stouthearted eight into a terrible clash. Before their determined onslaught, Travlor's soldiers fell.

Side by side, Ni-Cio and Evan fought in harrowing combat. Ni-Cio's crystal-enhanced energy, and Evan's telekinetic prowess, brought down scores of mercenaries. By deadly increments, Ni-Cio felt the weight of battle shift.

He tried to assess their progress. As his eyes circled the immense chamber, he glimpsed Travlor accompanied by his special contingent, entering the tunnel leading to the Council Hall.

Ni-Cio screamed maniacally. He grabbed Evan and broke into the open, "Travlor is going after Daria!"

Evan and Ni-Cio blasted a path toward the back of the Great Hall while Ni-Cio communicated his alarm to Daria, *"Travlor is in the tunnel! I am coming!"*

Travlor did not look back as he broke into the bleak corridor. From his elite squad he chose six men and underscored his order with an intense compulsion, *"Let no one through!"*

The men stopped and turned to guard the entrance. Travlor knew that the only route into the tunnel would be through his men and they would fight to the death.

He hurried through the passage toward the portal opening. He stalked his prey, and sensed that he was close, "The woman is not to be harmed. Destroy the others."

Travlor and his men were unopposed as they barged into the Council Hall. Daria stood alone in the center of the room. Travlor elbowed his way through his men and halted before his catch.

The woman met his gaze with an intensity he did not remember. "You may kill me, but Ni-Cio will never let you out of here alive."

Travlor lifted his face to the cavernous ceiling and chuckled, "Oh, you are mistaken, my dear. It is not your death I require. It is your life." He gestured to his squad, and they surrounded her with military precision.

He picked out two soldiers, "Blow that wall!"

The men bent to prepare the explosives while Travlor surveyed the hospital. He spied the biospheres, "I see you have provided a faster mode of transport. Very thoughtful." He motioned to another duo, "Once we are ready to leave these chambers, bring one of those biospheres with you. I intend to leave Atlantis in style."

He returned his gaze to the topsider, "Where are the others? I find it hard to believe you were left alone."

Daria stepped toward him, "There are no others. Once your killers acquired the Great Hall, everyone was called to fight." Her tone was different, it had elevated, just slightly.

Travlor scrutinized her face, then looked at his squad, "Spread out; look for…"

"We're ready, sir."

Interrupted by the soldier in charge of demolitions, Travlor reined in his anger and jerked his head, "Get everybody under cover."

The soldiers quickly overturned the beds. Huddled behind the mattresses, they used their bodies to shield Daria. Still encased in his own energy shield, Travlor stood, impervious to the detonation.

With a muffled WHOOOMP, debris rained down upon Travlor and his men, but they had created their avenue of escape.

Ni-Cio and Evan exerted a frantic effort to gain access to the tunnel leading to the Council Hall. Ni-Cio's crystal had cracked in half, so as Evan waged his telekinetic powers, Ni-Cio relied upon his skill of *Last Strike*. They fought through the Hall until they were close to the tunnel entrance where they were met by six of Travlor's elite soldiers. The odds did not favor Ni-Cio. He and Evan took cover behind one of the columns and Ni-Cio summoned Aris and Mer-An. He waited for them to come, but as the noise of the explosion reached his ears, Ni-Cio went berserk.

Grasping the jagged pieces of his broken crystal in either hand, he vaulted from behind the column and charged the defenders. His awareness narrowed to three soldiers. In a timed move of *Last Strike*, Ni-Cio raised both hands and rammed the razor-sharp crystals into the carotid arteries of two of his targets. With his right foot, he delivered a kick to the face of the third target. The man's nose cartilage was thrust up and into his brain, he was dead before he hit the ground.

Ni-Cio did not wait for Evan and the others to take out the last three guards. He raced toward the Council Hall.

Evan, Aris and Mer-An barged into the Council chambers to see Ni-Cio pulling people from under the dais. He helped Kyla from beneath the crawlspace and she jumped up to hug her brother.

"Ni-Cio, Travlor has Daria!" Kyla's gaze took in the others and she started to cry, "She would not let us stand with her. She made the children enter first, then Ylno with her group, and finally..." Tears left tracks in her dusty cheeks. She forced herself to continue, "She made me take her crystal in case we were found." Her shoulders shook and Ni-Cio tried to support her, but she evaded his grasp and Evan saw her fear. "Travlor has taken a biosphere. If we don't get to him, we may never see Daria again!"

Ni-Cio sprinted for the detonated exit, but Evan grabbed his arm, "Among the four of us we only have one crystal and no way to shield ourselves."

Ni-Cio cocked a fist, ready to fight. It took a tremendous amount of willpower to keep from hitting the topsider. Ni-Cio's roar vibrated through Evan's insides, "You do not understand! If Travlor kills Daria, nothing else matters!"

Ni-Cio yanked his arm from Evan's hold and grabbed a biosphere. He leapt through the open gap and pounded down the gloomy corridor. Evan and Aris chased his fleeing form and Evan's thought swirled into Mer-An and Kyla.

"Guard the children...we will do what we can to help Ni-Cio!"

Kyla's footsteps echoed off the tunnel walls, *"I am coming with you!"*

Having reached an exit that was still intact, Travlor began to prepare the biosphere. His remaining soldiers surrounded Daria and waited for orders.

"You know what to do. Finish the job for which you were hired."

Travlor stood and crossed to Daria. He took her arm and led her to the edge of the pool. But she could not wrest her gaze from Travlor's men. She watched in horror as they pulled yellow canisters and ugly masks from their backpacks.

Once they had acquired the necessary tools, the soldiers fanned out of the exit. Travlor lowered his mouth to Daria's ear and the sound of his venomous voice made her cringe, "Do not tax yourself attempting to reach Ni-Cio. I have blocked your thoughts." He pointed to the elongated biosphere, "Get in."

Daria tried to back up, "I won't go!"

Travlor gripped her arm in a powerful hold and shook her so hard that her teeth clattered together, "I do not have time to argue!"

Daria yelped with pain and struggled to break free. Yanking her off her feet as though she weighed no more than a kitten, Travlor hurled her into the biosphere. She clung to the sides. At last, her courage deserted her, "I don't know why you have to take me. I'm no threat to you!"

Travlor rapidly adjusted himself behind her and used his body as a restraint. The canopy materialized and Daria felt as though she had been sealed inside a coffin, "I need you to attend my health."

Travlor willed the biosphere into a descent. He flew the craft through the tunnel and toward the open sea and Daria squeezed her eyes shut. She tried to reach Ni-Cio but received not even the breath of a reply. She prayed that Travlor was blocking her thoughts. She refused to let herself think of the alternative.

Trying to suppress her fear, she took several deep breaths in an effort to relax and Na-Kai's words flowed from her memory. *"You are stronger than you know...events have unfolded as they should..."*

Travlor's breath scrabbled over her neck and the touch of his body made her skin crawl. She felt unclean. Daria was considering her options when a sense of defiance bloomed within her. She looked over her shoulder, "It won't matter where you try to hide. Ni-Cio will find me!"

Travlor's eyes opened wide and a malevolent grin parted his lips, "My dear, no one will be left alive *to* find you. With your departure secured, a highly toxic supplement to the Atlantean air supply is being released. You see, I have paid my men to be *very* thorough."

Daria squirmed, but Travlor easily pinned her down. She gave up, "Travlor, I'll do anything you ask, just call your soldiers off. You have no reason to do that!"

His dispassionate reply was worse than a slap, "Quite the contrary. I would not have you continue to hope for rescue. Better to have your undivided attention."

Daria could no longer contain her grief or her desperation. She lowered her head to the console and bitter sobs welled up from deep within her chest. Through great, choking breaths, she tried one last time to break Travlor's composure, "You cannot compel me. With everyone dead, what reason would I *ever* have to help you?"

His sigh came out with a rasp, "For my sake, I hope you are more aware than it would seem."

Daria pushed herself up and turned to face her captor. She swiped at her eyes, "What are you talking about?"

Travlor quirked a black eyebrow. His words chilled her to the marrow, "Why, the child you carry. Her safety alone should ensure your undying obedience."

CHAPTER
67

Ni-Cio carried a biosphere and found the only exit he thought Travlor could have used. He wasn't sure if Travlor's death squad still guarded the passage, so he made his way through the halls with as much stealth as possible. He encountered no resistance, and when he entered the pool area, he hurriedly prepared to leave. He had adjusted the length of the biosphere and was settled inside when Evan, Aris and Kyla dashed into the room. Evan stumbled to the edge of the pool and fell to his knees, "Ni-Cio, they're using gas!"

Ni-Cio scrambled out of the biosphere and grabbed Evan. "Kyla! In the biosphere!" Kyla jumped into the craft and looked back. "We have to get him away from the gas!"

Ni-Cio and Aris lowered Evan behind Kyla. The hatch materialized and Ni-Cio hit the side with his hand, *"Get him out of here…we will meet you at his compound…"*

He saw Kyla nod. The biosphere lit up and hurtled down into the black water. Ni-Cio grabbed Aris's arm and turned away from the pool. He sent an urgent command to the other Atlanteans, *"Full bioskins, now!"*

Encased within their bioskins, Ni-Cio and Aris fled the pool access as Evan's thoughts thundered back.

"I don't know what kind of gas they're using…and I don't how it will affect the bioskins…get everyone out immediately, and be ready to decontaminate topside!"

"Evan...the bioskins will hold long enough...look to yourself...I do not know how much you inhaled..."

Ni-Cio and Aris skirted dead bodies as they barreled toward the Council Hall. There were no signs of life. They rounded a corner. Ni-Cio slowed his pace and Aris followed his lead.

Ni-Cio stopped, shook his head and looked at Aris. His friend was lit with an eerie green from the light of the luminescent sticks, *"I cannot hear Daria's thoughts..."*

Ni-Cio glanced down the path they had just traveled and started to turn back, but Aris grabbed his arm, *"Ni-Cio, Travlor must not intend to kill her...or he would have done so..."*

Ni-Cio hesitated, torn between duty and love. He scowled. Aris did not move. Within the space of a single heartbeat, Ni-Cio made his decision, *"Agreed...let's move!"*

As one, they ran toward the Council Hall.

"Aris...we have to get everyone out...I do not know how long it will take for the gas to neutralize..."

"Affirmative..."

Ni-Cio issued an urgent order, *"Everyone to the Council Hall...we must abandon Atlantis...we must do so now!"*

Ni-Cio relayed the course heading to Evan's compound before he and Aris reached the hall. Through the ragged hole, Aris and Ni-Cio saw that the children were already prepared. Mer-An, having assigned some of the biospheres to be carried, was leading the youngest children out into the corridor.

Aris ran to Mer-An and took her in his arms in a ferocious embrace. Ni-Cio heard his anxious thoughts.

"Evan and Kyla will be waiting topside to help you and the children. You will be safe...Ni-Cio and I will come as soon as we can...by all the gods, I do love you!"

Mer-An raised a hand and caressed Aris's rugged face, *"Look to yourself...I need you safe and well..."*

She turned and guided her charges through the tunnel. Aris looked at Ni-Cio and he nodded in reassurance. He signaled

Aris to precede him as they waded through the exploded debris and entered the Council Hall.

They readied the biospheres for transport as people began to straggle into the chamber. The injured, and those with torn bioskins, were seen to first. Ni-Cio deployed them into groups, then he and Aris took turns helping everyone to the exit. Ni-Cio was relieved to see that most of the injuries were not fatal and that a good number of his friends were remarkably unscathed.

The last group to arrive was Rogert and his fatigued fighters. When he saw them, he did not need to be told how badly their home had been decimated. The brave-hearted Atlantean had brought up the rear, and as he hoisted two biospheres, Ni-Cio knew how deep Rogert's sorrow ran.

"That is all, Ni-Cio...we have only the children and one hundred seventy adults..." His face was etched with exhaustion, and deep lines ran from his nose to his mouth. They had not been there before, *"There are no soldiers to be carried out..."*

Ni-Cio grasped Rogert's shoulders, *"Get your men topside...we do our grieving later..."*

Rogert indicated one of the biospheres, *"I will leave this poolside for you..."* He turned and his men followed. They skirted the gaping hole and made their way to the exit.

Ni-Cio and Aris were the only ones left. Ni-Cio was reluctant to leave, *"Aris...I must go to the Great Hall...take this biosphere and leave..."*

Aris scowled and shook his head, *"We stay together..."*

Ni-Cio hesitated, *"Very well...come with me..."*

They made their way into the wreckage of the Great Hall. Bodies were everywhere. The sight nearly brought Ni-Cio to his knees. He wanted to scream, so great was the senseless loss. His body trembled and tears stung the corners of his eyes. Why was he still alive when so many were gone?

He met Aris's bleak stare and beheld a mirror image of his own grief. The deep blue stripes of mourning covered Aris's face and tears soaked his cheeks. At a loss, Ni-Cio lowered his gaze and looked over his fallen people. When he saw Marik's body, he knew what he had to do.

He wound through the room to reach the epicenter. When Aris followed, he was relieved that he hadn't left him to face this alone. They halted in the midst of the carnage and Ni-Cio raised both arms. With the greatest sorrow he had ever known, he performed his first duty as Council Leader.

He intoned the first notes of the heartbreaking *Song of Passing*. As his friend joined in, their thoughts drifted in a silent lament through the charred ruins of the Great Hall of Poseidon. The last of their grief-filled words sighed through their minds and drifted away. They stood in a silent tribute to the lives that had been lost.

At length, Ni-Cio wearily turned to Aris, *"Even in the midst of so much death, it is possible we find ourselves having come full circle...to another beginning..."*

Together, they left the Great Hall. They traversed the passages of their ancestral home. Their muffled footfalls were the only sounds that echoed throughout all of Atlantis.

Entering the portal, Ni-Cio shuffled to the pool. He grabbed the biosphere and wearily shoved it into the water. He settled himself at the helm and Aris slipped in behind him. The canopy materialized, and without a backward glance, Ni-Cio rocketed from their home toward a strange and different world. When the biosphere burst into the open sea, Ni-Cio looked back at Aris.

"By the gods, it is not over! I will find Travlor and I will rescue Daria! If this terrible end has brought us a new beginning...then let it begin...and may it be glorious!"

END

Coming Fall, 2017!

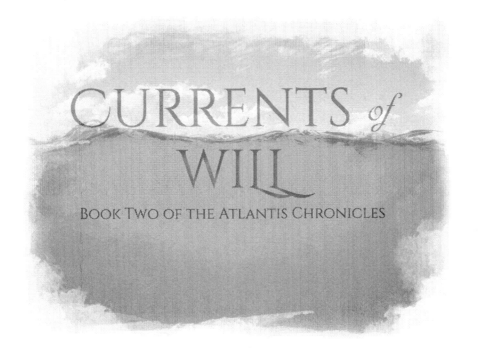

CURRENTS *of* WILL

Book Two of the Atlantis Chronicles

Susan MacIver

CHAPTER
1

*B*reathe in, breathe out. He could not talk. His heart still beat and blood still slid through his veins but the words would not come. With each contraction a band of grief tightened around his heart so that Evan didn't think it would re-expand and yet it did. Heartbeat, eye blink. Still, no words.

With practiced skill Kyla piloted the craft through the turbulent water. Behind her, Evan watched her movements. They had not spoken since their evacuation of Atlantis, but he felt the breaking of her heart as if it were his own.

On a course heading to his deserted compound, Kyla operated the biosphere with mechanical detachment. Her normally fluid motions were too quiet, too contained. She moved as though the weight of the dead, like remora, had attached themselves to her limbs and might never leave.

Evan reached to stroke her hair, then hesitated. He had no right. Her life had been shredded because of his father. And though he had tried to thwart Travlor's invasion, by every standard, he had been stunningly unsuccessful. He dropped his hand. "Kyla, when we are clear of this vessel, grab handfuls of sand, and as hard as you can, scrub it over yourself and your bioskin. It will help neutralize the gas."

A slight tilt of her head was the only acknowledgment he received. At last she spoke, but her voice was thick. She cleared her throat. "Evan, are you all right? You must have inhaled some of the gas. Do you feel any effects?"

He didn't answer. The ocean floor had risen to meet them and he felt the craft's deceleration. In the shallows Kyla halted the biosphere and when the hatch dematerialized Evan clambered out.

He gasped from the sudden touch of frigid saltwater. An incoming surge washed over his chest while he helped Kyla out of the craft and he tried to shield her body from the worst waves, but she was already soaked. He ducked underwater, grabbed handfuls of sand and surfaced. He scraped the abrasive grains over Kyla's back and shoulders. "Do this all over your body and keep scrubbing until I tell you to quit!"

Kyla followed Evan's lead and vigorously rubbed sand over her body. "What about you?"

Evan did not break rhythm. "Ni-Cio reacted so quickly I'll be all right, but I don't want you to take any chances."

During their ascent Evan had scoured his memories for anything he knew about nerve gas. Although he wasn't sure what agent had been released, he knew that copious amounts of soap, water, and forceful brushing helped decontaminate most poisons. He continued to scrub Kyla's back hoping the saltwater and sand would stave off any immediate effects. He needed to get everyone to the compound as soon as possible. The skies threatened and it would be dark soon.

"Kyla, I think the saltwater will be enough to neutralize the outsides of the biospheres, but your people don't have much time. As soon as they start surfacing get them out of the vehicles and out of their bioskins. Show them how to scrub each other down."

He stopped and looked at her. Sadness, laced with fright, stared at him out of beautiful topaz eyes. More than anything he wanted to take her in his arms and hold her until her grief

360

subsided and she was able to smile again. Instead, he blinked hard and raised his voice over the sounds of the surf. "The saltwater and sand should be enough for initial decontamination, but I have to go to the compound for extra clothes. Once the bioskins are off don't let anyone touch them. Use a stick to put the discarded 'skins into a pile then wait for me!"

Evan couldn't help himself. He raised his hands to her lovely face and kissed her full lips. He tasted salt and tears and longing. Astonished, he felt her arms wrap tightly around his shoulders. Kyla clung to him and her body trembled, whether from shock or cold or...it took every bit of his willpower to pull away. Evan held her quivering chin and used his other hand to brush the wet hair from her eyes. "I'll be back as soon as I can."

Kyla nodded and though Evan would have given his heart to stay, he turned and grabbed the biosphere. He slogged through the surf and carried the craft onto the beach beyond the high water mark. Once he had secured the biosphere he allowed himself a backward glance.

Alone, Kyla regarded him from shore break. He couldn't leave her. He started back, but Kyla's thoughts poured into him. *"Go, Evan...Please, we must help the others...I will wait here for you..."*

Evan turned and sprinted up the rocky, cliffside trail.

At the summit he stopped and gulped a few lungfuls of air then headed to the compound in an all-out run. He leapt over the withered branches of the defunct vineyard and slid down the hillside until he pounded into the courtyard in a cloud of dry, red dust.

He rounded a corner and flew past the kitchens where he sighted the sagging, used-to-be-red truck that had been used to ferry supplies. He skidded to a halt beside the vehicle and yanked the door open. He jumped into the cab. Searching blindly, he found the key still in the ignition. The starter ground and he pumped the accelerator praying that the old relic still had some kick. But the truck was stubborn and tired. A string of curses gathered force, yet Evan tried to cajole the vehicle to life. He ground the reluctant starter once more and it faltered. An angry expletive exploded from his mouth. The truck hesitated for the last time, belched blue smoke, and finally rattled to life.

Rusty gears protested being rammed into reverse but without another problem, Evan backed the truck into the lifeless courtyard. He swerved toward a set of cabins, jumped out of the cab and made it through the closest door before the old vehicle jittered to a stop.

Searching the empty room, it was as he had suspected. Two army issued duffels lay abandoned in a corner. He crossed the cabin's squealing floorboards and hoisted the bags. He shook the contents onto the lowest bunk. Seizing all of the clothes, he crammed them back into one of the duffels, slung both bags over his shoulder, and ran from the room. He repeated the process until he had ransacked all the cabins for every article of clothing.

At last, he rested against the side of the antiquated clunker. He pulled massive amounts of air into his lungs and surveyed the mountain of duffels he had launched into the truck bed.

Ragged gusts of winter-like wind whipped through the compound and Evan eyed the black clouds roiling overhead. Their bloated underbellies warned of the ominous birth of a monster storm.

He had to move. Evan stepped into the cab and alternating between vitriolic threats of destruction and promises of resurrection, the old jalopy bounced its way through the vineyard. The truck wheezed to a stop at the edge of the cliff and Evan pushed the door open. He jumped out and hurried to the back of the truck. Without breaking stride he grabbed an armful of bags, reached the edge of the cliff, and hurled the duffels over the side as his thoughts roared down to Kyla. *"Grab the closest bag and get out of that bioskin!"*

Drenched in an icy prelude of the approaching storm, Kyla shivered. Her life had turned surreal and Evan felt like her last link to reality. His strong arms tightened protectively around her and she could tell that he tried to shield her from the stinging nettles of ocean spray.

The wind had stirred the surf into a frenzy and they struggled to remain upright. Nevertheless, Kyla refused to go ashore. She had a terrible feeling that if she did she would never, again, see any of her friends or family. She would be the last and only survivor of the horrific holocaust that had been visited upon her people. That, she would not be able stand. So, she remained. Battered by the surf, she ceaselessly scoured the horizon for any indication that someone, anyone from Atlantis had followed them topside.

"I'm so sorry, Kyla...I couldn't stop him..." Evan's thoughts were heavy with remorse echoing a lifetime of unshed tears.

Ribbons of water coursed down Kyla's cheeks and spilled over her lips. She tasted the salt and neither knew nor cared whether the tears came from her own searing sense of loss or were merely by-products of the unremitting sea spray. She swiped her eyes and continued to search the massive line of swells that rolled across the empty horizon.

The genocidal rage that Travlor had unleashed upon her people had taken a catastrophic toll. And she knew that the cavern floors of Atlantis were littered with the bodies and blood of Atlanteans and mercenaries alike. However, she knew the lengths to which Evan had gone to protect her and her people. Her thoughts touched him with infinite tenderness. *"I do not know anyone who could have withstood the choices you have had to make...we both have lost so much...yet your safety alleviates a measure of my grief..."*

It seemed as though her compassion broke the very heart of heaven. Winds that had sung a mournful dirge escalated to an earsplitting keen and an explosive blast of thunder shook the ground.

Jagged shards of lightning ripped through the rain-engorged clouds and Evan and Kyla held each other before an onslaught that seemed as though every element of heaven and earth had joined in a vast primal wake.

Blinded by the storm's ferocious display, Kyla almost missed the faint shimmer of light. A biosphere broke from beneath the weight of the sea. Hammered by wild surface waves, it labored to reach shore.

"Evan, over there!" Kyla tore herself from Evan's arms and bounded through the surging tides into deeper water. Followed closely by the topsider, they grasped the slippery sides of the biosphere and steadied the craft as the canopy dematerialized.

Mer-An, cloaked in dark glasses and earplugs, dragged herself from the vehicle. She willed the canopy closed and clung tenaciously to the stern. Her thoughts found Kyla. *"Nine children inside...terrified...more are on their way!"*

They strained against the inexhaustible undertow and wrestled the biosphere to shore. The hatch dematerialized opening a new world to some of the last children of Atlantis. Even though their goggles and earplugs shielded them, when they were lifted from the biosphere, they were terrified to move. Seeing them lined up in a rigid silent row, Kyla's heart wept. *"Come to me...we must get you out of your bioskins and into topside clothes...Mer-An is here and we will take care of you..."*

Mer-An and Kyla helped the children out of their bioskins and guided them into the surf. They scrubbed their tiny bodies with sand while Evan threw the 'skins into the empty duffels and found clothing for them.

The storm raged even as Kyla helped the children to shore and into the ill-fitting topside garments. Mer-An stood alone in the surf slowly scrubbing her bioskin. Kyla could tell how tired her friend was by the woodenness of her motions. Evan waded out to help and his quick command seemed to re-energize her. *"Mer-An! Let's move!"* Together they scrubbed her down while Kyla found clothes to replace her 'skin.

Once Mer-An had been clothed, they huddled around the children in storm-forced silence. Relief was palpable when, at last, weary thoughts began to penetrate the numbness that had crept into their minds.

"We are almost there..."

"I am behind you..."

"I think I see shore break..."

"There are others that follow me..."

Through the driving sheets of rain, several dim beams of light could be seen as biospheres breached the surface. Evan and Kyla left Mer-An to safeguard the children and battled their way back into the crashing surf.

Too tired for thought, everyone worked mechanically. Each biosphere was intercepted, dragged to shore, emptied of passengers and secured well past the high water mark. Everyone helped each other decontaminate as best they could.

As the storm shrieked to its furious apex the final vessel emerged from the bitter depths. To Kyla, it looked as though Ni-Cio had lost control of his craft. The biosphere careened through the high seas and hurtled toward a lethal outcropping of volcanic rock. Evan bellowed in a voice heard above the storm. "They're not going to make it!"

He broke from the group and leapt wildly through the incoming surf. Twenty spent Atlanteans followed his lead. Kyla watched in horror as the men worked to gain a purchase on the slippery vehicle. They swarmed the craft and through their combined strength they were able to slow the deadly trajectory of the storm-driven vessel. At last, they stabilized the biosphere and the canopy disappeared.

Ni-Cio evaw Azaes rose from inside and jumped with weary grace into the storm surge. Even from her vantage point Kyla could see that fatigue had carved tight, grim lines into his handsome face. And the tired, encumbered movements with which he strained against the violent blows of the surf, spoke of the tremendous ordeal he had endured. She held her breath. In agonizing degrees he raised one muscular arm to offer aid to his best friend. Aris thrust his body from the biosphere.

Surrounded by Evan and the others, Ni-Cio and Aris were scrubbed down. At last, they waded through the waist-high water and stumbled upon the rocky beach. Kyla had their clothes ready, and once Ni-Cio and Aris were outfitted, they trudged over the sand covered rocks to stand before the shattered remnants of Atlantis.

Kyla moved next to her brother. She took his hand to comfort him and saw the questioning looks wreathed in shock and sorrow on the sad faces of her people. She knew that Marik had bequeathed a terrible task to Ni-Cio, a task that he had never wanted.

His entire adult life, Ni-Cio had resisted the fact that he was next in line to succeed Marik as Council Leader. He had never wanted to be tied down to such an obligation with its inherent responsibilities. His need for something different had been gratified with his job of collecting samples. Wandering the seas and surreptitiously stealing glimpses of topside life helped offset his desire for adventure.

Ni-Cio never suspected that Kyla knew his deepest secret, with his habitual need for wanderlust, Ni-Cio had been bored with life in Atlantis.

When Daria had come into his life, Ni-Cio's restless soul had found peace and fulfillment. His wanderings had ceased and he had felt secure enough in the new Healer's love that he had accepted his ascendency with less reluctance.

Now, everything had changed. Travlor had taken Daria, only the gods knew where, and Ni-Cio headed a displaced group of people who had no idea how to survive topside. As the existent Council Leader everyone looked to him for guidance and deliverance. And it was clear that Ni-Cio struggled with his own grief. *"Kyla, how am I to guide the needs of others when I could not even help Daria? I am not prepared for this...what can I possibly say that will help? What am I supposed to do?"*

Kyla raised the back of his hand to her lips. *"Marik chose you, Ni-Cio, no one else...I know it seems unbearable...but he died defending our freedom...his last words were..."Lead them well"...he knew that you would..."*

The storm began to play itself out and Kyla watched Ni-Cio slowly raise his head. His violet eyes blazed with an inner light and he tenderly released her hand. Stepping into the midst of their people his deep voice broke the stillness. It came, low and strong, with steady reassurance. His words were a soothing balm that imparted hope and comfort. "You fought well and bravely this day. That any of us remain is a testament to your courage and the strength of your spirits."

Hot, silent tears slid down Kyla's cheeks and mixed with the cooling caress of rain. She bowed her head in mourning. The wind subsided to a freshening breeze and Ni-Cio's voice rose with conviction. "We will find rest within the walls of Evan's home. And we will stay until we regain our strength. When we are ready we will leave to rebuild our home…but it is here and it is now that we begin to heal our grief."

Kyla felt the raw ache of his soul. Ni-Cio's voice trembled. "We cannot and we will not let our sorrow dishonor the memories of those who gave their lives that we might continue."

Ni-Cio lifted his face to the night sky. Drops of rain glistened on his cheeks and lingered upon his lips. Kyla, too, savored the sweet, pure taste of fresh water. When her brother began to intone the first tremulous notes of the sacred *Song of Passing*, she let the water christen her parched mouth. One by one Atlantean voices joined in a mystical, loving tribute and the grief in every heart found an outlet in the ethereal song.

Blanketed by soft mist, Evan stood apart from the group, his somber gray eyes closed and his head bowed. Kyla knew his anguish and she left the solemn press of bodies to stand next to the solitary topsider. She gently took his hand in hers. Her touch must have stirred depths of remembrance in Evan for together, they lifted their voices as one.

TOPICS to CONSIDER

- ❖ Is the Atlantis story more than legend? Is there any basis in fact?

- ❖ What evidence is there for Atlantis to have been in Greece?

- ❖ Do you have a "vision" of what Atlantis was?

- ❖ Can people of different cultures ever truly understand one another?

- ❖ Was Travlor unjustly held in Atlantis?

- ❖ Was Travlor a product of his time and place, or was he "contaminated" by contact with other cultures?

- ❖ Is the desire for power, such as Travlor has, a result of his contamination?

- ❖ What kind of inner struggles do you think the original Atlanteans had with the quest for power?

- ❖ Should alien cultures, such as the Atlanteans, be revered by topsiders or feared?

- ❖ What can topsiders and Atlanteans teach each other?

- ❖ Do you believe Ni-Cio's "love at first sight" experience?

- ❖ Where does love come from?

❖ *If you were given the opportunity to decide the most important rules under which a society should live, what would they be? Poseidon gave Atlantis only eight canons, is there any significance to that number? Can you think of any other canons could the Atlanteans have used?*

ABOUT the AUTHOR

Susan MacIver grew up in Roswell, New Mexico. She has stated, emphatically, that she knows nothing about *The UFO Crash*. However, since she claims that she never wanted to be a writer, it is curious as to where she got the idea for The Atlantis Chronicles Trilogy.

She attended The University of Texas in Austin, where she  enrolled in dance and acting. Her acting career was brought to a screeching halt when, at her first student audition, she was informed that she had quite a strong accent. She claims her accent was a by-product of southeastern NM, but it sounds suspiciously Texan.

Intervening years occurred and time passed. She was blessed with a son, Eric, who has been an entrepreneur since the ripe old age of three. He now resides in Los Angeles and, of course, has his own company.

Married to Duke Ayers, Susan says, "Duke has taught me more about unconditional love than any other human I've met." Sharing their love and their adventures in Arizona, she credits Duke with the fact that she is writing again.

If you would like to learn more, please visit her website at www.susanmaciver.com

45485944R00216

Made in the USA
San Bernardino, CA
09 February 2017